BRIXMIS

BRIXMIS

THE UNTOLD EXPLOITS
OF BRITAIN'S MOST DARING
COLD WAR SPY MISSION

TONY GERAGHTY

HarperCollins*Publishers*

77–85 Fulham Palace Road,
Hammersmith, London W6 8JB

This paperback edition 1997

First published in Great Britain by
HarperCollins*Publishers* 1996

Copyright © Tony Geraghty 1996

The Author asserts the moral right to
be identified as the author of this work

Map drawn by Hardlines

ISBN 978-0-00-638673-5

Set in Meridien

Mixed Sources
Product group from well-managed
forests and other controlled sources
www.fsc.org Cert no. SW-COC-001806
© 1996 Forest Stewardship Council

FSC is a non-profit international organisation established to promote the
responsible management of the world's forests. Products carrying the FSC
label are independently certified to assure consumers that they come
from forests that are managed to meet the social, economic and
ecological needs of present and future generations.

Find out more about HarperCollins and the environment at
www.harpercollins.co.uk/green

FOREWORD

Major-General the Duke of Norfolk KG GCVO CB CBE MC
President of the Brixmis Association

History, so it is said, is written by the victors. This is not invariably true. The history of the Viking assaults on England, for example, was largely recorded by their victims, the monks of Northumbria, for the simple reason that it was the monks who were literate.

Most of the secret history of the Cold War, so far, has been more exposed by representatives of the former Soviet empire than by those of us who played from the other end of the pitch. The memoirs of Sudoplatov (*A Soviet Spymaster*), Oleg Kalugin and Gordievsky as well as Kim Philby and John Cairncross pile up like bricks in a new historical wall. The only other British voice to be heard, from within the secret world, has been that of the MI5 veteran Peter Wright in *Spycatcher*. That is also a story of failure or suspected failure on the British side, a tale of penetration or suspected penetration by the KGB, a tale of suspicion and betrayal.

A trend of history has been created which is not the whole story. At this rate, the devil will have all the best tunes.

The reality was different and vitally included Brixmis, the military liaison mission behind the Iron Curtain which I had the honour to command for two years as an unexpected change from orthodox, regimental soldiering. The Cold War ended with a bloodless victory and the victory was ours. We got close enough to the Russians to respect them as people as well as to photograph their military secrets.

The work that follows is the official history of a unique military formation, representing all three armed services, working in isolation over an unfriendly horizon. It justifies its title, *Beyond the Front Line*.

Miles (Norfolk)
Arundel Castle, 1996

CONTENTS

ACKNOWLEDGEMENTS

I would like to thank those hundreds of soldiers, sailors, airmen, Royal Marines, civilian specialists temporarily invested with military titles, the wives and (occasionally) the children who took an active part in the work of Brixmis throughout the forty-four years of the Cold War, all of whom have contributed directly or otherwise to this history. Some were kind enough to give me access to their unpublished memoirs. The West should be proud of them and grateful for their hitherto unsung efforts in increasing our security while making a third world war less likely.

At a personal level, I want to express special gratitude to my friend Major Nick Angus BEM, who suggested this book in the first place; to Major-General Brian Davis CB CBE, Chairman of the Brixmis Association, who supported the idea, having had a close look at me over lunch at the Special Forces Club; to the Duke of Norfolk, President of the Association, who was kind enough to provide the Foreword.

Particular thanks are due to Lieutenant-Colonel Nigel Wylde QGM, Secretary of the Association, military scientist, linguist and much else, whose unstinting guidance and meticulous fact-checking finally amounted to a benign process of editing the emerging script. The book would have been the poorer without the fruitful collaboration that developed between us.

LIST OF ILLUSTRATIONS

Section One

Communist border guard leaping to freedom (Topham Picture Library).

East Berlin war memorial, built around a T-34 tank. (This photograph, and all those following, is reprinted courtesy of Brixmis).

Berlin, shattered capital of the Third Reich, in May 1945.

One of the first Mission tour cars.

An early social lunch (probably during the late 1940s) between Soviet and Brixmis liaison officers.

General Cassells is received at the Soviet East German headquarters with full military honours on 17 March 1961.

Brigadier Learmont, Chief of Mission from 1982 to 1984, and the Soviet Commander, General Zaitzev.

Major Willie Macnair, a Highlander, briefs visitors on the Plotzensee Memorial.

Section Two

Sergeant Ken Wike BEM (an Army tour NCO 1982–5) takes an impression of a gun barrel on the latest BMP-2 infantry combat vehicle.

A view of a BMP-1 Ksh regimental headquarters vehicle, from the cockpit of the Mission's own RAF Chipmunk trainer.

Mig-29 Fulcrum strike/attack aircraft, the latest in Soviet fast jets.

Hip-E helicopter gunship.

A file of T-64B tanks charges in a battle-run formation towards a concealed Brixmis observation post.

Mobile Soviet radar system unwittingly revealed by an unwary crew.

An SA-2 (anti-aircraft) missile, Nato codename Guideline, assembled by Soviet troops.

'Thin Skin B' height-finding radar, paired with an Interrogation Friend or Foe system.

Soviet Army traffic regulators or 'reggies'.

Russian soldier.

Section Three

The human face of the East German war machine, caught smiling, behind his army truck.

Stasi nark working a camera.

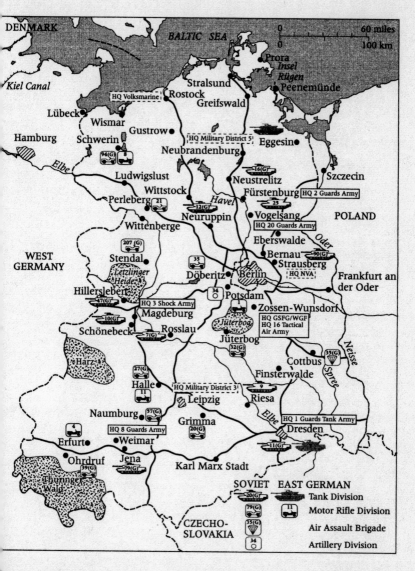

DENMARK

Kiel Canal

Hamburg

BALTIC SEA

Lübeck
Wismar
Schwerin
Gustrow

Stralsund
Rostock
Greifswald

HQ Volksmarine

Prora
Insel
Rügen
Peenemünde

Ludwigslust
Wittstock
Perleberg
Wittenberge

Neubrandenburg
Havel
Neuruppin

HQ Military District 5

Eggesin

Neustrelitz
Fürstenburg
Vogelsang

Szczecin

HQ 2 Guards Army

POLAND

**WEST
GERMANY**

Stendal
*Letzlinger
Heide*
Hillersleben
Magdeburg
Schönebeck
Rosslau

Döberitz

Eberswalde
Bernau
Strausberg

Berlin

Potsdam
Zossen-Wunsdorf
Jüterbog
Jüterbog

HQ 20 Guards Army

HQ NVA

Frankfurt an
der Oder

HQ 3 Shock Army

HQ GSFG/WGF
HQ 16 Tactical
Air Army

Oder

Neisse

Halle

Cottbus
Finsterwalde

Spree

HQ Military District 3

Leipzig
Riesa

Naumburg
Grimma

HQ 8 Guards Army

HQ 1 Guards Tank Army

Erfurt
Weimar
Ohrdruf
Jena
*Thüringer
Wald*

Karl Marx Stadt

Dresden

Elbe

**CZECHO-
SLOVAKIA**

SOVIET   EAST GERMAN

Tank Division
Motor Rifle Division
Air Assault Brigade
Artillery Division

he disposition of major Soviet and East German units on the European front
ne, c. 1987: secret locations which have been unpublished until now.

INTRODUCTION

Out of the winter bleakness of a Prussian night, a diesel locomotive looms large in the camcorder lens. The train's three headlights make an inverted V.

'Lights!'

The voice is British, unmistakably an NCO's played by Michael Caine or one of his ilk: intelligent, monosyllabic and full of controlled aggression. The car's headlights snap on, illuminating the train's cargo exposed on open flatbeds.

'Yes, kit!'

As the camcorder records the scene, another voice sings out a highly technical description of each piece of Soviet tracked and wheeled equipment as it flows through the headlights: 'MTLB . . . Two-S-One . . . again . . . again . . .'

It is mid-afternoon on a spring day and the lens reaches through the rain to feed on a long Soviet convoy of mobile Scud missiles (as used by Saddam Hussein in the Gulf War of 1991) travelling by road somewhere in East Germany.

'OK, taking the column from the rear. This is Scud resupply.'

'Give him a wide berth.'

Scud missile carriers, known as TELs (transporter–erector–launchers) are big beasts. If one of the TEL drivers, spotting the British spy vehicle in his mirror, decides to lurch over to the crown of the narrow country road to bump the intruder into a ditch at high speed, this will be nothing new. The British crew know they can do nothing about it because they are operating outside the law in a foreign country. They do not recognize the local police, the Volkspolizei, and can expect no help from them. Occasionally, the British drivers get angry. They are hard men and sometimes they arrange matters so that it is someone else's head which goes through the windscreen. The 'someone' tends to be a member of the Stasi, East Germany's secret police, tailing them too close in the dark, at speed, unaware that the British sometimes drive flat out without brake lights. The game can be lethal for all concerned.

'This one is NVA [East German Army] marked.'

Clack! The camcorder's sound system catches the brittle noise of the motor-drive on a Nikon camera.

'And again, Scud-TEL . . . again . . . a 27/66P small "r" . . . a GAZ 326, no markings . . .'

The acceleration past the convoy, seen through the single eye of the camera, is stomach-heaving.

'The fields left and right are both "Go".' (That is, clear for an emergency getaway.)

Down the road at Wipperow crossroads they stop at the edge of a Permanently Restricted Area (PRA). Crossing into it is extremely dangerous and requires special clearance. For the British, it is a potential killing zone . . .

It is late summer. Out of a clear blue sky above a Soviet Air Force missile range looms a flight of four big helicopters, fresh from their last successful appearance in Afghanistan. Members of the RAF, in a car at the very fringes of this live fire zone in East Germany, are checking the time and the tactical style of their potential enemy. It is not unknown for them to take their chances in an area under attack with live missiles and guns from the air. Yet the voice is as laconic as a cricket commentator on the village green.

'We are in the potato field alongside Gadow Rossow with four Hinds on the range. Time as shown. Nap of the earth flying, running in low, line abreast.'

The helicopters have to climb to avoid a line of tall trees. In the trade they call it a 'Pop-up' attack.

'There we go! Rockets off with a big puff of smoke. You can hear the impact. A Hip Charley is running in from the south, standard attack direction about zero-six-zero degrees. We have a pair of Hinds circling and a fast jet, a Fitter, in a co-ordinated attack. This could be impressive.'

Of all the operations run by the British, this could be the most easily compromised. The team is part of an apparently innocuous cadre of quasi-diplomats operating in communist East Germany with Soviet consent and Soviet passes. In one form or another they have been here since the defeat of the Third Reich in May 1945. They are unarmed, usually to be found wearing British military uniform, driving around the countryside in clearly marked official British cars. Their function, ostensibly, is 'liaison'. The word covers a multitude of interesting possibilities but espionage is not among them. Well, not officially. It is child's play for Soviet counter-intelligence to work out where an enemy would place a spy who sincerely wanted to snatch covert photographs of air movements at the right altitude and angle, since the possible flight paths are as limited. The RAF intelligence-gatherers know this.

They know also that the Spetznaz – the Kremlin's equivalent of the SAS – has squads on standby, waiting to corner them. If that happens, a severe beating and a few broken bones might be the least serious outcome. The soldiers on the British Mission can usually find some excuse, however implausible, for being where they are. But someone caught penetrating an air-base with the aid of a long camera lens can expect no immunity.

Until it was consigned to history on 10 December 1990, the unit's ponderous, official title was 'The British Commander-in-Chief's Mission to the Soviet Forces of Occupation in Germany'. The title was instantly shrunk to BRIXMISS and, later, BRIXMIS. In this history, 'Brixmis' and 'the Mission' are used.

Brixmis was one of the great success stories – some people would say one of the few – to emerge from the uneven fabric of British intelligence-gathering after the Second World War. Because the Mission was in the business of collecting or recording military hardware, and the way the Soviets handled it, there were no subtle distinctions, no shades of grey, when assessing its success or failure. This was the world of Bulldog Drummond rather than George Smiley. As one of its soldiers, later recruited by the Secret Intelligence Service (SIS, i.e. MI6) said: 'I am led to believe that the Mission – together with our US and French colleagues – was our prime source on the use of new weaponry in the Warsaw Pact forces and of the movements of the Group of Soviet Forces in Germany [GSFG].'

Some recruits to the Mission were surprised (not always

4

pleasantly, for they had not volunteered for the posting) to be told that they were to become spies. In time, almost 200-strong, the Mission had its own specialist map-making team, technicians capable of handling anything from vehicle repairs to electronics, signals experts, linguists, full-time photo-technicians, two light aircraft with dedicated RAF pilots and army helicopters on call to collect defectors. Brixmis became an arm of British Intelligence as distinctive as SIS (MI6), MI5 or GCHQ. It was the smallest as well as the most coherent of these. Yet, in spite of turning up regular intelligence scoops, many of which were sent straight to Washington, the information it obtained was automatically given a lower security status by Whitehall than the product of GCHQ. As one former Chief of Mission said:

> Our product was almost invariably classified 'UK Confidential'. The same product from GCHQ signals intercepts was 'Secret' or 'TS' [Top Secret]. This was a kind of snobbery. We knew that GCHQ could be misled, spoofed. On one occasion, to my knowledge, massive signals traffic by the Soviet Army in Germany was dismissed by Cheltenham [GCHQ] as some sort of exercise or counter-intelligence. In fact, the Soviet armoured divisions had deployed from their barracks and we watched them. This was not an electronic game but a real deployment. Brixmis used nine Indicators of Hostilities which we checked virtually every day. One day, all nine were signalled. They included the trigger number of 25,000 Soviet soldiers swarming from barracks to their assembly areas, from which they could launch an attack on the West. Cheltenham missed that completely as the actual deployment was conducted in radio silence. We were on the ground and saw it happen.

When, as sometimes happened, Soviet tank divisions massed on the Nato border in total radio silence under cover of darkness, the West was even more at risk from the combination of deception and surprise for which the Russians were deservedly famous. The only Western eyes and ears to witness the threat were those of the Mission. Complacent commanders in the British zone of West Germany sometimes did not believe that the Red Army could be that efficient. (They tended to be the same people who believed, in August 1969, that the IRA was a fading memory in Irish history and that the British would be home again by Christmas.)

This scepticism was encouraged by the fact that Brixmis was not originally intended to be any kind of intelligence agency. This was one of those triumphs of the dilettante, amateur British approach to spying. As one of its Russian-speaking veterans put it: 'The British military has always regarded the whole area of intelligence with some distaste and as not quite playing the game. Therefore in my day [the 1960s] a posting to Brixmis was regarded in my regiment as something of a sideline. It was not a "fashionable" posting. I remember the remarks made in my hearing and for my benefit by two retired brigadiers in the Buffs Canterbury Cricket Week tent: "The Brixmis team? Never heard of it, have you, old boy?"'

Another linguist recalled: 'The question of languages was more important than most senior officers allowed. I had fluent Russian and German but some people on the team had limited language ability or none at all. As one joke goes, "That's the third village called Umleitung [Diversion] we've been through today."'

Like other hardy, long-living growths, Brixmis had a mass of roots; it developed like a rhizome, rather than from a single bulb. One of its roots – a sort of founding charter – was an Allied document signed in wartime London on 14 November 1944 by the Americans, Russians and British (the London Agreement). The French were invited to sign in March 1945. Entitled 'The Control Machinery in Germany', the document confidently anticipated the defeat of the Third Reich.

Article 2 stated: 'Each Commander-in-Chief in his Zone of Occupation will have attached to him military, naval and air representatives of the two other commanders-in-chief for liaison duties.'

To begin with, these duties were mundane. The first teams were known as FIATS, that is, members of Field Information Agency, Technical; groups concerned with demilitarizing Germany. Each wartime Ally had one. By early 1946 a trade-off was emerging between the Soviets and their Western Allies. The Russians wanted to repatriate 150,000 displaced persons (DPs) who had taken refuge in the British zone, people whom Moscow claimed as Soviets by birth or blood. The list included Estonians, Latvians and

Lithuanians (the Balts), and Ukrainians. The Russians wanted most of them as labour to replace the millions of war dead. Since the vast majority had had experience of being Hitler's unwilling slaves, this would be no novelty for them. Even more urgently, the Kremlin wanted to get its hands on those DPs who had caved in under German pressure and had fought against the Red Army.

The British, French, Americans and Russians, in a re-run of the settlement that followed the First World War, all wanted to pursue claims against Germany for war reparations. The British were also determined to confirm the destruction of Germany's war machine. An essential prerequisite was access to Germany's industrial base in the East and, for that, on-the-spot teams of accredited British liaison officers would be essential. FIAT teams were the tools employed for this job. The British FIAT was tasked by a high-level group known as the British Intelligence Objectives Sub-committee, or BIOS.

The FIAT search teams were dedicated to various tasks. Not all were concerned with hardware; some went in search of British citizens whose fate was unknown. In a parallel but separate operation the Special Air Service regiment kept in being an SAS war crimes investigation team long after the wartime regiment was officially disbanded. Its highly unorthodox methods included impersonating Gestapo veterans and even occultism. Another part of the official war crimes investigation unit was run by the mainly Jewish 12 Force, all of whom had served in the German or Austrian sections of the Special Operations Executive (SOE) during the war. What these teams had in common was the pursuit of Nazi officers, German and French, who had murdered war prisoners.

Yet another FIAT group, the Enemy Personnel Exploitation Section, specialized in targeting the best German brains, particularly in the war sciences, for use elsewhere. According to Lieutenant-Colonel Nigel Wylde QGM, Secretary of the Brixmis Association, 'These groups were purely national with a little co-operation between the UK and US. Their task was to find leading German scientists and persuade them to work in Russia, Britain, France or America. Wernher Von Braun [architect of the V2 missile attacks on London] was a case in point.'

One veteran of that time recalled working on Operation

Matchbox, a secret smuggling route through which some of the best German brains were brought out and shipped onward to the USA. Meanwhile, as Wylde said: 'The Russians tried everything to "persuade" their people to return. Russian and Baltic newspapers were distributed in the camps. Films were shown. Some people were even kidnapped and returned by force.'

The freedom enjoyed by Soviet missions of various kinds to range through the Western zones of a now dismembered Germany was not reciprocated. Nazi war criminals were discovering that if they wanted to evade Western justice, the Soviet zone was the place to be, just as a later generation of German terrorists found sanctuary in the communist East. The SAS team had its own method of dealing with that problem. Major E. W. (Bill) Barkworth, a former intelligence officer of 2 SAS and a fluent German speaker, learned that his quarry was in Leipzig and therefore untouchable. One of Barkworth's colleagues, Captain Yurka Galitzine, recalled: 'Bill impersonated the [former] Gestapo chief, Wilhelm Schneider, on the telephone and he said: "I'm on to a frightfully good thing on the black market. If you meet me under the clock in Cologne railway station at midnight, I'll cut you in and we'll share the proceeds." This fellow fell for it. At the rendezvous the SAS team was waiting in the shadows and grabbed their prisoner.' (The real Schneider was hanged at Hameln, in the British zone, in January 1947.)

This kind of unorthodox solution did not address the main problem, which became apparent during the first year after VE Day. On 4 July 1946, Major A. J. Evans, Officer Commanding Search Team O, Prisoner-of-War and Displaced Persons Division (Search Bureau) headquarters at the Control Commission (then the effective government of occupation in Germany) in Berlin, sent a signal to the headquarters of British Army of the Rhine. He reported that he had just seen his Russian opposite numbers. He went on:

It seems that a new situation had arisen which may seriously impede our search. The personnel of the Russian Liaison Mission have changed. Colonel Yeaseyev has disappeared. The Colonel and the Major that I saw confessed they were new and ignorant and seemed frightened of the job.

The new rules are that routes, places and objects of search are to be submitted in writing and the search can only be authorized by a Russian General. This must mean serious delay ... We shall get new conducting officers who won't know their job and will work to a rigid brief. My experience is that this makes a search nearly impossible.

The time has come when there should be a comparative examination of the liberties accorded Russian Search Officers in our Zone and British Search Officers in the Russian Zone and a charter drawn up covering both zones.

This signal was the last straw for the frustrated British search teams. Within days and with Whitehall's backing, Lieutenant-General B. H. Robertson, deputy military governor with the Control Commission, spoke informally to the Russian top brass after a meeting of the Control Commission. Knowing the Soviets' fondness for precedent, he reminded them of the still-unconsummated London Agreement of 1944. He proposed exchanging missions as the agreement suggested. The Russians concurred and work began on drafting a charter for all the Allied Missions.

Meanwhile, on 9 July, five days after the Evans signal, the BIOS group – now one of a multitude of expert committees presiding over the corpse of the Third Reich – met to seek ways to sift through the rubble surrounding the corpse. BIOS had been unwise enough to invite each Whitehall department to draw up a list of what it needed to know about Germany's remaining industrial potential. The resulting document comprised thirty closely typed pages and included such items as dental supplies and fertilizers. At this point the Joint Intelligence Committee (JIC), then as now the powerful hub of the Whitehall intelligence network, became concerned about the likely manpower required to deal with this open-ended shopping list and imposed a limit on the business. It was to be focused strictly on the potential military capability of Germany.

The result was that BIOS concentrated on a single, over-arching issue: tasking the new British military mission which would represent the UK in communist-dominated Germany.

On 16 September 1946, the Allied liaison agreement of November 1944 ('The Control Machinery in Germany') was confirmed in

Berlin by Robertson for the UK Occupation Forces and by Colonel-General M. S. Malinin on behalf of the Soviets. Elsewhere, relations between the former allies were already deteriorating, with wrangles about the number of roads from the West to Berlin open to non-Soviet allies. The British had a particular reason to be suspicious.

At Yalta in February 1945 the Big Three wartime leaders – Stalin, Roosevelt and Churchill – had agreed that Berlin would be split into zones of occupation: Russian, American, British and (later) French. The British zone included the sprawling acres of Berlin Zoo, in the tower of which some of Europe's greatest art treasures were stored for safe-keeping. They included Schliemann's gold, the legendary treasure of Troy containing Helen's diadem. Soviet trophy brigades, specially formed to seize works of art and other war booty, broke into the tower on 2 May 1945. Almost three weeks later, in breach of the Yalta agreement, the hoard was spirited away to Russia. When the British asked for an explanation the Russians shrugged and blamed looters. The full story came to light only in 1995, but a rank odour of suspicion pervaded the affair from the beginning.

The Robertson–Malinin agreement (see Appendix VIII) the following year laid down approximate ground rules for both British and Soviet liaison teams. As Captain S. D. Gibson MBE noted in a monograph on Brixmis:

The agreement allowed reciprocal arrangements for freedom of travel and circulation in each zone, with the exception of some restricted areas to be notified to the respective Commanders-in-Chief. Wireless and telephone communications were guaranteed and couriers were granted diplomatic immunity. Each Mission was to be administered by the zone in which it resided in respect of accommodation, rations, petrol and stationery. Mission buildings were to be given full immunity.

The aim of each Mission was to maintain liaison between the staffs of the two Commanders-in-Chief and their Military Governments. The Soviet equivalent of BRIXMIS was known as SOXMIS and was set up in Bunde, West Germany. The simplicity of the agreement allowed for considerable flexibility of interpretation in the years to follow. This flexibility was regularly used to the advantage of both British and Soviet organizations. Indeed it was difficult [such was their inherent flexibility] to break the agreements.

Brixmis, as the reborn liaison unit was now called, had a total strength of thirty-seven all ranks, many more than the American or French liaison Missions. In time this would be of crucial importance to Allied espionage. Of the thirty-seven, thirty-one were issued with Soviet passes enabling them to travel throughout the Soviet zone. The American and French Missions jointly had a total of thirty-two passes. One effect of that was that the standard British 'liaison' crew, cruising round communist East Germany in the Mission car with its number displayed, was three. As the intelligence role increased, this evolved into a flexible formula comprising a driver, usually a corporal; a tour (i.e. patrol) NCO – sergeant or warrant officer – to record the type and number of Soviet weapons they spotted; and a tour officer, often a linguist and usually the cameraman. When, against the rules, the NCO and officer slipped out of the car to creep up on their objective, the driver was their backstop and look-out. The French and Americans, with two-man crews, were limited in the risks they could take, though some French teams took them anyway.

At this early stage, an inner circle of nine officers controlled the unit. Serving under Major-General G. C. Evans, the Mission Chief, were his deputy, Brigadier Hilton, senior naval and air-force officers, a senior staff officer (G-1), the Chief's aide-de-camp, a brace of interpreters and an officer commanding rear headquarters. The team was further enlarged by two civil service mandarins from FIAT headquarters. One studied the economics of communist Germany and would score an impressive intelligence success during the Berlin Blockade; the other was an agricultural specialist. Both were invested with temporary military identities. The economist, Mr L. S. Hodson, officially responsible for political and civil affairs, became Colonel Hodson. The agronomist, W. H. Spice, who described himself in a Top Secret Brixmis report dated May 1951 as 'Economic Observer', became Lieutenant-Colonel Spice.

With a little help from Mr Attlee's postwar Labour government, the unit's strength was cut to thirty-five in 1949. Tension generated by the Berlin Blockade was still running high. The team was further reduced to twenty-five in 1950, the year in which a Soviet–Chinese friendship treaty was swiftly followed by war in Korea and China's invasion of Tibet. Thus reduced, the Mission started to 'borrow' officers from various regiments and military units serving in Berlin to maintain the number of people entitled to carry Soviet passes at its original total of thirty-one.

Responsibility for Brixmis was transferred from the Foreign Office to the War Office (Ministry of Defence; MoD) in 1950. By then, a unique operating style had emerged, one in which inter-service rivalries were ignored and bright ideas and lateral thinking were welcome. (It was an NCO who revolutionized the Mission's analysis of Soviet tank tactics.)

As the postwar frost deepened into Cold War, Brixmis evolved to meet the circumstances in which it found itself, the only accredited British military unit lawfully operating in communist Germany. Brixmis was never a formal part of the British intelligence apparatus, that sprawling, sometimes quarrelsome empire embracing MI6 and GCHQ (Foreign Office), MI5 and Special Branch (Home Office) and Defence Intelligence (MoD). Brixmis, like Special Operations Executive during the war, was able to respond to the realities on the ground by making up its own rules within the broad charter governing the ill-defined 'Liaison'. Brixmis, like SOE, had its own idiosyncratic way of doing things, audaciously cutting corners and often getting away with breathtaking coups through sheer cheek.

Like any good regiment, Brixmis developed a folk memory for its earlier history. Its experience was often kept within the family, passed on carefully so that, after the first ten years or so, it had acquired a more certain touch when dealing with a potential enemy than had most other diplomats or spies. And because it turned over its personnel, bringing in new blood from more orthodox regiments and air squadrons, it retained its vitality and amateur enthusiasm.

Its great successes were not always acknowledged by London. Sometimes it was Washington that sent congratulations back to Berlin or Potsdam. Since ultimate power lay in the US capital, applause from Washington confirmed the strategic significance of what had started as an oddball liaison team, floundering in the wreckage of the Third Reich and politically out of its depth.

With its main office in a building that had formed part of the Olympic Stadium complex for the 1936 Games, in West Berlin, and a Mission compound in Potsdam, half an hour's drive away across the Glienicke Bridge, Brixmis soldiers and airmen and their families had to get used to the sudden change from normal life, as it was understood in the West, to the claustrophobia of communism. As Lieutenant-Colonel David O'Connor (Brixmis 1969–71) put it:

One of the most depressing aspects of the Iron Curtain was that it existed in so many Soviet officers' minds. In conversation they were unable to get beyond details of their families, home (always Moscow) and the weather. When you tried to get an opinion or the conversation on to abstract matters, down came the shutters . . . These men were at that time aristocrats of Soviet society and yet they were frightened mentally of Westerners, such had been their conditioning. If you met an officer who was smiling, relaxed and good company, you knew that he was GRU [Soviet Military Intelligence] or KGB . . .

The effect of this conditioning was brought home to me one day while waiting at the Glienicke Bridge to cross over into Potsdam. While the documents were being checked, I ventured some conversation with the Soviet sentry. It was November and a light snow was falling, so I tried, 'Nasty weather for sentries.' He considered this mournfully and said, 'Why?' I replied lamely that it was cold and sentries had to stand around in it. He turned and marched off the bridge. Suddenly he stopped and I saw a smile of triumph on his face. He came back and said, 'In some parts of Russia it is hot and in others it is cold.' It was only later that I realized that he thought I was trying to find out where he came from.

As time passed, the Mission spent less energy on liaison and more on espionage but the process of confidence-building at times of international crisis remained an essential part of its identity. The art of the game was to prevent a war by accident or misunderstanding. The Kremlin, isolated from the truth by its iron mask, needed to be sure that its own propaganda – that Nato would attack – was not going to turn out, one dark night, to be true. The existence of a British Mission on the Soviet side of the front line and a Soviet Mission (Soxmis) on the British side was the ultimate insurance against disaster.

At the British military headquarters in West Germany (HQ British Army of the Rhine) and the Foreign Office in London, tongues wagged regularly about the risks taken by Brixmis, running free and sometimes a little wild, beyond the front line. According to one veteran:

There was considerable naivety about the likely attitude of the Soviets to the Missions [when they were caught breaking the rules]. There was a fear that the Soviets would put an end to them, that if they were too successful in intelligence terms they would be finished. 'Play it safe and hold back,' was the motto.

There was never any chance that the Soviets would end the Missions, for two reasons. First, the Missions were part of the status quo of 1945, of four-power occupation in Germany, and the Soviets had a vested interest in maintaining that status quo. They have always understood well the logic of not changing anything, lest the whole should unravel. Second, the quid pro quo of Soxmis was much too valuable to them. Soxmis was an agent-running or agent-support operation. It gave them ease of travel [in West Germany] which their embassy staffs could not match.

There was another, more basic reason. Fearful of a Nato attack, calculating whether or not to launch a pre-emptive strike, the Soviets had a third option: to ensure that the Western Missions were able to see, at close range, their combat readiness. The Missions were an essential component in the Kremlin's version of deterrence.

For more than forty years, successive generations of Brixmis soldiers, airmen and occasionally civilians rode the tiger of the Cold War. Though Moscow would not wish to cut down the Mission completely, it did use considerable ingenuity to draw its fangs. The KGB and the Stasi, the East German secret police, tracked and ambushed Brixmis people in the field and beat or shot them. Mission cars were rammed and pushed off the road in 'forced traffic accidents'. The surprise was not that some people serving with the

Mission lost their nerve but that so few did. The Mission's airmen, adapting a rule that allowed them to keep their flight training current, used a pair of Chipmunk two-seater trainers as low-level reconnaissance vehicles from which they took brilliant photographs of sensitive military targets. From time to time the communists took a pot-shot at the aircraft which would land at RAF Gatow, in West Berlin, with another hole in it. The aircrew, like all airborne spies flying clandestine missions, were ordered to torch their machines if they were brought down in hostile territory.

Much of the time the job was mind-numbingly boring, bitterly cold in Prussian winters and, in one series of operations known as Tamarisk (see Chapter 8), stomach-churningly disgusting, even for the SAS soldiers on the team.

Lieutenant-Colonel Jerry Blake, the Mission's senior staff officer (G-1 or General Staff Officer Grade 1) from 1976 to 1978, recalled: 'Much of the work was dull and uncomfortable, watching a railway line for hours when nothing came; sitting in some wood when you hoped a field exercise would take place and it didn't and you were eaten by mosquitoes in summer [at 35 degrees C] or half-soaked and frozen at other times; or sleeping in the snow [at minus 20 degrees].'

In time, the unit became increasingly self-sufficient, supported by its own specialist staff. The Berlin headquarters spawned a series of sub-departments including Research (intelligence analysis); the Weapons Office, also known as Technical Intelligence, to interpret the value of hardware 'scoops'; the Spandau Prison translators' office; the Geographic (map-makers') Section; and the RAF Special Section of photo-technicians and archivists.

Every Brixmis veteran who helped in the preparation of this history described it as 'the best time I had', though some of the tour teams added: 'It was also bloody petrifying.' The reconnaissance teams (deodorized with the description 'tours') were uniquely free to make their own decisions and take their own chances once they crossed the Glienicke, that Bridge of Spies where the U2 pilot Gary Powers walked West one freezing morning in 1962 as his Soviet counterpart, Rudolf Abel, came the other way. It was part of the agreement that the tours had no radios, so they operated in total silence like any other clandestine special forces operation deep behind enemy lines. As Major John Parry MBE was told by his Mission Chief, Brigadier (later Major-General) D. L. Darling, in 1963: 'When you cross that bridge you are at war.'

Most Brixmis veterans admit that they were less fitted afterwards for a garrison army stuck with a garrison mentality. 'This,' one of them said, 'was the real thing short of World War Three.'

No one knew that better than the German civilians on both sides of the Iron Curtain. For them, the war did not end on 8 May 1945. Just before the Berlin Wall came down in 1989, Theo Sommer, Editor-in-Chief of *Die Zeit*, wrote that the aging rulers of East Germany could not grasp that a new era was dawning. He went on: 'Because they opposed Hitler bravely and knew then that they were in the right, they believe they are in the right today when they cling to their Stone-age socialism. The people of East Germany are Hitler's last victims.'

With even greater directness, Vera Low, born Vera Goedicke, survivor of RAF bombing raids on Magdeburg and Dresden, wrote: 'Magdeburg was taken by the Red Army. I had to flee again while my parents remained behind, starving, freezing and imprisoned again. For me, Hitler's war ended only when the Berlin Wall came down.'

Brixmis was the only British military team on active service in Europe during the long continuation of Hitler's war, operating in a dangerous twilight – 'no peace/no war' – that suddenly seems, on the countdown to a new millennium, medieval in its remoteness. But as its veterans remind us, preserving the peace of twentieth-century Europe was sometimes a damned close-run thing: 'It happened sometimes that all our nine Indicators of Hostilities read positive. We checked the situation on the ground, looked down their gun-barrels, made sure there could be no surprise attack, no war by accident. That was our major contribution.'

CHAPTER 1

Blockade

1948–52

Throughout most of its history, Brixmis operated from two bases: a main headquarters in the comparative freedom of the British sector of Berlin and an outpost in a compound at Potsdam.

Half an hour's drive from Berlin, across the Glienicke Bridge, Potsdam is an historic town surrounded by water and full of faded glory. Throughout the Cold War it was a major garrison for the Soviet Army in East Germany. Brixmis soldiers rapidly came to regard their little holding there as a staging post and occasionally as a place of asylum. It was not very restful.

The Mission took over the Potsdam compound late in 1946. Situated near the Wildpark railway station, it contained seven houses, two of which were to be occupied by the French liaison team. The other five comprised the officers' mess, the other ranks' mess, the Chief of Mission's house, an administration block with an apartment above the office, and a house split into two apartments. There were also three stables occupied by three horses and a motor transport area where, later, a corporal of the Royal Electrical and Mechanical Engineers serviced the Mission's tour cars.

The first expedition appears to have been on foot, around the Potsdam area, and the next on horseback, when the Mission was waiting to be supplied with cars early in September 1946. It was, arguably, the last time that the British Army rode horses on a military operation in Europe. The Red Army was not being co-operative in supplying passes at the time, possibly because the Robertson–Malinin Agreement was not signed until midway through that month.

The first passes, allowing freedom of movement throughout the Soviet zone, were issued on 28 September and the first Brixmis motorized tour set off two days later. It did not get far.

Lieutenant Colonel C. B. Critchley MBE, an intelligence officer who briefed Brixmis for 'their very first venture out on the ground', noted that the tour 'ended prematurely in Brandenburg, where it was detained by a picket and escorted back to Potsdam despite every kind of clearance from the Soviets'. The incident prompted the first of many protests by the British Mission Chief to Marshal Andrei Sokolovsky, the Soviet Commander-in-Chief. The protest, a mere pebble on the beach of history, was none the less a sign of the times. Only a year earlier, Lord Montgomery had formally invested Sokolovsky with an honorary British knighthood during a ceremony at the Brandenburg Gate. In a sense, the Soviet Chief was 'Sir' Andrei.

It soon became clear that even when the paperwork was in order, Brixmis patrols which ventured out of their compound were likely to have trouble. There was another impediment to 'touring', as the game of covert reconnaissance was coming to be known; this was the fact that, during the first three years of the Mission's existence, not everyone shared the same enthusiasm for spying on a former ally. As Captain (later Lieutenant-Colonel) Frederick Bonnart said: 'The original "story" of the diplomatic protocol was that we were there to benefit and pass on to each other our war experiences to help each other in training. We were still fairly close allies at that time. The Russians were allowed into our Naafi; we reciprocally were allowed into their shop where we could buy caviar and vodka. Some of them greeted us as "Usniki", our allies.'

Major-General Lionel Manners-Smith, the Mission's second Chief, advised his tour officers: 'You get on with the dirty work but I'm not getting involved in it.' Most of his successors led from the front, sometimes too exuberantly for the Russians, who declared them to be PNG (*persona non grata*) and successfully demanded their removal. Manners-Smith, by contrast, belonged to a generation which still regarded the Germans as the enemy and the Red Army as an ally. So did many RAF aircrew veterans, some of whom had very mixed feelings about flying missions in support of German civilians during the Berlin Blockade of 1948–

49. Shortly before that costly operation, a group of veterans had attended a war crimes trial at Hamburg. There, as Air Chief Marshal Sir Kenneth Cross later recalled: 'The trial was that of the eighteen [Gestapo] criminals who had murdered fifty RAF aircrew from Stalag Luft 3 [on 19 May 1944] ... Seventeen of those on trial were convicted and old Pierrepoint [Britain's official executioner] came over in an RAF Dakota with his rope and he hung seventeen of them down the road at Hameln. We hadn't got a great deal of affection for the German nation ... When it came to doing the Berlin airlift, it was a professional job and whether it had been Hindus or Germans, the Air Force would have done it.'

The majority of the Mission, however, cared no more for the Soviets than the Germans; they simply wanted to get on with the job. One of these, said Lieutenant Colonel Bonnart, was the first Chief of Mission, Major-General Sir Geoffrey Evans, who 'left very much in disgust because the Mission had been unable to kick off'.

When clearance for open-ended tours was not granted, Evans's successor, Manners-Smith, wrote to the Soviets, asking to meet Red Army district commanders. There were four or five of them. What followed was a sort of comic opera. Bonnart's recollection was that 'We went off to these meetings in convoy, the Chief in the Humber Supersnipe, we in Snipes: his aide-de-camp, myself as the Russian speaker. We were received royally, stopping at the local *gasthof*, but watched by chaps in suits with enormous shoulders who never let us out of their sight. We had dinner and a reception and we were shown things ... a china factory, a car factory, but never anything military.'

It was after one of these Ruritanian non-events, said Bonnart, that Manners-Smith gave the green light to others on his team to do the 'dirty work'.

It all began quietly enough for some, but the calm was deceptive. Jim Symes MC, a Royal Hampshire major and senior interpreter who had started learning Russian as an alternative to mind-rot while a prisoner-of-war at Oflag IX A/Z, joined the team in September 1948. He rapidly concluded: 'Those of us who lived in Potsdam were virtually prisoners ... There was not much to do on the liaison side. Probably the most important tasks were to ensure that the Chief's furniture at Potsdam was arranged for the better, and on one occasion to arrange for an intelligence officer from headquarters, British Army of the Rhine, to interview a British Army deserter. We were allowed to visit West Berlin (usually the Officers' Club) once a week, while our wives could go Naafi shopping, also once a week. We spent most evenings playing bridge . . . Soldiers and airmen [the Other Ranks] were unfortunate. They were allowed one evening a week in Berlin, but had nothing else to do.'

The Mission's first attempts at military espionage, as he shrewdly noticed, were 'pretty amateurish'. In London, the Director of Naval Intelligence wanted photographs of 'some extraordinary super-structures being built on some ships in Rostock', an ancient port on the Baltic. Undetected, in perfect weather and full light of day, a Royal Navy officer escorted by Symes shot a roll of film which, when processed, revealed thirty-six frames of black, opaque nothingness. The team was sent back to try again, having been instructed to remove the lens cover from the camera. At his second attempt, the senior naval officer again took thirty-six shots, 'but unfortunately, nobody had told him to aim and he got the sky mostly, though there were some shots of the superstructure.'

Various British intelligence agencies, including the Foreign Office, were anxious to direct the tour teams' energies but since Brixmis came under the direct command of the Commander-in-Chief, Germany, rather than the Ministry of Defence in London, unrealistic proposals could be deflected. To impose some order on the requests, a 'Targeting Book' was created, complete with a Brixmis editor, the first of whom was Major Symes.

There were to be many embarrassments in these early days, in line with the style of British film comedy of that time. It is all the more necessary, therefore, to note the first serious intelligence scoop in 1947, when experts, including Lieutenant-Colonel Tony Dangerfield OBE, senior staff officer at Potsdam, cracked the 'spiral code' of Soviet vehicle numbers. The spiral related code letters and numbers to the means to retrieve information and decode by a complex cross-reference procedure compared by one veteran to a message written on a sheet of paper and then wrapped around a walking stick. The 'message' could be read only if the stick were twirled, apparently sending the data up or down the stick in a spiral.

According to another intelligence officer who served with the Mission, Major Harold Gatehouse MBE, Dangerfield would have needed 'a pool of reports ... from military attachés, mission sources, reliable agents and photographs across the board in the Soviet armed forces'. When it was broken, the code was found to consist of one Cyrillic letter and five digits (for example, G3–15–01) which identified the military district to which the vehicle belonged. In time of tension the movement of number plates in one direction or another could be of critical importance.

As a subsequent intelligence officer put it: 'Our first task was to identify the other side's Order of Battle, the "Orbat". Apart from talking to Russian deserters, we sent back to UK records of all Russian military vehicle numbers we encountered. We learned that the "teeth" (fighting) arms had five letter/figure numbers, e.g., G3–24–02, that logistic/admin. vehicles had four letter/figure numbers, e.g., L–20–30. The clever experts at home with this and other information duly worked out the Order of Battle.'

This claim is challenged by Major Gatehouse. He asserted: 'To identify the military unit to which a vehicle belonged, there was no short cut other than the painstaking collection of vehicle registration numbers seen using a barracks or noted in a column of other vehicles belonging to the same unit.'

He also concluded: 'Dissemination of our knowledge of the system was probably made on too wide a basis. It was discussed in detail by various desk officers at a conference I attended in London in about 1954. Any mole who saw the minutes of the meeting, or attending it, would have been able to pass on the extent of our knowledge to the Soviets.' He also contended that such knowledge was of only limited value, particularly since the Soviets were unsporting enough to change the numbers just before a big exercise.

Dangerfield, a Royal Warwickshire soldier, later became Head of Intelligence Organization in Austria. It was just before he left the Mission in June 1948 that Brixmis began its 'unauthorized' tours. As Bonnart put it: 'Touring was made unannounced on the basis of the liberty of movement supposedly authorized by our diplomatic status and confirmed by our passes. Our vehicles were Humber Box cars, painted dark red with the Union flag all over them to ensure that we could not be accused of clandestine action. These were subsequently replaced by khaki-coloured Humber Snipes. Two Supersnipes were available for the Chief and his deputy. All cars' – a fleet of thirteen at the time – 'had the Union emblem on the bumper. We wore uniform at all times on tour and carried no arms.'

Symes was quick to note that Soviet barracks were visible in spite of their boundary fencing: 'They were surrounded by wooden palisades. We found that if you drove past at a certain speed the palisade effect "disappeared". It became a big, open flap and you could count everything inside.'

Manners-Smith's wily successor, Brigadier S. Curteis, told the Soviet liaison office that Brixmis was fascinated by the stirring history of how, during the Great Patriotic War, the Red Army had crossed the ice-bound river Oder early in 1945 so as to attack Berlin. The operation was launched from the eastern bank at a spot named Kustrin. Brixmis would like to see the spot for itself.

As Symes recalled: 'Lieutenant-Colonel Agamirov, head of the Soviet liaison office, got permission for our visit. He had been the senior staff officer of the Soviet division which launched the attack on Kustrin, so he could brief Curteis. I went with the party. We had an entertaining day. At the end of it, as we were crossing the plain on the west bank, we saw a JS2 tank which had been knocked out during the battle, lying some distance from the road.'

Curteis mentioned this hulk in his report to Rhine Army headquarters. The JS (for Josef Stalin) heavy tank was a useful find. 'Some days later we received a request from a branch of Military Intelligence [MI]. They were very interested in the JS2. Even three years later there were big gaps in the knowledge. An MI officer joined us on a temporary pass, bringing with him a long questionnaire.'

Symes now made a second, uninvited trip to the battleground, with 'Tom', the man from MI: 'Tom and I had a couple of undisturbed hours at the site. Tom did the measuring and I the recording. Our instruments were a ruler, tape measure and protractor.' Safely back in West Berlin, Symes and Tom realized that they had left their instruments littering the site. An angry deputy Chief, Colonel J. E. F. Meadmore, sent the two men back to find the gear. 'We dashed off and found to our chagrin that someone had been there before us and had taken the evidence away! Nothing more was heard. MI were very pleased with the detailed report.'

Economic intelligence was also collected by Brixmis at this time. Its agronomist was an ultra-laid-back war veteran named – appropriately, in view of his vocation – 'Lieutenant-Colonel' W. H. (Harry) Spice. The point of a Spice tour was to see how the harvest was going. A fellow officer recalled:

'As we left Berlin, Spice said to our driver, Trooper French, "Wake me up when we get somewhere near Dresden." As we rolled down the autobahn, approaching Dresden, French said: "We're there, sir."

'"Good," said Harry. He opened his eyes, looked up and, amid fields of bright yellow, said to me "Rape."

'I said, "Rape?"

'"Yes," he said. "You think that's mustard, don't you? But it's rape." Then, to the driver, "French, wake me up at Erfurt."'

A week passed. Symes, in Brixmis headquarters in Berlin, asked Vera, the secretary, if he could see a copy of Spice's report of their agricultural tour.

She replied: 'Here it is. It's the same as last year. Only the date has been changed.'

For all that, the Brixmis beginners did score one useful intelligence coup. The West, denied road access to Berlin, was learning the hard way what it cost to support a city under siege about 130 miles inside hostile territory. Nato's reprisal was to impose a counter-blockade on the East in September 1948. It needed to discover how effective that was, and how much punishment was being inflicted on the economy of communist Germany. So 'Colonel' L. S. Hodson, the economics guru with Brixmis, set about finding out. He used many sources including the remnants of the Third Reich's bureaucracy and expert defectors debriefed by that odd unit, the Enemy Personnel Exploitation Section of FIAT (British Element). Hodson also conjured up insider help in communist Germany using pressures and enticements still not disclosed. As official records indicate, Brixmis acquired stunningly detailed maps of Soviet-zone railways indicating track status, old war damage, regional control centres, sidings, numbers of locomotives, types and numbers of freight trucks, passenger carriages and much more.

The overall effect of this research was to show that East Germany's steel output was dropping catastrophically. Since the end of the war, Russian production had been propped up by the satellites, including the Soviet zone of Germany. From the end of 1948, Hodson could detect a dramatic increase in the amount of steel delivered from Russia to its German ally. A steel-rolling mill removed to Russia less than two years earlier was brought back again. In April 1949 he reported: 'The counter-blockade was a powerful but probably not decisive factor in inducing Russia to open negotiations with the Western Powers.'

As a final gift to Brixmis, Hodson (probably detached from MI6 and now on his way back to other cloak-and-dagger operations there) promoted the first 'Rail Watch' by the Mission. Hodson was interested in steel cargoes. In due time, Brixmis observers would widen the agenda.

In parallel with the first tours, playing the liaison card, the Mission talked to British deserters who, having crossed to the East, were now also deemed to be defectors. Such interviews, staged with Soviet co-operation in anonymous offices deep inside communist Germany, tended to be crisp and monosyllabic.

Some defectors, it is thought, are still in Eastern Europe. They were sent to the same obscure town in East Germany, taught the language and set to work in a factory for the rest of their lives. They are old men now, but they are still fugitives from British justice, officially deserters and liable to prosecution if they return.

None of the deserters whom Brixmis encountered went East for political reasons. Most were private soldiers or junior NCOs, in trouble because they were not very bright, looking for a new identity in the nearest convenient hiding place. A major who defected in 1947 was identified by MI6 in East Berlin in 1965, but as he was a mere 'Schoolie' – a member of the Army Education Corps – no one was very concerned. He was outranked in importance by another defector, an Intelligence Corps corporal subsequently spotted in the Baltic states. His desertion caused, as one veteran admitted, 'a terrific stir and made us revamp the vetting system'.

Some of the British deserters married East German women but when they later decided to return to the West, they discovered that they could not take their wives with them. One had to divorce and to renounce his East German citizenship before he could come back. In another case, Brixmis officers adopted a politically neutral line when it became apparent that they were not dealing exclusively with a British subject but his East German wife as well. According to one account, the deserter 'turned up at the Mission House [at Potsdam] in the 1950s and asked for political asylum. His wife was East German. He would not leave the country without her. He was taken secretly into Potsdam and released without being spotted by the police. He and his wife escaped over the border into Bavaria some weeks later.'

Between operations, time dragged in the Potsdam compound. In the wreckage of a starving Europe immediately after the war, navigation through the rubble of some German cities still needed a compass. It was a landscape of grey scarcity and bartering, where food was the principal currency. A bar of chocolate could buy a night with a girl or a performance of German *lieder*. At a British Army vehicle aid post just inside the Western side of the border, Lieutenant-Colonel Critchley wrote: 'half-naked German civilians would occasionally seek refuge, having been stripped of clothing and possessions by roaming Soviet defectors.' This gloomy situation – slightly deodorized in Britain by the use of the word 'Austerity' – was an irresistible challenge to the survival instincts of the British soldier.

Encouraged by Symes, Gunner Bentley, one of the drivers, started an unofficial pig-farm in a corner of the British compound in the East. The resulting bacon was traded for whisky at the Berlin headquarters and the whisky traded for Russian vodka.

Bonnart, a Russian interpreter from the Queen's Royal Regiment, was up early every morning, riding his horse before the working day began. He seems to have been less affected by the claustrophobia of Potsdam than most and celebrated Christmas 1949 by riding the animal into the officers' mess. Symes and the RAF interpreter, Alexei Yates, 'caught masses of perch and one tench' from the lake at the US Mission House nearby. The deputy

Chief, Colonel J. E. F. Beardmore, took the team to shoot boar in local woodland, with .303 infantry rifles, lethal up to about 1,000 yards, with German foresters acting as beaters in exchange for cigarettes. The only casualty was a fox.

Group Captain Eyres RAF, a senior Air Staff officer, went one step further as befitted a member of a service that had recently practised strategic bombing. According to Bonnart:

> We did not normally carry arms but on one occasion when I was touring with Eyres, I noted that he had taken a .303 service rifle. It was not my place to criticize senior officers so I kept quiet, but it was autumn and game was plentiful in Germany, particularly as the Germans were severely limited in any shooting activities.
>
> I also knew 'Groupy' was a keen and good shot. How good I was soon to find out. Near a bridge out in the country he shot a wild goose (admittedly sitting) at 200 yards right through one eye. We hung the bird in a cellar for a week and invited a French Air Force friend to Sunday lunch at the mess.
>
> The cook [a German] at first refused to put the green thing into the oven and thought we were mad when we insisted. But when she had been given a bite she admitted it had been worthwhile.

A reluctant cook was the least of their troubles with local staff, all carefully chosen for work at the UK Mission by the Soviet Liaison Mission. 'We assumed that all of them had been ordered to keep an eye on us and we behaved accordingly. In principle, "business" was not even discussed in Potsdam, although some of this was unavoidable. On one occasion, during a short meeting, Group Captain Eyres saw an eye at the keyhole and quietly opened the door to find one of our staff standing doubled up behind it. One of the maids tried to let us know that they were being forced to spy. We were able to reassure them by advising them to report whatever they saw. We received Soviet rations as well as British ones and were able to pass on a good deal of food to our staff, who were duly appreciative.' And, of course, discreetly bribed.

To 'ensure our protection from the public', Bonnart recalled, the Mission was 'guarded' by the increasingly oppressive presence of the Volkspolizei, or Vopo, the East German security force. For a time they occupied one of the two empty houses within the compound. Bonnart noted that the Vopo guards 'were clearly there to watch us and behaved fairly arrogantly'. So, in a gesture which might have come from the pages of *The Great Escape* or *The Wooden Horse*, he pounced one afternoon when one of the hated Vopo left his pistol lying on a table, unattended.

'I "confiscated" the weapon, put it in the safe and let him look for it. His lieutenant turned up the next day and I made him sweat a bit before returning the weapon. Soon afterwards our Mission Chief [Brigadier Hilton, replacing Brigadier Curteis] persuaded the Soviet Mission to forbid them the camp. They then stayed on duty, "guarding" us from the outside.'

For the Berlin Blockade generation, the isolation from normal life was underlined by an order excluding British wives from West Berlin during the crisis. London might have started to purge itself of its war psychosis but Germany was another matter as the blockade tension mounted. It would not be surprising if some British war veterans serving there in these immediate postwar years were becoming permanently marooned, culturally and psychologically, caught up in a foreign culture under siege like divers in an air bubble, faintly aware that their 'mother ship', England as they had known it before the war, had gone for ever. Symes was not the only ex-war prisoner to return to the scene of his captivity, but for him the trip ended in tears.

'I wanted to go back to Eisleben near Halle to see the farm where I was released from captivity on Friday 13 April 1945. I was [now with Brixmis] a tour officer and interpreter. As we pulled up in the courtyard we were arrested. My story was not believed.'

Even under siege, however, West Berlin was a honeypot of seeming normality, a free zone and a military clubland in which to shake off the oppressive drabness of the East. All manner of reasons were found to go there or to some other town in the West. Such journeys were often eventful. Alexei Yates, with his wife, was driving his VW car from a party in Berlin back to Potsdam when they came upon a Russian colonel and major, hitching a lift. Yates obliged but appreciated too late that neither of the Russians was sober.

'Then they recognized we were speaking English. As we drove

through a wood, the major said to the colonel, "Shall we do them in now?"' Yates, for whom Russian was as familiar as English, understood every word but he was still surprised when the major put an arm round his neck from the rear in a stranglehold.

'My wife took off her stiletto-heeled shoe and beat him with it. The colonel also controlled him. We bundled them out and drove off but I couldn't report the incident because I was in civilian clothes and that contravened the regulations.'

The mission Chief, Brigadier Curteis, wanted to visit a seaside resort on the Baltic with his wife, son and daughter. Yates, as interpreter, tried to negotiate diplomatic clearance for this trip. It was refused. With Yates as driver, they set off anyway. When the Vopo tried to obstruct their passage, Curteis said: 'Run them down.' Yates grazed past them. A further row followed at the resort hotel and the local Soviet command post.

'We were told to leave in one hour's time. On the way back to the hotel where his wife was staying the brigadier said, "Take the engine apart. Make the car unserviceable."'

When this was done, Yates telephoned the East German police and asked for a tow back to the hotel.

'We had three days at the hotel while spares were brought up from Brixmis.' The hospitality was not conspicuous. Even the compound at Potsdam seemed welcoming when they finally got back.

In all the gloom there was one reason for optimism: unlike so many of their contemporaries, they had survived the war. As the era of no war/no peace, the years that historians came to identify as the Cold War, rumbled forward into a new decade, this gratitude for small mercies evaporated. A later generation of soldiers on both sides had their sights set on the next war rather than the last, and they had rather more firepower available to them.

By the spring of 1948, both sides were developing a new form of conflict: conflict-as-communication, a political body-language that fell short of all-out war but was not bloodless either. It was shadow-boxing in which, sometimes, the shadow struck back. At the centre of this arena was Berlin, outpost of Western liberalism deep inside communist Germany. The horseman Captain Freddie Bonnart was one of the first Brixmis soldiers to be blooded by the crisis. In

March 1948, when the Russians first let it be known that the Magdeburg Bridge over the Elbe – a wooden construction at that time – was unsafe, cutting the autobahn route to Berlin, Bonnart used body-language rather than the Russian he had been expensively taught during an intensive six months at Cambridge.

The three Western commanders in Berlin – a sanctified trinity of generals – were to meet in the city. Bonnart, newly promoted to captain, was told to check the bridge and report back by 9 A.M. He reached the bridge early and waved aside the East German policeman who tried to stop him.

'I drove across it slowly and then at speed, returned the salute from the Vopo, who had [now] become respectful and set out again for Potsdam. Speeding down the autobahn we ran a wheel-bearing and had to stop but I succeeded in ringing the Mission and was able to report in time for the meeting that there was nothing wrong with the bridge.' This critically important call had to be made from a local public telephone.

The political atmosphere was not sweetened by an avoidable air disaster a few weeks later. On 5 April 1948, a British European Airways Viscount airliner approaching Berlin flew over a grass airstrip on the site of the 1936 Olympic village at Dallgow-Döberitz. The strip was used by Russian Yak fighters. One of these, performing aerobatics, hit the Viscount. Both machines crashed. The Yak created further chaos when it fell on the busy Heerstrasse in West Berlin. The Viscount hit the ground in communist territory with the loss of fifteen lives including two Americans. A Brixmis team went to the scene.

Mutual blame-laying followed. A Foreign Office file reveals: 'The British found that the Yak pilot flew under the Viscount and tried to loop back over the top of it. The Yak's tail was torn off by the Viscount's wing, with the Yak upside down. The Russians said that the Viscount was on an unauthorized flight and that it took the tail off the Yak as that plane was taking off. In fact, records show that the Russians had been informed in advance of the Viscount's approach.'

The tragedy provoked the only direct, personal protest by one commander-in-chief to another. On the evening following the disaster, General Sir Brian Robertson accompanied by the Brixmis

Chief, Major-General Manners-Smith, drove to Karlshorst, in East Berlin, to confront Marshal Sokolovsky. The British were icily angry; the Russians placatory, offering condolences and the promise of a joint inquiry. Robertson, still wary of the cowboy behaviour of Russian airmen, ordered RAF fighters to escort subsequent BEA flights to Berlin. Worse was to follow.

Road traffic between Berlin and the West stopped on 15 June when the autobahn road bridge across the Elbe near Magdeburg was closed for 'extensive repairs'; on 24 June the rail link was cut and so was the electricity. As the air bridge was developed and the three air corridors from the West became increasingly crowded, the dangers increased.

The root of the problem of access to Berlin was that, at the end of the Second World War in 1945, the US believed that its right of way into the former capital, through communist-controlled East Germany, was not something that needed to be written down. Written agreements covered only three air corridors into the former German capital. The implications of a land blockade came as an unpleasant surprise. As Sir Frank Roberts, a British diplomat who negotiated with Stalin during that time, recalled in a discussion staged by the RAF Historical Society in 1989:

So there we were, with this blockade. About two million Berliners in the Western sectors to be fed, quite sizeable Allied forces also to be maintained and fed. The first American reaction was from General Clay and from Murphy, his diplomatic adviser: 'We don't put up with this kind of thing, we push a land convoy through, and to hell with the Russians if they want to stop it.' In Washington they didn't like this very much, and certainly in London we didn't, because obviously you didn't want to be the first to fire and it was going to be so easy for the Russians.

There was the bridge already [across the Elbe] which you couldn't cross because they said you couldn't, and they only had to put a tree trunk across the road and then what did one do, get out of one's tank and say to the Russians, 'Will you remove the tree and if you don't, we're going to fire on you? . . .' Where we were strong was in our rights in the air.

To assert the West's rights of access by road, such as they were, a Brixmis car made a trial run over the Magdeburg Bridge each Monday morning. Symes recalled: 'We managed to cross from East to West by paying the guards at the Eastern end three cigarettes, trundling over and paying the guard at the Western end three cigarettes to get off the bridge. We went on to Hanover [in the West] to do some shopping and on the return trip, took the vehicle ferry below the bridge and inspected the bridge from below ... We knew it was being used, as a car with Dutch number plates crossed while we were there. We roared back. No change from last visit. Bridge usable.' Despite this, the bridge was not accessible to normal military traffic from the West until the formal end of the blockade on 12 May 1949.

The French, with more bravura than sense, tried to make their presence felt at the airport they constructed at Tegel with German labour gangs (almost half of them women) at the beginning of the crisis. A tall mast used by the Soviet Berlin Radio transmitter, a propaganda station, stood near the end of the newly constructed runway, obstructing the flight path. The French General Ganeval ordered his men to blow it up. A wrathful Russian Major-General Kotikov demanded an explanation: 'How did you do it?'

'With dynamite and French sappers,' replied Ganeval.

This was good anecdotal stuff, but the episode was not calculated to amuse Stalin personally, or the Red Army which had liberated Berlin three years earlier. Nor would it make life smoother for other Allied operations, including those of Brixmis. They were, as one veteran recalled, 'frequently involved in dealing with the consequences of planes that crashed whilst flying over East Germany'. The work included retrieving the wrecks which could be salvaged. There was no shortage of those. Between 22 July 1948, when Dakota No. KN213 crashed at Gatow, and August 1949, when a Hastings (TG611) was severely damaged at Tegel, more than forty RAF machines were recovered. Sometimes there was no wreckage worth salvaging. It was a matter of detaching identity tags from the aircrew's bodies to confirm the legal fact of death.

One man engaged in the macabre task of examining the dead was Flight Lieutenant (later Squadron Leader) Alexei Yates, born in Ekaterinberg, near the scene of the massacre of the Russian

32

royal family. The son of a British father and White Russian mother, Yates joined the RAF before the Second World War and served in wartime Russia with Britain's Military Mission No. 30. (All the RAF officers on that team, as it happened, were also born in Russia.)

Now, with the airlift at its height, Yates was on the ground in communist Germany, a Brixmis interpreter. He visited the sites of three crashed RAF aircraft. 'I cannot pinpoint any longer where they were,' he said. 'I could tell you how we stumbled through forests and found charred bodies. The aircraft would be scattered over hundreds of yards all over the place. Then we would come across the odd body which had been burned out completely, so charred it was horrible. We had to remove the identity disk.'

East German police would recover the human remains for repatriation, eventually, to Britain. Salvaging aircraft was another matter. Yates was permitted to bring technicians to assist but 'we were not allowed a crane and we had no tools'.

The most intractable case was that of a Meteor fighter which crash-landed in the East. Without tools, they tried to break up the machine for piecemeal recovery. The machine defied their efforts to take it apart by hand. It stayed where it was, and may still be in the undergrowth. As later events would prove, it was not necessarily an innocent victim. Nato was already preparing to fly spy-plane missions into Soviet-held territory.

The longer the operation dragged on (and at the time, no one could be certain how long that would be), the greater the danger. Aircrew and ground crew fatigue resulting from non-stop round trips against the clock as part of a crowded air programme conspired with long hours of winter darkness. The stress was given an extra, savage twist by Soviet provocation. What amounted to an orchestrated game of 'chicken' evolved in the sky along the three Allied air corridors as Soviet fighters and bombers flew deliberate, nose-to-nose collision courses against the lumbering Western transports, only to pull away a mere fifty yards short of disaster.

By 18 September, Allied aircraft running the Russian blockade of the city lifted a record 7,000 tons of supplies through fog, high winds and rain. In all, 895 machines touched down with food and fuel within twenty-four hours. As one observer noted: 'US pilots put on a special effort to celebrate Air Forces Day, flying in 651 times and carrying 5,572 tons of coal.'

Dakota, Globemaster and York transports were not enough. The RAF pressed into service its Sunderland flying boats to land on Berlin's huge Lake Havel. Civil airlines such as Skyways and World Air Freight joined the British Operation Plainfare running up to 2,000 tons of cargo per day. Even this was modest when set against the American operation, Vittles, which delivered almost 77 per cent of the total of 2.3 million tons flown to Berlin between late June 1948 and early September 1949.

The airlift finally broke the stranglehold on the Western presence in Berlin after fifteen months of blockade and at a cost of sixty-one British airmen's lives and those of thirty-one Americans and seven Germans. Hard-up Berliners raised a fund to support the families of Allied dead. The fund was still in being when the Berlin Wall came down in 1989.

Throughout the crisis, insulated by protocol and anaesthetized by alcohol, civilized contact between Brixmis and the Russians were sustained at official receptions. According to Symes, one of these parties took place in the glittering surroundings of the Cecilienhof Palace at Potsdam amid the usual haze of vodka, although the official record designates only two such occasions in 1948, both in the more drab surroundings of the Soviet head-quarters at Karlshorst in East Berlin. Either way, it was an unlikely setting for part of a military front line.

During the blockade, on orders from Downing Street, British absentees from Russian receptions included the UK Commander-in-Chief General Robertson, all the headquarters staff from British Army of the Rhine based in West Germany and the Allied Control Commission running civil affairs in the country. It was a symbolic snub, a diplomatic gesture of cold anger which ignored the dictum, 'There is no harm in being polite to a man even if you intend to kill him.'

In 1948, during the first great showdown between the wartime Allies, Brixmis stood in for the rest of the British establishment and was uniquely placed to assess the real temper of the Red Army high command in the front line, if not the mood in Moscow. The Red Army reaction to the death of Stalin five years later – an

event closely monitored by the Brixmis Chief of Mission, Brigadier
Dewhurst – revealed how impenetrable are such secrets in a true
dictatorship.

Symes recalled the historically important 1948 reception with
something less than gravitas. He was clear about the details,
however.

> The Brixmis party consisted of the Chief, deputy Chief, Senior Air
> Staff Officer and myself together with our wives. We had a briefing
> at the Chief's house in West Berlin beforehand (over a gin or
> two). The reception was from 1800 to 2000 hours. The Chief
> explained that we would arrive on time and most important of
> all, leave on time, so that the Russians could get on with their
> own celebrations. Wives would follow their husbands up the stairs
> of the palace. At the top, wives would be taken to the wives'
> party, while we four would be taken to the generals', colonels'
> and majors' rooms respectively. We would all meet at the cars
> promptly at 2000 hours.
>
> We were to be very careful about drinking vodka. Between each
> drink we must have a mouthful of bread and butter. If we felt we
> could not compete we must be firm and tell the Russians we did
> not want any more. The Russians would respect this. Generally
> we should do what the Russians did.
>
> In my room there was a Russian major . . . who picked up a
> chicken leg, ate it, and threw the bone over his shoulder. I did the
> same. Unfortunately I did not realize that Colonel General M. S.
> Malinin [second most senior Soviet officer in Germany] with our
> Chief, Brigadier Curteis, had entered the room to greet us all. One
> of us hit Brigadier Curteis in the chest. I think I got Malinin as a
> matter of fact.

So the reception ended and 'at 2000 hours only the Chief was
late'.

The Russians were still angry with the French who, pressured
by the threat of stronger protests than mere words, agreed to return
the Stolpe district of Berlin to Russian control. The Brixmis veteran
Bonnart shed some light on the motives which probably inspired
French recklessness.

The American and British Missions worked together on intimate terms. 'We were in permanent contact to such a degree that a certain amount of "um" [umbrage] was taken by the French because we were told not to pass certain details to them . . . because the French had communists in the government at that time . . . We had good relations with the French Mission Chief, a charming man and patriot, an airman who had fought with the [Free French air squadron] Escadrille Normandie, alongside the Russians, winning lots of decorations, a Russian speaker but not a communist, a patriotic Frenchman . . . But there we were, there was nothing we could do about it.'

The Berlin Blockade was followed, a year later, by the Korean War, ostensibly between the UN and North Korea but really part of a growing conflict between the superpowers. Brixmis sharpened up its act. Now under Foreign Office control, it was also answering demands for information from Nato's operational headquarters (SHAPE) at St Germain en Laye and from various parts of the British Military Intelligence establishment. As a result it became an omnivorous collector of information about the potential enemy, a vacuum cleaner that hosed up anything and everything, however trivial. Some of its Top Secret documents from this period combine the minutiae of wartime Mass Observation reports with the voyeurism and compassion of Henry Mayhew's accounts of the underclass of Victorian London. The Germany Brixmis knew, the Soviet zone of occupation, was a cheerless place in which 'the only town clearance [of bomb debris] was that necessary to provide bricks for rebuilding the factories'. As the relevant report also noted: 'from 1945 to 1951 is a long time, but not long enough to rebuild a country the size of Eastern Germany, whose industrial and economic expansion is leaping at such a speed.' Beneath the bricks, occasionally, they still found victims of the Second World War.

The Mission's monthly reports ran to fifty pages and covered eight topics: General; Soviet Army Order of Battle and Military Activity; Paramilitary Police; Air Information; Naval Information; Communications; Inter-communications; Economic, Industrial and Agricultural Information. In May 1951, the Air Report's thirty-nine observations (signed by Wing Commander M. H. de L. Everest AFC) included:

Miscellaneous: Eberswalde – 23rd May (1100 hrs, visibility good)

Following Soviet Air Force Personnel seen on road between EBERSWALDE and HOENFINOW:

1 NCO [non-commissioned officer]
  and two ORs [Other Ranks] walking
1 NCO and OR in horse and cart
1 OR on horseback
3 ORs with picks and shovels

The other thirty-eight items in this report addressed more serious stuff, including detailed records of the movement of Mig-15s, Ilyushin-10s and Yak-14s. Collecting such intelligence was, inevitably, risky, though sometimes the risk consisted of being bored to death rather than being shot. Commander J. C. Pearson RN experienced near-terminal tedium. Picked up with his interpreter Flight Lieutenant B. Bliss RAF by German paramilitary police outside their barracks at Prenzlau on 14 May 1951, he found himself in front of the local Soviet commandant. The Russian was 'somewhat flushed with wine, his manner by turns suspicious, pompous and ingratiating'. He said, 'You are all preparing a war. You are against the Soviet Union. But we're not afraid, no matter how many there are against us. You have the Marshall Plan, the Schuman Plan and the atom bomb, but we have nine million soldiers and victory will be ours.'

The commandant's lieutenants 'were less hostile, more open-minded and reasonable men ... they were not convinced that the West had aggressive intentions against the Soviets ... They considered unanimously that the late Mr Ernest Bevin [Britain's Labour Foreign Secretary] was an honourable man.'

Pearson's analysis concluded: 'Many Soviet officers, particularly the younger ones, are interested to meet and talk to British officers in a friendly way if they can do so without political risk to themselves. The British officer must have sufficient understanding to give the necessary lead. A sense of humour with considerable patience is a good line of approach and some direct experience of the Soviet Union provides a valuable talking point.'

Had the Prenzlau commandant been allowed to study a Brixmis report just a year later, his suspicions about Western intentions would have been confirmed. The Brixmis summary for May 1952, classified Top Secret as usual, described the latest exploration of the Baltic coast near Rügen as follows: 'Beach reconnaissances have been carried out in the vicinity of ZINGST and WARNEMUNDE with a view to assessing the usefulness of this area for possible future landings and separate reports will be rendered.' 'Here', the Brixmis authority Lieutenant-Colonel Wylde later confirmed, 'is Brixmis preparing for the next war.'

The 'Economic Observer', Lieutenant-Colonel W. H. Spice, was confounding critics who alleged that he merely recycled his reports, changing only the date. In a detailed round-up of the state of East German industry in May 1951 he produced a map of the country which identified thirteen zones of development as if they were the prime cuts on a butcher's diagram of a cow. He was rewarded with a trip to Buckingham Palace to be invested as a Member of the Order of the British Empire.

An exhaustive, unsigned report on the state of East Germany generally, dated October 1951, analysed the numbing effect of relentless state propaganda, adding:

It very much looks as if the DDR [German Democratic Republic; GDR] has come to stay, and the descent from a free and democratic Germany into a subservient satellite of Moscow is the policy which Russia has decided upon. Nor is there much opposition . . . Little evidence of strikes . . . and few demonstrations . . . propaganda notices neither pulled down nor disfigured . . . Almost every bridge on every autobahn carries a notice, 'Ami [Americans] Go Home', 'Peace Through Friendship', 'Follow Stalin to Prosperity', 'All Germans Round One Table' . . . Germans have swallowed other slogans like 'Strength Through Joy' . . . but Hitler propagandized what he accomplished . . . and the Russians have given little, as yet. They have big plans for the future.

38

The Soviets' main problem was to find a way to create a communist German army that could be relied upon not to bite its creator. According to one of the Brixmis monthly reports: 'An adequately armed and trained German division will probably be much more efficient than its Russian equivalent. The Russians know this and do not relish the prospect of having to create a German army . . . The Russians are sensitive to a degree about concealing the activities of paramilitary police [precursors of the East German Volksarmee] from allied observers, and it seems as if they do not wish evidence to be amassed which will serve as a provocation to the Western powers to go ahead with militarization.'

From time to time, the Russians attempted to tame the Western Missions by withdrawing their passes and substituting more restrictive ones. The British, who usually turned the other cheek, uncharacteristically hit back in the summer of 1950: similar limitations were imposed on the Soviet Mission (Soxmis) in the British zone of West Germany. The status quo was restored. One violent episode during that time reassured Brixmis that the Russians did not want to cut the liaison link entirely. In October, at Bochum in the British zone, a Red Army lieutenant-colonel and driver from Soxmis were, as a Brixmis report put it, 'subjected to force by [West] German police'. The Soviet Major-General Vinogradov used the incident as a counter to complaints about the East German Vopo harassment of Western Missions. The Brixmis summary of this row concluded: 'If the Russians wished to end the exchange of missions, this would have afforded a fair pretext. Up to now, there has been no reprisal in kind against this mission.'

The Russians were not unhappy about the way things were going. Unlike the Western Missions, Soxmis dabbled in the dangerous business of running agents as part of a hostile and predatory spying operation in West Germany. Senior officers were involved, as a Brixmis Chief discovered during a confrontation in 1952 with the Soviet C-in-C, General Chuikov.

A Soviet pursuit car had tried to force a Brixmis tour off the road at high speed. Replying to that complaint, 'Chuikov harped back to the occasion when his officers had been handcuffed at Solingen. (It will be recalled that West German police trapped them at night, in plain clothes, in an unnumbered car, meeting a worker by pre-arrangement: i.e., caught red-handed.)'

This merely confirmed what everyone knew. The wartime Allies, who had spied on one another before, were at it again.

Just after 9 A.M. on Thursday 12 March 1953, two RAF Lincoln bombers took off from Leconfield, Yorkshire, ostensibly on a routine 'fighter affiliation' exercise with four RAF Vampire jets based at RAF Celle, in Germany. For one of the two bombers – Lincoln No. RF531 'C' of the Central Gunnery School – this was a doomed mission: all seven crew members died. Three of them perished (if official sources are to be believed) because their parachutes were defective in some way. Three others went down in the Soviet zone of Germany with their aircraft in a hail of Soviet Mig machine-gun fire. The seventh man jumped, apparently without a parachute, from 10,000 feet. In the mysterious, lethal world of Cold War bluff and counter-bluff, the disastrous end of RF531 remains one of the most enigmatic stories of air espionage.

It was not a unique incident, however. During this period of the Cold War, when the West still depended on a bomber force to deliver its nuclear strike, with no satellite photographs to identify targets, both the RAF and USAF probed and tested Warsaw Pact air defences with manned aircraft. For a time the RAF was in the front line of clandestine air operations because President Truman would not allow the USAF to fly them, following the loss of a US Navy Privateer aircraft off Latvia in May 1950. From June 1951 the RAF ran a top secret RB-45c Tornado Special Duties Flight, using the latest US reconnaissance aircraft. The targets were Soviet strategic missile sites. The RAF sorties started in the Baltic and ended, if they were lucky, in Iran. They survived many near-misses. In 1953, for example, a modified Mark II Canberra taking part in 'Project Robin' photographed a missile launch site at Capustin Yar in the Soviet Union. The Canberra limped into its base in Iran scarred by Soviet shots. When the Americans resumed such operations, they again took heavy casualties. Around forty US aircraft were shot down in Warsaw Pact airspace between 1950 and 1970. More than 250 aircrew were lost, of whom around 100 are still officially posted missing.

Many of these intrusions from the West crossed East Germany to reach Soviet airspace. The Soviet Air Force, fearing a pre-emptive nuclear strike, was ordered to shoot down any alien aircraft which refused to land. If gunnery was insufficient then the Soviets were expected to ram the Westerners. When disaster occurred over communist Germany, as it did in the case of the Lincoln, Brixmis had the grim job of collecting dead and wounded, repatriating prisoners and cleaning up the debris.

One of the first casualties of these secret air missions was Flight Lieutenant Driver. On 28 September 1950, his Meteor Mk VII, WA695, crash-landed about thirty miles inside the Inner German Border (dividing East and West Germany) some seven miles west of Ludwigslust.

The same day, the deputy Chief of Brixmis, Lieutenant-Colonel P. R. Mortimer, with Alexei Yates as his interpreter, visited the local Russian headquarters. There the Soviet commandant, also a lieutenant-colonel, contrived to look surprised as he delivered a pre-scripted line: 'What aircraft? There is no aircraft here.'

On their way back, Mortimer and Yates took the opportunity of gathering a little intelligence of their own. They noted heavy tank tracks around Neuruppin and propaganda slogans, painted in English and French on roadside hoardings (perhaps to greet a Western invading force): 'The Atlantic Pact means bombs on Great Britain and France', and 'Our Youth is fighting for peace and prosperity'.

Nine days later, after much diplomatic activity, the senior RAF Brixmis officer, Wing Commander Everest, tried his luck in obtaining Driver's release. He, too, was accompanied by Flight Lieutenant Yates. This time the Brixmis representatives were taken promptly to the site, which was guarded by twelve armed men. The Meteor rested on its starboard wheel, nose wheel and starboard wingtip, with the tail in the air. The port wing was wrapped round a birch tree.

'Marks on the ground indicated that the pilot had landed in a grass field ... overshot ... through a hedge and ditch at the far end, coming to rest in a field of root crops,' Everest reported. 'The Russians told us that a cow had been killed in the landing and that the cowman with it had escaped injury by jumping into a ditch. I looked carefully at the aircraft to try to ascertain to what extent the Russians may have examined it and came to the conclusion that it had not been tampered with in any way apart from the possibility that the hatch on the nose marked "CAMERA" had been opened.'

Everest found no conclusive evidence that the Meteor had been shot down, 'apart from a jagged hole about 3 inches by 2 inches in the leading edge of the starboard main-plane inboard of the engine which could conceivably have been made by flak'.

The Russians said that 'such fuel as was in the aircraft when it crashed had since leaked out'. They 'could or would say little else. They did not know where the pilot was.'

Later, the Chief of Brixmis had two meetings with Major-General I. Vinogradov, Soviet deputy Chief of Staff, about 'the questions of British personnel in Soviet hands, Soviet deserters and freedom of movement'. His report noted: 'No visit has yet been permitted to the [Meteor] pilot, whose detention is linked by the Soviet staff with that of Bystrov, the Soviet officer deserter in British hands.'

In October, there were three meetings about the RAF captive as well as a British soldier, Sapper Bennett, also in Russian hands. Both men were eventually set free on 24 November. The Meteor was recovered by an RAF salvage team on 1 December. Bystrov, a political refugee, did not return to Russia. It would seem that Flight Lieutenant Driver had got away with his flight on the basis of a Soviet 'non-proven' verdict. Others would be less lucky.

No aircrew survived the Lincoln crash, less than two years later. History must rely on circumstantial evidence, and the Soviets' account, to make an intelligent guess about what happened. Such evidence as there is – including guns and spent ammunition cases inside the Lincoln – suggests that there was an aerial gun battle in which an RAF gunner opened fire on Soviet interceptors deep in communist airspace. The unusual openness and courtesy of the Russians with whom Brixmis had to negotiate afterwards suggested that they had nothing to hide. An RAF Court of Inquiry later blamed the navigator for error and asserted that the bomber was unarmed, a fact denied by what Mission members saw at the crash site.

The Mission's Top Secret reports of this episode reveal that Brixmis was alerted just after 8.15 P.M. on 12 March 1953 by a telephone call from the headquarters of 2 Tactical Air Force (TAF) in West Germany. This instructed the Mission to get details of casualties and visit the crash site as soon as possible. Brixmis officers, with a Soviet escort, reached the area on the afternoon of 14 March and spent the rest of the day collecting the bodies. These were driven through the night to a British military hospital at Hamburg, in the West.

A Soviet liaison officer, Colonel Ignatiev, gave a crisp account of the action:

The Lincoln flew over Arensee, Perleberg, Parchim, Gustrow to Rostock [a Baltic port well inside East German airspace] where it circled. It was met by the Migs here. The Migs flew alongside the Lincoln, then one flew in front, waving its wings and breaking to port and descending to indicate that the Lincoln was to follow and land.

The Lincoln made no attempt to comply. This was repeated three times in all and on the last occasion the Lincoln opened fire on the front Mig and subsequently on the one flying alongside. This occurred at 6,500 metres (20,000 feet) over Butzow. The Migs gave warning fire and subsequently fired mixed ammunition at the Lincoln, which continued to fire. The Migs followed the Lincoln down to the point near Boitzenburg where it crashed.

Four days later, said the Brixmis documents, 'Mission party accompanied salvage party into Soviet Zone. Met by Colonels Tveretnikov and Ignatiev and Lieutenant Makarov who, with approximately twenty other Soviet officers remained with the party all day.' Tveretnikov, Ignatiev and Makarov were familiar faces at Brixmis diplomatic parties, the most recent of which had taken place in Berlin little more than a week earlier. Surrounded by the Lincoln debris, they kept their party manners. It was an eerie encounter: 'Once again the Russians were only too anxious to help and supplied a crane and forty Other Ranks. They recovered the engine . . . and accompanied by the RAF Interpreter, the leg of the undercarriage.' Near the main crash site, the British team were shown a 'pile of ammunition which Soviets said had been collected from the surrounding area, lying near remains of mid-upper turret with two cannon. Permission readily given for technical representative to take nine rounds of ammunition which he noted bore mark of striker pin and also breech block of one machine gun from rear turret. Soviets said no ammunition for rear gun had been found.'

The Top Secret Brixmis monthly report for March 1953 reveals that, in spite of the work generated by the Lincoln affair, twenty-three tours went out. They covered, among other targets, twenty-one active Soviet airfields and two inactive ones. As to ground forces, 'our main efforts have been directed to making continuous barrack checks and watching training areas for formations moving into them ... Ten out of twenty-three tours were not followed and two more managed to evade their pursuers,' though one mission car was detained briefly in West Germany by an RAF sentry who claimed it belonged to 'a foreign mission'.

A report on technical intelligence disclosed: 'Most of the types of weapons and military equipment in use in the Red Army have been seen during the month. Clear views have been obtained of the signals/command vehicle on a Soviet chassis which is being produced for the Red Army in East Germany and of the 100mm anti-tank gun. The new East German Army "jeep-type" vehicle and the new half-ton "Phänomen Granit" have been seen. The latter is definitely fitted with four-wheel drive.'

There was also the usual crop of deserters: 'Missing RAF Personnel: The Chief of the Mission wrote to the Soviet Liaison Officer on 10 March asking for the return of two RAF personnel who had stolen an RAF car and driven through the Helmstedt barrier into the Soviet Zone ...'

CHAPTER 2

March on Berlin

1953–54

On 5 March 1953, the Brixmis team entertained members of the
Soviet External Relations Bureau (SERB) and other Soviet officers
at a reception in West Berlin to mark the impending departure of
the British Mission Chief, Brigadier C. H. Dewhurst OBE. As one
veteran put it: 'You couldn't say we threw a party because it wasn't
that unrestrained. We smiled politely and touched glasses.'

Brixmis officers' wives, who had not attended the Russian
language course, were prepared to greet the guests with pidgin-
Russian greetings. These easily memorized phrases were put into
their mouths at a special training session and included 'Does-yer-
arse-fit-yer?' (said quickly, translating as 'How do you do?'), or
'Manchester-Rovers' ('Your good health!') and 'Dusty-dancer'
('Goodbye').

The Russians were charmed, for they had little to celebrate. In
Korea, their airmen were engaged in a secret war against Americans
flying under the UN flag. Only three days before Dewhurst's party,
5,000 German refugees from the East had voted with their feet for
a better life and crossed into the West. While back home in Moscow
people were struggling to make sense of the mystery of 'the
assassins in white coats'.

Some months before the Brixmis party, nine eminent doctors
on the staff of the Kremlin hospital had been arrested by Beria's
secret police, the NKVD. The doctors were accused of killing Stalin's
purge-master, A. A. Zhdanov. The 'Jewish Doctors' Plot' was born.

A statement issued under Stalin's name in January 1953, two
months after the arrests, asserted that the doctors had assassinated

party leaders on the orders of Western intelligence. That was not the way they read the situation at Brixmis. The Mission's conclusion was that the 'plot' was a useful nonsense, a bluff, and perhaps the precursor of a real and deadly one. As Dewhurst later revealed:

> The Doctors' Plot had, I believe, as its objective the severance of Stalin from his capable and trusted physicians, perhaps leaving the way open for the introduction of other, more pliable material . . . If, as was naturally presumed at the time, the Doctors' Plot had been invented by Stalin himself and made public on his orders, then what precise purpose was it supposed to serve? It looked as if it were an anti-Jewish measure . . . but only one of the top few was, in fact, a Jew. Moreover, the doctors never came to trial at all. Instead they were exonerated and their accusers arraigned.
>
> The Plot, if organized by Stalin, had accomplished nothing . . . If, however, it were part of a plan prepared to pave the way for Stalin's demise, then a purpose was certainly accomplished. Firstly, it got rid of Stalin's immediate protectors. Secondly it covered up Malenkov's liquidation of Zhdanov, his notorious rival and number two to Stalin up to 1948, by announcing that the doctors . . . 'had succeeded in murdering A. A. Zhdanov'. Thirdly it prepared the public for news of death in high places.

Dewhurst had his own evidence for doubting the Kremlin version of the Doctors' Plot. One of the doctors' other alleged targets, if the Kremlin announcement was true, was the Soviet Chief of Staff, General Shtemenko. But, Dewhurst recalled: 'I met Shtemenko at a reception in East Berlin just about the time when the doctors must have been active and I have never seen any officer in such robust health . . . The next step was to get rid of Stalin's Chief of Bodyguard, Lieutenant-General Kosigin. His death went unnoticed . . . [Finally] on or about 23 February, Stalin, in my opinion, "died".' No announcement of the death was made at that time, however, though 'precautionary measures were noted in Moscow, including the movement of troops. There were moves to a "state of readiness" by Red garrisons in certain satellites. There was uneasiness in Potsdam.'

In fact, it seems unlikely that Stalin did die quite so soon. There is reliable evidence that he suffered a stroke on 2 March and died three days later, as Dewhurst held his farewell party, an event at which political paranoia filled the air as if someone had let off a stink-bomb. Major Tony Hall, the intelligence officer and Russian translator with Brixmis at the time, recalled: 'The Russians came in fair numbers. The party was very strange because everyone knew that Stalin was extremely ill. Officially we took no notice of this. So the Russians came to the party and then, in a very abrupt way, without warning, lined up and said they regretted they would have to leave. They gave no reason. Only afterwards did we learn that on their grapevine they had discovered that Stalin had just died.'

Dewhurst, with a little time left before he finally moved on, pondered what he should do. He wrote later: 'As Chief of Mission accredited to Russia's most important Army, I certainly expected to be asked to some ceremony, parade, or to have the opportunity of expressing my official condolences. The letter of condolence which I wrote was never acknowledged or answered. The matter of Stalin's death was thereafter taboo.' In Moscow, he noted: 'Stalin was hurried to his last resting-place with the minimum possible ceremony consistent with decorum.'

If, as Dewhurst believed, Stalin was assassinated, it might reasonably be asked why the Soviet top brass, having tolerated Stalin for so long, would choose the spring of 1953 to end the life of Europe's leading executioner. Stalin was an unrepentant Marxist, believing that war against the capitalist powers was an inevitable part of an historically-determined process from which Soviet socialism would emerge victorious. His was a dangerously messianic view at a time when the USA had just exploded a hydrogen bomb. He had to go. As the veteran British diplomat Sir Frank K. Roberts observed in 1987: 'Stalin's death in 1953 broke some of the ice of this Cold War ... Khrushchev [Stalin's successor] realized that war ... was in the nuclear age no longer an acceptable part of Marxist–Leninist ideology.'

Worse, Stalin was isolated by madness, and by fear of wolves and his closest colleagues alike. Senior ministers on his personal hit-list included Molotov, Mikoyan and Voroshilov. It would be no surprise if they determined to eliminate Stalin before he eliminated them.

The change of Soviet leadership was a political earthquake whose shock-waves rapidly rocked the East German regime of Walter Ulbricht. According to André Fontaine's *History of the Cold War*, Ulbricht was described at that time as a rigid doctrinarian, without finesse or eloquence, hampered by his Saxon accent, a goatee-bearded clone of 'the wretched Professor Unrath in *The Blue Angel* (that is, the aging, doctrinaire professor destroyed by his lust for a nightclub singer), obedient to Stalin's orders in every situation'. Ulbricht was also a naturalized Soviet citizen following a fifteen-year exile in Russia. Brixmis, as well as the East German people, would live with the anachronistic, hard-line Stalinist style of Ulbricht for most of its operational life.

Ulbricht's reaction to the changed party line was a charade of reform. 'Errors' were admitted by government. The enforced collectivization of farmland (a policy which had already turned the agricultural areas of the Soviet Union into abattoirs for the massacre of small farmers) was dropped, temporarily. Public opposition to religion would end in theory, if not in practice. A few political prisoners were amnestied but others rotted in prison for years to come. This 'New Course' was propped up, like the old one, by the 'Ivans', the despised heavies of the Soviet Army of occupation.

The New Course had its price: higher production norms, announced on 28 May. The workers did their sums and discovered that, in real terms, their pay was being cut by 10 per cent. The result was an explosion of resentment. On 16 June, 2,000 construction workers of both sexes, building palaces for bureaucrats along the Stalinallee in East Berlin, were ordered to increase productivity to the new norm. This, in a city where two million people had just been arbitrarily deprived of ration cards entitling them to basic foodstuffs, was unwise. The workers downed tools and marched on government buildings at Wilhelmstrasse. Soon a crowd of 100,000 had assembled. The scene was now set for an explosion of German resistance to communism. It was something which neither the Soviet garrisons around Berlin nor knowledgeable Brixmis observers had expected, though it *was* something which

Western propagandists – from broadcasters at Radio Free Europe to the West German leaflet artists who sent their message eastwards with the help of balloons and the prevailing westerly winds – had done their best to stir up.

The first intimation of trouble in Berlin reached the Brixmis team at Potsdam courtesy of an East German maid. Tony Hall, the Mission's intelligence officer, remembered: 'At first we hardly knew it had happened. We got hysterical cries from our maid who said she had heard something on the local wireless. Bearing in mind that Berlin is a very large, spread-out city, we saw smoke rising from various areas in East Berlin.

'My staff captain and I went off to the Brandenburg Gate where we were politely turned back by the Russians. Beyond we could see serried ranks of anti-aircraft guns and tanks lined up ... By and large, it died down so quickly that it really didn't have much impact.'

That first evening, the East German Politbüro met to wag a finger of rebuke at the 'provocateurs', the trouble-makers, who had made a mountain out of a molehill. In passing, the new pay structure was abandoned, in the embarrassed, furtive way an earwig might be picked out of the bean soup. It was not enough. Communist Berlin was about to create a historical paradox by being the first area of postwar Europe to adopt the orchestrated riot as an instrument of political protest.

Next day, 17 June, and for several days after, many thousands of Berliners stamped round the city demanding freedom. The Volkspolizei charged and were hurled back. The Soviet Army moved T-34 tanks and armoured cars of the 1st Motor Rifle Division on to the streets, shuddering as rocks and scrap metal bounced off their vehicles.

At 11 A.M. around 100,000 protesters were marching towards government buildings in Wilhelmstrasse and Leipzigerstrasse when the tanks appeared. In this febrile atmosphere only one half-brick hurled towards the enemy was enough to start a riot. The Russians opened fire. No one knows, even today, how many Germans died in the shootings that followed. A low estimate suggests thirty. The Soviet sector commandant, Major-General P. T. Dibrowa, reinforced by an additional infantry division of 10,000 men, proclaimed martial law and curfew from 9 P.M. to 5 A.M., banned meetings of more than three people and sealed off the eastern sector.

'Some arrests were made, and a few executions took place,' said a laconic French account of the affair which (unsurprisingly) lays some of the blame for what happened on American propaganda broadcasts. These included transmissions from RIAS (Radio in American Sector) which presented life in the West as a consumerist Camelot. As things turned out, the Berlin workers' revolt was crushed so effectively that within a week or so, on 12 July, martial law could be lifted with hardly a bloodstain to show that anything was amiss, just like a scene from *The Threepenny Opera*. ('On the sidewalk, Sunday morning, lies a body, oozing life . . .').

Denied access to East Berlin, Brixmis watched and counted as the Red Army went into action from its bases outside the city. What it observed was a chaotic but quick response. The Mission gave the operation a high mark for effectiveness in spite of the chaos. The Mission's report, signed by Brigadier Julian Meadmore OBE, said: 'Moves evidently took place at very short notice, and tanks and vehicles were often seen in a very muddy condition, having apparently come straight out of training areas. Units did not move in tactical groups. Wireless trucks were seen moving together in one block.'

The Russians left behind their rockets and artillery but brought their bridging equipment, in case the rioters destroyed Berlin's bridges. They brought tanks, self-propelled guns, scout cars, anti-aircraft guns, mortars and armoured personnel carriers. The march-in combined advance with rout:

Although it was daylight, columns of 1 Mechanized Division moving through Potsdam often lost their way and were seen turning in back streets to regain the correct route. Vehicles were being driven too close to each other with the result that sudden checks caused collisions. Single vehicles and short columns overtook other vehicles in order to regain their positions. Along the side of the road small trees were knocked down and larger ones had their bark scraped off. Moderate speeds were not adhered to, and little or no effort was made to keep proper intervals.

This poor march discipline led to many accidents. A petrol tanker was seen burning at one point; no fire extinguishers were being used, but troops were shovelling earth onto it, while the rest of the column waited for the fire to die down before passing. Some tanks and SP [self-propelled] guns lost their tracks . . . Many of the tank casualties were caused by armoured fighting vehicles running off the road at high speed. Accidents and broken-down vehicles averaged about one per kilometre, even in the short moves of 40 to 60 kilometres carried out by 1 Mech. Div. and 14 Guards Mechanized Division. It is, however, estimated that about 90 per cent of the armoured fighting vehicles reached East Berlin within 48 hours of the start of the move.

Within a day or so, three divisions – an overwhelming show of strength – sat on East Berlin: 'The Russians did not employ more than a small part of the force. The intention seems to have been to make a big display of force while using only the minimum necessary.'

With defended positions sited on key crossroads in the city, Dibrowa, the commander, standing up in his vehicle, waving his hat and smiling at the angry crowds, led a demonstration column: 'Despite intense provocation by the crowds there was no firing at this juncture and it appeared that the Soviet troops were well disciplined and under strict orders.'

When the Russians did shoot, Meadmore reported:

it is possible that on some occasions blank ammunition was used . . . The withdrawal of troops from East Berlin (between 27 June and 13 July) was efficient and orderly . . . The discipline of Soviet troops in East Berlin seems to have been excellent. The troops were kept well in hand and did not react to intense German provocation. As a result, casualties were low and the civil populace was not further angered.

Probably rather more than half of the line divisions in the Soviet zone have been affected and have lost two to four weeks of their normal training. On the other hand both the troops and the higher command have gained valuable experience.

Compiling a considered study of the affair a month later, Mead-more wrote to a friend in London: 'I hope that the [Soviet] Sector is not going to be closed to us again . . . If only it were possible to have an air recce things would be much easier.'

The limited use of force in Berlin matched the carefully measured response of the Soviet Air Force in dealing with the RAF Lincoln bomber's attack three months earlier and, almost certainly, for the same reason: the Kremlin, for the first time since the creation of the Soviet state, was unsure of itself and was not looking for trouble. In both cases, the only reliable observations on the ground of the behaviour and attitudes of the Soviet military came from the Western Missions, led by Brixmis. The effect was to reassure the West that this particular local difficulty could be contained without an international crisis.

One of the political casualties of the Berlin uprising was the Soviet Commander-in-Chief in communist Germany, General Chuikov. Meadmore's successor, Dewhurst, had crossed him more than once.

As soon as Stalin died, I wondered what would be the fate of General Chuikov in East Germany, for there was no doubt he was a typical Stalin protégé . . . He had a brilliant, ruthless record culminating in Stalingrad's great defence, where he took personal orders from Stalin.

He never really recovered from that ordeal and has been often described as 'punch drunk' ever since. He was an immense drinker, and I often noticed how terrified of him was his staff the morning after! I was always glad that, unlike his own generals, I had diplomatic protection from his anger. And yet, like most bullies, when one stood up to him one could sense that he appreciated it . . .

When an official reception at the Berlin Embassy was over, I often used to see him escorting Pieck, the President of the 'German Democratic Republic', Walter Ulbricht or some official into an adjacent salon, where the real party à la Chuikov would begin. That would mean vodka, dancing and songs till dawn. I smiled at their apprehensive faces, wreathed in sycophantic smiles, as they were escorted away . . . Chuikov was dismissed for 'mistakes' in the interpretation of Soviet policy in Eastern Germany. These 'mistakes' amounted to implicit obedience to, and fulfilment of, Stalin's German policy. It must be difficult indeed to serve a country where this year's Party Line is next month's heresy, and where the Saviour of today is the Forgotten Soldier of tomorrow.

For Chuikov the story did not end badly. Fourteen years later a Brixmis veteran met him in Moscow, where, somewhat mellower, he was his country's civil defence supremo.

Dewhurst, among others, noted the sudden change in the temperature of the Cold War with the death of Stalin: 'Within a few weeks, almost days, appeasement became the watchword. Steps were initiated for an armistice in Korea; talks on Berlin's air corridors began; pressure was diminished on East Germany; under an amnesty a British Embassy "prisoner" [presumably in North Korea] was released; American reporters were invited to visit the USSR; the attitude towards my Mission changed; the travel embargo was lifted for diplomatic personnel in Moscow – and so forth. Each day revealed some new concession.'

The consensus in Brixmis at the time, as Captain S. D. Gibson MBE, a Brixmis officer, suggested, was that 'a faint glimmer of hope emerged from the now openly demonstrated hatred of East Germans for their government and its shallow-rooted, albeit strongly enforced, control of the population'.

Meanwhile, in the USSR, the doctors whose 'plot' had signalled the latest convulsions were released. *Pravda*, of all newspapers, acknowledged that they had been tortured into confession on Stalin's orders. It was hardly surprising that the Russians with whom Brixmis had to deal were touched by the pervasive fear which was part of the Soviet way of life. They had learned that, in a somewhat capricious empire, it paid to be polite even to those whose aircraft they were shooting down.

The preceding two years, 1951 to 1953, while Stalin sank slowly, identifying enemies of the state within his inner circle, had been rough for everyone. For the Brixmis team they were by turns tense and preposterous, reflecting the ambiguity of the time. As Dewhurst put it: 'If things went on as they were, my Mission might have had to withdraw, for life was being made almost impossible for us. A withdrawal of the only Mission in close contact with the Red Army would have been a serious step on the downward path.'

The late N. L. R. (Nick) Griffiths, a Royal Marine major (the equivalent of an army lieutenant-colonel), joined the Mission in 1951. He occupied a magnificent flat in Berlin, hired a retinue of five German servants for 15p (or one shilling and sixpence in the old coinage) per day and sent his four-year-old son to school in the bulletproof limousine that had once belonged to Field Marshal Kesselring. His wife was one of the first targets of a technique used by communist agents against many of her successors in Eastern Europe.

'While I was out on tour,' Griffiths wrote later, 'she would receive telephone calls designed to upset her. She would lift the receiver and only heavy breathing and grunts would ensue. I often got back from tours six or seven hours late and sometimes a day or several days late. The Russians never admitted any knowledge of our whereabouts when we were "held" by them.'

In Eastern Europe later in the Cold War, nuisance telephone calls, pursuit and groping on the streets by strangers were aimed at reducing the morale of British diplomatic wives to a point where they insisted on going home. The husband, usually a military attaché, was now alone and, they hoped, open to 'honey-trap' propositions.

One Brixmis wife got her revenge for such treatment by naming her cat 'Kozlovskii', after the chief Soviet liaison officer. One Mission veteran recalled: 'when her husband was the duty officer staying overnight in the Mission House in Potsdam, she went with him and telephoned a neighbour near their home in West Berlin, assuming that her call was monitored by the communist authorities. She told her neighbour to keep an eye out for Kozlovskii, adding that she would return home later, in time to let him into her house through the back door. Soon afterwards, the liaison chief disappeared for a couple of months. The rumours flew that he had been interrogated and exiled to Siberia but he came back, having been on leave in the Soviet Union.'

Many Brixmis veterans question the 'honey-trap' stories but they acknowledge that harassment came in many forms. As Griffiths observed: 'Staying in hotels overnight was quite an experience.

We always knew the car' – theoretically protected by diplomatic immunity – 'would be searched and sometimes it was all too evident next day. We were disturbed in the night and hotel staff would try to get into compromising conversations.' Similarly, bags left in the tour team's hotel room were invariably searched without consent.

Like most tour officers, Griffiths evolved his own techniques for repelling narks, the plain clothes security police who at this time were Russian. With his driver, Royal Marine Corporal Dye, he was followed on one mission for several hundred miles. In a small market town they spotted 'a man on the pavement with his back to us, wearing a good overcoat which could only be bought from the Party store'. This stalwart of the Communist Party they now used as a decoy. 'We approached him from behind and stopped the car. So did our "tail". I called him over, holding up the map, making sure the tail could see what was going on. I asked the man in the overcoat for advice about the route back to Potsdam. He was only too pleased to help us.'

Griffiths drove away. The narks behind him, convinced they had detected high treason, pounced on the man in the overcoat. By the time they had sorted out the confusion, said Griffiths contentedly, 'We were on our own.'

Griffiths also recalled a 'rather rugged' tour in June 1951. Six Brixmis cars swept out of the Potsdam compound simultaneously, then fanned out on to different routes. The object was to confuse the ever-present narkwatch. Griffiths's car was the one the narks chose to tail. An eighty-mile chase ensued. Corporal Dye drove through a ford in his efforts to escape, but at the next town, a Red Army base, the two men were arrested.

'As usual, I asked the sentry to let me use the lavatory urgently.' This was a Brixmis operational procedure, for lavatories were sometimes a repository of useful information. Old copies of *Pravda*, recycled for use in the loo, might bear the name of the Soviet officer entitled to receive the newspaper. Also, 'we were less likely to be searched after visiting the loo. They presumed that anything incriminating had been thrown away, even though the cistern that flushed was rare.'

A long period of detention under armed guard followed. The

two were escorted to a point where the Soviets claimed (wrongly) the Brixmis vehicle had passed a notice that said, in English: 'Off limits.' Griffiths reproached the Russians for their poor use of English. 'I explained that, among soldiers, this meant that we could buy alcohol there but we could not consume it on the spot.' A conclave of Russian interpreters put their heads together and agreed that, just maybe, in a military context . . .

Meanwhile, as the hours ticked by, Lieutenant-Colonel Philip Mortimer, deputy Chief of the British Mission, was putting pressure on the Soviets and the Foreign Office in London. The British side threatened reprisals against the Soviet liaison team in the British zone. This did the trick. Griffiths was released.

In January 1952 a British concert party lost its way in Germany. The group should have travelled from Berlin to Helmstedt, on the West German border; instead it found itself in a small market town near Leipzig, deep in the East. It was stopped by the Vopo (Volks-polizei). The incident made news since it was led by Gracie Fields's manager (the same Gracie Fields whose colloquial, street-soprano had raised the spirits of the wartime British). The party was spirited back to the West, under cover of darkness, by Griffiths, who kept quiet about it.

The road show manager, who had created the original mess, now boasted that he alone had led his people to freedom. The press took up the story. That in itself generated a new quarrel between the Brixmis boss, Brigadier Dewhurst, and General Chuikov.

A British transcript captures the comic-opera nature of the affair. It does not reflect the problem faced by the British interpreters, one of whom (Lieutenant-Colonel J. M. Laing) said: 'The trouble with Chuikov was that he had practically a full set of steel teeth which seemed to be permanently shut when he was talking. Russian speech is difficult enough for a non-Slav, but when the sounds are muffled and come out at odd angles it's impossible to catch.'

This, then, is a brave attempt to reconstruct what was said:

CHUIKOV: This newspaper says you came to interview me about
   some British persons who deviated from the official autobahn.
   You did not come about that.

DEWHURST: No, General, I did not come to see you about that.

CHUIKOV: But the newspaper says you did.

DEWHURST: That is so.

CHUIKOV (incensed): Then how do you account for it?

DEWHURST: I don't account for it. I came to see you about another matter and the press guessed the subject wrongly.

CHUIKOV: How did the press know you visited me?

DEWHURST: Because they probably saw my car on the way. Our reporters are allowed to see and guess what they like.

CHUIKOV: But the report is not true. It's a lie. It seriously embarrasses our relations.

DEWHURST: I agree that it's not true and I am sorry if it should embarrass our relations.

CHUIKOV: But the paper precisely says it's true.

DEWHURST: Yes it does.

CHUIKOV: Then you must have told them.

DEWHURST: On the contrary. No one in my office, except my adjutant and secretary knew the subject matter.

CHUIKOV: I think that there must have been a crow sitting on your shoulder when you wrote in your office!

DEWHURST: In that case the crow would have seen the truth and known exactly what our conversation was about.

CHUIKOV: Anyway, the paper says you came here to speak to me about a certain subject – which was not why you came. That is a very bad thing.

DEWHURST: I don't see why it's a bad thing to have a free press. I regret their mistakes but I cannot muzzle them. We don't believe in that.

CHUIKOV: You should stop such reports.

DEWHURST: But I have just said, General, we have a free press. Why should they listen to me?

CHUIKOV: We have a free Press too but [as an afterthought] they listen to me. They don't print lies. Anyway, I see you do not wish to do anything. You may go.

Dewhurst said later: 'Chuikov would never believe that I had not invented a story and given it to the press. It was, to his mind, a purposely misleading one and what aggravated him was that neither he, nor his advisers, could make out exactly why I had contrived the whole affair.'

Like his predecessor Curteis, Brigadier Dewhurst became interested in the Baltic coast, particularly the island of Rügen, 'in view of all the restrictions that the Soviets had placed round it and the rumours'. Dewhurst gave advance warning of his trip, to allay Soviet anxieties. His gesture had the opposite effect. He reached the unremarkable little town of Stralsund on the Baltic coast one winter evening and dropped in on the local Soviet commandant. He admitted later that when he entered the bare, cold room he was shaken by the fact that the Russian commander, Lieutenant-Colonel Mamir, was a clone of Stalin, whose portrait glared down from the wall above the colonel's desk. A windy night on the Baltic and Dewhurst felt he was being interrogated by two Stalins. In spite of that, Dewhurst's amazing memory for dialogue did not fail him.

MAMIR: Who are you?
DEWHURST: I'm the Chief of the British Mission at Potsdam and this is Major Reynolds RM, my naval officer.
MAMIR: Then why are you here?
DEWHURST: Because I want to see Rugen Island.
MAMIR: There is nothing to see.
DEWHURST: I'm glad to hear it. I want a holiday.
MAMIR: It would be better to return to Potsdam.
DEWHURST: That is not my opinion. I would prefer to see Rugen.

After a night in a hotel, during which Mamir telephoned in another vain attempt to persuade them to leave, Dewhurst returned to the Stralsund commandant's office. He was asked to show his Red Army pass. Mamir glanced at it and pronounced it 'incorrect'. 'But it was correct last night,' Dewhurst protested. 'How can it be incorrect now?' Mamir produced another pass bearing a different signature. 'But this pass has the signature of a colonel who has only just arrived in Potsdam,' Dewhurst said. 'Ours were signed before he arrived.'

Mamir smiled with satisfaction, happy to reach the door at the end of a Kafka corridor. 'That is why your passes are invalid,' he said. 'You must return to Potsdam to get them renewed.'

The row about the team's legal status intensified when Dewhurst said he would stay a second night and Mamir was obliged to threaten to evict him 'by force of arms'. Dewhurst quit the hotel but doggedly continued his journey towards Rugen. He was halted at the lift-bridge linking the island to the mainland. The bridge was up. To ensure that the English brigadier did not attempt to swim across, his way was also barred, as a colleague later put it, by 'three Soviet officers, three special motor cars containing twelve "narks", and the bridge-elevating team.'

When, at last, Dewhurst turned south again to return to Potsdam, he was tailed by three vehicles. His driver took to the back roads, spraying so much mud over the nearest chase car that it had to halt. Next in line was a Stasi-driven Chevrolet, specially imported for the job. Dewhurst dealt with that problem by driving at 20 m.p.h. until the Chevvy overheated and blew up. While the pursuers paused to discuss tactics, 'the Mission car took to its heels and vanished into a wood and by a circuitous route returned to Potsdam unescorted'.

Such apparently childish games had a serious political point: the British were determined to make the liaison agreement work, and work to their advantage. The Soviets, caught between a desire to observe 'correctness' and halt the virtual piracy of the liaison teams, sought to rewrite the agreement by precedent and case law, the creation, in a famous Zionist phrase, of 'new facts'. When one side or the other pushed its luck too far, a high level inquiry usually concluded that orders had been 'misunderstood'. A few ritual victims were disciplined by their own headquarters or declared *persona non grata* (see Chapter 3) and sent home, but not necessarily in disgrace. Sedgwick recalled a wing commander, RAF, who left Brixmis after an 'airfield incident'. The man would not have been reprimanded, for his team had spotted the first Soviet Mig jet in Germany to replace the wartime twin-piston-engined TU fighter, a major coup which 'caused a sensation back in the Ministry of Defence'.

After the row and the inquest, the whole game usually began afresh, but in Stalin's dying months additional pressure was put on Brixmis. Mission teams were detained five times during October 1952. In one episode the deputy Chief and his crew were held for thirty-four hours. Brixmis targets included a uranium mine at Aue near Zwickau in southern East Germany as well as the artillery and tank-training areas at Letzlinger Heide, west of Berlin.

It was in this inflamed atmosphere that two more Brixmis officers (the Royal Marine Major Reynolds and his Royal Artillery colleague, Major Vincent Harmer) started to take a serious interest in the ultra-sensitive Baltic island of Rügen, whose facilities included an important Russian artillery range. More to the point, though Reynolds did not know it, the island concealed the Orwellian secrets of its recent history as a Nazi holiday megapolis and a Soviet death camp. Housed in a monstrous concrete building shaped like a knuckleduster, it ran along the Baltic coast for six kilometres. It was the biggest as well as one of the ugliest buildings in the world (see Appendix IX).

Reynolds suspected that it was now home to an East German mechanized infantry divisional headquarters. What required no guesswork was the probability of detection and detention. Reynolds's predecessor as naval officer, Major Griffiths RM, was detained so many times in the area that he got to know the local Soviet command structure better than General Chuikov.

Rügen drew other Brixmis people like a fabled island. The man who really broke through and cracked its secret was Reynolds. First he foxed the East German watchers outside the Mission compound by leaving lights on outside the building as if he were about to go on tour. After several nights of this the watchers' attention lost its edge.

In a Top Secret report, Reynolds described how he and Major Harmar drove at speed out of the compound on to snowbound roads in the early hours of 17 December 1952. The two were preceded by Mrs Reynolds, in a separate car, acting as decoy for the waiting nark. For once, Lieutenant-Colonel Mamir at Stralsund had not been alerted. Twice the British officers and their driver had to dig the vehicle out of deep snowdrifts, but the bridge to the island was down and manned only by half-frozen Vopos who waved the intruders across.

Virtually the whole island was a secure zone, as the team

discovered between sessions of digging itself out of snowdrifts. At one point the car swung into a wood. There Reynolds and Harmer, pushing their luck, got out and prowled on foot around a former naval mine depot, an area measuring 700 by 1,000 yards. 'It was ruined and silent, with all its bunkers still blown up and there was no sign whatever of rebuilding,' Reynolds reported.

Had it been otherwise, they might have been shot. In high-level negotiations with Brixmis a few weeks earlier, a senior Russian staff officer, Colonel L. S. Sergeev, explained that a Soviet sentry 'was taught not to allow anyone, including Soviet officers, to approach his post unless accompanied by his Guard Commander . . . He would fire if necessary . . . the fire would be aimed.' Even Sergeev said he had recently noticed a change: young soldiers were halting him and demanding to see his papers. A sentry could also order an approaching officer whom he did not know, 'to halt and lie down'. Even then he would fire 'if necessary'.

Unaware of this, Reynolds, Harmer and their anonymous driver continued their exploration of Rügen, taking in a deserted beach and a medieval castle occupied by the Red Army. Near the main town of Bergen, they were intercepted by a Soviet jeep. At 3.30 P.M., just before dusk, after twelve hours on the road, they were taken to see the Soviet commandant.

Lieutenant-Colonel Lunivov, a youthful forty-something, asked why they had come. Harmar, with Brixmis panache, replied that at this time of year he always planned his summer holiday, so he was looking for a nice spot beside the sea. Lunivov, glancing out at the freezing darkness, said most people did that job with maps at this time of year, in the comfort of their own homes.

A confused, four-hour negotiation followed in which Reynolds and Harmar were accused of ignoring 'Keep Out' signs. As usual, the offenders were asked to sign an 'Akt' (a legal statement akin to an affidavit) admitting the offence and, as usual, they refused. During the long stand-off that followed, they talked of home leave and families in Moscow.

When the power failed and the lights went out, Reynolds cheekily offered to take the Soviet team for a drink in the local hotel. The offer was stiffly refused. Candles were brought. Negotiations continued. At 2040 hours, the team was bundled out and told to leave.

On the way back they were repeatedly stopped by angry German policemen, one of whom drew his pistol when the British driver declined to show him any papers. A Soviet jeep arrived to halt the pantomime. The Russian's order was: 'You will follow me precisely, whether there be hotel, restaurant or cabaret on the way.' The Brits became interested: 'A cabaret, did you say?'

The final run home was a nightmare that included a 100-yard skid on the ice and three more Soviet checks. The team reached the Potsdam base at 0345, after twenty-four exhausting hours. Reynolds, perhaps understating the case, said: 'We had a feeling that our future presence on Rügen Island would be unwelcome.'

If some people, such as Dewhurst, never quite reached their intended destination, others found that like most military bureaucracies, the Soviet Army's had some interesting holes. Major (later Colonel) W. T. Sedgwick, a Gunner officer with enigmatic prewar experience in Estonia, where he had learned Russian, joined Brixmis in 1949 as the General Staff Officer Grade 2. (The G-2 was usually the unit's intelligence officer.) He recalled that, while touring, he would drive into Soviet military transit centres. There 'we were able to check in, receive two blankets and settle down for the night. We were often asked to hand over our pistols which we said we didn't carry, to their surprise. Since we wore duffle coats I suspect they had little idea of who we were. On one occasion we found ourselves in a large convoy of Russian vehicles and we travelled with them several miles, being waved on from time to time by their traffic control and eventually finished up in a field, where we joined a large number of soldiers being addressed, or rather harangued, by a general after the end of some exercise.'

Sedgwick drank in every word of this 'hot wash-up' (instant debriefing session) at the conclusion of the Soviet exercise (its 'endex'). 'It was only after the general's talk that a Soviet officer spotted us and he started to confer with others. We slid off to our car and, assisted by the traffic controllers, sped off, expecting to be pursued ... We managed to our surprise to get back to Berlin without trouble.'

Relations with the communist German security teams – both the

Volkspolizei (Vopos) and the Stasi narks – started badly and got worse over the next forty years. Hall remembers a tour with Harmer:

> We were approaching Leipzig along a main road with a railway embankment on our left and the nark very close on our tail. We had a very good driver, Corporal Stokes, and as we came to a viaduct, Harmer said very quickly, 'Turn left!' The driver swung the wheel round left. The nark tried to follow. At that moment a large East German lorry came down the road towards us. As we went under the bridge we heard the most appalling crash of tortured metal, and sailed on our way rejoicing. Two or three days later, having got the number of this car, we saw it in East Berlin, very bashed up, the whole of one side painted with red lead.

Soon afterwards, sniffing round a Soviet airfield, Hall pulled into a wood for lunch. The nark followed. The British team laid brushwood on the boggy ground to make sure the Humber would not get stuck. The nark, parked nearby, ignored this precaution. When it was time for Brixmis to move, the car inched forward, cautiously, gathered speed and escaped. In the rear-view mirror Hall 'saw the nark sink gently to his axles and remain there'.

It was the first of many similar duels. Communist security teams wished, at the minimum, to keep Brixmis under tight surveillance. Even better, they preferred to find a pretext, a pretended or real breach of the liaison ground rules, to stop the Allied teams, take them into custody and hand them over for questioning by the Soviets. The Westerners never recognized the authority of the Germans. The British in particular wrote their own rules of conduct and if it was necessary to take risks on the road, then they would do just that. Not surprisingly, a history of such duels built up. The cult of the car chase was born. Collisions and rammings at high speed were routine. For some of the riders, the game was the last they played.

Once a year, Tony Hall or another G2 member of the Brixmis squad would attend a dedicated Military Intelligence conference in London. This was run by the operational side of intelligence-gathering, MI3. From the mid-1950s, the meeting, now known as the Warsaw Pact Intelligence Conference, was held every six months. Later still came the MI (or DI, for Defence Intelligence) 60 Allied Land Warfare Technical Intelligence Conference. It was very much an Old Commonwealth affair, limited to the AUSCANUKUS group (that is, Australia, Canada, UK, US) plus New Zealand. Both still continue, though the Warsaw Pact meeting has been given a new title.

Useful in themselves to the Cold War effort, such conferences were also a reminder, if one were needed, to Brixmis tour officers that their operations in obscure parts of the East German countryside, often in the dark, were not an adventure but part of a huge machine encompassing clandestine reconnaissance flights, the running of agents and debriefing defectors. Keeping one's eye on the ball, as they used to put it, was what the car-chase game was ultimately about.

In October 1953, a Brixmis team eluded its pursuers to reconstruct an entire Soviet battle exercise. With the Soviets still in a state of political shock after Stalin's death, the Mission reported: 'A total of sixty tours was carried out during the month, easily a record . . . Brixmis touring cars covered 25,100 miles . . . After a Soviet army exercise had finished a tour was usually despatched to go over the area to reconstruct the battle and to collect any useful articles which might have been left lying around.'

The 'useful articles' brought home in the back of the Brixmis car included a live anti-tank mine and two wireless valves. Combined with other trophies, they enabled the technical intelligence teams of MI3 to conclude: 'no indications have been seen to suggest that the Soviet High Command has considered the threat of atomic weapons, either airborne or artillery projected, in the planning or execution of their major exercises.'

The Soviets, it seemed, were still relying on their nine million soldiers to be victorious whatever the odds.

By the time Hall finished his tour in 1954, Stalin's successor, Khrushchev, was floating an alternative to historically inevitable war between the two dominant economic systems. Khrushchev called it 'peaceful coexistence'. This boiled down, in practice, to détente in Europe and confrontation in the 'Third World', fought through surrogates. In Indo-China, at Dien Bien Phu, France was being whipped by General Giap and losing an empire, appealing to the United States to fly nuclear missions against the communists. The Americans were half-inclined to agree to Operation Vulture and even smuggled agents into the doomed outpost until Churchill told them not to be so stupid. The world was getting smaller and, as he pointed out, such an attack would lead to a nuclear counter-attack against US bases in Europe, particularly the USAF bases in Britain.

The West, responding to the German passion for reunification, was preparing to create a political sop, a halfway house. On 5 May 1955, the Allied Commissioners who had run the country since the end of the war abolished themselves and granted the fledgling West Germany the powers of a fully sovereign, independent state including the right to a defence force. West Germany would become an odd mixture of historical repentance, incipient pacifism and military readiness. Bonn symbolized the change. Its focal point is the statue of a composer (Beethoven, because he was born there) rather than a soldier-king such as Frederick the Great; a monument, furthermore, set in an unpretentious market square, rather than the urban pomp of an Unter Den Linden or even a Potsdam. Yet this provincial corner of which few had heard would also be armed by the ferocious firepower of a new German battle tank called the Leopard.

For the Soviets, the emergence of the West German army, '*das Heer*', cast a long and frightening shadow. They responded on 20 September by giving similar recognition to the rival Democratic Republic. The bite was about to come on Berlin once more. The Soviets said they would retain control of military convoys bound for Berlin only temporarily, while Ulbricht, their creature, announced that the four-power status of Berlin was 'without any foundation'.

In the minds of some of the most informed and thoughtful Western observers on the spot, particularly in Brixmis, one question nagged: which way would German loyalties go in the event of a conflict? Many Germans, for their part, were not ready to trade in a growing postwar prosperity for the privilege of becoming the principal killing ground in another world war. What was more, they yearned for reunification.

Squadron Leader (later Group Captain) Hans Neubroch OBE, an Austrian-born airman who achieved the unusual distinction of receiving an OBE while still a squadron leader (the award usually goes to higher ranks), expressed the German problem bluntly in a prize-winning essay published by the Royal United Services Institute three years later, as he was about to join Brixmis: 'Western Germany's defection from the Nato alliance, with all the calamitous results of such an event, is very much within the realms of possibility. Her reliability as an ally must remain suspect.'

CHAPTER 3

The Scorched Flag

1956–59

In an increasingly unstable world, in which the great powers reassured themselves that a deterrent policy known as MAD (Mutual and Assured Destruction) was as reliable as any other form of suicide, it is not surprising that the warriors of Brixmis encountered fists, boots, shoulder charges and gun-slinging at the same time as they were being offered canapés, garnished with some old-fashioned protocol, at diplomatic parties.

Chris King was one of many young National Servicemen who spent most of their two-year military service learning Russian. He was a midshipman, a Royal Navy officer-in-waiting who found himself, in the summer of 1956, in his early twenties, doing the 'silly jobs' for Brixmis.

When his tour officer ran out of patience with the East German Vopo tail car following them throughout one day, the Brixmis men manoeuvred themselves behind their pursuer.

We chased one of these cars at very high speed on a normal road, not motorway, and after about ten minutes we came to a level crossing. The Volkspolizei car got stuck there because the barrier came down to allow a train through. So I was deputed to go and unscrew the number plates off the car. They had a stack of number plates and to try to deceive us they would change them from time to time. They were only held by butterfly nuts. Then the tour officer went to photograph so as to complain about the Volkspolizei car. I was quietly unscrewing the number plates at the back. One of the German policemen got out and rugby-charged me. I flew

into a ditch. Our driver drew a knife which he always carried and
we beat a careful retreat.

There were other entertaining tasks. From time to time, the tour
would come upon a 'Mission Restricted' sign, indicating a military
no-go area for liaison teams. 'Being the youngest person in the
car, the Opel Kapitän, my job was to get out and take the sign
saying "Restricted Zone" and put it in the ditch and then explain
why we hadn't seen it.' (King and others treasure a necktie to
commemorate such episodes, depicting 'Mission Restricted' signs
and made by the gentleman's tailor Gieves & Hawke of Savile Row,
at the suggestion of the Duke of Norfolk.)

The pressures on Brixmis came from two sources of Cold War
tension: local and international. When the two came together, even
a Mission Chief could find himself in a brawl. There was mutual
paranoia between the two blocs, but equally fierce was the anger
of those Germans who were trapped by their recent history in the
East. Those who could not escape (and around three million did
so) found it hard to be treated as serfs in their own country.

Brixmis people played jesuitically on some of these tensions.
When it was useful, they appealed to the Russians' respect for the
Great Patriotic War and the old alliance against the Nazis (all those
millions of war dead . . .). Alternatively, when it suited the case,
they stressed their sympathy with Germany's need for nationhood.
This was not merely cynicism; it recognized that Germany was still
a battleground on which blood was still being shed. Politically, the
unresolved status of postwar Germany continued to be the most
likely cause of war between the wartime Allies.

Brixmis was not entirely untouched by the virus of betrayal
among people on both sides of the Cold War, running scared for
the future. On the whole, however, the amateur gumshoes of
Brixmis emerged from this period of the Cold War with more
credibility than the espionage professionals, not least because they
were professionals in their own field of military reconnaissance.
Their reports contained a depth of military understanding not available elsewhere.

In keeping with the confrontational spirit of the age, in the
autumn of Suez and Hungary, the Mission suffered its first case of

PNG. To be *persona non grata*, in the diplomatic corps, is like being the target of a non-proven verdict in Scotland. But to be PNG'd is not without its penalty. The diplomat caught out doing something he is not licensed to do must be recalled, perhaps instantly, by his own government under a cloud that might, or might not, have its silver lining. We are never told.

Some people were given the boot by their own governments. Two NCOs who got drunk in Potsdam were PNG'd by Brixmis in the 1950s. An RAF officer was sent home in 1953. A lost notebook, a loss of nerve or temper could provoke the silent wrath of military caesars, sitting on high, giving the thumbs up, or down, to the gladiators struggling for survival in the ordure of the colosseum. Some people got away with it. An officer who left a roll of film under his pillow at the Elefant Hotel at Weimar confessed what had happened. It was fifteen years before a Brixmis team returned. When they did, the same manager was in charge and he had kept the film, intact, to hand back to them. None of these unfortunate little accidents has the same flavour or resonance of a full-blooded government-to-government PNG divorce.

The facts of the first diplomatic rumpus were clear enough and they had their origins a long way from Germany. On 26 October 1956, Hungary revolted against Soviet occupation. The Red Army, using reserves based in Czechoslovakia, crushed the uprising. On 31 October the RAF bombed parts of Cairo as a preliminary to an invasion of Suez. On 7 November (celebrated by the Soviets as October Revolution Day) the senior staff officer with Brixmis, Lieutenant-Colonel Mark Askwith, took a tour to Bernau, to look at barracks no. 4243. His car stalled as it turned outside the main gate. A Brixmis account describes what happened next:

> Askwith was soon surrounded by several Russians, including a number of curious but drink-happy officers who had been celebrating the Revolution. They asked Askwith what the British imperialists were doing at Suez and Askwith retorted by asking what the Russians were doing in Hungary. So it went on, until a considerable and heated altercation developed.
>
> Askwith was hauled off to the local kommandantura, and then to the regional kommandantura in Eberswalde, accused of making

false statements about Soviet policy. The Soviet liaison officer, Colonel Sergeev, was summoned to the scene. Askwith was escorted back to Potsdam. A few days elapsed. Then a letter was received from Soviet headquarters, Germany, saying that Askwith had exceeded his duties as a liaison officer and that he was no longer acceptable as a member of the Mission.

Unfortunately for Askwith, he had been involved in a similar incident only a few days previously, after a detention near Riesa ... Whilst under detention there, he told some officers in the kommandantura that Group of Soviet Forces in Germany [GSFG] had just moved five divisions up to the Polish frontier (which he had actually seen them do) during the uprising in Hungary. The Riesa commandant professed to know nothing of this and took Askwith over to Leipzig [a superior headquarters] for questioning.

Things livened up after that. The newly arrived Chief of Mission was a charismatic pirate named Brigadier Denys Wynn-Pope, of whom his colleague Lieutenant-Colonel C. B. Critchley MBE said: 'Never happier than when touring three days a week, driving himself ... having relegated his driver to the back seat, usually for not taking sufficiently rapid action against the narks.'

Wynn-Pope had a cavalryman's approach to life in the field. The tour ration box included, if not the Lancer's champagne, caviar, vodka and smoked salmon, as well as adequate supplies of Scotch as irresistible bait for reluctant Russians. Wynn-Pope did not so much drive his tours across communist Germany as charge. His instruction to colleagues was: 'You just glide them to leg, my dear fellow; glide them to leg.' This was his way of describing his technique of deliberately driving perilously close to anyone who, in his view, was improperly obstructing him. The targets included narks, Vopo and Soviet Army traffic regulators also known as 'reggies'.

Following his forays, the telephone lines were hot with complaints. When his name was mentioned at GSFG headquarters, they would scowl. Was he not the British Military Attaché in Moscow who had broken virtually every rule of protocol? He was. But the Brixmis posting was controlled by the War Office, not the Foreign Office, as (doubtless) the FO tried to explain. His reputation preceded him. It was customary for the new Brixmis Mission Chief to be received with elaborate courtesy, at the start of his tour, at the Russian headquarters at Zossen Wunsdorf. Not so Wynn-Pope, and it rankled. If they would not give him his due recognition, then they could forget their 'Mission Restricted' signs.

To make matters worse, as part of the recognition of East German sovereignty the Russians were handing over the task of narking to Ulbricht's emerging Stasi agency. The Russians denied that there was any change of control. Wynn-Pope decided to prove them wrong by producing the (preferably living) body of a Stasi agent in the office of the Soviet liaison officer (SLO), Colonel L. S. Sergeev. On a fine summer's day in 1957, with Critchley as observer, he took the wheel and drove around in the hope of being spotted and followed. He was, for two hours, in Potsdam, by two Stasi vehicles. Critchley identified one of the opposition as 'a particularly aggressive character named Fritz Pix'. The Cold War didn't get much more personal than that. Events were now about to take a distinctly Laurel-and-Hardy turn.

Critchley said:

We lured one of the cars into Rembrandtstrasse, a one-way street and outside the Soviet liaison office the Chief (still driving) suddenly reversed rapidly and crashed the rear of our Opel Kapitän into the front of the following EMW. The EMW collapsed with a broken front axle and radiator from which clouds of steam gushed out ... The two narks sprang out brandishing tyre levers and started to batter the Brixmis car.

Wynn-Pope seized one and dragged him into the Soviet Liaison Office while I grappled with the other, who was Fritz Pix. He hit me on the head with a tyre lever, but my balmoral [the headdress worn by a Cameronian] took the force of the blow and he fell in the gutter where our driver sat on him.

Sergeev, the SLO, passed the buck and the affair was treated by the East German police as a traffic accident caused by the movement of the Brixmis car the wrong way down a one-way street. This was technically correct, even if the Brixmis car was facing the right way. The fact was it was reversing at speed. No mention was made of the narks.

A few days later, Wynn-Pope received a personal letter from Sergeev, saying that the sentries at the Glienicke Bridge checkpost had orders not to accept his pass.

Wynn-Pope retired from the army, prematurely, soon afterwards. He was the first big 'scalp' taken by the Stasi.

In the increasingly tense atmosphere, locally as well as internationally, Brixmis and their Russian hosts needed an emollient. The army needed a safe pair of hands and looked towards Windsor Castle. There, the Honourable M. F. Fitzalan-Howard MC, later to become Duke of Norfolk, was commanding his regiment, 2nd Grenadier Guards, on one of its periodic rounds of royal and ceremonial duties. Miles Fitzalan-Howard was a soldier's soldier. As a subaltern he had commanded the regiment's anti-tank platoon during a hard-fought rearguard action against the Wehrmacht at Calais in 1940. By the time the war had turned, he was a brigade major of the 4th Armoured in the bitterly-fought Italian campaign all the way from Sicily to the Sangro. Equally useful, from Whitehall's point of view, he was untainted by any intelligence background. He had no 'form' so far as the KGB was concerned. At short notice, he was posted to Brixmis.

He broke the ice with a joke. At his official reception, receiving his credentials, one of the guests was a Soviet parachute commander named General Epanchin, now running Soxmis. 'I said to him, "You know, I am very sad to see a young officer like you so bald." He walked behind me and said to the interpreter, a suave character called Romanov who'd learned his English at Oxford, "Just tell the Brigadier I am bald at the front because I work so hard; he is bald at the back which means too many women!" From then on, I could make jokes – rude jokes – with the Russians and it didn't matter. The Russians were real soldiers, infantry soldiers, full of jokes, you know?'

Fitzalan-Howard found there were many fences to mend after Wynne-Pope's charges. The French and the Americans had to be soothed. Eventually, the three Mission Chiefs (American, French, British) started meeting to co-ordinate tours for the first time, 'to delude the narks, sidetrack them'. There was a fatal flaw in this scheme, but it had nothing to do with the men on the ground.

The co-ordinated tour·programmes, including targets identified by London, Washington and Paris, were circulated among several desks including that of MI6 in Berlin. Berlin, however, was 'a nest of spies and counter-spies where you could see MI6 officers briefing people in cars'. One member of the MI6 team in that city was George Blake. Fitzalan-Howard noted that whatever his team targeted was well covered by the Stasi narks. He tried decoys, to draw the narks away on a false trail across the Glienicke Bridge while another team made its way to the real objective elsewhere. When it got near the objective, 'there was always another nark ready to meet it. They knew where we were going. We should have spotted this but we didn't. It was several years later that I realized that Blake was in that mission at that time and was giving a copy of all our tour programmes to the East Germans.' (George Blake was arrested for spying in April 1961.)

RAF veterans of that time are not so sure that the problem started with Blake. They concede that he would have had access to tour programmes circulated to the MI6 station; but by adopting a lower profile, they argue, air tours were rarely detected. The basic issue was whether a tour should have as its objective a high-profile, protocol-laden right of passage under the terms of the Robertson–Malinin Agreement, or the theft of Soviet military secrets. As Group Captain Hans Neubroch OBE put it recently: 'My own instinct is to postulate cock-up rather than conspiracy . . . When tours were undertaken primarily for exercising and, if need be, enforcing what the navy would call the *right of innocent passage*, gaining intelligence was by way of a bonus. The primary aim implied an element of confrontation and this explains a great deal that went on (and wrong) in the Mission.'

Another veteran, Major Gatehouse, said: 'In my day, individual tour officers tended to be reluctant to divulge the routes they had found into targets and OPs for fear that these would be compromised by others . . . Tour officers did not often stick to the routes they had planned, for instance, when they came across unexpected signs of movement. It seems unlikely to me that Blake could have been effective in betraying Mission tours once they had set out, but he could have caused SERB [Soviet External Relations Bureau] to improve the security of sensitive targets.' Much later – long after Blake was caught and locked up – the Soviets did refine their defences against Brixmis intrusion to a point where tours were ambushed and savagely beaten.

Fitzalan-Howard was himself a regular victim of what he later perceived to be the Blake betrayal. Ignoring pressures from White-hall to command the Mission from his desk, he routinely went touring and was detained, along with Critchley, about ten times.

Fitzalan-Howard's period of command ran from 1957, the year in which the Russians demonstrated their technical missile superiority by putting the first astronaut into space, to 1959, the year of the second Berlin crisis. At times, the tension dramatically penetrated the comparative calm of the Mission's compound at Potsdam. The main house was so infested with eavesdropping devices that 'we went into the gardens to whisper and even then, the flowerbeds were probably bugged'. In the wide world beyond the compound, this was a time of anti-left witchhunting in the US, a period when Anglo-American relations were convalescent after Suez, one in which Khrushchev struggled for absolute power in Moscow while CND protesters, fearing the worst, became a serious political force in Britain. Amid such instability, it would be easy to jump at shadows and report Red Army activities in colourful terms. Fitzalan-Howard would have none of it.

'I never believed there would be a real invasion. We saw the Red Army manoeuvres but if it was the real thing one would see the vast echelons of ammunition and supplies of fuel moving forward. They were not there. I never thought there was going to be a war, ever, and that was the tenor of my reports to my headquarters. At parties back home, when we heard people talking about the Russian threat, we said it was rubbish, they had no intention of attacking.'

Not even Fitzalan-Howard's sang-froid could prevent the near-destruction of mission buildings in his second year of command. It was a vivid example of the impact of the external conflict upon Brixmis and its local demons such as Fritz Pix.

On 14 July 1958 a clandestine, pan-Arabist 'Free Officers' Group' seized power in Baghdad to topple a royal dynasty created by Britain in August 1921. King Faisal, aged twenty-one, and his powerful uncle, Abdulillah, were murdered. So was the manipulative Iraqi premier, Nuri-es-Said. As he tried to tiptoe away from

Baghdad dressed as a woman, a mob spotted him and kicked him to death. Political shock-waves shuddered through British-protected Gulf oil states in one direction and Lebanon in the other. From Lebanon, President Chamoun sent an SOS to the White House.

As it happened, the British Foreign Secretary, Selwyn Lloyd, was in Washington on that day. He reported secretly to London, 'complete US solidarity with us over the Gulf'. President Eisenhower let it be known he was prepared to protect Chamoun with nuclear weapons. In the event, the US sent 10,000 Marines to Lebanon while the British put 2,000 Paras into Jordan to support another client, the Harrow-educated and Sandhurst-trained King Hussein. Bahrein was reinforced with troops based in Kenya.

Russia and its satellites were furious. The communist media reported, falsely, that the RAF and USAF were bombing women and children in Amman and Beirut. On 18 July, in a carefully orchestrated riot, this anger was directed at the British and US compounds at Potsdam.

At that time the mission included Squadron Leader Hans Neubroch. From the RAF Staff College he had hoped to take command of a flying squadron, but instead, in May 1957, he was sent to Brixmis. Now, fourteen months later, he called at the Mission's Berlin HQ following a tour to be told by Fitzalan-Howard that 'there's a bit of a riot going on in Potsdam'.

Neubroch found a crowd of around 200 in the mission compound at Potsdam. Near a damaged Brixmis car, Major Chris Hallett held his ground, his uniform apparently blood-smeared. He had retrieved the Union flag after a failed attempt to burn it. Most of the windows in mission buildings had been smashed. As the mob hammered on his own car, Neubroch calmly noted slogans painted on walls: 'Hands Off Middle East!'

Neubroch now pulled off a political conjuring trick. He got out of the car and argued patiently and in perfect, idiomatic German with the demonstrators. A careful student of German military history, he made an instant assessment of the opposition: 'Really quite good-humoured ... factory people and young girls out for the lark of an outing from work on a lovely summer's day ... an "intellectual" element (party people and students from the party school) ... a handful of activists.'

A discussion ensued and the 'intellectuals' invited Neubroch to address the crowd. For them, the rally was a familiar ritual; for Neubroch it was thin political ice, made more fragile when he was introduced as 'this Anglo-American terror bomber prepared to inflict atrocities on women and children in Lebanon with atom bombs'. Absurd as this claim was, Neubroch was aware that he was in RAF uniform and that they were a mere three hours' drive from Dresden.

Neubroch began with a lie: 'How very nice to see so many of you here in the British Mission compound.' To his own surprise, his impromptu address succeeded in winning them over. After much political gesturing, he undertook to convey the people's protest personally to the British government. The crowd dispersed.

Enter, as a finale, the Soviet Town Commandant of Postdam led by the arm by Brigadier Miles Fitzalan-Howard who said to him: 'You promised me personally that there would be no violence against the Mission. It was a solemn promise from a soldier to a soldier and you broke it.'

Fitzalan-Howard's reproof had a dramatic effect: the Soviet colonel was crying.

That night, at the Officers' Club in Berlin, there was a party at which the Brigadier handed out portions of the scorched Union flag. It was a gesture in keeping with the outpost-of-empire bravery and absurdity of that day.

It was the end of the original Mission site. Brixmis moved to new, more secure premises. Damages were claimed. Almost exactly a year later, Sergeev asked Fitzalan-Howard to come down to the Soviet liaison office at Potsdam. There, he produced a pile of crisp, new English fivers and slowly counted out £1,200 owing in damages. He did not even ask for a receipt.

The attack on the Mission compound was not an isolated incident but part of a growing policy of pressuring the Western Missions, amounting to an attempt to throttle the life out of them. In 1957, as Lieutenant-Colonel Critchley put it later: 'We were entering the era of Khrushchev's threats of naked aggression against the West and a determined effort was made by the Soviets and the East Germans in collusion to undermine the position of the Western powers in Berlin by any means available. One such means ready to hand was the three Allied Missions, which became a collective target for insult and opprobrium, since their very presence on the "sovereign territory" of the German Democratic Republic was a constant denial of the sovereignty which it claimed to possess.'

Peter Goss, an Intelligence Corps officer with Brixmis at that time (though still badged as a Royal Fusilier, his old regiment), argued that 'the FCO [Foreign and Commonwealth Office] were the masters in deciding any response to the Soviets and in this respect they decided to do nothing and so the thing mushroomed'.

Containment came in various forms over the next two years, from the quasi-legal to the use of firearms. Official signs declaring vast training areas out of bounds to mission patrols proliferated from 450 throughout the GDR in 1955 to 2,500 by 1960 and 4,000 by 1972. The instruction to Brixmis from the headquarters of BAOR (British Army of the Rhine) – amid the many creature comforts of a free West Germany – was to obey the new signs or face the consequences. In practice, mission patrols chose to take their chances. Some Brixmis soldiers even collected the signs to be taken home to Britain as souvenirs.

East German narks took over the game of tailing patrols from 1956 and added intimidation to the repertoire. The new generation of narks, Critchley recalled, were of the same timbre and temper as the Hitler Youth a generation earlier: 'The scum of the East Berlin underworld, tough, dangerous, indoctrinated young hoodlums . . . Apart from attempting to drive one off the road they were up to every kind of beastliness . . . spitting at, throwing garbage, knocking drinks out of one's hands, banging on car windows, shouting obscenities.'

When Squadron Leader Jim Cade hit one of them, the nark ran to complain to the Soviets, whose liaison officer obligingly accused Cade of acting like a hooligan in striking 'an authorized citizen of the GDR'. The phrase had an Orwellian tinkle. It stuck. More than once, when complaints flew in the other direction, Brixmis protests would drily refer to 'an authorized citizen'.

The Stasi were equipped with new, fast cars, some of which were confiscated from unwary Westerners using the authorized autobahn 'corridor' through East Germany to Berlin. The vehicles were BMW, Chevrolet and Mercedes SL fitted with radios and accompanied by Soviet instructors. Then they waited at the predictable exit points from the mission compounds to intercept the Western vehicles. The line of Stasi cars reminded one Brixmis veteran of a taxi rank. A 100 k.p.h. (62 m.p.h.) speed limit was imposed on autobahn traffic which Brixmis was expected to obey. If it did so, its cars were now overtaken by the narks and forced to halt.

In November 1958, soon after the attack on the compound, Khrushchev served notice on the West to leave Berlin. In a 6,000-word note, he said that the agreement on the Berlin occupation, sharing responsibility, was obsolete. Any violation of East German borders would be considered aggression against the Warsaw Pact. For good measure, he told a press conference in Moscow that West Berlin had become 'a sort of cancerous tumor', in need of 'a surgical operation'. The surgeon, he made clear, would be the USSR.

Ulbricht, faithful to his master's voice, declared that when the different zones of occupation were established in 1945, 'Berlin did not become a fifth zone . . . all of Berlin is located within the territory of the GDR.' Western areas of the city relied on the Potsdam Agreement for their legality and, in rearming West Germany, the West had breached that treaty. Therefore, the three Western powers no longer had any right to be in Berlin.

Taking their cue from Khrushchev and Ulbricht, the watchdogs started shooting at Western patrols in East Germany. A Brixmis tour led by Major Pilsbury encountered a Russian officer in a training area near Brandenburg. The Russian promptly drew his pistol and started shooting, though not straight enough to hit. As the Soviet liaison office put it when complaints were made: 'All Soviet soldiers can shoot straight enough to hit you if they intend to do so. These shots are to warn you not to come any closer.'

Soon after the Pilsbury affair, Captain Moser, a young officer with the French Mission, was 'running' a Red Army convoy (passing it at speed and noting the types and numbers of vehicles in it) when he was spotted at Vogelsang by an army traffic regulator. 'Reggies' were planted at crossroads in advance of the convoy and picked up by the last vehicle to pass. They were armed and often bored. Vogelsang, a suburb of Stralsund on the Baltic coast, was a particularly dangerous place for mission patrols. On this occasion, the 'reggie' decided to shoot at the French car. Moser was seriously wounded.

A Brixmis source commented later: 'These inspired incidents made the missions realize that the rules of the game had changed to our disadvantage; things were never going to be the same again.'

Fitzalan-Howard, the safe pair of hands, was limited by the caution that verged on appeasement on the part of his own headquarters at BAOR. Yet he had to do something if the mission was not to be emasculated or, in a euphemism popular at that time, 'Finlandized'. He noted that lack of co-ordination among the three Western teams often meant that an East German hunt stirred up by the patrol of one Western ally would compromise another.

As Critchley put it: 'Some profitable or popular tour areas were over-toured, whilst others were left largely neglected. It was not unknown for a tour from one mission to run innocently into a hue-and-cry caused by another mission whose whereabouts had been unknown to it.'

Fitzalan-Howard's initiative meant integrated tours 'more clearly defined and specially allocated week by week. Tour programmes were planned jointly a week in advance (except for ad hoc emergency tours and those involving special targets on behalf of other agencies) and all tours were debriefed at the US mission office before returning home.'

It took another year to integrate the individualistic French into the system but Fitzalan-Howard talked them round. Mission reports were set out in a uniform format and a comprehensive data-base created. Greater co-ordination led to the circulation of around twenty copies of the joint tour programme. This, as we have seen, probably gave the British spy George Blake access to the system.

Critchley noted:

My tour was making for the Wittstock training area and I was quite certain that we had got clean away from Potsdam, when to my disgust we were picked up by a waiting nark car on a minor road. The narks that day were disposed to be chatty and quite friendly. When the tour eventually stopped for a short break, they pulled up close behind us. One, whom I knew of old and who was never offensive, said: 'You thought we wouldn't find you today, didn't you?', to which I replied, 'Well, sometimes you do, sometimes you don't.' The nark then said, 'We can find you whenever we want to. We always know in advance where you are going.' I was amazed that he should have said it so openly.

The pressure had its effect on many members of the Mission. When Fitzalan-Howard left at the conclusion of his period in command, he handed over to Brigadier John Packard, who lasted just a year in the job. Then, like Wynn-Pope, he left the army completely. His first wrangle, in February 1960, involved a Soviet attempt to switch existing mission passes for new ones recognizing East Germany. During a stand-off that lasted a month, no Western patrols went anywhere. Lieutenant-Colonel Wylde explained: 'The US would have given up their mission rather than give formal recognition to the GDR on Soviet-issued passes. The status of Berlin was at stake. They were not going to accept changes that might threaten West Berlin.'

The Soviets, having tried a little elbow-wrestling, restored the old wording with a shrug and a reference to 'a little misunderstanding'. Meanwhile, they exercised no control over the East German narks. In June 1960, Packard, in his distinctive staff car identifying him as a one-star general, took a short cut shortly after leaving Potsdam to avoid waiting narks. Another mission vehicle blocked the pursuit of the Stasi. Packard was stopped in woods on the edge of an East German army training area by a sentry armed with a machine-gun. Soon his escape was blocked by two East German army trucks and two Stasi cars whose occupants were furious that they had been fooled. Next, the nark leader Fritz Pix – the man who had tried to reshape Critchley's head with a tyre lever in Rembrandtstrasse in 1957 – arrived, leading a squad of hand-picked backstreet thugs in four cars.

Pix took charge. His men systematically scoured the area for large rocks and stout branches. For the British party – Brigadier Packard, Lieutenant-Colonel Critchley, Squadron Leader Harry Nunwick and two drivers – the message was ominous and clear.

It was to be warfare of the bare-knuckle variety. It was not a good day for diplomatic immunity.

Critchley wrote: 'On a given signal they rushed our two cars simultaneously and swarmed all over us, bashing in door locks and windows, and wrenching open the sunshine roof. We were all hauled out bodily, roughed up a bit and forced to stand by while both cars were stripped and searched from stem to stern. The narks seized all our kit and touring equipment, we were shoved back inside again, and the narks made off with their loot, at about 1130 hours.'

The affair provoked an international storm. About a week later, the East German leader Ulbricht presided over a televised news conference in East Berlin at which the tour's equipment was displayed. Some of the team's maps revealed areas that were highlighted in yellow. For Brixmis purposes, they indicated towns whose population exceeded a given density. Ulbricht identified them as 'areas earmarked by the fascist imperialists for extermination by germ warfare'. Other routine map symbols were interpreted as cabbalistic signs for sabotage parties. As a follow-through to this performance, to ensure that Brixmis got the message, the Soviet Army headquarters in Germany informed General Cassels, the British Commander-in-Chief that Packard's safety could no longer be guaranteed. It was a shrewd exploitation of the original confrontation. Packard was relieved of his command. No retaliatory action was taken by the British. Yet again, it seemed to the men on the spot, there were disturbing indications of something amounting to surrender on the part of Western governments when faced with a degree of bullying that just fell short of an outright declaration of war.

It is far from certain that Packard left the army because of the beating he took from the Stasi. Packard was described by Critchley as 'a true gentleman and one of the nicest family men of my acquaintance, but he was basically a man of peace and the rough hurly-burly of Brixmis life was not for him.' A later authority, Lieutenant-Colonel Wylde, sees it differently.

Packard had been an intelligence officer all his life. Before the war he had lived in Germany until August 1939, next to an

SS barracks, reporting back on what was happening in the Rhineland area. He arrived back in the UK just before the war [declared in September 1939] and joined the British Expeditionary Force [in the Battle of France] as their intelligence officer. He went through the war as a German specialist, in intelligence.

The moment Cassels refused to stand up to the Russians . . . Packard said, 'Enough is enough.' He didn't tell Charles Critchley or his staff any of this. They thought he had just decided to resign because of the roughing up. He felt that the only way to obtain protection for the Brixmis staff was to put a new Chief of Mission in place. So he resigned. He never criticized Cassels. It was very sad. He told me the story in June 1993, two months before he died. He had bottled it up out of loyalty for thirty years.

Not all, or even a majority, of Brixmis soldiers and airmen were as pliable as commanders who may have taken their cue from a government, headed by Harold Macmillan, which was negotiating a trade agreement with Russia while telling the British people they had never had it so good. In April 1959 (a month before the Anglo-Russian deal was signed) Critchley, with Major Chris Hallett – the technical intelligence officer who had been involved in the attack on the mission compound – penetrated an East German Army May Day ceremonial parade. The event was a nice photo-opportunity but they were spotted and drove off down the autobahn. The lead parade vehicle, flying 'an enormous GDR standard', took up the chase. The other parade vehicles, caught unawares, followed. Buster Keaton might have created the scene that ensued.

The whole column was moving faster and faster as our tour car tried to keep ahead . . . Then the saluting base came into sight on our right, a small stand packed with VIPs, mainly East Germans with a few Russians among them. As the GDR standard-bearer approached, the spectators all rose to their feet, no doubt wondering what the strange car in front was.

As we drew level almost nose-to-tail, would-be salutes changed into violent shaking of fists . . . I only wished we could have photographed that scene in the grandstand. But we were too intent on getting off the autobahn again by the only escape track before the end-barrier at Satzkorn . . . The memory of that hilarious occasion more than compensated for many less enjoyable incidents involving the East Germans and their evil narks.

Major Peter Goss, at the start of a long and successful career in military intelligence, developed a formidable repertoire of conjuring tricks to baffle the opposition. 'I never took a nark on tour, ever,' he said. 'If you had a nark with you and you saw something interesting you couldn't do anything about it so the best thing was to get rid of him right at the beginning. If I couldn't get rid of him I came back and went out again a few hours later.' Goss, among others, favoured the stealthy approach. He had several favourite, pre-surveyed shake-off points off-road, in the pine forests near Berlin, 'with sandy soil that was muddy in winter, very churned up, and dusty in the summer.' In summer he used sudden acceleration into the shake-off area and a cloud of dust to camouflage a sharp turn into a side track. Sometimes he would deliberately drive into an area of soft or boggy ground, a 'sandsplash', where – to the initial amusement of the narks – he would become bogged down. Goss, though, always carried a winch. A slow pantomime act would follow: 'You'd winch yourself out and if he was going to follow he'd also bog down and stay there, as we drove away.'

Another variant was to drive at speed over a carefully chosen spot where tree trunks could foul the underside of a pursuer's car; Brixmis cars were fitted with plates to protect the vehicle's underside. The bladder test required empty bottles in the car: 'Eventually, the narks had to stop for a pee. We didn't.' There was also the chauffeur camouflage ploy:

We ran administrative runs down to the Mission House at Potsdam. People who were not on tour would drive down and deliver some stuff to the Mission House. The visitors might stay and send the car back to Berlin, with just the driver. East German sentries watched us and knew the form. They weren't going to waste the time of a Stasi team following an empty Brixmis car back to its headquarters in Berlin. So we simulated these runs to conceal the start of a tour. We'd turn up like other visitors, get out of the car, creep back into it from the blind side and lie on the floor as it drove away again. The Stasi would see only the driver. I remember pulling this trick with Brigadier Tom Pearson [Chief of Mission from 1960 to 1961]. By that time I knew Potsdam so well that I could navigate the tour blind, from the floor of the car.

Out in the field, there was constant risk of accidental discovery. 'I was at the end of my tour and probably getting a bit reckless,' Goss recalled. 'Early in 1961 we were watching a river crossing by the Soviet Army, complete with tanks.' Since any invasion of West Germany would require a series of river crossings to succeed, this manoeuvre was of key importance to both sides. 'Getting out of the car was not a good idea but I got out anyway, and went forward on foot to get a better sight of what was going on. I got about a quarter of a mile from the vehicle. We wore duffle coats and flying boots because it was bloody cold. Then I was spotted by a PT-76 semi-amphibious troop carrier on the other side of the river. It was then a race between us to reach the car first. He was looking for a ford to cross over and snatch me. I was floundering about in flying boots. I just made it in time.'

The Brixmis RAF staff, meanwhile, was undergoing a quiet revolution. In 1956, the senior RAF job was upgraded to the post of deputy Chief of Mission in the rank of group captain, equivalent to a full army colonel. It was also made the preserve of the RAF's praetorian guard, the General Duties (Flying) Branch. Until then, the senior RAF officer had been a wing commander of the Secretarial Branch, which included administrators and intelligence specialists.

The officer chosen to establish this new, more aggressive and more directed style was Group Captain F. G. (George) Foot. Foot had recently achieved distinction as British Air Attaché in Hungary. A native of Winnipeg, he had paid his own fare in 1937 to travel from Canada to England, so as to join the RAF. As a flying-boat captain and navigation expert, Foot flew several wartime missions to Arkhangelsk and Moscow, and brought Soviet VIPs to England. Later he studied Russian at London University and, after the war, became a diplomat in Budapest. When he joined Brixmis, as his colleague Neubroch recalled, Foot 'was determined that every RAF tour would be planned, briefed, conducted and evaluated with the

84

same meticulous professionalism as an operational flying mission'.

RAF veterans of that time say that the control and reporting chain ran directly from the Air Ministry's Technical Intelligence branch (DDI Tech) to the RAF element of Brixmis. Simultaneously, the Air Ministry's air 'orbat' (order of battle) specialists in DDI3 and the Intelligence Branch of headquarters, RAF Germany, would receive copies of all reports.

Foot's brief was to collect intelligence on the men and machines of the Soviet 24th Air Army in front-line Germany. A secondary target was the East German Air Force. Foot was not concerned with right-of-passage or other issues of protocol. His first priority was to acquire technical intelligence, a job he and his team were to do brilliantly. The principal weapon would be the long-lens camera, using stereoscopic techniques. Neubroch explained: 'In the early 1950s touring officers had made pencil sketches of their objectives. Foot insisted that photography would be the primary means of validating intelligence. No item was to be "credited" unless there was a photograph to support the claim. We used a Leica M. 3, 400mm Telyt lens on land and a 200mm lens from the air.'

Targeted airfields were allocated routine monthly surveillance by Brixmis, concentrating on flight line and radars. The pictures were taken from concealed observation posts (OPs) or from adjacent roads, standing on the touring car roof if a perimeter fence obstructed the view. Occasionally they were spotted and warning shots were fired.

Foot's golden rule was photography first, then considered visual observation if there was time. In the summer of 1957, Foot and Neubroch darted into a position overlooking an airfield at Neu Welzow and legged it back to Berlin with a photographic panorama of the Soviet flight line of Fresco and Flashlight fighters.

'Only on his return,' said Neubroch, 'when Foot checked stereoscopic pairs of the Flashlight machines did he realize that one aircraft had its nose-cone removed, exposing the AI radar dish inside it. The photograph gave us technical details long sought by Allied intelligence, including the Flashlight's radar intercept capability.'

The Mission also wanted detailed photographs of the underside

The most popular – if unsanctioned – sport in sport-minded East Germany was called escape to the West. Some people tunnelled. Some built their own hang-gliders, light aircraft and balloons. This photograph, of a Communist border guard leaping the wire to freedom during the first hours of the Berlin Wall, went round the world as a testament to the average German's fundamental appetite for freedom from his Marxist utopia. *Topham Picture Library*

The Russians renamed streets and entire towns to emphasize the new Soviet order in Eastern Europe. Chemnitz, for example, became 'Karl Marx Stadt'. Other symbols included this war memorial, commemorating the loss of thousands of Russian lives in the nine-day Battle of Berlin, built around a T–34 tank. The memorial was in place less than six months after the war ended as this photograph, taken in late 1945, shows.

Berlin, shattered capital of the Third Reich in May 1945, was also the start-point for post-war military liaison between British and Soviet wartime allies. Ostensibly the purpose of their liaison was to clean up Europe politically, with an emphasis on human rights. In practice, Soviet expansion had already started.

One of the first Mission tour cars – slow, highly polished, easily followed, this left-hand-drive model, probably war booty, belonged to the Senior Naval Officer and carried an Admiralty insignia on the front bumper as well as a Brixmis number plate. This high-profile vehicle – Protocol-on-Wheels – embodied a 'right of passage' philosophy. It was not compatible with a subsequent emphasis on low-profile intelligence gathering.

Above: An early social lunch (probably during the late 1940s) between Soviet and Brixmis liaison officers. The Second World War medal ribbons, lean bodies and austere table were part of a shared experience which the Russians identified as 'the Great Patriotic War'. Simultaneously, Brixmis was learning the realities of the Cold War. They included spying on an 'ally'.

Below: So long as the rules were obeyed, etiquette was strictly observed. Here, the British supremo in West Germany, General Cassells, is received at the Soviet East German headquarters with full military honours as he calls on the Russian Marshal Yakubovski on 17 March 1961. In Britain, the Lonsdale ring of five Soviet spies was being interrogated. So was the master spy, George Blake.

In public, meetings between the two sides were ritualized, even when no immediate cause of tension existed. Here, with the Soviet War Memorial near the Reichstag in Berlin as a background, Brigadier Learmont, Chief of Mission from 1982 to 1984 and the Soviet Commander, General Zaitzev, converse through an interpreter.

Liaison with the Russians was trapped in a 1945 timewarp regardless of real time. Maj Willie Macnair, a Highlander, briefs visitors on the Plotzensee Memorial, a prison whe Hitler ordered executions as a pre-dinner entertainment. The son of a Russian prisone murdered in this fashion was visiting the site of his father's calvary when this photogr was taken. The participants, left to right front row, were: Colonel Alex Rubanov, chief SERB; Major Macnair (Staff Officer, Operations, 1979–82); Group Captain RD Bates A Deputy Chief of Brixmis, 1981–3; Soviet Captain Dimitri Trenin, a translator (now an occasional BBC commentator from Moscow); the Russian (name not recorded) whose father died in Plotzensee. At rear, right, is Captain (later Colonel) Peter Williams MBE Coldstream Guards, who participated with Sergeant Wike in the apple episode (see chapter ten).

of targeted aircraft, from which aerials and other equipment could be analysed. The team's problem was that film shot upwards, against a bright sky, usually darkened the underside of the aircraft so badly that no details emerged. 'In a trial, Foot exposed dozens of films and determined that for the best results it was necessary, on a clear day, to take light-meter readings against the horizon and then over-expose by two stops on the lens, always with a filter.'

Special developing techniques enhanced the pictures remarkably, raising 64 ASA film to the equivalent of 1600 ASA. The experiments also showed that clear pictures could be obtained from carefully chosen OPs 3 kilometres from either end of an operational runway, where aircraft would be flying at about 700 feet. 'One chap would photograph the aircraft. The other would get an identification of the aircraft number and type.'

For the new strategy to work, it was imperative that the RAF's hidden OPs should remain undiscovered. One officer, designated 'tour navigator', would be in tactical command on the route to and from the target while the other would keep constant watch for unwanted followers.

'Foot recognized that we had to avoid or shake the narks. If we failed to do that, the tour as planned was abandoned in favour of some less sensitive activity, such as picnicking in the woods or talking to the locals, a practice euphemistically known as "gaining political intelligence", or exploring new trails through forests as potential, future escape routes. Our army colleagues, by contrast, might complete an entire tour of barracks and training areas accompanied by the opposition.'

The narks were waiting most mornings on the six or seven exits out of Potsdam. 'they were in EMW or ancient Mercedes cars. We knew their registration numbers and their faces . . . Their normal method was to follow us at a discreet distance – as much as 2 kilometres behind us on the autobahn – and once they were able to guess at our likely target, to telephone or pass by radio a warning to the people guarding that site, that we were coming.'

Foot, Neubroch and others developed their own repertoire of nark-shaking tricks. Trick no. 1: Spot Them First. 'They would accelerate from a standing start while we were travelling at 35 m.p.h. We could then accelerate to a turn-off point before they could keep us in sight.'

Trick no. 2: Acceleration. 'We would take the narks to the nearest autobahn, cruise gently at 50 m.p.h., the nark maybe half a mile behind.' Approaching a long incline, the Brixmis driver would change down and accelerate hard, uphill. 'The clapped-out East German car, with its low-grade petrol, was no match for the immaculately maintained Opel Kapitän with its high-octane Western fuel. We usually lost sight of the nark long before we turned off at one of the autobahn exits.'

Trick no. 3: The Lay-by Ploy. Some lay-bys, noted in advance, led off the autobahn but were not overlooked by the road and also provided some sort of exit to the local countryside.

Trick no. 4: 'The Wives' Tale.' 'In December 1958 Group Captain John Boardman, Foot's successor, and I spent a night with our wives at the Potsdam Mission House. Next morning one car, with the ladies, en route to Leipzig, "picked up" the guard nark at one of the Potsdam exits. John and I followed five minutes later along the same route and had a clear run. The ladies spent the day shopping in Leipzig, leading the narks a merry dance on the escalators of the Konsum department store; John and I did our day's work and we all rendezvoused at a hostelry in Eisenach.'

Foot recalled: 'In two years of touring I was stopped and taken to a kommandantura only once, when I went on an army tour to ascertain, as deputy Chief of Mission, how the army carried out their tours. The Soviet liaison officer in Potsdam, with whom I always spoke quite freely, once asked me how I was able to shake off the German followers. I replied that I was a colonel, whereas the German was merely a chauffeur. If I couldn't shake off the nark, I should give my "scrambled eggs" [service dress cap, decorated with oak leaves] to my chauffeur!'

Some months later, Squadron Leader Terry Harrison went out with an army tour. He asked how they prepared their approach to the target. 'We make sure we have our hats on,' his guide replied. Neubroch confirmed it: 'Though this caused a certain amount of mirth among the Light Blue, there was a serious purpose about the wearing of correct uniform in the target area. The senior army touring officers then serving in Brixmis had earned their spurs in the immediate postwar era in both Austria and Germany, when tours were undertaken primarily for exercising and if need be enforcing right-of-passage ... George Foot was probably the first to see that exercising one's diplomatic rights and gaining intelligence were largely incompatible and needed quite different tactics. Everything the RAF element subsequently achieved flowed from that.' (It should be remembered, though, that the RAF's use of stealth was not unique: it had already been adopted by the Intelligence Corps officer Peter Goss, among others.)

Brixmis was never ordered to obtain specific intelligence but, said Neubroch, there was 'a wish-list, detailing objectives with various degrees of priority'. Routine touring was modified to take account of the wish-list but it was entirely up to the team whether or not to go for a given target. Since the 24 Air Army flew only on Tuesdays and Thursdays, 'we would plan to spend those days photographing aircraft of one particular regiment'.

The team consisted of two officers and a driver. Maps, like those carried by special forces on operations, were never marked with objectives. Important, secret data had to be memorized.

If the wish-list left the choice of objectives to the men on the ground, this did not rule out some friction between the team and the intelligence godfathers. During Neubroch's tour HQ RAF Germany, at Rheindahlen, 'maintained they had evidence, presumably from Elint [electronic intelligence], that the Soviets flew much more than we said. This included considerable night flying, of which we had little evidence.'

To get at the truth, the team staked out the sensitive operational base at Gross Dolln for an entire working week from a main OP near the ruins of Goering's former official home, Karinhall. 'Although there were scares when Soviet military were seen wandering through the woods (sometimes in pairs, holding hands), the entire schedule was completed successfully, with flying observed by day on Tuesday and Thursday; minimally on Tuesday night.'

The conclusion was that the RAF's electronic intelligence team had been spoofed by the opposition transmitting false signals. Nigel Wylde subsequently stumbled upon a prime example of the Soviet art of *maskarovka* (deception): 'I was tasked to view an exercise in two training areas near Berlin. After several hours of searching I finally found three GAZ-66 trucks each filled with a number of big reel-to-reel tape recorders and some very bored soldiers playing back an old exercise.'

Neubroch, eager as a bird-watcher to complete his Red Air Force collection, went after the photographs of the Soviet air regiment at Neuruppin. His hide was in a marsh, among reeds which concealed him completely, though his flying boots developed a slow leak. With his colleague, Flight Lieutenant Huw Madoc-Jones, he emerged to find the team car and driver surrounded by armed Russians, snarling at them to stand back. Madoc-Jones, the Russian speaker on the team, growled back and pulled rank. Neubroch, he pointed out, was a major, and senior to the Soviet lieutenant so a little respect would be in order. While the argument continued, Neubroch slipped into the car to conceal the compromising camera and spare film.

'Huw told me that the lieutenant had sent for a major from the airfield, to deal with me on equal terms. To pass the time I asked could the Russians perhaps do a song-and-dance routine. To our delight, the Soviets obliged . . . all within ten minutes of threatening to shoot us.' The major, when he arrived, declared his hatred for Germans and sent the British team on its way with a smile and a wave.

Brixmis's growing photo-library proved to be a success. According to Neubroch: 'By the time I left the mission at the end of 1959 we had high-grade pictures of about 85 per cent of 24 Air Army's front-line strength.'

As well as photographs, the team brought home debris and maps from a wrecked Beagle Ilyushin-28 light bomber which had apparently crashed on the Brixmis OP 3 kilometres from the runway.

The RAF, which was to develop airfield destruction using a specialized ordnance known as JP233 as its Nato party piece, was hungry for knowledge about the structure of Warsaw Pact runways. Brixmis air tours took a loving interest in those still being constructed, before the RAF prepared to deconstruct them. On-the-spot surveys checked the direction and dimensions of the runway, its composition and even the subsoil.

To get direction we used an RAF landing compass. To assess length
we drove over it, taking a reading from the vehicle's mileometer.
We collected soil samples for analysis back home. We took photographs of the runway depth against a matchbox so as to measure
the depth later.

On one airfield, still under construction, we started off at full
speed. We sank into the soft soil. We were trying to extricate
ourselves with planks, gear and tackle when a Soviet GAZ-69 [a
jeep equivalent] approached and also sank in. The occupant called
to ask what we were doing . . .

[Neubroch] offered to help him out if he did the same for us.
Two more vehicles appeared. They also sank. I had visions of an
entire Soviet army formation all sinking into this runway. After
several hours we extricated ourselves. By then we were working
together and had become great friends. We were sent on our way
with the merest warning not to come back.

During Khrushchev's controversial visit to Berlin in 1959,
unruffled by the international tension it provoked, 'we knew the
East Germans were on the point of test-flying their first postwar
civilian jet aircraft, built on the lines of the Comet 1. So we went
to where the aircraft was kept and right enough we only waited
half an hour when it took off. We didn't see it land. In fact it
crashed on the approach. The entire Junkers test crew was killed.'

When Neubroch was not burrowing under Soviet runways he
was flying over them. The unit was equipped with its own basic
trainer, a two-seater Chipmunk clearly marked with RAF roundels
and kept at the RAF-manned Gatow airfield in Berlin. He said: 'I
flew this thing about once every ten days with an army officer.
We could legally fly anywhere within the Berlin air safety zone,
twenty miles around the Berlin air safety centre. There were more
Soviet barracks, personnel and kit in that area than we had in the
whole of Rhine Army. Within forty minutes you could cover a
large part of the Soviet "orbat" from a Chipmunk. The Soviets
protested about this from time to time. They were told that the
squadron leader had to earn his flying pay and the only way he
could do it was to fly the Chipmunk every ten days.' Nothing was
said about the rear seat passenger equipped with a camera.

Flights within the air safety zone were authorized by the Potsdam Agreement but had started only in 1956. In later years the pilot occupied the rear seat, reversing the usual arrangement, giving the observer, with hand-held camera, a clear view while leaning out of the open canopy as the pilot banked on one wing in stomach-lurching turns over the target.

The crews sometimes reflected ruefully that they could have done a better job but for Lord Montgomery's excessive nationalism at the 1945 Allied Potsdam conference. There the commanders-in-chief agreed that a twenty-mile radius should be fixed for training and air control flights over greater Berlin, measured from a pillar at the centre of the air safety building. Should the miles be nautical or statute? 'Statute, of course,' Montgomery said brusquely and, with one word, imposed an unnecessary limit on the Mission.

A later generation solved the problem by making clandestine trips beyond the permitted flying zone. In 1959, Neubroch got word of a new SAM-2 (surface-to-air anti-aircraft missile) site at Glau, just outside the permitted area. 'The missile itself had been photographed at the May Day parade in Moscow but no one had yet seen its associated radar, which would reveal the system's full operational capability. Our electronics expert, Harry Nunwick, had made several attempts to photograph the radar from the ground but he was unable to get close enough. We decided to try from the air. Harry and I started the flight as a routine circuit of the permitted area but when we approached Glau, I took the Chipmunk down low.'

Flying as close to the ground as he dared, to avoid detection without hitting the tree tops, Neubroch ensured that Nunwick got excellent close-up photographs of the secret site. 'The mission was on a Wednesday morning. During the afternoon – sports afternoon – we called in our corporal photographer to process the material. Then we called in the group captain who was over the moon. He said, "Right, Hans. Tomorrow you and I will fly up to show this stuff to the Commander-in-Chief." We did. The stuff was immediately flown down to Frankfurt, to the Americans. We had a letter of congratulations from the Americans. We were also told that the pictures were on President Eisenhower's desk the following Monday. We felt good about that.'

Neubroch's flights invariably culminated in a Biggles-style flourish: 'I would end up usually by offering to do a few aerobatics. The only army officer who regularly took me up on that offer was Brigadier Fitzalan-Howard. He was very keen on his aerobatics, was the Brigadier.'

CHAPTER 4

Harry Nunwick, His Fiddle Fund and the Blake Effect

1959–61

When Brigadier Packard was ambushed by Fritz Pix's Stasi thugs, Squadron Leader (later Wing Commander) Harry Nunwick MBE blamed himself. He had chosen the route to the ambush spot. He was the wily fox in the undergrowth who usually slipped away unscathed. He also spoke colloquial German and that often helped. Furthermore, the soldiers of Brixmis had asked him to act as a decoy to ensure Packard's clean getaway. But as Packard's predecessor as Chief (Brigadier Fitzalan-Howard) discovered, there was something not quite right about the security of the mission tours. Only after three years of living dangerously with Brixmis, being regularly intercepted by an enemy that seemed possessed of almost occult powers, did Nunwick put two and two together. In May 1961 he was back on regular RAF duties in England, and George Blake was being tried and sentenced to forty-two years' imprisonment for having, as Lord Chief Justice Parker put it, 'rendered much of this country's efforts completely useless'.

Blake was working at the MI6 station in Berlin when Nunwick was being betrayed. Nunwick followed the trial avidly. He wrote later:

Now I knew who the mole was. He had been six doors away from my office on the same floor, behind the top security barrier (manned night and day), behind a heavy, grilled access with self-closing and locking grill. Security clearance was required for each access. All windows to this section were barred, with frosted glass and with curtains across notice boards. This chap was one of the recipients of copies of every report I made and all were highly classified.   You can imagine my feelings towards this chap, knowing that he had also been responsible for the disappearance of more than forty brave men, some of whom I knew of by the output of their work. He only served six years in gaol before making a sensational escape.

Nunwick got off lightly. Proximity to the former Royal Navy officer and diplomat could be bad for the health. For four years Blake had an official flat in the Charlottenburg area of the British sector of Berlin. Four floors above, in the same block, MI6 kept a 'safe house'. For a time it was occupied by a valuable KGB defector, but not for long. The defector, drugged and barely conscious, was collected by car and driven to East Berlin, where he died under interrogation.

Even before his posting to Brixmis in June 1958 from his previous posting as Commander of the RAF Signals Squadron at Gutesloh, a forward Nato air-base, Harry Nunwick took a lively interest in the intelligence war. He particularly admired an Anglo-American interception of Soviet military communications launched from a cemetery. In a personal, unpublished, memoir (*The Nightriders of Berlin*) he wrote:

Before I joined the Mission, one of our US cousins reasoned that the main prewar underground trunk telephone link from Berlin to Leipzig was probably intact and in use by the Soviet military GHQ at their Karlshorst/Zossen Wunsdorf complex to the Leipzig command headquarter areas. If so, this would pass within 350 metres of the fortified, patrolled and floodlit fence between East and West Berlin. A joint US/British operation was mounted to dig a tunnel, half a mile long, from a graveyard in the British sector.

The Soviet trunk route was used for both voice and high-speed data transmission. In silence, a cavern was constructed around the trunk cable network and every cable core was tapped. Monitors were inserted and all traffic was recorded. Fortunately, Western watchers were constantly overlooking the road above the cavern because, in 1956, Soviet Army engineers arrived suddenly and started to excavate the road above the cavern. It was a close call. As the Russians broke through the roof, Allied staff were scrambling back through the tunnel to the safety of West Berlin. This betrayal was the work of a British traitor.

For those with robust nerves, this was fun, but a sense of humour was no guarantee of survival, as two more of Nunwick's stories demonstrate.

A member of the International Panel of Jurists lived and worked in West Berlin, gathering evidence of atrocities committed in East Germany and Warsaw Pact countries contrary to Human Rights agreements. He accumulated statements from victims and witnesses for use at future trials. One day, at breakfast-time, he answered the front door bell and two men stood there. After confirming his name they shot him carefully through each thigh . . . He was then bundled into a waiting car which drove away at high speed. He was never seen again.

In the centre of Berlin is Lake Havel. It is several miles long and about a mile wide. It was used for dinghy sailing by various clubs but one half was in West Berlin, the other in the East. A barrier of buoys and heavy cables marked the division. So did warning signs. To approach the barrier too closely was to risk being shot by Vopo guards. One morning a dinghy was spotted, overturned by the barrier and with the body of a man entangled in the sail. The man was known to us. His death was reported in the local press as a simple sailing accident. There were several snags with this version. He did not own a dinghy. He could not sail. He did not belong to a sailing club. No one in his right mind would have approached the barrier. He had also helped us. At the time, there were a number of unexplained deaths and disappearances from West Berlin.

By the time Nunwick was posted to Brixmis, the Mission was occupying new premises in Potsdam. The new Mission House was

a pre-war mansion, once owned by a millionaire, on the banks of a large and lovely lake. It had many bedrooms and a huge ballroom, with two huge, cut-glass chandeliers. This was our main area for diplomatic entertainment. Opposite the entrance in the side road which led to the Mission House was the familiar 'goon-box': a large, wooden, heated hut standing on the pavement covering all approaches to the Mission House. East German guards monitored our movements through a slit left in the green-painted windows. These guards, a mixture of Vopo and people dressed as civilians, were all armed.

All servants and cleaners in the Mission House were provided by the Soviet Army and relayed information on what we were doing and saying . . . We did hold cocktail parties occasionally for Soviet soldiers and airmen – not East Germans, whom we didn't recognize – and always with their wives and children. I found the children to be delightful: well dressed, very well behaved. We had a separate room for them with all the usual 'goodies' which children the world over enjoy. Like locusts, they cleared the tables in quick time as they were very short of 'luxury' foods, which we took for granted.

No matter how well a party was swinging, 'at some hidden signal' the Soviets would all get up and go, 'clearing the place in a matter of minutes, marching out as a crocodile'.

As he became familiar with this routine, Nunwick decided to mock the Soviets' departure ritual with a gentle joke. The Mission still had its own mini-farm, its pigs and its chickens. With another RAF officer he went through the terrace doors from the ballroom to the chicken run, the side pockets of his uniform full of corn and chicken feed. Then they wandered across the broad lawns, leaving a trail of corn, up the shallow steps into the main ballroom, where the cocktail party was in full swing.

In due course, the chickens pecked their way to the centre of the ballroom and stopped the party. Important conversations were silenced. Frowns and stern looks abounded. The day was saved by a French officer, a great friend of ours. He gently took hold of a chicken, turned it upside down and tucked its head under its wing. He then swung it like a pendulum between his feet and laid it upside-down on the floor. The chicken lay there, feet in the air, absolutely still. Some accused him of killing the chicken. He proved that wrong, gently pulling the bird's head out from under its wing. It then shook its feathers and continued to feed on the corn. Before long, the whole party started playing this game of 'hypnotizing' chickens.

I caught the eye of the Chief of Mission, a Coldstream Guards brigadier. He wasn't hypnotized. He fixed me with a gaze that said I would know more of this later. Next morning, not for the first time, I was treading the long, narrow carpet leading to the front of his desk in the Olympic Stadium headquarters in Berlin. I got the usual, gentlemanly ticking-off . . . but it was with a half-smile. He told me I was lucky to get away with it this time and asked me not to do this sort of thing again.

Since Nunwick was one of those officers who wanted to make his name touring rather than dancing a slow pavane of protocol, this was no great setback. He took to the road like a happy highwayman. His brief was electronic intelligence-gathering. How he did that was left up to him and some of the agencies he serviced direct. Soon he was adding to the existing repertoire of nark-shaking and other evasive options used by the Mission. His army colleague, Major Chris Hallett MBE MC, showed him how it was done: 'On a minor country road we approached a roadblock manned by Vopos. Waved to stop, Chris reduced speed as though to comply, then made a 180-degree turn and accelerated away. The Vopo officer took potshots at the rear wheels, as I watched through the rear window . . . Later I asked Chris if this happened often. "Oh no, only about once a week."'

Hallett was an old hand at fun and games. Just before joining the Mission, he had disguised himself as an Austrian window-cleaner and, according to his obituarist, 'complete with ladders, bucket and bicycle, went forth into the Russian zone to obtain photographs of the latest Russian tank'. As a mission officer, he was one of the first to snatch photographs of amphibious Soviet armour.

When Nunwick started touring without Hallett, he was trapped by East German soldiers and handed over, after some hours, to the Stasi in the isolation of a pine forest. He stayed inside his vehicle until the combined opposition smashed their way into it, using rocks to break the windows. He was then dragged out of the car and punched in the face. 'This resulted in my top teeth coming through my top lip. Back at Potsdam Brigadier Fitzalan-Howard took me to confront the Soviet liaison officer, Colonel I. Kozlovskii. We got nothing out of it, even though the car was ransacked.'

The nark driving technique involved trying to box in the tour car front and rear:

> To prevent that on minor country roads I usually swerved from verge to verge, dodging the oncoming traffic. On the autobahn we drove at about 75 m.p.h., took a corner on a sliding turn with violent acceleration on to a minor track through the undergrowth, followed by more violent acceleration and frequent changes of direction to escape away across-country by minor tracks . . . Speeds of more than 90 m.p.h. were frequent. Nothing was normal and East German laws were ignored . . .
>
> Towards the end of my touring I knew the forests better than the narks . . . It was important to keep them off-balance and keyed up. I knew what I was planning to do. They didn't and it caused them to take erratic action. The greatest was to cause them to crash now and again. It was also important not to be too clever or use excessive speed, or endanger the public. We left that to them. Occasionally, they would get too excited, draw guns and shoot. If that happened I took that as a failure on my part.

It was during a reflective moment in Berlin that he spotted, on a medieval map, long-forgotten fords across the River Elbe. He and a crew made a quiet, unobserved reconnaissance of the crossing. They walked the ford, measured the crossing, and looked afresh at the manually-operated winching gear they carried to extract the tour car from deep snow or bog. Usually, this was done by hitching the winching cable round a strong point, such as a tree, at one end and the towing point on the car. Then the slow business of cranking the winch handle by hand began, the ratchet mechanism drawing a slow but certain method, long used by mission crews. Nunwick's contribution was to link the winch to a river crossing, under the noses of the narks.

I motored down a minor country road along the Elbe with two nark cars close-tailing me. I turned off into a field, through a gate which I had removed some time previously. We bumped our way across a field to another gateway and down the second field, to the river bank. The narks gleefully slewed one of their cars across the gateway, blocking it. Then they got out to watch the fun, joking and laughing, all six of them.

My car coasted down the bank at about 17 m.p.h. and into the water. We cracked the rear doors open to allow water in quite deliberately, to ensure that the car did not drift off course. The ford was under our wheels and that was fine. The driver then got out, moved to the far bank, waded to a tree there with a long wire strop. I and my assistant then got out, our trousers rolled up above our knees, boots and socks removed. The narks were beginning to latch on to the fact that all was not well, from their point of view.

Next, we opened the car boot and out came the special light-weight winch with its extended strop. This was attached to the front of the car, paid out and connected to the wire around the tree. The car's engine had been stopped at a predetermined point in the river to make sure no river water was ingested into the sump or the carburettor. We then slowly winched the car across the Elbe. We were in midstream when I glimpsed the narks, two of them struggling on the ground, one trying to draw his gun and the other trying to stop him. It seemed at that moment that maybe what we were doing was not too bright an idea. Never mind. We crossed without trouble, disconnected the strop in the shallow water on the far side, started the engine – which fired first time – and we were on our way.

His next evasive short-cut was less successful. It also confirmed the old military wisdom that time spent in reconnaissance is never wasted.

We were in the Standal/Travemünde area, on cart and field tracks in open country, when Soviet Gaz-69 vehicles appeared from various places. All had radio aerials. They were herding me towards a main road where they could box me in and arrest me.

I eventually became somewhat desperate. I hadn't experienced a pursuit like this before, co-ordinated by radio. I was driven into a very large collective farm, which I'd wanted to avoid in case I was stopped by a herd of cattle. I scooted into the farm centre, about the size of a large village. I wanted elevation, to see what was around us, and spotted the answer: a platform about 6 feet high, with pine-post sides with a sloping ramp leading to it, ideal for a vehicle. I told the driver to take us up there quickly. As he did so, I opened the sun-roof so as to stand up and use binoculars. We didn't stop in time and drove into the biggest and sloppiest manure heap I have encountered. It also appealed to my sense of humour that anyone watching would see a senior RAF officer popping his head out of the top of a large manure heap from time to time.

We were deep in the fertilizer business half-way to the top of the car windows ... We stayed there for half an hour and let the opposition get on with it. Then we crawled out and made for the nearest woods and a quiet spot beside the Elbe. We sluiced the car down, inside and out, for an entire afternoon. It made no difference. We really could not stand the stench and I finally had to throw away this tour and creep back to Berlin, to hand the car over to the long-suffering maintenance staff for more than two days' steam-cleaning. Some of the upholstery had to be replaced and our uniforms required repeated cleaning.

On another occasion, Nunwick found an OP position from which to study a radar station when, without warning, a Russian rose from a drainage ditch close by, draped in weeds and mud and dripping water, aiming a Kalashnikov rifle at him. Nunwick immediately raised his hands in surrender. The Russian pressed the trigger, but the gun jammed on the first round. Nunwick seized the opportunity to rush back to the tour car, yelling to the driver to move off fast.

It was at this phase of his tour that Nunwick realized that he was getting 'clobbered' regularly, far beyond the realms of coincidence. In 1960 alone he was arrested and detained about sixty times. Almost certainly he was one of Blake's last victims, for the Soviet spy was preparing to move to his next posting in Lebanon.

West Berlin was thronged with refugees from the East, many of them dispossessed farmers. More than 5,000 of them flooded in during the Easter weekend that year. Tension was rising. Nunwick needed all the luck he could get.

Near Magdeburg, I was doing a reconnaissance in depth to find out how to close on a very sensitive target and escape afterwards ... I had steadily 'eaten' my way into the area. I had found a hidey-hole within walking distance of the perimeter fence around the target. My planning was now complete. I decided to withdraw and leave the target area fallow for some months before we went in hard. We were easing the car out quietly when we heard a 'click' somewhere inside the transmission and we stopped. The half-shaft, transferring power from engine to rear-wheel drive, had broken. We were totally immobile.

Nunwick's team pushed the car under tree cover and added some camouflage. He left the crew with instructions to stay silent. In the political climate of the time, he felt he had a sporting chance of coming across someone with pro-Western sympathies. It was imperative to get a tow to somewhere less sensitive. The nearest collective farm was three miles away. He took a route to it across fields, following the dead ground, avoiding roads, then walked into the complex of farm buildings.

The site manager was alone in the office. I told him I was an RAF officer whose car had broken down. Could he help me? He looked hard at me and asked where I was. I said I could not read a map so I was not sure. If I could have a tractor I could lead the driver to the place and he could tow me to the nearest town. He wasn't sure. If he was caught helping me he would disappear, his family would be thrown out of their house and on to the poverty-line. He was looking hard at me and I was watching his hand, wondering whether it would reach out and lift the telephone on his desk to report me.

Suddenly he said, 'Come with me.' We walked to the cow sheds. He said, 'This is my prize herd. We keep these for breeding.' We were leaning across the back of one of the cows and our faces were a few inches apart when he whispered, 'All right. You are in a jam. Now where are you? Are you on the site of the big radar up there, near the bunker?' I admitted I was, since this was the moment of truth. He continued, 'We must wait until dusk. I will drive the tractor myself.' We shook hands and grinned. I cannot describe how relieved I was.

As the sun was setting, the two men slipped out of the office and drove the tractor to the car. The manager hitched a rope to the car, towed it seven miles to the nearest town and left it in a multi-storey car park. Nunwick offered him a generous reward but he would accept nothing, not even Western currency.

As their rescuer swept round a corner out of sight, Nunwick found the nearest Soviet kommandantura. The commandant inspected their car himself, noted the oil seeping from the cracked rear axle and was convinced that Nunwick was telling the truth, for a change. A call was made to the Brixmis Mission House in Potsdam and the crew was towed back. 'Six weeks later,' wrote Nunwick, 'I was able to crack the target very successfully, without being seen or identified.'

As a change from military targets, Nunwick was asked by one of the agencies to find an Englishwoman said to be living in poor conditions at a block of flats in a small town in the north of East Germany. She had been there for many years and was in some sort of trouble with the local authorities. She was thought to have a German name. That was all that was known. Could he find her and assess her condition? By now, Nunwick had his own network of informers, a network lubricated by a financial slush-fund operating in several currencies which he called 'Harry's Fiddle Fund'. Nunwick juggled happily with US dollars and sterling as well as two sorts of Deutschmark, to say nothing of gifts in kind. His tour crews knew that they could depend upon meal stops at which the best prime steaks would be served to them.

I put out the usual feelers through various sources available to me. I asked for a plan showing the layout of the building where she lived. In time I learned that she lived alone in a tenement block guarded by a concierge at the entrance. She lived on the second floor and usually rested in the afternoon. I did a reconnaissance of the area, in stages. My advisers had done me proud, as they always did. I had all the information I needed.

When I went in, I carried two heavy briefcases, which cut down my mobility . . . My crew dropped me in the town in a 'running drop', the car slowing to walking pace as I jumped out, leaving my assistant to slam the door from within as the car left. I went down an alleyway. The car and crew were to hide up in a wood and return at an agreed time.

I scuttled into the tenement building, past the sign instructing me to report to the concierge, past his window and up the bare stairs. The place looked like a dosshouse. On the second floor, I knocked on the door. It was answered in German by an old lady's voice, asking who I was, what did I want. I replied in English: 'I am an RAF officer. I am English. I would like to come in since I don't think it wise to talk through the door. I mean you no harm, I assure you.'

Bolts were drawn, top and bottom. The door opened a fraction, still chained, and one eye peered out at him. Then the chain rattled and he was admitted. The woman was dressed in a plain black dress with a white lace ruff at the throat and at the end of long sleeves. Her hair was raked back into a bun on top of her head. The flat was a one-room, prewar bedsit, poorly furnished. There was a stone sink and a single cold tap, a single gas-burner and an old iron kettle; antique double bed, a small table with two upright chairs and two tattered armchairs. Nunwick did not need to check her name or identity. A large Union flag covered the whole of the chimney breast above the fireplace, secured firmly to the wall.

The conversation began in English but then reverted mainly to German. She no longer thought in English. Nunwick learned that she had married a German seaman before the First World War. By the start of the Second World War her husband was a naval captain. She was living on a small state pension. Asked whether she wanted to return to England to spend the rest of her days there, she thought carefully and then said: 'You see I am now too old. I have no relatives in England. I cannot even speak English now. What friends I have are in this town.'

So why was she in trouble? Every year she insisted on flying the Union flag outside her window on the Queen's birthday. In the past, 'they' had broken into her locked flat and had confiscated the flag. Then she had to make another one, sewing it herself. She could ill-afford this on her small pension.

Nunwick told her that he could not come again, since it would compromise her. 'I then opened my briefcases and took out two kilograms of real coffee, the same of real butter, two or three pounds of good tea, a kilogram of prime bacon. All these had been unpacked and rewrapped in plain paper, for security. I warned her against cooking the bacon in the flat as the smell would travel around the tenement and for that alone she might be reported. She told me she had a friend in an isolated house and she would share it with her.'

The assignment was now complete. Nunwick paused at the top of the stairs, listening. There was no sound. He skipped down the steps, out of the building. He emerged from the alleyway as the tour car cruised towards it.

By this stage in his Brixmis career, as Nunwick himself recalled, 'I was jittery and uptight due to the constant arrests, detentions and the general uncertainty of life. I had taken to sitting with my back to walls and we always travelled with the car doors locked.' Mrs Nunwick, too, had endured her share of stress, from being followed and jostled in shops by Stasi agents to the discovery that her sanitary towels were systematically cut open in their married quarter in West Berlin. On one occasion, her husband had persuaded her to dress in a Scottish sergeant-major's bonnet and tunic, travelling as a decoy in his car as he lured narks away from another Brixmis tour. More often she endured long nights alone, sometimes until dawn, studying the clock on the kitchen wall and waiting for a husband who was overdue again, and probably in trouble.

Serious trouble was narrowly avoided on a Chipmunk reconnaissance flight at low level out of the West Berlin air traffic zone in a deliberate breach of the Robertson–Malinin Agreement, in an attempt to photograph a particularly significant target from the air. Wing Commander Hans Neubroch was at the controls.

> We jinked around it as if we were really lost, crossed the target, circling it at least twice at less than 200 feet. It was not possible to photograph from the rear cockpit without kneeling sideways on the seat and without wearing the safety harness. We decided to accept this ... The Soviets were chasing around pointing at us and getting in a real tizzy. At one stage I shouted, 'Drop your wing,' and we did a vertical bank. He kept me in the aircraft by centrifugal force. We were able to get the pictures with a telephoto lens, then shot off almost at ground level back to West Berlin. We'd got away with it, but it was not impossible that one squadron leader, complete with camera, could have been launched into free-fall. It was an irresponsible thing to do.

According to Neubroch, there would have been no breach of the Robertson-Malinin Agreement but the rules governing flights around Berlin, laid down by the Berlin Air Safety Centre, might have been broken. All but five of the seventy-five minutes in the air, he says, were 'completely routine; throughout, there were no unusual manoeuvres.'

Nunwick had completed three years in a job which most people did for two years. In London he was asked to start another three-year tour with Brixmis: 'I had only had one period of leave in three years. I knew I was going stale. I asked to be excused this. To the RAF's credit, they immediately agreed to my request to be allowed to return to UK to a normal RAF posting where we could resume family life. I had had enough of hiding in bushes and sleeping rough, of having to inform our security staff in advance where I was going in West Berlin, with my wife, during off-duty hours.'

Nunwick's departure was a strange and ambiguous affair. He and his wife planned to pack their Mercedes with the treasures of three momentous years. Nunwick would drive the vehicle home. Mrs Nunwick, with their small daughter, would travel light and take the sealed British military train from Berlin, across East and West Germany to the Hook of Holland, there to take the ferry to Harwich. Following the customary instruction, Nunwick telephoned the British security services number in Berlin to notify them of his plans. He should have begun to wonder by now why he was obliged to report his every movement in advance, even while off-duty in West Berlin; why his married quarter was so thoroughly turned over, apparently by his own security people. He did not know, until much later, that the hunt was already on for a master-spy somewhere on his corridor in the Olympic Stadium headquarters. Nunwick, stopped with such deadly regularity by the Stasi, was about to be arrested again, if more politely, by his own side.

This is how he described the return journey. Having made their plans, Nunwick telephoned the 'discreet' number.

> However, 'they' altered the plans. On the day of departure, with one briefcase only, I was to stay behind in our married quarter and await visitors. My car would be delivered to Hanover airport by the British Army. My family, much earlier, would be whisked off to the train. They were the only occupants of a first-class carriage. An armed guard was in the corridor and the doors were locked. The guard left at Helmstedt [on the border with the West].
>
> I stayed behind in our bare married quarter. This was the loneliest time of my stay in Berlin, denuded as it was of all the bits and pieces which made it home for us. After some time, with a screech of tyres, two cars stopped outside. Two burly civilians closed on me at the front door. An Army lance-corporal took the keys of my Mercedes. As we drew away, the second car close-tailed us at a fast speed.

The destination was the US-controlled Tempelhof airport. As an RAF officer, he might have been forgiven for preferring RAF Gatow. This time, he was not flying with the RAF. At Tempelhof, 'I was rushed at a trot through side passages, giving a nod to Customs & Immigration. A BEA civil aircraft had been awaiting my arrival with engines running. All doors were closed except for the one giving access to the pilots' cabin. I was never provided with a ticket for the flight. That had been "arranged".'

The flight was a short one, to Hanover in West Germany where, in due course, the lance-corporal who had collected Nunwick's car in Berlin arrived with the vehicle. He handed the keys back to the squadron leader, who was now free to drive to Calais. No explanation was offered for this unorthodox departure. It is possible that

Nunwick was wrongly suspected of being the Soviet mole at the heart of British Intelligence in Berlin. At the time both British and US counter-intelligence agencies were so plagued by an obsessive and paranoid search for the enemy within – sedulously cultivated by KGB disinformation – that they had little time or energy left for anything else.

The Soviets had a problem where Brixmis was concerned. This was that it did not form part of the regular British intelligence 'orbat'. Yet it was proving an increasingly dangerous adversary, from a Soviet standpoint. The Mission, furthermore, was staffed not by lifelong professionals dedicated to a single agency but by military people who were posted elsewhere every two years or so. As a political target for long-term penetration it was as accessible as an amoeba. From the Kremlin's perspective, Brixmis was the one that got away, while MI5 expended its energies on non-existent moles and MI6 was betrayed by real ones. Arguably, Nunwick's experience was an attempt to introduce the Spycatcher virus into Brixmis.

There is another, more benign, explanation for the close cover maintained by British security on Nunwick. This is that, for reasons unexplained to Nunwick then and perhaps still unknown to him, he had been targeted by the KGB's 'Wet Affairs' (assassination) unit as a British agent whom they would wish to liquidate. As others had discovered, too late, the 'Blake Effect' was usually lethal. If Nunwick did not know that at the time, his own security people were assuredly moving towards that conclusion.

As things turned out, Nunwick resumed his RAF career in London and, in the fullness of time, retired honourably. Blake, like Philby, went to Beirut. Blake was at Shemlan to learn Arabic. Philby, under a cloud of suspicion, had left the Foreign Office to become a freelance journalist covering the Middle East. In Beirut, the two spies were able to compare notes for a short time. Then the Foreign Office recalled Blake to London 'on a matter of urgency'. This turned out to be his arrest and trial, and a forty-two year sentence which he did not serve thanks to a remarkable prison escape. Philby, cool as ever, remained in Beirut for two more years until he sensed the hounds closing in. Then he, too, legged it to Moscow.

CHAPTER 5

The Night They Shot Corporal Day

1962

Only a few – the *cognoscenti* – heard the whispers, though everyone knew something would have to be done about the tens of thousands of Germans now fleeing from the East into West Berlin in the summer of 1961. In 1960, 197,000 East Germans had defected to the West. During the first six months of 1961, the total touched 153,000. But that wasn't the whole story. There were also more than 10,000 political prisoners, most of them honest critics of the regime but some of them spies convicted of working for the West German foreign intelligence service (the BND), or the CIA, or the French DST or the British MI6. Negotiating their release was a delicate game played for high diplomatic stakes.

One of the few who knew not only what was going to happen, but when, was Wolfgang Vogel, the East German lawyer and spy-broker. On Thursday 10 August, Vogel got the hint from a KGB source and – at some risk to himself – warned a friend that it was time to move the family silver westward. The new policy of *Abgrenzung*, or fencing off, was imminent.

Even when it happened, it came as a surprise. Only the very wide awake saw the military teams swoop on the Brandenburg Gate just after midnight on Sunday 13 August, to dig a ditch with pneumatic drills. Elsewhere, soldiers of the Volksarmee were setting up barbed-wire fences for all the world as if they were about to replay *All Quiet on the Western Front*. Insomniacs tuned in to the American sector's German-language radio station, RIAS, got the word an hour later.

An SAS hell-raising veteran of the war in Occupied France,

Lieutenant-Colonel Ian Wellsted, now a senior touring officer with Brixmis, had noticed 'bags of cement and building materials being assembled close to the inter-sector boundary'. He assumed that the East German authorities were about to begin the long overdue building programme to repair war damage.

As American and Russian tanks squared up to one another in the centre of the former German capital, the risk of a war by accident was never higher. Wellsted, as it happened, was Brixmis duty officer in Potsdam that night.

It was evident from the activities of the Soviet military that some unusually large manoeuvre was afoot. I consulted with the US Mission's duty officer and we decided it was probably the start of a big exercise. He agreed to follow it up immediately and to brief me at first light. As dawn broke, we met up and he said: 'There's an awful lot of stuff out there.' It rapidly appeared to us that elements of three Soviet divisions were deploying to the West of Berlin.

I returned to West Berlin, made my report and learned that a barricade was being erected along the length of the boundary between the Soviet and Allied sectors of the city.

My immediate reaction was, 'Ah! So that's what all the activity has been about! The Soviets are prepared to seal off West Berlin if the Allies react. They want to be sure that the Allies know, so that there can be no war by miscalculation! Everything we saw, we were meant to see so that the message is unequivocal! That's just what the Allied military missions were for! Maybe in this moment of time we have in our own minuscule way played our part in preventing the Third World War!'

The telephone woke Squadron Leader J. H. (Dickie) Dyer, an RAF member of the Brixmis team, a navigator with a background in Military Intelligence, at 7.45 A.M. The night before, in common with many other Westerners serving in Berlin, he had enjoyed a good party. He had turned in at about 5 A.M. Now a voice with barely controlled urgency told him to get dressed, have breakfast, listen to the British Forces Network news and report to the ops room in half an hour. Dyer telephoned RAF Gatow, the British air-base in Berlin, and passed a message in code that meant: 'Prepare the Chipmunk immediately.'

When Dyer and his boss, Group Captain Gordon Young, reached Gatow, the aircraft was ready. Beneath their greasy overalls, the ground crew still wore their pyjamas. Allied air-power was about to be expressed with a light trainer aircraft.

It was the start of the working day in London, the early hours in Washington as statesmen were jolted by the news. For some it was an almost physical experience, like stubbing one's toe on leaping out of bed to answer the telephone. Was this what Khrushchev had recently threatened, after his first meeting in Vienna with the young, untried President John F. Kennedy? Was it the first step in occupying the whole of Berlin? How far did the operation extend? At what point would it stop? At the Dover Strait, perhaps?

With Young at the controls in the front seat of the tiny, unarmed Chipmunk, and Dyer, navigator and photographer, behind him, they flew over the action at 500 feet, one wing down, canopy open. Dyer's logbook suggests that they took off at noon and flew for one hour twenty minutes. Under the heading 'Remarks' the flight details, for security reasons, were opaquely described as 'Local Flying'. They followed a leisurely, anti-clockwise route first to the south where the autobahn was packed with Soviet vehicles: 'The impression we got was that the Soviets had moved a lot of stuff between the East German barracks and Berlin and they were doing their stuff' – that is containing an operation for which they would not take responsibility.

The RAF team confirmed 'the arrival of large numbers of additional troops with their tanks and armoured vehicles, brought in at short notice from the Soviet Union and their careful positioning between the East German barracks and the city itself. This appeared to us as a good indicator that the Soviet Union was intent on preventing any trouble or possible sector border infringements within the city still legally controlled by agreements among the four occupying powers and out of bounds to East German military forces. In the car afterwards we agreed that the Soviets didn't approve of what was going on. Otherwise they wouldn't have moved all this stuff in.'

Back at the British headquarters, the intelligence staff accepted that assessment and drafted a signal proposing that 'the obstacle' be removed that evening.

As Dyer wrote later: 'When our findings were reported back to the Head of British Army Intelligence, authority was sought from President Kennedy and Prime Minister Macmillan to use the dozen or so available Allied tanks to bulldoze down, before the end of the day, the embryo barbed-wire structure that preceded the laying of concrete blocks. Sadly, no reply was received for more than forty-eight hours when it was too late to undertake such an operation. Who knows what course history might have taken had the Wall been destroyed at birth?'

As train services between the two parts of the city were halted and 50,000 East Germans who usually worked in the West were turned back, a riot began. A shout arose: 'Hang old Goat-beard!' (a contemptuous nickname for Walter Ulbricht). At the Brandenburg Gate, 4,000 West Berliners jeered at the NVA troops. Elsewhere, as they trampled down the barbed wire, communist soldiers advanced on them with bayonets fixed. East German police waded into protesters at the closed crossing points with hoses, truncheons and riot-gas. Dyer was not alone in being disconcerted by Nato's weak response. Those close to Willy Brandt, then Mayor of West Berlin, observed that he was shaken by the West's reaction, which one commentator characterized as 'confused, hesitant, blustering and entirely ineffectual'. Brandt, concluding that this confirmed Germany's status as the potential superpower battleground, adopted a policy of creeping détente, or 'small steps', in his relations with the East from the moment he became West Germany's Chancellor in 1969.

A young president had been blooded after seven months in office and he had failed his initiation rite. Or had he? More than thirty years later, Brixmis veterans of that turbulent week disagree about the reaction of Downing Street and Whitehall. Dyer and others saw it as an inexplicable, unnecessary surrender to communist bullying. Wellsted, a tough guerrilla with much experience of going for an enemy's jugular, acquits the West of weakness. The Chipmunk reconnaissance, he believes, took no account of what was happening outside Berlin, between the city and the border with the West. The Red Army, he argues, was not out in strength to contain East German aggression; it was there in support of it: 'The RAF report does not appear to be aware of the far more sinister Soviet deployments to the West of Berlin. Had those embryonic barbed-wire structures been bulldozed down, the Soviets were poised to react very fiercely. They were ready to react to any Allied intervention should it take place. Our missions passed the message which undoubtedly the Russians wanted us to pass. I believe that on this occasion Kennedy and Macmillan were absolutely right!'

Instead of a bulldozer, the British high command, in the form of the General Officer Commanding Berlin, Major-General Sir Rohan Delacombe, sent in a Trojan horse to test the Allies' continued right of access to the barricaded Eastern sector. 'Jumbo' Delacombe was not famous for his subtlety. With his aide-de-camp, he had once frog-marched a Fleet Street correspondent out of his headquarters and on to the pavement outside. The Trojan horse he now unloosed upon East Berlin was an official British staff car, carrying two Brixmis wives. Their mission: to buy tickets for the East German Opera and return unscathed. They did not know that they were being used as pawns in a dangerous game of diplomatic brinkmanship. The wives chosen for this mission were Colonel Wellsted's wife Diana and Squadron Leader Dyer's wife Pat. They did not ask any questions, and that, said Ian Wellsted, was just as well. Diana Wellsted explained:

Pat Dyer and myself used to go regularly into East Berlin to buy opera tickets for the whole of the British Mission. [The state-subsidized East Berlin Opera was a cultural gem.] On this particular occasion we had heard that there had been an 'incident' the night before in which an American VIP had been denied entrance because he hadn't shown his pass. So the Brigadier decided we should go in a Brixmis car with a driver and not in our own cars.

As we approached the [newly erected] Checkpoint Charlie [one of the main crossing points from West to East Berlin], I was astonished to see a column of American tanks on the left-hand side of the road, with a line of American troops in front, and about thirty yards further on another line of East German troops in front of the half-built Wall, with a barrier across the road.

We just showed our passes in the car window, kept closed, as we normally did and they raised the barrier without any problems. We just had to negotiate a couple of tank-traps and we were into the city.

Opera tickets were purchased from a ticket agency in a side street, the sort of discreet place, out of sight of the Stasi, where other deals might be struck. As the Brixmis wives emerged from the agency, tickets in hand, 'A very distressed German woman came up to us and said she had a sick mother in West Berlin and could we please take her over in the car with us. We explained we couldn't possibly do that because we had to show passes and she wouldn't have one. And so she said, "Oh, well, put me in the boot." Whether this was really a genuine case or whether she was just trying to have us on I don't know. We certainly couldn't take the risk of making our husbands *persona non grata* and so we had to harden our hearts and say no.'

Pat Dyer, confronted by 'this little woman, weeping and carrying on', concluded: 'I didn't believe a word of it.'

Dickie Dyer was less than amused to learn that the wives had been sent where tanks feared to tread: 'Neither Ian [Wellsted] nor I were aware of what was going on. I discovered by some means that morning. I went to see Sir Rohan to ask him "What the hell is going on? Why put our wives across there?" He admitted to me that basically this really was a try-on to see whether the Four Power Agreement on Berlin still held.'

This version is confirmed by the Brixmis historian Captain S. D. Gibson MBE, who asserts that it was the General Officer Commanding the British garrison in Berlin who 'sent two Brixmis wives holding Soviet passes on the genuine pretext [sic] of purchasing opera tickets, thereby testing the reaction of East German authority to the British exercising their rights of unrestricted travel. With the world's television and press looking on at the Soviet and American tanks squared off against each other and the head of the British RMP [military policeman] patrolling with revolver at the ready, the [wives'] crossing was made without incident.'

This was a case of no news being big news. The use of two officers' wives as a test of strength was assuredly less inflammatory than driving a tank through the Wall to assert Allied rights. Equally, had Diana Wellsted and Pat Dyer softened their hearts to a hard-luck story, the Mission's continued rights in a new situation could have been compromised from the very beginning.

An odd precedent was now being set. Before the Wall was built, Brixmis visited East Berlin's Opera and restaurants, like other Berlin-based Allied servicemen, but in such a way as to avoid frightening the horses. Afterwards, in order to show the flag, regular visits were made by members of the Mission, resplendent in full mess kit with medals up. As Wellsted explained, the West was making a point, 'to emphasize Allied right of access to the eastern half of the divided city'. The new ostentation, Gibson recounted, 'clearly antagonized the East German hierarchy who also liked to be seen at the Opera. When it became known on occasion that Brixmis had booked the best seats, the programme was rapidly changed from the advertised classic to a heavily indoctrinated and politically accented modern piece. The redeeming feature of such torture was the excellent champagne and cabaret of assorted opera-goers encountered during the interval.'

A few yards away from the Opera, a theatre of another kind was playing, a theatre of cruelty in which the blood and death in public were real. In August 1962, almost a year to the day after the Wall was built, Peter Fechter, aged eighteen, raced across the gap between East and West and was brought down by a burst of machine-gun fire a few yards from the border. As he screamed for help, no one moved. The East German guards watched with clinical interest as he took an hour to die, like schoolboys observing an insect impaled upon a pin. A guard on the Western side threw the casualty a bandage.

Fechter was one of the first of 200 such victims. An American journalist, Edmond Taylor, noted in *The Reporter*:

Sometimes immensely complex issues suddenly become simplified to the essential, reduced to the size of a human person, to a point where a passing episode acquires the clarity of eternity. This took place recently in Berlin when that boy lay dying for one hour a few yards away from the western sector while American troops looked on and an American officer failed to send him a doctor to relieve his pain or a chaplain to bring him the Cross . . . The test is coming when we can no longer act as if the death of that young man, indeed the fate of the East Germans, were no business of ours.

Such sentiments were in macabre contrast to the jauntiness of the British Prime Minister, Harold Macmillan. During the first, most energetic, phase of Wall-building in Berlin, he was intercepted on the Gleneagles golf course in Scotland. Asked if the situation, with guns facing guns, frightened him, he replied: 'I think it is all got up by the Press. Nobody is going to fight about it. But there is always danger of folly. I think the way it is going on is very worrying but nothing more.'

Captain Stuart Money, Somerset & Cornwall Light Infantry, reported for duty at the Mission's Berlin headquarters on 15 August, just two days after the wire was laid across Berlin. Teams of East German labourers and soldiers were now mixing concrete and creating a more solid structure. Money said: 'I couldn't find a soul anywhere because the Allied Missions had been caught with their trousers down. Russians and East Germans had deployed troops round Berlin. Missions had woken up to this rather late, then covered thousands of miles of East Germany looking for deployments elsewhere . . . If not absent, touring the countryside, they were exhausted. They were not waiting for a new arrival.'

Wellsted disputed Money's assertion that the Allied Missions were caught with trousers down, but he confirmed, 'once the Wall was up we had every man we could muster out on tour'.

Money recalled that there followed two-and-a-half years of 'the most remarkable and fascinating time of my life'. As a bachelor, he lived in the British Berlin Brigade officers' mess, and was briefed in Berlin by a Canadian operations officer working in conjunction with the American and French teams. He went out with the Chief, 'Brigadier Tom Pearson, a great Boy Scout, who taught me how to do it: sleeping in woods. He'd be up first, brewing tea and cooking breakfast while the rest of us were collecting our thoughts.'

Every tour started with a visit to the US Mission to see the 'headlines' from the previous day; and ended with a call at the same establishment to report the 'highlights' of that trip. That process 'was exhausting if you had been out forty-eight hours; it was the middle of the night and before you could go home in your hungry, tired, unwashed, filthy state you still had to go down to the dungeons of the American Mission and write down the highlights.'

He was not exaggerating. Wellsted, the SAS war veteran, concluded that the stress of operating in enemy territory as a guerrilla and his time with Brixmis were similar experiences beyond the front line.

Both were potentially lethal games of cops-and-robbers, which I enjoyed. It's much more fun being the 'robber' than the 'cop'. When I was parachuted into the Morvan [in Occupied France, 1944] I was a raw young officer on my first campaign; by the time I came to Brixmis I had had my fair share of playing the part as a 'cop', hunting terrorists in Palestine and Malaya. So I had a wider understanding of what I was doing and of its political implications.

Also the stakes were very different. In France, I knew that if caught, I would be tortured and killed unpleasantly. In East Germany, I hoped that my adversaries knew that they were not allowed to shoot me and that probably the worst fate that could befall me would be to be declared PNG.

Events would soon demonstrate that this was an over-optimistic assessment.

On the other hand, there were close similarities. Sitting hour after hour in a suitable coppice in the GDR, waiting endlessly for convoys which never came, was very similar to laying an abortive ambush in Burgundy. In any active confrontation with the enemy, the adrenalin is flowing and one does not feel the stress. It is during the periods of anticipation that one feels the stress and it is after the action is over that one feels the reaction.

I think that I found Brixmis more stressful than the SAS, partly because I was older and less resilient and partly because it was more prolonged. When my time came to return from behind the lines in the Morvan, I wanted to stay on with the more recent arrivals, even though I had already been there longer than any other member of the Squadron. When I left Brixmis, I felt that I had been through an exciting experience that I would not have missed for anything, but I was not sorry it was over.

I well remember one evening when I had just dropped, utterly exhausted, on to my bed after a hectic three-day tour when the telephone rang. There was an unexpected emergency. I knew that I was the only person available who could deal with it. I put down the phone and literally burst into tears. Then I got up, got out and got on with the job. That never happened in the SAS!

For every low moment, there was a high. Captain Money, warming to the robber's role, was pursued into the ancient town of Cottbus and drove round and round the same block of streets, the narks still on his tail. The trick was one he had learned from Wellsted who had used it in Leipzig at rush-hour: 'A crowd built up on the pavements. Their sympathies were clear. The narks pulled out. We tried to escape down a side street and hit the main road again. There were the narks again. We had to resume the exercise . . .'

On one of his tours, Money spotted the first T-62 main battle tank on a railway transporter.

[We were] woken shortly after dawn one summer morning, after a night in a cornfield, by the noise of armour moving. Out of the cover to our left, moving straight across our front, went a whole battalion of Soviet armour. It was useful from many points of view. It confirmed the organization of one of these battalions. I remember the armoured cars, then the amphibious reconnaissance tanks and the armour itself, the tanks, with the tell-tale baffle on the barrel. There in front of our eyes was the T-62 tank.

It wasn't very difficult to follow them. We found them in an assembly area, totally engrossed with their own activities, breakfast, a bit of maintenance. We were able to get quite close, nobody paying any attention to us, take some photographs – I have to say that in the excitement the photographs were not a great success – but we stuck around all morning as they moved on.

Afterwards, the team was interrogated by Allied intelligence and, 'in the face of considerable scepticism, stuck to our story about tanks with gun-barrels using muffles or baffles and we were credited with having seen a trainload of the new tank'. The photographs were later used in the British Army recognition manual covering such matters.

The military significance of the find was considerable. As the Brixmis authority Nigel Wylde explained: 'Soviet tank guns were always less accurate than those in the West. On late model T-55s they put a fume extractor at the end of the barrel. This had two objectives, firstly to keep the fumes out of the tank and secondly to reduce barrel wear and thus improve accuracy. On the T-55 this was an afterthought, but on the T-62 it was built into the design of the new 115mm smoothbore gun. Such changes made for good technical reasons were quickly memorized by Brixmis tourers as recognition points.'

Wellsted's own tours were no less eventful, full of studied deceits camouflaged as spontaneous gestures, the 'little things adding joy to our days'.

'An East German army squad came doubling across the fields to stop us. I told my driver to slow down. As he did so, I whipped up a smart salute, whereupon the whole squad halted and tried to present arms. I then said, "Speed up." By the time they got their arms down we were off.'

Pulled up because he was caught in an area allegedly off-limits to Western Missions, accused of ignoring warning signs, he would ask, 'What mission signs? Sorry, I didn't come that way. We came across country.' Asked to explain why he would do this instead of using the road, he said blandly: 'Your countryside is so beautiful.'

Wellsted had a knack of hitting trouble in Potsdam as well as in the countryside. Sometimes Wellsted's family – his wife Diana and daughters Sandy, aged twelve, Roxy, aged nine, and seven-year-old Gail – was also caught up in the turbulence of Cold War confrontation. On 17 April 1961, Cuban right-wing exiles, backed by the CIA, invaded their homeland, now run by the hard-line communist dictator Fidel Castro. The Bay of Pigs affair was a fiasco which did nothing to sweeten relations between President Kennedy and Khrushchev. Khrushchev made threatening noises. JFK responded: 'I have taken careful note of your statement that events in Cuba might affect peace in all parts of the world. I trust that this does not mean that the Soviet Government . . . is planning to inflame other areas of the world.' Kennedy hoped that the Kremlin 'has too great a sense of responsibility to embark on any enterprise so dangerous to general peace'. The words were to prove prophetic.

While the row was at its height, the Wellsteds went shopping in Potsdam. 'In fact, we were buying fishing rods. I was duty officer, in full uniform – Sam Browne, the lot – and the family were there carrying their purchases when down the street came a great rentacrowd, filling the whole street, carrying signs saying "HANDS OFF CUBA". So I just charged into the crowd saying, "If you don't let me through, you'll have no one to protest to."'

The crowd opened and let them through. The first target for the protest was the US Mission. It struck Wellsted that the British Mission would be next. Recalling the 1958 attack, 'We went up to the top stairs and barricaded ourselves in. I rang the Soviet liaison officer and said we held them responsible for our safety.'

Of the children, Gail, the youngest, recently admitted: 'I was genuinely scared. It was a dark room. We were all told to be quiet. It impinged on me that there was a genuine danger.' Roxy thought it all 'very boring' and wondered, as if this were a school detention, 'when we could leave the room'. Sandy found it 'all rather exciting'. The expected attack did not happen, but the threat was all-pervasive.

The girls developed a taste for spy-spotting as they drove round the country with their father, ostensibly on shopping or sightseeing jaunts. On the road, they became skilled at identifying Red Army vehicle numbers. In cafés, they identified the narks around them with the *élan* of successful bird-watchers. (So, later on, did Wylde's eleven-year-old daughter, who photographed them.)

On May Day, Wellsted was duty officer and took Sandy along with him on the Potsdam Local (a routine trip), to look at the decorations. 'Quite unexpectedly, as we approached the railway yards we encountered a complete squadron of Soviet tanks, which had just detrained and were lined up along the roadside. There was no turning back. The driver of the leading tank, grinning from ear to ear, revved up. "Quick! Wind up your window," I said.

Sandy didn't understand why but she did as she was told, in the nick of time. As we came level with the tank's exhaust, which faced the road, each driver revved up the engine and cut it as we passed. This sent clouds of exhaust over us. They'd recognized us and were having a great time.'

In Berlin, in spite of the creature comforts of the Western sector, the political atmosphere remained distinctly edgy. Newspapers were read avidly for information about the deepening crisis between the superpowers, now personalized as a contest between the foul-mouthed, broad-shouldered bully Khrushchev and his youthful, war-wounded opponent Kennedy. The twitch could happen at unexpected moments. Captain Money and his bride went shopping in East Berlin one cold, foggy November afternoon.

> We went through Checkpoint Charlie in the normal way; did our business and by the time we came back the Russians had done what we hoped they would do: deploy armour and troops on the border at the checkpoint [to replace East Germans, not recognized by the Mission]. When we got through to the Allied side we were set upon by military policemen of the three Allied nations. They lifted our car to one side, bodily, as an American tank came charging down Friedrichstrasse and jammed on its brakes, standing on its nose in the face of the opposition. It was impressive tank-driving but a very childish exercise all the same.

The Americans even arrested Lieutenant-Colonel Wellsted in the crisis atmosphere that now lay like a depressive fog over Germany. Just before 8.30 A.M. on 10 February 1962, in biting cold, the ill-fated U2 pilot Gary Powers, the man who did not press the 'destruct' button on his aircraft before he bailed out over Sverdlovsk, was released by the Russians and exchanged for the Soviet master-spy Colonel Rudolf Abel in the middle of the Glienicke Bridge. Approaching from the East, Powers was flanked by two heavies. From the Western side, the American convoy was led by Abel's American lawyer James Donovan. Abel also had a bodyguard, 7 feet tall. The last part of the journey was on foot. At that moment, also approaching from the West, came Ian Wellsted: 'I just happened to turn up at that particular moment to go across to our Potsdam Mission House. The Americans were all terribly sensitive about this, and unfortunately the American Mission hadn't warned us. I was duly held on the roadside until such time as the exchange of prisoners had taken place, by which time one of the US Mission had come up to rescue me.'

Wellsted's nose for trouble was consistent. That same winter he encountered an East German tank regiment moving through Potsdam. Wellsted found himself hemmed in between two tanks. An NVA soldier told him to stay in his car. Since it was British policy never to obey any East German instruction, he got out. 'It was bitterly cold, with snow on the ground. I walked up and down to keep warm. As I moved away from the car a German soldier was put on to following me. That was fine, except that he had a loaded sub-machine gun in his hand. When I went in one direction he was behind me. When I turned the other way I had to push him quietly backwards with the muzzle of his gun in my stomach ... I knew he wasn't allowed to shoot me. I wasn't certain if *he* knew that also.'

If the Wellsted girls were enjoying their games of 'Spot-the-nark', some of the Mission's drivers were not so happy. Corporal Duncan Reid was the commander-in-chief's chauffeur at a time when Brixmis needed an intelligent tour driver. He was asked if he would like to join the organization. He told them: 'Not really, because I wouldn't want to treat a car the way your boys do. I like limousines. I have more respect for a car.' They talked him round. He stroked farewell to the general's limousine, a treasure defended, for diplomatic reasons, from every last speck of dust, and took the wheel of an Opel Kapitän fitted with long-range fuel tanks and a variable array of rear lights to spoof pursuers after dark. The Opel would be discarded, from new, after a mere six months. It was a two-wheel drive vehicle, not ideally suited for high-speed work across country. Reid was often teamed with Captain Money, whom he regarded as 'a bit of a bloodhound in those days'. (He was with Money on the T-62 hunt.)

On another trip deep in East Germany, the team saw a dust cloud approaching. From it emerged an American mission car whose driver screeched to a halt and shouted: 'Hey man, you'd better get outa here. I got a Sov on my ass.' With the brigadier as his passenger, this time in an area that was assuredly off-limits, the results of a detention could have been embarrassing. There was no room to make a three-point turn, so Reid reversed, flat out, for about a mile-and-a-half.

Reid recalled: 'My Brigadier was D. L. Darling. He was a hunting man. His farewell comment about Brixmis was that he hunted foxes with the Duke of Beaufort. He said, "Here in Germany the Communists had the finest set of hounds hunting the fox in their territory and we won."'

It was a fine sentiment, but not entirely correct. The tensions building up towards the Cuban missile crisis late in 1962 were reflected in the increasing violence of the East German frontier guards after the Wall was erected. During that year it was not a question of whether one of the Brixmis team would become a casualty of this dangerous game of deceit combined with hide-and-seek, but when. Regardless of hunt rules, someone was about to shoot the fox.

From Berlin the Wall developed extensions to north and south like some sinister Lego kit. Work on converting communist Germany into a physical prison went on at a manic pace into 1962. So did German resistance. In the immediate aftermath of the closure, a correspondent reported from Berlin: 'As the wall builders strive to close off every loophole refugees are still finding secret ways through war ruins, gardens and backyards which run right up to the border. Two families have swum across the city's canals to freedom. Ominously, border guards are now clearing strips of wooded country in the outskirts to give themselves a clear field of fire.'

In the countryside, entire villages were razed to create a kind of cordon sanitaire. Watchtowers, machine guns, guard-dogs and infra-red sensors linked to SM-70 automatic fire systems were used to tighten the political garrotte round the East. A secret Brixmis report noted: 'There has been a considerable importation recently to the East German frontier forces surrounding Berlin of a type of heavily indoctrinated young Communist, who can be relied upon to fire at his own countrymen and who has only a highly distorted conception of the world outside, or the position of the GDR in it.

As they also lack training and discipline, so long as they continue to be armed the risk to anyone travelling in the area is bound to be considerable.'

The German resistance hit back with the Girrman Organization, an underground movement dedicated to helping escapers, along the lines of Britain's wartime MI9. Girrman specialized in building tunnels to freedom, and it would kill to preserve their integrity. At least one East German police officer paid for an accidental discovery with his life. The Girrman culture developed its cult heroes, people such as Wolfgang Fuchs, a West Berlin student soon known as 'The Tunnel Fox'. Fuchs squared the Syrian consul, who obligingly smuggled refugees out of East Berlin in his white Mercedes 220, protected by diplomatic plates.

It was in this climate that Lieutenant-Colonel Wellsted despatched the Brixmis duty officer and driver from Potsdam at 11.15 P.M. on Saturday 10 March 1962 on a mission described in a contemporary, secret, report as 'a specially requested night tour of the Stahnsdorf area'. Some thirty-three years later Wellsted did not recall anything special about this operation. 'I probably thought that it was important that the "Potsdam Local" tour, on our own doorstep, was maintained and no regular touring officer was available.'

The duty officer at Potsdam that night, as it happened, was Nick Browne, a former Royal Navy officer, now a Foreign Office economist invested with the temporary, local rank of lieutenant-colonel. His driver in mission car 15 was Corporal Douglas Day, RAF, aged twenty-six and single. Their designated route took them through the snow along Karl Marx Allee and into Ernst Thälmann Strasse in a Potsdam suburb known as Klein Machnow. Ernst Thälmann Strasse was a mere 500 metres from the border with West Berlin and therefore an area which the frontier police (Grenzschutzpolizei, or 'Grepo' for short) or the Border Brigade (the Grenzbrigade) could be expected to treat as a free-fire zone. Much worse, 'Unknown to Colonel Browne, a detachment of Grepo had been established in two requisitioned villas on the west side of Schlusen Weg about 100 yards south of the junction with Ernst Thälmann Strasse. Thinking they had missed their road in the darkness, the tour stopped at the junction and turned around. The area is rather deserted and peters out at this point.'

Wellsted's recollection in 1995 was that 'the East German border guards had erected a checkpoint on a side street close to the border. Nick had taken a wrong turning. He was looking at his map and did not see the checkpoint. He ordered Corporal Day to turn round and go back. The border guards, probably temporarily blinded by the car's headlights, did not realize it was a Brixmis car and thought that it was someone trying to escape.'

Five months later a defector told British Intelligence that Grepo had expected an escape attempt. They had received a tip-off that 'a car containing six would-be refugees was going to attempt a break-through to West Berlin from the Klein Machnow area. Patrols from 2 Frontier Brigade had been sent out with orders to stop all cars they encountered and to fire at any failing to acknowledge signals.'

The Mission, of course, declined as a matter of policy to acknowledge any instruction, including signals, given by the East Germans, since to do so would be to grant Ulbricht's government diplomatic recognition of some sort. All the elements were now in place for a disaster.

The contemporary British report described what happened next:

The car had been turned and was just driving away again, eastwards down Ernst Thälmann Strasse when several bursts of machine-pistol [sub-machine gun] fire were directed at it from the right rear. The large and distinctive Mission number plate was fully illuminated.

Corporal Day was hit by the first burst of fire. There were no warning shots. Further bursts followed and he was hit again, several times, but as the car had not yet gathered speed he was able to bring it to a controlled halt on the right side of the road about ten yards from the junction. Colonel Browne got out and ran round the car to the Corporal's assistance. The firing ceased. It was clear that the Corporal was severely injured. A wound was found on the left side of his back, the bullet having torn a hole in his belt. Bleeding was mostly internal. He was assisted into the back seat of the vehicle. By this time a party of men in uniform had come running up.

Another bullet had split the car pass where it rested in the chest pocket of Day's tunic. This round did not touch his body but it was a near miss that could be measured in millimetres. Even so, he was in a bad way. It was more than half an hour before the East German ambulance arrived. The rear tyres of the British car were flat, full of holes. The petrol tank was also holed. Day, the report observed, 'must have been aware of the seriousness of his condition and was clearly in great pain, but he conducted himself in the presence of those who had injured him with a discipline and fortitude so exemplary as to command their obvious respect. His bearing was an invaluable contribution to the situation.'

Meanwhile, 'Colonel Browne ... told the Germans to send for a Soviet officer. Their attitude at first was hostile and bullying. Further physical violence was threatened.'

Browne was not allowed to travel with his injured driver. He remained with the car. The Vopo arrived. 'Flashlight photographs were taken. Colonel Browne's map-case was stolen (furtively) from the interior of the vehicle and a pair of maps which he was holding were snatched by someone creeping up behind him. This man then ran off towards the [Grepo] unit headquarters at full speed like an urchin with a scrumped apple. Fortunately the car contained no compromising material, not even a camera or binoculars.'

At 5.30 A.M., the Soviet team appeared: three full colonels, a lieutenant-colonel, a major and a captain. Their leader, Colonel Kozlovskii, separately interviewed the Grepo team and Browne. He asked Browne if his driver could have ignored the Grepo signal for them to stop. Brown pointed out that they were driving away when the bullets ripped into the car.

Wellsted recalled the events of that day: 'The first we knew of the incident was when the Soviet liaison office informed us in the morning. I went into Potsdam in a furious temper, thinking that the whole incident had been set up and made my views known in no uncertain terms. Obviously, the Soviet liaison office thought that *we* must have been up to something. Nick was adamant that he had seen no East German soldiers or police and the first inkling he had of their presence was when a sudden burst of automatic fire partly buried itself in the spare wheel behind him and a shot hit Day.' (This would explain why, in his initial analysis, Wellsted had concluded that the vehicle had backed into a side street to turn about and was then fired upon without warning.)

Kozlovskii drove Browne back to Potsdam, pausing at the civilian hospital in Stalinallee, to check whether Day had been taken there. Browne, a German speaker, was told that Day had already undergone surgery and his condition was stable.

By 9 A.M. Wellsted was at the hospital accompanied by his colleague Lieutenant-Colonel R. J. Bond (a translator from the Royal Army Education Corps) and Bond's wife, a doctor who was the British Families' Medical Officer in Berlin. Attempts to evacuate Day by ambulance or helicopter were rebuffed by the Soviets acting, they said, on 'medical advice'.

At 11 A.M., Wellsted, with a team of non-commissioned officers and a Soviet officer, Lieutenant-Colonel Serov, tried to recover the Mission's car. This was now outside the Grepo headquarters where a truculent East German lieutenant overruled Serov. Serov, out of his depth, made an excuse and left. While two sergeants changed a wheel on the damaged car, Wellsted and his Regimental Sergeant Major, Boyde, walked towards the corner where, Browne had told them, they had made their three-point turn. Immediately the Grepo senior lieutenant 'began screaming orders in an almost hysterical manner'. Wellsted and Boyde both found their paths blocked by Grepo guards. They recovered the car all the same and itemized the damage: one bullet hole in each rear tyre; two bullet holes through the body in front of the right-hand door and a ricochet mark on the door; three bullet holes in the rear bumper; thirteen bullet holes through the back of the boot; three bullet holes through the suspension; and eleven richochets on the back of the boot. Another bullet had smashed the rear left light and there were 'unmistakable signs of an unsuccessful attempt to break into the boot with some form of wrench'. All the bullets were calibre 7.62mm, a cartridge newly supplied to the Soviet Army.

A later forensic report would show that the first shot, which the Grepo claimed as a warning round, 'penetrated the right-hand panel and hit the right foot of the driver'. The second round went into the car's transmission tunnel and was fired by someone squatting or kneeling as the vehicle passed. Another bullet had been fired from a range of just 3.85 metres (about 14 feet).

Back at the hospital, a sort of siege was now beginning. Dr (Mrs) Bond remained at Day's bedside as permission was given for his removal to a British hospital and then withdrawn, ostensibly to assist Day's survival. A conference, involving the hospital director, the German surgeon in charge of Day's case, a British army doctor (Captain Dyer RAMC, senior surgeon, British Military Hospital, Berlin), Dr Bond and Lieutenant-Colonel Bond was actually held around the casualty's bed. Also present, but just out of sight, was a squad of Stasi secret police.

It was now 5 P.M. Day drifted in and out of consciousness. This was not surprising in view of his wounds: four perforations of the small intestine; one perforation of the large intestine; surface wound in right thigh; loin wound requiring removal of the left kidney; compound fracture and dislocation of the left big toe; undisplaced fracture of right big toe. He had not wanted to join Brixmis, he had told the RAF Mission officer, Squadron Leader Dyer, because he preferred driving cranes to driving officers around in staff cars. Dyer had reassured him: 'We go out across country and things like that.'

Day's Brixmis posting had started inauspiciously. Answering a call of nature in the Potsdam loo on his first morning, he was rudely interrupted by shattering glass behind him as a British defector made the dash for freedom into the same loo. He was accompanied by his pregnant, East German girlfriend. The intruder was desperate to get home, so desperate that he started to cut his arteries with the broken glass. Day, showing great self-control, adjusted his dress and hauled him before the unit's sergeant-major. The woman was handed over to the East German police. Dyer then drove the defector to West Berlin and handed him over to the RMP. From that first hour, Day might be forgiven for believing that crane-driving was a better option after all. Although Dyer had told him, 'You have nothing to worry about. You'll be perfectly all right with Brixmis,' he was now fighting for his life.

Next morning, Brigadier J. R. Holden CBE DSO, the Mission chief, strode down the hospital corridor towards Day's ward to find a trio of Soviet officers just outside it. An embarrassed Colonel Kozlovskii said: 'We asked the hospital director's permission to put one question to Corporal Day ... We asked him whether he saw the police before he stopped the car and he said yes.'

By now, a rota of British wives was at the bedside. Diana Wellsted was present when Kozlovskii entered with his interpreter Zhelanov. As Lieutenant-Colonel Wellsted himself later explained: 'In fact, Day was in a serious condition. He had tubes of all sorts sticking out of him. It was only skilful nursing by the East German medical staff that pulled him through. Kozlovskii interrogated him because he thought we had been up to something.'

Mrs Wellsted did all she could, under the circumstances. She listened attentively to what was said. A contemporary official report recorded what she heard as the two Soviet officers leaned over Day's bed, attempting to keep their voices as quiet as possible:

KOZLOVSKII: Did you see them?
DAY: Yes ... I tried to stop ... I reversed.
KOZLOVSKII: Was there a warning?
DAY: No.
[Unintelligible question.]
DAY: They were military, not [civil] police.

A British inquiry concluded that Day, because of his condition, was mistaken. The report noted: 'The vehicle did not and could not reverse during the incident because the first burst of fire hit Day. It is evident that his mind is confused.'

After the Russian interrogation raid, a British military guard was placed by Day's bedside until he could be moved to a British hospital. The RAMC doctor, Dyer, even brought supplies of British blood for transfusion through specially imported British equipment. Though no one said so out loud, this may have been to ensure that no so-called 'truth drugs' could be added to the plasma. A 'No Entry' notice was posted on the door. Later that day, the German and British doctors, in a carefully circumscribed, strictly professional conference, agreed that Day was unfit to be moved and should remain where he was for some days.

The surreal contrast between the efficiency of communist medical care of a man they had almost killed and their willingness to interrogate him, even as he fought for life, was yet another lesson for Brixmis about the fine, ambiguous path they trod between one role as spy and another as accredited diplomat.

It was six days before Day was deemed fit to be moved. He was taken by RAF ambulance to the Glienicke Bridge accompanied by Group Captain G. Young, the deputy Chief of Brixmis; an RAF interpreter, Flight Lieutenant R. A. Stark; and his doctor, Captain Dyer. At the bridge, US military police were out in force to control a crowd of journalists. West German police cars formed a protective convoy around the ambulance on its way to the British Military Hospital at Berlin. Day, with an impish humour that had been his trademark throughout the affair, said his journey was 'like a gangster's funeral'.

Paralleling Day's treatment, diplomatic wrangles were conducted with stiff formality and were carefully minuted. The day following the Russian penetration of Day's ward to question him, the Soviet Chief of Staff, Lieutenant-General G. I. Ariko, told Holden: 'This incident happened because Lieutenant-Colonel Browne, for reasons not known to me, at a very late hour at night, was in the immediate vicinity of the border, moving along poorly lit streets where everybody knows there are Grepo patrols and when he met one of these patrols he did not react to their demands . . . He tried to escape . . . I do not consider the actions of Lieutenant-Colonel Browne were correct: to go for a run along the border at night. We are all military people. We know what soldiers do when on duty with a mission to carry out. Grepo did not know it was a British Mission car until after they had fired.'

His liaison officer Colonel I. Kozlovskii backed him up: 'I personally had to clean the mud off the rear number plate to ascertain the number of the car.'

Ariko added: 'Of course we all understand that with such dirty, muddy roads the number plates are bound to get dirt on them. I am not trying to defend anyone . . . Browne was driving in an area in which he had every formal right to be, but he ignored the demands of the Grepo in this frontier area to stop the car.'

Next day, at an even higher diplomatic level, Marshal of the Soviet Army I. S. Konev, commander of the Soviet forces in Germany, reinforced the point: 'We are all soldiers and we know what border guards do; even your own troops might shoot you.'

It was not until the following August that Gerhard Senft, a defector from 2 Frontier Brigade, revealed to British Intelligence what had really happened: 'Various patrols had been sent out with orders to stop all cars and to fire at any which failed to acknowledge signals. The Brixmis car had then appeared, was not recognized as such and failed to stop when shouted at. The order to fire was given by the platoon commander . . . who then paid no attention to the British officer's appeals in fluent German to help his driver who was bleeding.' The company commander came on to the scene. The British officer (Browne) refused to leave the Brixmis car until the Russians arrived to help his driver. 'At this the Company Commander went almost berserk . . . [drawing] his pistol which he began waving at the British officer who refused to budge even when the Commander suddenly grabbed a map-board which the officer carried.'

Wellsted's considered view, after he had talked to Day long after the incident, was that 'Douglas Day had seen the East Germans but was ordered to turn round by Nick, who was still looking at his map and had not seen the Germans. Douglas reversed to turn round and then, as he drove away, the Germans opened fire.'

Meanwhile, the escapes continued. On 9 April, almost a month after the Brixmis car was shot-up, two East Germans drove a truck through a checkpoint. On 5 May, eleven elderly East Berliners, including four women, emerged from a tunnel one yard inside West Berlin at Frohnau. Their tunnel had taken two weeks to construct, they said. It was 6-feet high. Asked why they had built such an imposing, tall escape hole the team leader, a man aged eighty-one, replied: 'We did not want our wives to crawl, but to walk unbowed to freedom.' The sentiment might have come from Beethoven's opera about darkness and light, incarceration and freedom, *Fidelio*.

Throughout that year, darkness lay ever more heavily over the northern hemisphere. The fear was of universal extinction, and it was valid. For two weeks in October, the world held its breath as the US Navy blockaded Cuba to prevent Soviet ships from delivering medium-range ballistic missiles to the communists' Americas outpost. Some missiles were already in place, photographed by

American U-2s and satellites. President Kennedy had not intervened when the Wall was constructed. Would he now have to react, or even over-react, if he was not to be perceived, in the crude, strip-cartoon politics of the time, as a wimp president unwilling to fight the bully, Khrushchev?

It is seen with hindsight by historians such as Professor Christopher Andrews as 'the most dangerous moment in the Cold War'. Over the Atlantic, as Paul Johnson has noted, 'were ninety B52s carrying multi-megaton bombs. Nuclear warheads were activated on 100 Atlas, fifty Titans and twelve Minuteman missiles and on American carriers, submarines and overseas bases. All commands were in a state of "Defcon-2", the highest state of readiness next to war itself.'

At the eleventh hour, Khrushchev backed off. The missiles were shipped back to Russia. Khrushchev was now publicly ridiculed by the other communist giant, China, which dismissed the Soviet decision to withdraw as 'simply another Munich'. US Secretary of State Dean Rusk hurrahed: 'Eyeball-to-eyeball and the other fellow just blinked.'

Khrushchev now turned his anger back upon Berlin, a city he liked to compare – historically – to Sarajevo. In a visit to the city three months after the Cuba crisis, in January 1963, he proclaimed an apocalyptic vision of nuclear war which would kill 800 million people, eight times the body-count anticipated three months earlier by Robert Kennedy. To guarantee that his threat was real, Khrushchev revealed that Russia now had a 100-megaton nuclear bomb.

In June it was Kennedy's turn. He told a million cheering Germans: '*Ich bin ein Berliner*.' He went on: 'There are some who say in Europe and elsewhere, We can work with the communists. Let them come to Berlin. And there are even a few who say that it's true communism is an evil system, but it permits us to make economic progress. Let them come to Berlin.'

J. F. Kennedy, murdered in Dallas on 22 November, seemed to many, in the tortured paranoia of the age, to be the first victim of the renewed conflict as Russia struck back. The alleged assassin, Lee Harvey Oswald, a Marine Corps veteran and marksman, had defected to Russia and was then permitted to return to the USA. 'The effects of such complete polarization were felt in Brixmis,' wrote one of its scribes, Captain S. D. Gibson. 'They expressed a subtle but distinct reversal of the Mission's key roles. Whether this change in emphasis was debated and imposed deliberately is ... possibly irrelevant. The upshot was a necessary switch in emphasis from the liaison function to the intelligence-gathering, observing and monitoring function. Secrecy, heightened tension and restrictions on movement placed the Mission in an even greater position of significance by reason of its unique rights of access to an expanding, modernizing Soviet forward force.'

In practice, the switch towards intelligence-gathering had been authorized in 1948, following the Berlin blockade. The change of policy after the 1961–62 crisis was, as Wylde argued, 'a recognition by MoD and BAOR that an increase in Mission touring and support staff was needed. From then on the Mission increased in size – in spite of the Establishment Committee's closest scrutiny!'

For Corporal Day of Brixmis there was an ironic postscript to his near-extinction. Day recovered from his wounds, in spite of having lost a kidney. He finally retired from the RAF as a respected Warrant Officer on Christmas Day 1991, after thirty-five years' service. The Cold War was already history. The Gulf War had come and gone as had a popular little campaign in the South Atlantic. Only the Irish question remained unresolved, but Day had still not been compensated for his injuries. Soon after the event, in 1961, the Russians said the East Germans were responsible. No action was taken by the British government to press the matter at that time, as one veteran noted, 'so as not to compromise the Mission's status'.

The use the Soviets made of 'their' Germans as a means of testing Western resolve was a familiar trick. As a shrewd American diplomatic writer, Joseph Alsop, put it in 1962: 'The Soviets seem to be reasoning: "If we push forward the East Germans as pawns and the Western Allies do nothing about it, then we shall have won the whole Berlin game and maybe the world as well. If the Westerners try to assert their rights on the access routes and the East Germans give them a bloody nose, we shall still be the gainers. And if the East Germans get the bloody nose, as seems more likely, we shall at any rate know what Western intentions really are; and we shall also be free to make a settlement without a big war, as in Korea and the Quemoy crisis."'

Day had been a small pawn in a very big game and, with the end of the Cold War, memories proved remarkably short. But the Brixmis Association, representing Brixmis veterans, did not forget and used its formidable intelligence-gathering skills to promote a damages claim for Day in 1993. Lieutenant-Colonel Wylde drew to the attention of the Special Investigation Branch (SIB) of the Royal Military Police a secret British signal logged soon after the shooting, which said: 'We consider persons responsible were probably from 9 Company 3 Battalion of 1 Regiment of 2 Grenzbrigade.' In January 1994, the SIB disclosed that it had withdrawn the request for help it had lodged initially with the Public Prosecutor in Berlin. It added: 'The prosecutor's office now feels obliged to pursue its inquiries through Interpol with the civil police in the UK.'

As if to underscore the continuing sensitivity of the dark side of the Cold War, the SIB added: 'Our attempts to identify Mr (Local Lt. Col.) Browne have proved fruitless to date.'

Day still has a souvenir of the incident that nearly killed him. This is a bullet in his liver. It was discovered after his transfer to a military hospital in West Germany. Removing it now would put his life in danger. He has a British war disability pension assessed at 20 per cent. In cash terms, that is worth £19 78p per week.

With the unequivocal, physical division of West from East – the building of the Berlin Wall in 1961 – the Mission's intelligence-gathering was given a harder, predatory cutting edge. In this picture, Sergeant Ken Wike BEM (an Army tour NCO from 1982–5) uses his lunchtime apple to take an impression of a gun barrel on the latest BMP–2 infantry combat vehicle. The BMP was on a military train at the time.

A view of a BMP–1 KSh regimental headquarters vehicle, this time from the cockpit of the Mission's own spy-plane, the seemingly innocuous RAF Chipmunk trainer. The low-flying aircraft was not welcome as it wheeled around its quarry, one wing tip down. One Soviet soldier (circled on photograph) raised his assault rifle, started shooting and hit the aircraft.

Above: This Mig–29 Fulcrum strike/attack aircraft was the latest in Soviet fast jets when it joined the Warsaw Pact front line. Within days, a Mission team had got its photograph and its number. That was just the beginning. The next list of intelligence requirements ran: 'Imagery of all weapons carried ... Details of ground attack profiles ... Intro into EGAF (East German Air Force) airfields other than Preschen.' This particular aircraft is now in service with the unified German Air Force.

Above: Air tours, usually manned by RAF personnel, targeted Soviet Air Force bases and machines, some of which, like this Hip–E helicopter gunship, repaid the compliment by flying perilously low to swat the Mission's watchers with a powerful downwash.

Below: The Soviet FTX – Field Training Exercise – was an ideal opportunity for the Mission's spies to snatch pictures of the latest Russian equipment and evaluate Russian skills in handling it. Here a file of T–64B tanks charges in a battle-run formation towards a concealed Brixmis observation post.

Radar was a favourite target of Brixmis. The first of this series of three pictures was snatched by Major Peter Goss, an Intelligence Corps professional, from a position just across the sangar wall surrounding the target. The rear door of the mobile system had been opened by an unwary crew, to reveal useful detail within.

..s photograph of the ..embly of an SA–2 (anti-..craft) missile, Nato ..dename Guideline, by ..viet troops on exercise was ..en at close range, from ..hind a screen of trees, by ..ptain Roy Hunter MBE, a ..r officer from 1984–6.

..in Skin B' height-finding ..ar, paired with an ..rrogation Friend or Foe ..tem, captured on film by ..RAF team under Group ..ptain Keith Harding OBE, ..puty Chief of Mission, ..6–8.

Soviet Army traffic regulators – 'reggies' in Mission jargon – were placed at
intervals on Soviet convoy routes to point the way ahead. These human
traffic signs were not the Red Army's intelligentsia but they were strong,
durable, patient and apparently weatherproof. They were as useful to Mission
spies as to their own officers in an army that issued virtually no maps.

For some regulators there was a possible escape from the endless wait for the
next convoy: a journey of the mind into the oblivion of sleep. The perception
of one Mission Chief was: 'When you saw traffic regulators, opportunity
knocked.'

CHAPTER 6

One of Their Aircraft is Missing

1966

At 3.30 P.M. on 6 April 1966, at the beginning of the Easter holiday, the Soviet Air Force's newest interceptor, the Yak-25 Firebar, crashed in British-controlled territory. The Firebar was a long-range aircraft carrying two air-to-air missiles to a maximum speed of 1,200 m.p.h. and an operational ceiling of 60,000 feet. For once, this loss was not part of an undeclared air war; that continued, with regular losses as American aircraft sneaking into communist airspace were shot down.

On 10 March 1964 a USAF RB66 had been brought down over East Germany. Three months later, an American T-39 was shot down in the same area. In those circumstances, secrets of the Soviets' latest interceptor were of more than passing interest to Nato, whose intelligence services regarded it as manna from heaven when one of these machines crash-landed into Lake Havel, in the British sector of Berlin. Short of flying his aircraft to RAF Gatow, the Soviet pilot could hardly have done a better job of compromising the secrets of his aircraft. This pilot was not defecting. His machine was crippled by an engine failure known as 'flame-out'. He had sought permission from his own air control to make an emergency landing on a Nato airfield in West Berlin but was ordered to ditch on the lake instead. As one Brixmis veteran put it: 'The aircrew were refused permission to save themselves.'

For the British armed forces, that Wednesday, like all Wednesdays, was sports afternoon. The Chief of Brixmis, Brigadier David Wilson CBE, an Argyll & Sutherland Highlander, was playing squash partnered by his tour officer Captain Nigel Broomfield

(17/21st Lancers) in a needle-match against the Green Jackets. Another Brixmis operator was playing snooker at the Berlin Naafi Club. He was Junior Technician Eddie Batchelor, from the administration office of the RAF element of the Mission. From the snooker room, Batchelor strolled into the bookshop.

'I overheard the manager say that he had heard that a Russian Mig had just come down in the Havel. I immediately phoned our RAF operations officer, Squadron Leader Maurice Taylor and told him what I had heard. He asked if I had a car or a camera. I had neither. He said he'd go to the crash. I was to open the office at our Berlin HQ and call in the photo-technicians.'

Word rapidly reached the brigadier. By now, the Royal Military Police had thrown an armed cordon round the crash site. About 100 yards from the bank, the tail of the aircraft was visible above the water, and two aerials projected from the tail. The Soviets also reacted quickly. Within an hour, they had brought to the scene a bus full of armed troops from ceremonial guard duty near the Brandenburg Gate under the command of Soviet Air Force Major-General Bulanov. A potentially dangerous stand-off began.

Anticipating that they might be called on to undertake salvage operations, the Berlin garrison's resident Sapper unit, 38 Field Squadron, arranged for their store-keeper to release the unit's heavy ferry to the squadron. Divers would be needed, instantly. The answer was the Berlin Brigade Sub-aqua club, led by Captain (later Lieutenant-Colonel) Roger Eagle. He was one of 38 Squadron's people but the team included fun divers from other units including the Royal Signals and Royal Military Police. They were told to report to their club-room at the Olympic indoor swimming pool to charge up their air-tanks and make ready to dive.

At the British diplomatic Mission in West Berlin, Brigadier Wilson and Captain Broomfield, still in squash clothes, joined a council of war chaired by the acting General Officer Commanding the British Garrison in Berlin, Mr Peter Hayman, a Foreign Office minister. They promptly sent Major (later Colonel) Angus Southwood to the crash site with a letter from Hayman to Bulanov, telling him that his armed troops must be removed from the crash site within the hour. Southwood recalled: 'The Russian general calmly read the letter and said: "Go back to your General and ask him if he is threatening the Soviet Union."' After the bark, the bite did not follow. The Russians withdrew the guns and were allowed to maintain an observation party on the lakeside throughout the recovery.

By now it was getting dark. Taylor, the RAF operations officer, obtained a small boat and quietly rowed out to the wreck with his camera. There he took a flash photograph of the aircraft tail. The Russian observers, congregating behind the RMP's protective white tape, were suspicious. They knew what the aircraft was and what secrets it contained. So far, the British did not. That soon changed. Taylor's photographs were processed and Batchelor, who had a good eye for detail, was told to check through the air intelligence manual supplied by the Ministry of Defence and frequently updated.

'I sat down in our ops room with the photographs and our manuals,' Batchelor said. 'I knew basically what sort of aircraft it was but I was stumped by the two aerials on the tail. We hadn't seen anything like it before.'

The only photograph that matched had been supplied by the US Mission about a week earlier. Batchelor said to his operations officer: 'I think you should see this, sir.'

Taylor noted the match. The aircraft was almost certainly the Firebar, not seen outside Russia until now. Junior Technician Batchelor's identification promptly triggered off one of Britain's more audacious, and ruthless, espionage operations. Taylor sent a 'Flash' signal, the highest priority, to the Defence Intelligence Secretariat duty officer at MoD, London.

Two separate, parallel, operations had to be orchestrated by the British during the seven days it took to gut the Firebar. One was the 'liberation' of its secrets; the other was a diplomatic quadrille so as to give the 'salvage' team time to do the dirty work. Each of these represented a facet of the ambiguous Brixmis function, though the dirty work, much of it under water, was a matter of which Brixmis officially had no knowledge.

While Brigadier Wilson played it cool at a dinner party, the heavy ferry was sailing through a complex of canals and locks, towards the lakes. One of the diving team recalled: 'At first light on 7 April, the heavy ferry, with crane, majestically appeared out of mist on the lake and anchored close to the wrecked aircraft.'

The Soviet bodies were still inside, strapped into their ejection seats which were armed with a powerful explosive charge. One false move on the part of the divers could have blown more than their cover. They got to work all the same, cutting into the machine to remove the Firebar's radar from under the feet of the corpses.

The Russian watchers now included Colonel Lezzov, deputy Chief of Soxmis, who said he 'just happened to be passing' the crash site. A Brixmis document described how Lezzov, 'a professionally suspicious man, observed the movement of divers and a small boat around the aircraft. He was in a high state of agitation.' Squadron Leader Willis, the duty interpreter, pleaded ignorance, adding that he was aware that the military police were using a boat to guard the wreckage during the dark hours.

Blocked one way, Lezzov (a Hero of the Soviet Union) tried another approach. He protested direct to the BAOR headquarters at Rheindahlen. It made no difference. By now, however, Brixmis had compiled a roster of Russian-speaking officers to provide a twenty-four-hour liaison service with the Soviets at the site. Their efforts to ease the tension were a vital part of the operation.

After dinner that first night with Major (later Colonel) Geoffrey Stephenson (a Russian-speaking Royal Signals officer using the title 'Economics Officer' as his cover), the brigadier went to the site and reassured the Russian general. This was a mistake, however, as early next morning he was summoned to the Soviet HQ.

Through the night, a succession of ever more senior Russians appeared on the banks of the Havel, as if on some pilgrimage. Shortly before midnight it was Mr Billetski, first secretary of the Soviet embassy in East Berlin. He was sent away with a polite diplomatic flea in his ear, since this was not his part of the protocol network.

Stephenson, now a retired colonel, recalled in 1995: 'I wrote a confidential report at the time describing how the Russians were jumping up and down on the bank, eloquent but impotent while they observed the rape of their youngest electronic daughter. That's exactly what was happening.'

His view was confirmed by Angus Southwood. 'At first,' he said, 'relations were extremely frosty, with General Bulanov making hourly protests that they were not being allowed into the recovery raft. The Russians were particularly incensed that as pieces of the aircraft were recovered by British divers, they were photographed and bits were sawn off and taken away for analysis. After a couple of days, they realized that they were not going to get their way and the whole party appeared to relax.'

At mid-morning next day, Wilson, with Colonel Pinchuk, boss of SERB (Soviet External Relations Bureau), answered a summons from the Soviet commander-in-chief at Zossen. Pinchuk 'looked as if he had been through the mangle after a week in a nightclub'. They were both carpeted by the Soviet deputy C-in-C, General Belin. 'At that stage', according to Wilson, 'we had not recovered the bodies of the Soviet aircrew. I think the Russians were very anxious as to their fate, suspecting that we had them in captivity.'

General Belin told Wilson to pass on promptly the Soviet protest about British obstructionism. Wilson, a model of courtesy, assured him that it would be done, 'but I also said that on our way to his headquarters, passing through Zossen village, two clueless traffic regulators had tried to stop us. They were armed and I was sure they would stop us on the way back, unless we had an escort.'

Belin bridled at the suggestion that mere 'reggies' would not know the name of their own deputy C-in-C or fail to grovel when it was uttered. This suited Wilson, who needed to put a plausible brake on the process of handing over the wreck, if not the bodies. They left the office, feeling as if they had been given six of the best by the school head. 'Nigel Broomfield said that the experience was like getting "a good swishing from the beak". Pinchuk, whose English was good, overheard this and said he didn't understand what we were getting at. It was too idiomatic. We didn't enlighten him.'

As Wilson had anticipated, the British party was stopped at gun-point in nearby Zossen village. Having made the arrests, the Soviet 'reggies' didn't know what to do next. 'When we mentioned Belin's name they replied, "Never heard of him!" That played straight into our hands. We now waited for an hour or so, well past the time that BAOR would have knocked off for Easter. Then Nigel found a telephone and contacted SERB in Potsdam.'

There the news that the British negotiators had got no further than Zossen village, and that, as a result, no official Soviet diplomatic representations were being made that holiday weekend to speed up the return of the Firebar, caused 'a sort of atomic explosion of horror'. Thirty minutes later a Soviet Army jeep appeared 'like a Formula 1 racing car . . . A furious Russian colonel leapt out and clobbered the senior traffic regulator with his fist.'

The Russians now had to live with the fact that, at an official level, the British were well into the somnolent, holiday peace of the Easter weekend, even if some of them were exercising in boats on the Havel. As Wilson disingenuously told them, he 'very much doubted that the British C-in-C would get the Soviets' urgent message until Tuesday'. Wilson now returned to his own headquarters, satisfied that 'we had achieved exactly what we wanted. We had gained a very great deal of time for the Staffs to sort things out.'

That evening, Royal Engineer divers continued their 'salvage' operation from the heavy ferry. The Russians were still kept at arm's length as the bodies of the two Soviet aircrew were recovered, floated away to a safe haven and their pockets searched. Every document they carried was photographed and every personal possession noted. The bodies were then put back into their flying suits and smuggled back to the site to be handed over to the Russians. Later that night 'Chief Brixmis was authorized to inform SERB that the bodies had been found and would be handed over with ceremony in due course . . . Salvage operations would continue and all parts of the plane returned, once recovered.' (And, he might have added, after they had been lovingly inspected by Western Intelligence.)

The Soviets responded with a ploy of their own. As Colonel Stephenson put it: 'They tried every bloody ruse to get to the aircraft. They invented a "rule" that it was part of the protocol in such cases that their military band should play the Dead March beside the aircraft as the bodies were extracted, to pay due respect. It was finally agreed that the band could be given access down a little track as far as the water's edge. The handover was at midnight. The bodies were already placed on the bank. Before they accepted the bodies from us the Russians insisted on removing bandages on the faces so as to identify them.'

The Russians insisted on documentation. A crude 'handover certificate' for legal transfer of the cadavers was handwritten on a grubby sheet of paper, with the bonnet of a GAZ-69 as a desk and a flickering hurricane oil-lamp as office lighting.

When the handover finally took place in the early hours of 8 April, it was at an eerie ceremony which mixed grief with Cold War wariness. The Soviet party included Major-General Lazutin, Assistant Chief of Staff, Group of Soviet Forces in Germany; General of Aviation Bulanov and a party of Soviet Air Force officers in ceremonial dress who acted as bearers; a band and a party of thirty motor rifle division soldiers. Among the British party were the deputy Chief of Brixmis, Group Captain Ted Colahan, the Berlin Brigade commander, and a senior staff officer, Lieutenant-Colonel Peter Dryland. The Royal Inniskilling Fusiliers provided an armed guard of an officer and twelve fusiliers with a piper.

For one of the divers, the most delicate part of the operation was still to come. Western intelligence officers, some flown from the US especially to get near the wreck, wanted access to the engines. Although most of the debris had been extracted and stacked on the heavy ferry, the engines were lying deep in soft mud, somewhere on the bed of the lake. A single member of the amateur team, whose identity is still a secret, working in total darkness, burrowed into the mud until he identified the engines by touch. As Lieutenant-Colonel Eagle, the dive leader, put it, the man 'achieved the remarkable feat of squirming into the mud and applying lifting strops'.

In a silent, secret operation, the engines were lifted to a point just below the surface, then towed by tug to a lakeside jetty a mile away. The jetty was conveniently close to the RAF's Gatow airfield. From there they were flown to England to be stripped down and examined in detail before being reassembled. Within forty-eight hours they were flown back to Berlin, 'returned to the crash site and quietly deposited on the bed of the lake'. The day after that, the engines were located officially and publicly by the British divers, and lifted on to the heavy ferry.

While this was going on, General Bulanov had broken through the cordon to the water's edge, to protest anew. At various times, almost from the beginning, the Soviets brought in a small fleet of antique army lorries fitted with flexible canvas sides. When the canvas was raised, after dark, massive searchlights on the back of the trucks lit up the salvage work. Recovery stopped immediately. The Russians were told to stop this harassment if they wanted the aircraft back. They grudgingly agreed but still sometimes switched on again, briefly, when they heard the sounds of the work. Colonel Stephenson remembered: 'The third attempt to light up the area was completely hidden from view by craftily-contrived canvas screens on floating pontoons . . . More Sapper ingenuity! The lamplighters and their ramshackle trucks played no further part in this drama and left the scene.'

The protests and the stratagems were all too late. What Stephenson had described as a rape was all but complete. Wilson was summoned back to the Soviet headquarters at Zossen. There, he found 'the handover of aircrew bodies had calmed everybody down. The traffic regulators had caused great loss of face. The Soviet headquarters band was practising, very expertly. The atmosphere was very different.'

The way to a good Russian's heart, as Brixmis knew, was through a whisky bottle. The Russian speakers on the team passed the time innocently discussing the merits of Scotch and vodka, as well as more mundane matters such as pay-scales and pensions. One evening towards the end of the recovery operation, Major Southwood arrived at the lakeside to take over the interpreter's night-shift from Captain Tony Huddlestone.

'Southwood,' said one Brixmis report, 'was surprised to see the Brixmis car with all the windows misted up. Opening the door he found Huddlestone flanked by two Soviet Air Force colonels in the back seat. They had all been clearly doing some serious analysis of the merits of Scotch. This task continued into the small hours with liquid comparisons with vodka and East German brandy until the party finally repaired to the Russians' GAZ-69 jeep for a gourmet treat of cold liver and cloves of garlic.'

Southwood's driver did not appreciate the atmosphere of garlic and alcohol that swirled around his boss when Southwood returned to the Brixmis car. It paid off. As well as diverting attention from the Mission's latest burglary, it gave Brixmis officers a rare chance to hear the uncensored voice of the Russian soldier and to hear about Soviet standing orders for detaining Allied tour cars.

Not even Brixmis could please all the people, all the time. After a further row on the lakeside next day, the chief Soviet negotiator, Major-General Lazutin, exploded with anger and walked out of the latest round of talks. Two days later, a Brixmis major was sent round to the Soviet liaison office offering to move the wreck by raft. Exactly a week after the crash, 'two rafts, one from the British and one from the Soviets, joined together and discussion commenced on the signing of a suitable document'. At some Cold War conferences, it was becoming fashionable to argue whether the table should be square or round. The shape of the raft does not appear to have presented a problem on the Havel, though the Russians insisted that the vessel should be exactly over the line dividing the British part of the lake from the Soviet part. There was also a last-minute wrangle about the parts of the aircraft, as distinct from the main airframe, that the British still retained.

The British stuck to their guns and the Russians accepted, reluctantly, a two-phase deal. The main wreck was handed over just before midnight on 13 April. On 2 May a handover of all remaining recovered parts took place at the same spot and with the same representatives. Almost the last items to be returned were the engines.

Stephenson recalled two memorable moments during this process. 'Bulanov was on the raft and I was standing beside him. We lifted the engines over very unceremoniously and plonked them down. Bulanov ran his fingers over the stumps of about seven rotors which had been neatly cut off for metallurgical examination. He ran his thumbs over these and looked at me. He didn't say a word but his expression said, "I'm screwed."'

The Russians compiled an inventory of what was returned by Brixmis.

They said, 'We are at a loss to understand why, in an accident of this sort, one significant item seems to be missing while the other, surrounding parts are all intact.' We scratched our heads and said, 'We truly don't understand what you are getting at.' The Soviets were not going to say exactly what part they were talking about, just in case we hadn't got it, which we had. It was part of the radar kit.

We then drafted a protocol on the raft. It said, 'The salvage work is now complete. No further parts are to be found.' The Russians bridled at that. They knew this one piece was missing. They amended the draft to read, 'The British say there are no further parts to be recovered.' We had nicked it and couldn't return it because it was a very intricate item.

Brigadier Wilson shrugged off the tension around the episode: 'There was a great deal of toing and froing between Zossen [Soviet HQ] and SERB during this period. I did the high-level stuff and Ted Colahan, my deputy, the nuts and bolts ... Once the initial shock and panic had settled we really had no problems with our Russian opposite numbers.'

All the same, the commander of the British Berlin Brigade, Brigadier Alan Taylor, had posted a platoon of infantry marksmen in discreet fire positions on the bank overlooking the raft, to deal with any Soviet skulduggery. When he saw the sharpshooters take up position, Geoffrey Stephenson tried not to dwell upon what rules of engagement they had been given.

The Firebar affair occurred during an interesting phase of the Cold War, a time of shifting gears and perceptions. The years between Cuba, 1962, and the 1969 SALT talks (a device to cap the superpower nuclear arms race) pointed towards a kind of deterrence that the small-fry satellites of both sides in the Cold War did not much like. This was the emerging deal between Washington and Moscow, that the first salvoes of the Third World War would fall on Europe and leave the motherland and/or fatherland, untouched. It was Russian roulette, played away from home or, in the words of a song popular in the trenches of the First World War, 'The bells of hell go tinga-linga-ling for you but not for me'. As one GI of German extraction put it when he was posted to Germany about then: 'Gee, I'm glad to be here. I wanted to see the old country before it got nuked.'

Signposts on the road to a crude but exclusive survival pact between the two major powers included a telephone 'hot-line' linking the White House to the Kremlin (1963) and adoption by the US of 'flexible response', emphasizing tactical nuclear weapons on a localized European battlefield rather than the MAD strategy of inter-continental missile war. By 1966, the US had moved 7,000 nuclear warheads into Europe, guarded by armed sentries ordered to kill any intruder suspected of getting too close to the stockpile.

The small fry broke ranks. In 1966 France withdrew from Nato and obliged the alliance headquarters to move out of the leafy elegance of Fontainebleau and Paris to the freezing dust of Brussels, a suburban Siberia. More serious for war planners was the uncertainty of France's position in a sudden crisis. It was debatable whether French territory and airspace would be denied to Nato if Soviet tanks invaded West Germany, where a French garrison remained, no longer assigned to the alliance. While uncertainty was a deliberate component of the new 'flexible response' doctrine, this was an ambiguity too far. With Germany divided, France was the biggest nation, geographically, in West Europe.

Although British governments stood firm (and they included the socialist administration led by Harold Wilson after 1964), the other ranks were rebellious. CND burgeoned among the young and created 'spies for peace'. The idea caught on. Germans on both sides were busy leaking their masters' secrets to the opposition, thus imposing an unauthorized arms control mechanism of their own. The MI6 mandarin Kim Philby turned up in Moscow, to be hailed as an official Hero of the Soviet Union. The American war in Vietnam, stoked by Defense Secretary Robert McNamara, got no military support from Nato Europe. Student protesters at Oxford included the future president, Bill Clinton. When, thirty years later, McNamara confessed that he had got it wrong in making war against Vietnam, Clinton said well, that just vindicated his role as a refusenik, along with Mohammed Ali and others.

In 1968 the Czechs, Yugoslavs, Romanians and Albanians also rebelled against Big Brother. Warsaw Pact divisions dominated by the Soviet Army crushed the Prague Spring, while the West looked the other way. Czechoslovakia, as someone once said, is a far-off country of which we know little.

There was one hitch in the superpower understanding. Their agenda for self-preservation through détente was derailed, time and again, by the Vietnam War. In Washington, there was a degree of bitterness about the refusal of the West Europeans to join in. The effect of the war on Moscow was more profound. As the Institute of Strategic Studies noted in its 1966 survey: 'The deepening American involvement in Vietnam provided fuel for Chinese charges of Soviet collusion with "imperialism", alleging that Soviet pursuit of peaceful co-existence in Europe facilitated reorientation of American military resources towards Vietnam.'

The architect of the Soviets' limited understanding with America was Khrushchev. He it was who had denounced Stalin's brutality (having served the great leader faithfully until the great leader was safely dead and buried). In 1964, in a new October revolution, Khrushchev was deposed by an old-guard faction led by Leonid Brezhnev.

Brixmis was nicely placed to experience the impact of Europe's political schizophrenia. The Mission's first priority was to fight the good fight alongside Uncle Sam, against the Red Menace, within the arcane rules of the 1946 Robertson–Malinin Agreement. This was the world according to Ian Fleming, whose James Bond hit – *From Russia With Love* – was premiered in the same month (May 1963) as a British amateur spy, Greville Wynne, was imprisoned in Moscow. But there was a grey area. As well as its own form of licensed spying, the Mission's alternative agenda was liaison, the art of making friends with everyone in a changing world.

With Khrushchev's removal, his successors took a hard line on Berlin. The West invited trouble in March 1965 when it consented to a meeting of the West German parliament in Berlin, against Soviet wishes. Soviet reaction was prompt. Major David Bird, on his way back to Potsdam from a routine patrol in the north-west of the GDR, cut on to the normally busy Helmstedt–Berlin autobahn at an emergency exit. The Brixmis Association account says that Bird 'was immediately struck by the fact that the autobahn was completely devoid of traffic. He therefore took up an OP in woods bordering the autobahn and was soon rewarded by the sight of a complete division moving west towards Helmstedt on both carriageways. The troops looked grim-faced.'

Bird tried to get back to Potsdam unobserved. He was picked up by pursuing narks but after 'some very hazardous driving' managed to reach the Mission House where everyone remained 'hemmed in for a couple of days'. By then, a new Berlin blockade had started. All land routes to Berlin were closed. West Berlin was 'subjected to an almost continuous barrage of sonic bangs caused by Soviet aircraft'. Western civil and military aircraft were buzzed by Soviet interceptors along the air corridor from the West. A complete airborne division flew from Russia to make a mass drop into a favourite exercise area near the Inner German Border known as Letzlinger Heide.

As usual, the Mission's corporal-drivers were the unsung heroes of dangerous confrontations. Major Harold Gatehouse, serving between 1962 and 1964, recalled with gratitude Paul Puckey, 'on his first tour when we were surprised and shot at by two Soviet soldiers on foot in a wooden area overlooking the tank track leading from Wittenberg to the Forst Glucksburg training area. The paths were covered in pools of rainwater and were tricky driving . . . Puckey did well to get us away without stalling the engine while I peered anxiously out of the rear window at the advancing, gesticulating Soviets.'

To confirm its right to stay in business as pressure came on Berlin yet again, Brixmis sent out twenty-four tours during the next few days. Every one was detained for questioning by the Soviets. Major Angus Southwood, under the tutelage of Major John Parry, was sent on his first tour to patrol the autobahn. He remembered seeing another Brixmis car on the other side of the autobahn hemmed in by about six nark cars. The tour officer, Major Peter Chitty, was outside the car and being manhandled by the narks. As he appeared to be holding his own, Parry and Southwood sped on, only to be detained in a similar fashion a few miles further on.

This was not the whole story. According to Major (later Lieutenant-Colonel) Chitty:

I had managed to get on to the closed autobahn by using an emergency route (already recce'd) past the Olympic-standard athletics track outside Potsdam. On this particular day they were conducting the national athletics selection and we had to drive 'discreetly' through about 200 surprised athletes and officials. I held my own with the narks until I backtracked under an illegal turn-off between two military training areas and found that a

Soviet divisional tactical headquarters was already operating in the track leading beneath the autobahn. By now I had lost some vital lead time over the narks. As I emerged on the Berlin-bound side of the autobahn, where the slip-road led through a petrol station, the narks spotted me. Three vehicles came across the centre strip of the road and into the service station, where one's brakes failed and he slid into the only pump, writing it off completely, with petrol being sprayed around.

I was soon surrounded by both narks and Soviets. When Angus went past I was holding my own from a horizontal position, being kicked in the ribs (etc) by the narks and by some of the Soviets. Back in Berlin I was forbidden by the G-1 [senior staff officer] from mentioning the Soviets in my report on the treatment I had suffered as it was expected it would make things worse if raised at a diplomatic level.

In the end no mention was allowed in my report of the whole incident, save that I took much delight in circumventing the G-1 by sending a technical report to MI10 [military technical intelligence] in which I described how I had 'trialled' the new Soviet army boot.

Some days later, Major Parry was detained again, at an autobahn exit, just in time to see the Soviet paras going home by road. It was a signal that this crisis was now over. Brixmis soldiers, frustrated and fatigued, must have been relieved to learn that, in spite of everything, the sang-froid of Britain's Rhine Army headquarters was intact. 'All the Indicators of Hostilities on the HQ BAOR list had been fulfilled but nobody had seemed very worried,' as one of them put it. The purpose of the list was to prompt the flow of some adrenalin and to stir up a few contingency plans, but on Wednesday that week – sports afternoon – it was tennis as usual on the immaculate hard courts of Rheindahlen, shaded by plane trees and safely distant from the uncomfortable realities of the Helmstedt autobahn.

The crisis passed and, for the Mission's hard core, it was back to business as usual. Major (later Lieutenant-Colonel) Peter Chitty MBE, the tour officer spotted by Southwood, 'holding his own', was by now an unusually well-qualified part of that hard core.

One way or another, Chitty had already acquired a more than nodding acquaintance with the Mission for eight years, an unusually long time, first on detachment from BAOR's technical intelligence team, later as a tour officer. He had seen at first hand the rough trade of Wynne-Pope's management of relations with the Soviets; served under Fitzalan-Howard during the 'Blake Effect' period. From 1963 to 1965, he was back as an intelligence specialist under Brigadier (later Major-General) 'Duggie' Darling CB, DSO, MC as Chief of Mission and with Darling's successor, Brigadier (later Major-General) H. E. N. Bredin CB, DSO, MC. Between those tours he had enjoyed an educative time with the Ministry of Defence technical intelligence arm, MI10, where he got to hear about Soviet weapons systems not yet seen anywhere near the front line. Their very existence, in some cases, was 'laughed out of court by the experts until I photographed them'. This edge gave Chitty's later Brixmis tours an added 'tingle-factor', since Chitty, now on his mettle, had his own intelligence 'wish-list'. As he put it later: 'Many of my intelligence "coups" were of a personal nature as I had been following up their cases from well beforehand and then struck lucky to sight them on the ground.'

His first target was the T-54 semi-amphibious tank, fitted with a breathing tube known as a snorkel, which enabled the tank to cross waterways 14 feet deep. He explained:

I knew from London that there had been tests on snorkels within Soviet Russia and was therefore spending some time on, around or occasionally in river training sites near to the more 'high profile' divisional garrisons. Having been unlucky after a depth recce of a site where I had found tracks entering the water the previous day, I was quietly photographing some hoopoes – my wife and I being keen bird enthusiasts – when a GAZ-69 raced down the road to arrest me. The usual demand for cameras was made and refused. We were arrested and taken to the kommandantura and there I quite honestly protested my innocence.

As a palliative I showed them some earlier photographs I had taken in the local town of storks nesting on the church steeple that the Soviet commander could see from his office. Eventually I was allowed to go. When my film of the hoopoes was developed

. . . surprise, surprise, in the distance, coming out of the wood was a column of the first snorkel T-54s.

Next, Chitty wanted very much to confirm that the Soviet forces in Germany were equipped with a portable, folding pontoon bridge, or PMP. (Ten years later, the Egyptian armies were to use the system for a successful attack across the Suez Canal.) Chitty's first close encounter with the PMP went like clockwork; the second was a bit of a pantomime.

'I was not the first to sight the PMP bridge but was alerted to it and thundered down towards Magdeburg where I managed to get some good photographs. However, some weeks later, during an exercise in the Letzlinger Heide Training Area, a PMP pontoon bridging regiment was deployed to bridge the River Elbe . . . We managed to get down to the site after dark with no lights and lay up in the woods bordering the embankment.'

There was much shouting and cursing among the Soviet soldiers as Chitty's crew waited under cover for the action to start. It did not. Chitty learned later from 'Sigint' that the exercise had been put back a day.

The first fraught situation came late in the evening when a signals detachment laid battle cable along the embankment . . . The two 'mujiks' [peasants] doing this job managed to drag the cable over us where we lay in the undergrowth. The bridge-build took place all night. By dawn an apparently completed bridge was in place across the river. Then we were discovered by two 'mujiks' who were looking for some quiet spot where they could be interested in one another. Soon we were flushed out by two BTR-50Ps [armoured personnel carriers]. We had to take the only way out, which was to drive down on to the floodplain in our vehicle and go for broke.

Trouble loomed large everywhere. As we became more firmly corralled I took a gamble on the only possible escape route. We drove on to the newly constructed pontoon bridge itself as the far end looked open. Naturally . . . the pontoon engineers had loused up on their initial recce. The bridge was short of two floating bays. It fell short of the far bank. We had to come to a grinding halt with our wheels inches away from a drop into the Elbe. Arrest followed but the pontoon engineers were amused, in the end, by the fact that I, too, was an engineer, ready to tell tales of my own engineering failures.

Chitty was an old hand at the detention game. 'In Bernau, the Russian commandant challenged his Brixmis prisoners to a game of snooker before he released them. The game was loaded in that the prisoner's cue was tipped with a boot stud . . . I was caught on the way to Dresden and spent a quiet six hours or so in the downstairs loo of the city kommandantura. This was a tactical mistake by the Sovs. I was locked inside their only loo. The staff had to go out into the compound and pee or defecate against the wall whilst I remained in possession of their much-needed facility.'

With a sure instinct for psychological warfare and 'to pass away the time – for there is not much reading material in a Soviet loo – I pulled the chain every five minutes or so to break the monotony and to draw their attention to the fact that I was still in there'. This almost certainly reminded those who needed to go that they could not. The irritation grew too much for the Russians, 'who in desperation came in and removed the chain'.

He was released to eat with his crew, who were still waiting in the yard outside, with the tour car. 'We had been provided with self-heating tins of soup. This miracle of decadent Western technology attracted several of the kommandantura staff. We had not been briefed on the self-heating system and lit the element without making a hole in each tin. The pressure built up inside and the inevitable disaster happened. The three tins exploded pretty well simultaneously, covering the Russians, but not us, in tomato soup with bits of meat added. For me, it was back to the loo.'

By the time he left the Mission, Chitty had acquired a special reputation among the Soviets. He could not take up a subsequent appointment as an assistant military attaché in the Soviet capital: 'I was PNG'd from that job even before I got to Moscow!'

Chitty's Chief of Mission, Brigadier Bredin, was as active on tours as his juniors. He was with Major David Bird, 14/20 Hussars, when they spotted a train arriving, apparently carrying ore. Major Bird pointed out that there was snow on top of the wagons. This was odd since there had been no report of snow in Germany. The train halted and was left unattended. Bird clambered on to it, and collected some lumps of earth and rocks. The samples were sent to the Ministry of Defence for analysis and were found to be radio-active.

Car chases continued to be part of everyday life. Major Harold Gatehouse, an intelligence professional, and Corporal Moore, chased on the Dresden autobahn by a nark, opened a gap between the two vehicles.

> I told Corporal Moore to increase his speed, to flash his indicator as if turning off right as we approached an autobahn exit and then to switch off all his lights when he reached the fly-off [emergency exit]. Mission cars were fitted with switches to turn off their brake lights as well as headlights and sidelights. Moore continued at high speed in the dark for several hundred yards until we saw the nark car's headlights swing off the autobahn behind us, chasing into a training area and hoping to catch us out of bounds.

On another occasion, Major John Cormack, a Royal Engineer and intelligence officer, paused with his driver under fruit trees for morning coffee. Soon they were joined by a Stasi Mercedes.

> We drove on. I had a very fine driver called Jackson. We came to an area which was half wood and half open space, with a ditch, running right across the field. There was no bridge over it. It was only a small ditch. I said to Corporal Jackson, 'How about it, if we went flat out, could you bounce that?' He said, 'No problem, sir.' So we took them round for a while, wandering, until they got a bit dozy, till we hit this open area. Then Corporal Jackson revved up and did a sort of American television thing, a flying leap over the ditch and then drove off into the woods leaving the Mercedes stranded behind the ditch.

Beyond that ditch, and others, there were big fish to be caught. As part of the superpowers' implicit Battlefield Europe plan, the Soviets deployed a new, 175-mile-range mobile rocket armed with a nuclear or chemical warhead. It was carried to its launch site by heavy lorry and could be fired at the target after a mere sixty seconds' preparation. The weapon was known to Nato as 'Scud B'. Its introduction into Eastern Europe was a significant event in the Europeanization of the nuclear battlefield. It matched Washington's decision to up-gun the armoury of the American 7th Army in Germany with more Honest John missiles and the 400-mile, nuclear-capable Pershing.

When Scud-B went operational, Cormack joined the party, uninvited. 'I was driving on a fairly routine tour with Corporal Broe and Bombardier Knight along the edge of a PRA. We were on the way back when we spotted an A-frame. An A-frame is a piece of kit you associate with missiles. We thought, "This looks very interesting."'

Cormack hurried back to the Potsdam Mission House to get clearance to break the rules by penetrating the PRA. The senior staff officer, Lieutenant-Colonel Tony Caulfield OBE, was an artilleryman. Gunners love ground-based missiles. He gave his blessing.

> So we refuelled, got some extra grub. My wife was used to creating picnic meals at short notice. We shot straight back and got there in the very early hours of the morning and set up an OP. I had the long lens on my camera. After waiting a considerable time we heard noises and there, sure enough, we saw a Scud missile through the trees, the first one that had been seen on the ground [that is, a potential battleground]. It was an early dawn, in late summer. I got some reasonably good pictures of it.
>
> It wasn't the technical quality of the pictures that mattered so much as the fact that we had identified the kit on the ground. It showed that they were deployed with units in Germany and not just put on parade. The implication might be that those on parade were dummies or brought in for the occasion. Some people would argue that way.

As the Gulf War was to demonstrate almost thirty years later, mobile missiles of this type were almost impossible to detect, until they had been fired. Cormack's team was now in a position similar to that in which SAS teams found themselves, Scud-hunting in Iraq in 1991.

'At first, we didn't realize we were surrounded by armed sentries. We were lucky: they didn't appreciate who we were. They saw us as we were leaving. We got out without any trouble. When we came back over the Glienicke Bridge from Seestrasse [where the Mission House was sited after the destruction of the original in 1958] our first port of call was the American Mission headquarters. We checked in there and gave them the "highlights". This time they were over the moon. Then I went straight back to the Mission and handed my films in for processing and got down to writing my report.'

In the summer of 1965, Cormack came back for more. A joint operation was mounted by the three Western Missions around the outskirts of Berlin to trace the routes taken into the May Day parade by Warsaw Pact forces. Cormack spent a day under cover near an approach route to the Juterborg training area. 'It wasn't until the evening that the fun started and they all came trundling down, Scud missiles and everything. We watched them and we counted them as best we could. Then we tried to tail them.'

Cormack's team was spotted by a Soviet field security vehicle, a GAZ-69 carrying a distinctive black-and-white number plate. 'We reversed uphill as fast as we could. It was a fairly bumpy track. Unfortunately we bounced on to a large stone and stalled. He parked his vehicle in front of us. We were stuck until dawn the next morning.'

His next quarry was the 'Halle Gun'. This was a new 120mm field artillery weapon. Someone in Brixmis had already caught a glimpse of this beast at Halle (hence the nickname), but as yet no one had snatched a photograph of it. With Lieutenant-Colonel Peter Badger, Cormack went hunting for the gun as it was moved by rail. His vantage point was a railway bridge. His problem was that a nark had followed them and was closing in.

I got out of the car, left the door open to cover what I was doing and took a series of pictures as the railway trucks came underneath with all the guns lined up. I was so busy taking pictures I didn't actually see what I was filming. I was concentrating on taking clear pictures, in focus, and watching what might be coming the other way. I got a whole series of pictures of the train and they were all in excellent focus.

The team drove away at speed and shook off the nark,] . . . but they had radios and they were setting up a roadblock. In those days we wore battledress and RAF flying boots, topped by a leather flap. I carried a couple of exposed films in my tour kit which were useless. As soon as I got back into the car I rewound the good film, took it out of my camera and passed it to the driver, who put it down his boot. I then got a dummy film out and loaded my camera.

As we drove on it was clear we were being followed. Suddenly a tractor with a couple of trailers of beet or whatever drove across the road. We were completely blocked. The Soviet commandant was waiting there, livid. He accused me of taking pictures. I said yes, I had been taking pictures, all concerned with local culture: pictures of churches and cathedrals and interesting buildings. This was part of my great 'kultur' approach.

He said he didn't believe me and wanted to see my film. I ostentatiously held up the camera, opened it, took the film and pulled it out. I said, 'Here you are.' It ruined the film. Of course, this was the dummy; but if you gave them even a blank film you could never be sure that they might not take pictures themselves and then use them as evidence against you. I had to expose the film to prove it was useless anyway. He wasn't best pleased.

One of Cormack's drivers was Corporal Colin Brierley, a kit-oriented soldier who concluded that the RAF flying boots were 'smart when polished but impractical when floundering about in mud'.

A lot of our work was straight across fields and woodland. The cars – Opel Kapitäns painted matt olive – were simply tools. Any damage they sustained was not accountable in the army's usual meticulous system for reporting the merest scratch to an official vehicle.

On one of my first tours we were following a Soviet convoy. I was instructed to pass it. When I started overtaking, one of the Russians tried to force the car off the road. I took evading action but I couldn't avoid knocking down marker posts. All my training had been against that but now I was told very sharply to 'get past: the Soviet drivers often do that'. Now I knew the rules and I never looked back.

It was a bit cops-and-robbers. I was on a tour with Major Parry. We were being chased by a Soviet one-ton truck. This would not be a problem, normally, but this time, as we approached a level-crossing, the barriers dropped to let a train pass. The 'Sov' truck driver parked his vehicle broadside, across the road, boxing us in. He had a big grin on his face. He was on the ball. I was not happy at being bested and turned the car round, back end facing the railway. Train passes. Barrier lifted. Soviet officer runs to gate to have barrier dropped. He gets no co-operation from German signalman. I put car into reverse and race 100 yards or more, well above normal reversing speed, around cars and onlookers and over the level-crossing, past more cars and into the entrance to a field, where we turn and get away. All the while Germans are laughing at the Sovs' embarrassment. My passenger said nothing to distract me but he knew that even Brixmis could not get away with running over civilians.

Regrettably, civilians did become casualties occasionally. One of the first cases occurred on Christmas Day 1949, when a driver, Leading Aircraftman Franklin, hit a German cyclist. According to Major Symes:

Franklin set off from the compound to pick up Brigadier and Mrs Curteis in Berlin to bring them back to their house in Potsdam so that they could spend some time with the troops. Just after leaving the compound there was a narrow alley, along which a drunken German was riding his bicycle. He shot out on to the road and was run over. Franklin was stone-cold sober.

The problem was what to do with the body. Rashly, someone decided it should be taken to the British Military Hospital in West Berlin. He was put in the boot of the Brigadier's car and taken through the checkpoint. He was dead.

I am not sure what happened to him. I think the body was returned to Potsdam. Franklin, I know, quickly left the

Mission for his own protection. Some time later the Russians sent in a bill for 1,000 Marks. Payment was refused and the incident died.

Twenty years later, Symes was a senior intelligence officer at the British Rhine Army headquarters in West Germany. 'A signal was received from Brixmis stating that a German had been run over by one of the drivers and the Russians were demanding monetary compensation. What should they do? I told the G-1 what had happened in 1949. A signal was sent to Brixmis saying, "Do not pay." We never heard anything more.'

There were other cases. Midshipman Chris King, a National Service sailor with the Mission in the 1950s, admitted: 'We knocked over a child at one point in one of the towns, down south. We just stopped and stayed there. The police came. The Russians came. Then we were allowed to go.' In the 1980s, Corporal Paul Hartley, a virtuoso driver, had some near misses 'driving at 120 m.p.h. through towns congested with traffic'. Captain Bob Longhorn, before he was PNG'd, hit a tractor, injuring the driver.

By the time Brierley joined Brixmis, the cars were modified with two hooks front and rear. The petrol tank was reinforced to protect it from obstacles hit in rough terrain. The boot held a reserve tank containing 100 litres of fuel. Though he did not say so, it is clear that a fully-laden tour car was a potential bomb in a serious crash. Switches on the dashboard could cut out the stop lights and the tail-lights. The tool kit included a winch and other 'de-bogging' gear as well as sand boards, ground anchor pins and a sledge hammer to drive them home. Several pairs of heavy leather gloves were carried to avoid 'frost burn' on hands in very cold weather when handling the winch and wire rope.

For nourishment, on a two-day tour, the team carried three glass-lined Thermos flasks filled with hot water. These occasionally blew up inside the car. They also had self-heating cans of soup and an army camping cooker, used when they were held at a Soviet kommandantura.

We often stayed out overnight. To handle harsh central European winters we were issued with two sleeping bags. There were those who could not get properly rested sitting up in the car and those who found they were with a heavy snorer. We would then sleep out on the ground.

I often woke to found myself covered in deep snow. I never felt cold. The 'modus' when you woke was to get out of sleeping bag into car, drive with heaters going full blast until we were thawed out, then halt for coffee and a sandwich. If there was a heavy snowfall overnight we would spend the first hour or so getting warm by winching ourselves out instead of having breakfast.

In time, it became normal practice for the driver to sleep in the car while the tour officer and NCO roughed it in 'bashas', bivvies or barns.

Good kit was indispensable but the most effective weapon available to a tour driver was quick wits. Brierley remembered:

I was on a tour with Colonel Badger. We were followed all day by a Stasi BMW. After midnight we stopped for a pee. The Stasi, parked twelve inches from our rear bumper, did likewise. Then we got back into the car and had coffee and a sandwich before settling down to sleep. I lay back and relaxed, one eye on the rear-view mirror. The narks obviously thought we couldn't get away without alerting them and they dropped off to sleep. I asked the Colonel if he wanted to get away and got a 'Yes'. I waited for the next big truck to come thundering past us. When it was making the most noise I hit the starter and we were away. The narks were zizzing contentedly, unaware that they had the lay-by all to themselves.

From time to time, Brierley was allocated to RAF tours which 'had a more difficult task because their interests (airfields, planes) were mostly in no-go areas and they had to be more pushy. They had two Land Rovers which were slow, but able to cross rough terrain.'

Life back at the Mission House was also eventful:

A scruffy character jumped through the open window of the ladies' room (no one was enthroned there) and was chased by a Vopo guard from the goon-box across the road who pulled his shoe off as he got into our building. We called the RSM. He alerted our duty officer in Berlin [John Cormack] and the American duty officer. They took the man upstairs to interrogate him. It turned out he had deserted some years earlier from the US Army and defected. We closed all shutters and windows, sent the domestic staff home (they were Soviet plants) and locked the doors. The man was released at the bottom of our garden after dark. There was nothing the Americans or we could do to repatriate him. We understood the Americans would try to get him out via East Berlin but we heard no more.

On 22 August 1968 the Soviet Tass news agency reported: 'The people of Czechoslovakia are showing gratitude for the timely arrival of Soviet troops.' Their gratitude took strange forms. Ordinary men and women fought against tanks with rocks, telegraph poles and anything else they could find to express their joy at the appearance of yet another invasion force on the streets of Prague. Like Neville Chamberlain's 1938 proclamation, 'Peace in our time', the Tass announcement was one of the great official lies of twentieth-century Europe. The betrayal of Czechoslovakia by Britain and France and their surrender to Hitler in 1938 foreshadowed the West's acceptance of the Soviet-led invasion of Prague exactly thirty years later.

In the 1960s, the Czechs did not dare hope for freedom as it was understood in the West. The defenestration of their Foreign Minister, Jan Masaryk, by communist assassins in 1948 had taught them caution. All they sought was 'socialism with a human face'. The new Soviet dictator, Leonid Brezhnev, detected in that desire a threat to the whole repressive apparatus upon which the myth of Marxist-socialism rested. As the ISS *Strategic Survey* for 1968 put it: 'The developments in Czechoslovakia threatened to disturb an equilibrium which was already precarious. There is little evidence to suggest that the process of democratization inside Czechoslovakia was regarded as a threat to the security – in any immediate sense of the word – of the Soviet Union or the Soviet system; much to indicate that it was regarded as a threat to the ability of the other governments to contain their own internal changes; few of them were prepared to contemplate the increased uncertainty which might have followed upon the success of the Czechoslovak experiment.'

The answer to this little local difficulty was the Brezhnev Doctrine, the use of jackboot and bullet to suppress any dissent in the Warsaw Pact satellites. Combined Warsaw Pact manoeuvres began on Czech soil on 20 June. It was low-profile stuff to begin with, a Staff exercise to test communications and procedures, a process known to Nato as a CPX or Command Post Exercise. Soon, tank and motor rifle divisions were also on the move. The CPX had become an FTX, a Field Training Exercise. In a sickening re-run of the Nazi invasion of 1938, some of these divisions were from Prussia.

The first hint that Brixmis had of what was in the wind was the Soviet announcement of temporary restricted areas (TRAs) excluding the Mission from three areas in the south-eastern corner of the GDR adjoining the Czech border. The three Western Missions combined forces to run patrols through the only routes still available to them. These were the autobahns.

From mid-July, Brixmis patrols spotted columns of stores vehicles and fuel tankers rolling at night down the Dresden and Karl-Marx-Stadt (Chemnitz) motorways. The Soviet 19 Motor Rifle Division swept out of its barracks at Dallgow-Döberitz at the end of the month, destination unknown. This move, whatever it was, was not the pell-mell rush regardless of security which had followed the Berlin Uprising of 1953; but it had an edge, an urgency, that did not go with an exercise either. Roy Giles, then a junior staff officer with the Mission, recalls seeing 19 Grenadier Motor Rifle Division, a crack East German unit, driving out of its barracks taking everything, including vehicles which had broken down. These they towed, adapting the decorative red-and-white chains from the barrack gates as improvised tow-lines. Soon after that, the regiment's families were evacuated. It seemed to Giles and others that they were watching the first steps towards a real operation, not a mere exercise. British higher command, however, would not believe it. As Giles put it: 'We said, "They are going to fight." Higher command said, "But you don't invade another country in Europe in the '60s."' '

Denied access to some of the key transit areas, Brixmis adopted a policy of intelligence-gathering through an observation of what could *not* be seen. The barracks of the Red Army's 71 Artillery Brigade and 6 Grenadier Motor Rifle Division at Bernau were reported empty on 22 July. The silent emptiness of a huge barracks at Halle suggested that the East German Army was also taking part in whatever was going on.

At the end of July, the Czech praesidium and Soviet politbureau met and defused the crisis. Or rather, the Soviets adopted a form of words amounting to a military deception plan. The Czech Communist Party would have 'the leading role' in the country and the Soviets 'would not interfere in the internal affairs of another socialist country'. On 3 August, it was announced that the last Soviet troops had left Czechoslovakia, though none of the Western Missions, including Brixmis, noticed that. A week later, the Czechoslovak communists made the mistake of recognizing the rights of minorities to hold dissenting views.

This was political suicide. The Soviet high command saw to it that Czechoslovakia was invaded across four frontiers rather than the 60-mile border shared with Russia itself. The ISS assessment was that the invasion force totalled 400,000, three-quarters of them Russian, with 50,000 Poles, 20,000 Hungarians and East Germans and 10,000 Bulgarians commanded by the Red Army General Pavlovsky. This army was still 10,000 fewer than the number of American GIs committed to war in Vietnam.

A typical news report said: 'People in Prague can be seen climbing on Soviet tanks and arguing with the men inside. Emil Zatopek, the Olympic gold medallist, appeared in his Colonel's uniform and told a crowd that the Russians had to go home. When Russians arrived to take over Prague radio, crowds blocked their way. An ammunition lorry exploded, setting fire to buildings and Russian tanks.'

The political significance of what happened largely under cover of darkness on the night of 20–21 August was later spelled out by *Pravda*. There was a new party dogma, the 'doctrine of the Socialist Commonwealth' combined with the 'doctrine of limited sovereignty', through which Moscow now asserted a right to intervene wherever socialism was threatened by the internal developments in one of its allies. In due course, the impact of the Brezhnev Doctrine would be felt far beyond Eastern Europe. The absence of a Western response could be explained only by US acceptance, tacit but real, of the Brezhnev Doctrine, a mirror-image of which, imposed from Washington, stoked French scepticism about American intentions.

If the Czechs were surprised by the Soviet invasion, Nato should not have been. The liaison missions were counting them out. An unofficial Brixmis memoir recorded: 'In conjunction with the French and American missions, the south-east autobahns were now being regularly patrolled twice in every twenty-four hours. During the nights of 20 to 25 August the missions observed 65 ambulances, 62 fuel bowsers, 192 medium tanks, several FROG [missile] elements including a minimum of four launchers, 22 anti-aircraft guns with associated radar and some 1,100 assorted logistic and support vehicles. All of them went south towards the Czech border and did not return.'

The Mission did not enjoy an uninterrupted view of the build-up: 'From the end of July through to the end of November, Vopo and nark security measures on the Dresden and Karl-Marx-Stadt autobahns were extremely severe. All fly-offs were guarded by armed Vopo, autobahn roadblocks were set up and mission cars were followed by up to six-vehicle nark teams at any one time.'

Nimble minds in Brixmis found ways through this problem. Squadron Leader Don Wistow wore a fur hat decorated with his RAF officer's eagle and oak leaves and an RAF greatcoat buttoned up to the neck. The effect was close to that of a Soviet uniform – so close that some Warsaw Pact forces saluted him – but not illegal. He and others, including Flight Lieutenant Peter Hearmon, a Russian speaker, discovered that it paid to have a British symbol on the tour car. East German truck drivers and even soldiers slipped notes to them, days in advance, saying: 'We are going to invade Czechoslovakia.' The warnings were passed to BAOR headquarters and elsewhere and disappeared into a political void.

In spite of the restrictions, Hearmon snatched good photographs of Soviet Mig-21 fighters, their fuselages marked with red bands just in front of the tailplane. These tactical markings, similar to the white bands on Allied aircraft over Normandy in 1944, were a signal to friendly gunners on the ground not to shoot at their own air force. The Czech Air Force flew the same machines, without the tactical strip. The implication was clear. The Czech Air Force might just defend Czechoslovakia against the Warsaw Pact invasion.

Harry Alderson of the Yorkshire infantry regiment, the Green Howards, was posted to Brixmis in January 1966 as a touring sergeant. He well remembers the Czech crisis.

As soon as we left the Glienicke Bridge the Stasi were waiting. From Potsdam there were about four routes. There were cars on every route. They would escort you, one in front, one behind. As soon as you saw a BMW you knew they were Stasi people from East Berlin. They always had their leather jackets on a coathanger inside the car and they always wore dark glasses.

In Karl-Marx-Stadt we counted between eight and ten cars, all Stasi. They didn't seem to know each other. They were trying to overtake one another to keep with us. They had Stasi cars on parallel routes to us as well as in front and behind. We saw them changing number plates. You'd try to lose them in woodland perhaps 30 kilometres from the intended target area, then hide out overnight and go and do the job next morning. You left the autobahn and swooped across country. Before and after the Czech revolution a network of informers developed throughout East Germany. You'd see people running to phone as soon as they saw one of our cars.

The Russians involved in the invasion were demoralized. Initially, some thought they were in Germany. One whole regiment had to go home. The Czech people were saying, 'Your fathers were liberators. Why are you killing us?' Lots of [Soviet] soldiers would not attack so they had to pull some [unsound] units out and bring others back in from Russia.

The warriors of Brixmis were anything but demoralized. They perceived the invasion as another great opportunity to catalogue the Soviet Army's secrets. A complete Scud brigade was watched, its order of battle carefully noted. A gas-mask and its nuclear warfare accessories, carelessly dropped from a convoy, were scooped up.

New electronic boxes added to the T-62 tank were photographed. So were two new battlefield detection systems, code-named Long Track (surveillance radar) and Thin Skin B (height-finding radar).

The Soviets were careful to leave a larger military presence in the 'northern tier' of Warsaw Pact territory, including East Germany, after the Czechoslovak crisis. Brixmis, a target for budget-cutters and others who regarded the Mission as a curious waste of military know-how, was back in fashion at Nato headquarters.

The ISS noted that year: 'The Czechoslovak invasion shattered the image of a mellowing, pacific Soviet Union and created the impression of Soviet unpredictability which, together with the Brezhnev Doctrine of limited sovereignty used to justify the invasion, helped give the Nato alliance a fresh sense of its relevance to European security . . . It also prompted the United States to begin mending her relations with her European allies.'

CHAPTER 7

The Double-cross Years

1969–74

On 21 October 1969, the Mayor of Berlin, Willy Brandt, became the first Social Democrat (that is, liberal) chancellor in Germany for thirty-nine years. A darling of the Left, and of the ladies, he scraped into office by two votes above the necessary minimum. Behind the joking philanderer there was a serious politician dedicated to improving the human condition, a charismatic man described by one Brixmis officer who heard him (Group Captain Jim Corbishley OBE AFC) as 'a magnetic, electrifying speaker'. Supported by democratic socialists throughout Western Europe, including Britain, Brandt set about Ostpolitik, the delicate process of offering an olive branch to the Soviets and their German clients. The trick was to get them to accept the olive without pulling him down, branch and all. Brandt was not to know that he would be pushed into the mire from behind.

The agency that betrayed Brandt over the next four years – mocking his Nobel Peace Prize – was HVA, or Hauptverwaltung Aufklärung, the East German intelligence service, headed by General Markus Wolf. Wolf was very good. His toy-boy Stasi agents seduced aging secretaries in West Germany's key ministries and were rewarded with state secrets.

One summary of this penetration includes: Technology Ministry, 1970; Social Democratic Party headquarters, 1974; Foreign Ministry, 1976; Defence Ministry, 1978; Christian Democrat headquarters, 1979; Chancellor's office, 1985 and 1988; Economics Ministry, 1985; and President's office, 1985. Wolf was also the benign uncle, for a time, to such plagues as Carlos the Jackal. And he planted Gunter Guillaume, a former Hitler Youth volunteer, on Brandt. Guillaume became liaison officer between Brandt and his Social Democratic Party.

Guillaume was one of around 7,000 Stasi agents in West Germany. His wife Christel was another. They had been working for the Stasi since the early 1950s. Guillaume's father returned home from a British war prison in 1948, found his wife living with another man and killed himself. Guillaume, it is thought, discovered a father-substitute in his father's contemporary Paul Laufer. Laufer was an HVA colonel. Thereafter, by extension, the party became Guillaume's parent. He was not the first or last spy to betray his country as a reaction to parental shortcomings; Philby was another.

Gunter and Christel Guillaume arrived in the West in 1956, just after the Soviet Communist Party had denounced Stalin, the year the Soviets invaded Hungary. These events did not deter Guillaume who was a spy by temperament rather than conviction; his knowledge of Marxist theory could be comfortably accommodated on a microdot. But by following the ground rules of strategic espionage, of which patience is the most important, he established a one-sided relationship of trust with Brandt. He was with Brandt on the famous election campaign train that criss-crossed West Germany in 1972. He was Figaro to Brandt's Count, with dangerous knowledge of the Chancellor's nocturnal life. Through Guillaume, journalists covering the campaign were admitted to the presence, one by one, on the train. One witness of the process recalls, 'The last reporter sent in was always the prettiest girl from the press corps.'

When Brandt became Chancellor, Guillaume was his link with the party and the trade unions. With access to Brandt's trust as well as his inner office, the HVA agent was ideally placed to interpret much of Brandt's thinking. That was intelligence not to be found in a barracks or a laboratory. It was priceless. The top-secret telegrams Guillaume read in the Chancellery were a mere bonus.

Brandt's resignation on 6 May 1974, for what he himself described as 'political negligence' prior to Guillaume's arrest, stunned the West and severely damaged Nato confidence in its German allies. This was a time when the Russians identified their three major adversaries as the US, China and West Germany. Brandt was a greater prize than, say, the British Prime Minister Edward Heath.

The Chancellor's crash did not surprise many people in Brixmis, who for four years had been reminded of the need 'to be more mindful of the risk of upsetting the new relationship'. Simultaneously they were asked to work harder than ever to verify arms control and missile treaties. The most important of these had some link with Brandt's Ostpolitik and its fruit, détente.

There were apparent gains from détente, in the short run. The Americans, scaling down their forces in Vietnam, emphasized the need for conventional weapons to defend Europe. Nato offered something called 'Mutual and Balanced Force Reductions' in such weapons. A four-power agreement in 1971 clarified the right of Berlin to exist as a free city with open transit through the GDR to West Germany.

Meanwhile, the East German Army re-equipped at a hectic pace, watched by Brixmis. In February 1970 Brixmis noted the first joint field exercise involving the East German and Soviet air forces. A Mission report recorded: 'The NVA [East German army] were observed carrying out night river crossing exercises with tanks fitted with both snorkels and mine ploughs: hardly a defensive act of war.' Joint Soviet–GDR nuclear warfare tests followed soon after.

Brixmis was being pressed to enhance its 'train-spotting' expertise, to become more sophisticated. As well as the latest SPG-9 recoilless gun and SAM-4 missile, what was wanted was 'an element of analysis and assessment at all levels'. As a British ambassador to Nato once said: 'We know what the Warsaw Pact's capabilities are. But what are their intentions?' The question which Guillaume was able to answer from the intimacy of the West German Chancellor's office, on behalf of the HVA, was essentially the same question that was implicit in the new Brixmis agenda of 'analysis and assessment'. In both cases, one side was trying to second-guess the other's intentions as well as capabilities. Unlike the HVA, Brixmis had to guess harder, starting with changes in patterns of weaponry and their use. Guillaume had only to listen to what Brandt said and read the Chancellor's highly secret signals.

Brixmis could also make some very good guesses. The SAM-4,

for example, was the Soviets' standard high-altitude air-defence missile commonly found guarding sensitive high command centres. 'The electronic signature from this SAM's radar was a way of pinpointing the headquarters,' one veteran said.

The Brixmis RAF squad opted for a high-risk strategy: moving into the target area by vehicle, as usual, having shaken off the narks, completing the approach on foot, or on all fours, through barbed wire, a mile away from the diplomatic and physical cover of the tour car. The chief exponents of this new tactic were Squadron Leader Rod Saar, a navigator with a taste for commando warfare, and his engineering colleague, Squadron Leader Frank White MBE. Saar made it clear to his team that what he proposed to do often broke all the rules and carried with it the potential penalty of being shot dead by Soviet sentries. Some of his men agreed to go with him. Others, exercising a legitimate right not to put their lives at risk by breaking the rules, did not. Two of his favourite targets were spiced with the additional risk of being bombed or machine-gunned from the air. There were the Gadow Rossow range used by the Soviet Air Force for live bombing practice and the Belgern range used for air-to-ground machine-gun and missile sorties.

On one such mission they set off at night, creeping into a pre-surveyed hide, hitting the target at dawn. Then, 'We sat on the ranges while they were actually bombing and used a cine-camera for the first time. We collected some of the hardware including 30mm and 21mm ammunition. We wanted a better understanding of the 21mm cannon fired from the new Fishbed J,' he said.

Next time they brought home an even larger souvenir. This was a special practice bomb, the detonator of which was armed by a small propeller on the nose. It was a primitive but effective piece of equipment, almost 5 feet long, containing a modest but lethal charge of 12lb of high explosive. It had been used in a raid on simulated hangars and had failed to explode. When he got close to it, he saw that the propeller had jammed. He decided to take it home.

One of the team was on his last Brixmis adventure before moving to his next posting. Saar, mindful of the need for consensus in sharing a calculated risk, asked his colleagues how they felt about taking it. They, like their boss, decided it would be a shame to leave a useful piece of kit lying around. It took three men to lift it: 'We couldn't get it into the boot of the car very easily and decided to lay it on the floor inside the back of the vehicle. Two of us sat in the back with feet resting on the thing. We didn't think the risk was any less if it had gone off in the boot or inside the vehicle proper. The result would have been the same.'

The journey to the Mission's Berlin headquarters took ninety minutes. Nobody said much. When they reached the building, they staggered to the lift. There was not much room to spare. The lift creaked slowly to the top floor. The door clanked open and the three sweating men puffed out, with the bomb, on their way to the RAF end of the Mission. They were met on the corridor by a senior officer.

'Hello, Rod, what've you got there?' he asked.

'Unexploded bomb, sir,' the Squadron Leader answered cheerily.

The arrival of the bomb in the air force office caused some disruption. The office was emptied while bomb-disposal experts were summoned to take it somewhere safer, but only after Saar had photographed it. He went on leave. When he got back, he found an Ordnance Accident Report on his desk, 'with a polite note from the Brigadier asking me to read it, advising me not to bring any more UXB's back to the office'.

Saar asserted that there was a good reason for such operations: 'We wanted to get a message across. When the Russians got into the space race we built them up as giants. In fact, much of their fighting equipment was terribly crude. We wanted to illustrate that and we succeeded.'

Others, including Lieutenant-Colonel Nigel Wylde, wince at this 'foolish heroism'. Wylde, an ordnance expert who won a Queen's Gallantry Medal for dealing with terrorist bombs in Ulster, recalls other, similar cases. His advice was to photograph any spare bomb or shell they found, with a note of its location, so that a specialist could inspect the bomb on its own ground.

An even more spectacular (and risky) operation was to photograph a Fitter bomber as it dropped a simulated nuclear bomb on Gadow Rossow range. This was an air-burst weapon that produced a mushroom cloud. During the same reconnaissance, the team also photographed the first tactical air-to-surface (TASM) missile seen by the West attached to a Fitter. Saar's debriefing after that was at the headquarters of RAF Germany, conducted by Air Chief Marshal Sir Michael Martin, the Dambuster veteran then commanding the Allied air forces in Germany.

The high-risk penetration of bombing and machine-gun ranges (on to which spent cartridge cases as well as live bullets rained) guaranteed that the work was uninterrupted by the Stasi or other security teams. As Saar explained: 'The narks didn't appreciate that we were foolhardy enough to sit on the range while it was active. They were in the vicinity but they didn't come any closer. We sat under the flight path of attacking aircraft, just short of the bombing range.'

When Saar used the same approach to stalk radar arrays directing SAM-2 anti-aircraft missile batteries, the risk of detection was greater. Saar climbed inside these sites. 'They were surrounded by first, wooden fences, then electrified fences, finally by three separate rings of barbed wire. There was a distance of 300 to 400 metres from the inner to the outer fence, surrounded by pine forest. If you wanted a good [photographic] shot of the radar, you had to climb through the wire.'

He used forked sticks to hold the barbed wire high enough to crawl beneath, following dead ground, in a manoeuvre reminiscent of some of the RAF's great escapes from captivity during the Second World War. This trick he used three times on one installation near Dresden. By breaking in at first light, or lunch time, and timing his exits during those periods, he was, he thought, safe enough. These were the times when the guards tended to be less alert. Nevertheless, he had 'the odd fright', such as the time when 'an East German officer and a soldier were between me and my way out. They did not see me . . . [but] I could have got shot.' The car was a mile away or more, concealed in undergrowth. 'My instruction to the team was that if it got hot, they would have to hop it and return an hour later.' The E & E (Escape and Evasion) drill, with its emergency rendezvous agreed in advance, was bread-and-butter routine among special forces; less usual within the RAF except for those deadly exercises in Arctic escape and survival usually conducted in Bavaria, in winter.

At night, Saar and his men used night-vision equipment

developed for the Vietnam War to examine tactical, dispersed air-strips for use by the Soviets in wartime and warlike exercises. Nato needed to know the maximum weight these strips could sustain. They were basically constructed of specially prepared grass. What type of fighter with what fuel and ordnance loaded could fly from them? How easily could they be put out of action? The Brixmis squad, using a special tool, bored holes every 100 yards to a depth of 10 inches, drawing samples from the earth which were sent to a London laboratory for analysis.

Things did not always go according to plan, even when Saar was undetected. Soviet Fishbed reconnaissance aircraft had been fitted with a new pod, full of interesting electronics, beneath the fuselage. All the Allied Missions had been trying to get a close-up photograph of the pod. Then they heard that the aircraft was visible at Allstedt airfield.

Saar got in close inside the airfield with a 500mm lens on his camera. The lens was relatively light and easily trained on the target. He shot many frames in good light, trying to concentrate solely on the job in hand. 'Only when the film was developed did we find that the pictures were blurred through camera-shake. This was due to my own physical nervousness. The airfield was very exposed, with just the odd bush for cover. A Russian soldier and officer were nearby, walking the perimeter close to my tracks in the grass ... They could have spotted me and opened fire any moment.'

While Brixmis watched the garrisons, the Stasi, as usual, watched Brixmis. The attack on an RAF team which included the Mission's newly-appointed deputy Chief, Group Captain Corbishley, re-minded the team that, regardless of the spirit of détente elsewhere, it was still playing a risky game. Saar had developed a novel tech-nique for getting the narks off his back which was about to get him into trouble.

Like a buffalo that stalks its hunter, he would move on foot in a circle to surprise the Stasi from the rear, then charge at them, yelling war cries. They were apprehensive and officially embar-rassed, since their status as 'authorized citizens of the GDR', and nothing more, was as dubious as the right of the Brixmis team to penetrate a high-security airfield. So when Saar bounced them, the shock was usually enough to induce them to run for it; usually, but not invariably.

In the early hours of 6 September 1972, a Brixmis air tour cruised cautiously towards a well-established Soviet Air Force base at Welzow. The team comprised Squadron Leader Rod Saar, his new boss, Group Captain Jim Corbishley, and their driver Corporal Donald Calvin RAF. This was Corbishley's first experience of the sharp end of Mission operations. To ease him into the techniques of covert work, Saar took him to a well-established observation post, used many times during the previous two years. That, as events were to prove, was not a good idea. Both the Stasi and Soviet KGB were beginning to target people who repeatedly used the same route to the same hides. In some cases, the Russian equivalent of the SAS, the Spetznaz, were on call to deal with such cases.

Saar's tour had followed the usual de-narking drill and was satisfied that no one had followed it. The surprise was that someone was already waiting. Around lunch time, the tour driver, who was keeping watch for signs that they were compromised, said he thought someone was in the bushes. A Brixmis account of the event described later how 'the tour climbed into the car, covered up all the equipment and Squadron Leader Saar went to investigate'. Saar himself said:

It was important to get the Group Captain used to the idea of being tracked, without pushing things to the limit ... I left the others in the car and ran at what I could see, something lying down. I thought I had a nark. I did not realize this was a platoon of armed Soviets with an officer who had already drawn his pistol.

I charged, shouting vigorously. They rose from the ground. There was no way to escape. As I turned tail they ran towards me. They pinned me to the ground and stuck an AK [Kalashnikov assault rifle] into my neck. They then smashed the driver's window of our car and knocked the driver, Corporal Calvin, unconscious with a rifle butt. They left the Group Captain alone. They knew what we were. The night before we had been seen by a local on a motor-bike and he had tipped off the authorities. That was our problem.

The Soviets – almost certainly Spetznaz – removed all the equipment from the car. They were particularly interested in a Russian-made 1,000mm-long lens which the team had procured, via a diplomatic bag, from Moscow. Shortly afterwards a Soviet photographic team arrived and photographed the car, its crew and all the equipment. 'Then,' said a Brixmis report, 'the local Commandant arrived and the atmosphere cooled down somewhat as everybody present embarked on the "normal" round of accusations, counter-accusations and denials, during which the "Akt" [an admission of guilt] was produced and the tour duly refused to sign.'

Brixmis was aggrieved that the car should be broken into. 'It was always considered "inviolate" and it came as a severe shock that the Soviets should behave so brutally to a tour which was carrying out, by normal standards, a routine RAF operation.'

From a Soviet standpoint, the operation was anything but routine. A secret British report on the de-brief of a Stasi defector analysed the opposition's tactics:

Sometimes the Soviets would provide the MfS [Stasi] with prior warning of a new equipment entering the GDR in order to protect it. MfS would then mount an operation deploying surveillance teams . . . Such operations could last several weeks. Surveillance operators would live in tents or caravans in the area of the target and deploy from there. The team would be briefed on the basis of an appreciation by the Analysis Cell in Potsdam. They would consider who, from the Allied Missions, would be likely to attack the target based on perceived specializations and how the target would be approached by the Mission crew based on routes, Op locations, etc.

Another role of the mobile surveillance teams was to photograph or video mission teams photographing targets . . . One of the main aims of mounting deliberately planned detention operations was to prove a direct link between the Missions and national intelligence services in the form of captured equipment or documents . . . If a Soviet Mission crew was detained in the FRG [West Germany] the order would be passed to the MfS by the KGB department in Potsdam to attempt a reciprocal detention . . . Alternatively, if a member of the Mission was deemed to set patterns whilst touring that could be exploited, he would be targeted. An officer in the French Mission was successfully ambushed and detained because he persistently approached an identified OP from the same direction. A special squad was set up based in Zossen Wünsdorf [the Soviet military HQ in East Germany] composed of either GRU [Main Intelligence Directorate] or Spetsnaz personnel ... The special detention squad would be supported on the ground by MfS personnel dressed in Soviet uniform.

Saar's compromised air tour could have fallen into several of these categories. The bruises healed and the usual protests were exchanged. Saar was declared *persona non grata* by the Soviet high command at Zossen. As Colonel-General V. Yakushin said in his protest: 'Squadron Leader Saar, having violated earlier the provisions of the Robertson–Malinin Agreement, can no longer remain a member of your Mission.' Under the rules of the game, Saar was removed from the Mission, but on paper only. Ostensibly posted a short distance away to RAF Gatow in Berlin, he remained at the Mission headquarters for a year. The joint headquarters of RAF Germany and BAOR retaliated by sacking, on a tit-for-tat basis, one of the stars on the Soviet Soxmis team in West Germany. Among other signals, this action removed any taint of failure on Saar's part. As one of his colleagues put it: 'Rod Saar was PNG'd for being too good at his job.' Saar was also awarded the MBE.

Saar's adventures were matched by those of Staff Sergeant (later, Major) Mike Seale. Seale was a Parachute Regiment veteran slowly recovering from wounds suffered during the hidden war in Oman. He could travel through most of East Germany without touching a metalled road and was never detained by either Stasi or KGB in more than two years with the Mission. He moved stealthily with a car that had been specially reconstructed in Britain. Apparently a normal Opel Senator saloon it was, in practice, a four-wheel off-road vehicle that could travel anywhere. When stealth did not work, he rammed the opposition.

Seale also made a practice of leaving his driver and car concealed far from his target before going forward on foot, sometimes for hours at a time. He varied his routes and times so much that his approach always caught the opposition by surprise.

Seale's greatest coup was to obtain clear photographs, at close range, of radar controlling the SA-6 missile (the same weapon that shot down an American F16 fighter in Bosnia in 1995). He recalled:

We had unconfirmed reports about a new 'Sam' missile being brought into East Germany from Russia, half confirmed by the silhouettes of cargoes carried by goods trains coming from the East. Then, passing a Soviet barracks at Magdeburg, I caught a glimpse of something interesting.

I planned the operation so that the vehicle got into the general vicinity of the target in darkness. I then went on foot to arrive at the wall surrounding the barracks as dawn was breaking. We had carefully watched the sentries and knew that they were on 'stag' [static guard duty] for three hours and off for six. And they were conscripts. What did that add up to? It meant they were fairly alert at the beginning of the shift; more than ready not to get involved in anything when it was time to knock off and get to bed.

This was particularly true of the dog watch that ended just after dawn. Armed only with a Leica camera and 500mm lens, Seale scaled the high wall as if it were just another training aid. He looked carefully over and was warmed by the sight of the new battery and its radar, thinly covered by a camouflage net. A young, weary sentry glanced in his direction. Their eyes met. Seale was certain the man saw him but fatigue was the winner. The sentry carefully turned his back and walked away as the camera focused on the Soviets' latest secret.

As a hardened, clever NCO he led newly-arrived tour officers on their first patrols. Since the heart of the job was information collation, impeccable reporting of long convoys and fast-moving train cargoes was imperative. With a throat mike fitted to a tape recorder, one man (usually a senior NCO) called the type and number of each vehicle while a second (usually the officer) used a motor-drive camera. One system backed up the other in producing an exhaustive written report back at the Brixmis headquarters. 'We never

returned from a tour with less than twenty rolls of exposed film,'
Seale said.

Intensive homework followed the reports. Each Friday, tour
crews which were not in the field were expected to attend recognition classes at 10 A.M. sharp, to revise and polish their knowledge
of Warsaw Pact weapons systems. These included every type of
hardware imaginable, from motor-cycles to tank transporters and
the numbers or symbols identifying the unit from which they came.
In the afternoon, at 3 P.M. sharp, there was a test on the morning's
work.

During the Mission's final phase, another veteran recalled, 'Recognition' with a capital R took place every morning from 0830 to
0900 hours. Everybody was issued with a Recognition Manual in
fifty-seven sections. This covered every known piece of equipment
used by the Group of Soviet Forces in Germany. One section was
covered each day by a tour NCO with a box of fifty slides. Recognition was the responsibility of the staff officer grade 2 (Weapons).
Afterwards, a short test was held. Everybody, from the Mission
Chief to the newest driver, attended. Each month a written test of
100 items was staged. Those not reaching a very high mark 'went
through a series of interviews to encourage them to improve'. They
always did.

Throughout the next two years the détente bandwagon continued
rolling in Europe, apparently untouched by the explosions just
over the horizon. These included the Middle East oil crisis and the
Yom Kippur War. The Soviet leader Brezhnev backed the Arabs. US
President Nixon sustained Israel. That apart, Brezhnev and Nixon
smiled at one another over an increasingly sceptical Europe. They
had reason to smile. The year 1973 was the first since the Second
World War in which one of the major powers was not directly
involved in bloodshed. From now on, for some years, hot wars
would be fought by surrogates in the Third World.

Europe hunkered down to its own affairs. The UK at last joined
the European Community and tried political band-aid in Ireland.
Milestones were laid in relations between the two Germanies,
including a treaty between East and West for 'good-neighbourly
relations' (December 1972) and simultaneous membership of the

UN by both (September 1973). Britain recognized East Germany in February 1973 and opened an embassy in East Berlin a few months later.

One officer, a fluent Russian speaker who spent four years with Brixmis, promoted his own personal form of détente which he described as 'town touring' to pick up political gossip. It led to overnight stops in hotels, visits to bars and restaurants and even dances at the Soviet officers' club at Potsdam (where his British uniform was misidentified as Polish). It occasionally led him into trouble, and once into a brawl not of his seeking. These events yielded no intelligence coups, as he confirmed. His overall view of the Mission's work was: 'I don't believe we gained much that was not known anyway by other methods from the '70s onwards. It was useful confirmation and possibly led to some material being given a lower security classification.'

The Chief of Brixmis at this time was Brigadier David Baines MBE, a forthright leader who told his teams to ignore most of the signs posted by the authorities warning Brixmis tours to keep away from military training areas and others deemed sensitive by the Soviets or East Germans. The signs, for the most part, were invalid and, as he said, 'were being used wholesale to keep us out of places where we had every right to be'.

As one veteran of that period put it: 'David made it clear we should go through the signs but not if we were being followed by narks.' Some signs were collected by the tours as souvenirs. The Brigadier was a collector himself, but he encouraged a low-profile approach to such activities to reduce the risk that the Soviets would protest to BAOR headquarters in West Germany for, as he put it, 'it was my firm view that the less our beloved HQ knew about certain aspects of our affairs, the better'. Nevertheless, the wrangle about the 'Keep Out' signs prompted a 'narkfest', a campaign of pressure on the tours, in March 1973. Tour cars and other mission vehicles were held for hours at the roadside by Stasi patrols.

The existence of a full-blown British embassy in the GDR added a new layer of communication and complexity to the work of the Mission. As Brigadier Baines noted later: 'There was no [official] link between Embassy and Mission, but even before the Ambassador [Curtis Keeble] arrived, his Head of Chancery started to attend our weekly Mission briefing sessions and sometimes provided interesting intelligence following journeys through Permanently Restricted Areas [which even Baines had to acknowledge] which were inaccessible to us ... We were keen to maintain the closest possible personal contact with the Ambassador and his staff for obvious reasons.'

The Head of Chancery was a talented, elegant woman who later represented Britain at the Vatican. 'She was,' said Brigadier Baines later, 'always a welcome visitor and not just because she had a fondness for see-through blouses. She would happily agree to drive through Permanently Restricted Area signs and then tell us what she had seen.'

Some incoming diplomats were puzzled about the Allied Missions' self-contradictory roles of friendly liaison and predatory spying, creeping up on the Russians in the dark of a training area while entertaining them with the film version of *The Sound of Music* at the Mission House. There was a third, deeply secret, *raison d'être* which no one explained to them but which, some Brixmis soldiers believed, was the most important in those days and for long after. This was that Brixmis was the ideal cover for other sources of intelligence which had to be protected from accidental compromise when their 'product' was circulated within the Allied intelligence community.

Those ultra-sensitive sources needed a plausible alternative to the agency from which their highly secret data originated. Attributing it to one of the Western Missions operating behind the front line deflected embarrassing questions about the true source. In that sense, Brixmis was a stalking horse or, at the very least, a collateral against which to confirm information gleaned from other, more sensitive sources. Major (later Lieutenant-Colonel) Mike Wiskin recalled: 'While the Mission carried out its basic functions highly effectively, it was most pleasing for pro-Russians like myself to improve relations and fête the Sovs wherever possible. Mission House receptions were always a success ... *The Sound of Music* where the enemy was common to both of us and the music and scenery sufficiently *Kulturnij* [aesthetic], was a howling success. The Babushkas wailed into their hankies whilst a slack handful of generals commented approvingly on the Caucasian landscape.'

Wiskin followed through such contacts to identify the anglers among the Soviet officers: 'In return for relatively minor favours, such as bits of uniform and badges, I provided quality fishing accessories to several Sovs including a likeable rogue called Captain Yuri Sakharov, who found it difficult to control his hormones when confronted by Western women.'

At the 1973 Christmas party at the US Mission House, Wiskin and a Russian officer, Major Andrei Malavko – both Gunners – swapped uniforms in the men's room. 'We emerged truimphantly at the top of the stairs and joined the assembled throng to applause. The whole thing came unstuck when a senior Russian, who had left earlier, returned for some reason and an embarrassing scene ensued, after which we were forced to revert to our proper uniforms.'

Wiskin liked most Russians because 'they were like us: good at improvising, extremely cynical with a great sense of humour and an endless appetite for drink and tobacco'. He did not think a Warsaw Pact invasion of the West likely at that time, 'though if the Soviet leadership perceived it was beginning to slip behind militarily, or that it faced an unacceptable threat, it might be tempted . . .'

Nevertheless, he did what was necessary as a tour officer, and more. While he and his crew watched a tank division flowing past on military trains at Wittenberge, they 'were surrounded on three sides by a Motor Rifle Divisional HQ, with the commander's BTR-60PA [armoured vehicle] only a few yards away. On several occasions we thought we had blown it when soldiers came for a leak in the clump of bushes where we were hiding. Amazingly, we got away with it, by extending the tour for forty-eight hours. Before finally leaving we had a most productive rubbish scavenge around the Div HQ position.'

Life on tour was enlivened by the unexpected. On a dirt track near Satzkorn, Wiskin's car was overtaken by a motor-cycle, at high speed. The occupants were not wearing crash helmets. The crew surveyed the local area and, on the way back, saw the motorcyclist kissing goodbye to his erstwhile passenger. Seconds later, 'the bike roared past us again, trailing a massive dust cloud . . . Suddenly we came upon the bike, on its side, the rider motionless beside it.' Among many standing instructions to Mission crews, one said they should not stop for an accident unless it was imperative. Wiskin was not prepared to drive past an injured man. In this case, the casualty's skull was smashed, brain tissue exposed, but he was still breathing. Wiskin inserted a shell dressing to keep the wound clean while his sergeant ran to a nearby house for help. The man died on his way to hospital. Unusually, the People's Police sent a thank you to Brixmis.

The new diplomatic contact between London and East Berlin was to lead to some interesting adventures. For years, Mission officers and their wives had visited the huge trade fair at East Germany's second city, Leipzig. The consumer goods were drab by Western standards but, on the industrial side, the Soviets had a long lead on the West in metallurgy. There was usually some interesting nugget of intelligence to be collected there. Furthermore, as Brigadier Baines put it: 'One stayed at the reasonably comfortable Astoria Hotel and although the exhibition itself was of no great interest, the social atmosphere was convivial and relaxed and at various receptions and dinners we would meet British MPs, business visitors and the occasional Soviet trade minister.' Such left-wingers as Ian Mikardo and Jo Richardson 'were regular visitors'.

Britain's new ambassador in East Berlin, Curtis Keeble, had four tickets for a gala performance at Leipzig during trade fair week, to be attended by Erich Honecker, the GDR leader who had taken over from Walter Ulbricht. Keeble could not attend. Could Baines go? The brigadier could. The embassy team urged the brigadier to go along in civilian dress. This was not the way Brixmis usually operated; as Flight Lieutenant Yates had learned twenty-seven years earlier (see Chapter 1), it could provoke misunderstandings and worse.

'Major Michael Cawse was the Mission's technical intelligence officer. He and his wife Mary were staying in Leipzig with my wife, Honor, and myself . . . Michael and I put on our dinner jackets and drove with our wives in the Chief's black car [with British emblems] to the Opera House, parking in the square outside.'

An odd atmosphere developed around them as the evening dragged on from one ballet excerpt to the next political speech and back again. The British party were aware of a growing presence of

Soviet soldiers round them. As they left after the performance they were corralled by a phalanx of Russian soldiers. On the square, their car stood isolated and alone, guarded at all four corners as if it were a funeral bier. Dozens of other limousines had gone.

The row – essentially about the protocol of British military men dressing as civilians – continued into the early hours. The two British wives refused to leave Leipzig before the shops opened next morning, so that they could retrieve goods they had paid for. They won their point. Next morning, the Soviet escort back to Potsdam made an impressive convoy, but the Russian leading it could not read his map. Baines obligingly took over the navigation. His black limousine flying the Union flag led the caravan until it was nearly home. 'There we halted, briefed the young officer carefully on the directions to the Soviet offices and let him lead us for the last mile or so.'

One Soviet officer was happy to navigate his own way out of East Germany. With the help of Brixmis, he was about to defect from the KGB, to the West. Captain Aleksei Myagkov, aged twenty-nine, was the political officer attached to three battalions of the 82nd Motorized Rifle Guards Regiment based at Bernau, twelve miles north-east of Berlin. Myagkov was good at his job, which was to blackmail military officers into acting as informers on one another. For this, he required a talent to simulate friendship. The 'friendship' was invariably a prelude to betrayal. Myagkov developed a bad conscience about the raging corruption that touched every part of the Soviet army. He decided that the best way out was to become an agent of Western intelligence. This he did for two years, from 1972.

Early in 1974, he sensed that the game was almost up. A meeting with his MI6 contact in East Berlin almost ended in disaster. The rendezvous was elaborately staked-out by Stasi officers who did not recognize him, but knew his contact. He spent the next five hours or more eluding them.

On 2 February, with a waterproof cape under his officer's great-coat – a prelude to disguise as a civilian – a pistol in his pocket and a briefcase loaded with top secret documents, he joined the soldiers' bus trip to West Berlin. It was a cultural visit in which there were only two official stops: the Charlottenburg Palace and the Soviet

War Memorial near the Brandenburg Gate. His plan was flawed. While he watched the soldiers, two other KGB men watched him.

As the group paused in front of the palace for photographs, Myagkov bolted into the building, scurried through corridors towards the rear of the building, locked himself into a small back room and breathed hard. Slowly, he realized he was not alone. An elderly German was quietly munching his lunchtime sandwich. Myagkov wrote later: 'I said, "Everything is all right, daddy. Enjoy your meal." Despite the seriousness of the situation, I burst out laughing.'

Myagkov told the German to telephone the police, telling them that a Soviet officer wanted political asylum. It was a long time before they arrived. They explained that because this was the British Sector, the British had to be consulted. By the time he was picked up by an easily identified Brixmis car at the police station opposite the palace, the KGB prowl cars were waiting. They followed the defector to the gates of the Brixmis headquarters in the Olympic Stadium building. Myagkov quietly cursed the indiscretion that might set him up as a target for assassination.

It was 4 P.M. before a British official, other than an armed guard, arrived to tell him that London was aware of his case. The officer added: 'Your presence here is like having an atom bomb on the premises. It will be best for everyone if we get you out of here as quickly as possible.'

Myagkov, who had now handed over his gun, was not reassured. His joke that the razor brought to him, so that he could shave, might be an invitation to suicide, was not well received. The guards removed the razor. Just down the corridor, a diplomatic tug-o'-war was in progress. Myagkov had hardly removed his coat when the Chief of Brixmis, Brigadier Baines, took a telephone call from Colonel Ivan Skurikhin, deputy chief of SERB.

'Skurikhin always looked as if he had nothing to do and drank quantities of vodka to relieve the boredom,' Brigadier Baines remembered. 'He was now being harried by Colonel-General Yakushin, the Chief of Staff at Soviet Army headquarters, a brutal individual who was a member of the Supreme Soviet.'

Skurikhin wanted to call on Baines at the Berlin headquarters. 'Their aim, of course, was to see the defector Myagkov and persuade him to return. Ours was to get him out of Berlin as quickly as possible, before too much diplomatic pressure or publicity could build up.'

As a compromise and to play for time, the Brixmis boss invited Colonel Skurikhin to his official home at Stuhmer Allee in West Berlin. The Russian arrived just at 7 P.M. Skurikhin's version of the case was: 'while travelling through the British Sector, Captain Myagkov had a breakdown in his car and went for help. He has remained somewhere in the British sector. We request you to do whatever is possible to return him to the Soviet sector.'

While the brigadier ostensibly searched for Myagkov, the brigadier's wife, Honor, with a Brixmis intelligence officer, Major Roy Giles, entertained the Soviet colonel and the colonel's interpreter, a young captain. Brigadier Baines and his wife knew Skurikhin and others on the Soviet liaison team well. They found 'the lovely sense of humour of the Russians made them much more like ourselves than the Germans'. Honor Baines regularly went to Soviet celebrations with Seraphima Nyurin, wife of the head of the Soviet liaison team. (Seraphima was 'a splendid lady who had fought as a sniper in the war'.) They had seen Skurikhin at an American party, dressed for fun in British officer's uniform, 'carried out to his car by the three Soviet generals he was supposed to be looking after, being thrown in the back and driven off by the trio of generals in the front, with no repercussions afterwards'.

Abruptly, with the defection of Myagkov, the party was over.

There ensued a difficult six or seven hours. Honor and Roy Giles ... did their best to keep Skurikhin under control, if not exactly happy, with copious supplies of eggs, bacon and alcohol, while every now and then I had a telephone conversation with him, repeating the official line that Skurikhin would be taken to see Myagkov provided Myagkov agreed to see him, which of course he never did.

At 10.30 P.M., two sets of civilian clothes were brought to the office where Myagkov and his escort, a captain, waited. Myagkov was told that they would leave the building at 11 P.M. and get into an unmarked car. He would sit in the rear, between two escorts.

The car would take the party to a helicopter in which, with his captain still minding him, he would fly to Gatow, the RAF airfield in Berlin. Myagkov wrote: 'These precautions were taken because of the very real risk of an attack by Soviet agents who might try and kidnap me. The British had alerted one of their units to strengthen security during the operation.

'We left the building; got into the car; drove fifty metres and stopped at the helicopter which was waiting with its engine running. Around us could be seen British soldiers in full battle-dress, with automatic weapons in their hands and tense faces. With the captain, we got into the helicopter quickly and it took off immediately.'

At this stage, Brigadier Baines said, 'Honor remembers rather strained discussions on comparative salaries, education and housing. Skurikhin found it difficult to believe that 10 Stuhmer Allee [a mansion] was a house for just one family.'

The whipping, rhythmic roar of the helicopter engine ended the small talk. 'The helicopter was heard flying in and, moments later, taking off directly over the house. Skurikhin's face, always pale, turned green and Honor thought he was going to be sick. But he pulled himself together, said a few words of thanks and left.'

The defector Myagkov was not out of the wood yet. From Gatow, he was transferred to a fixed-wing aircraft with two escorts and two pilots. None made any attempt to conceal the tension they felt. As Myagkov noted, 'The aircraft was of Second World War vintage and had a maximum speed of only 280 km (175 miles) per hour. We were flying over East German territory. Despite our two escorting fighters, there was a real chance of being shot down by a Soviet missile, by 'accident'. At last the long flight over East Germany was over and as we crossed the frontier into West German air space, the atmosphere in the aircraft brightened noticeably. Everyone began to smile. The captain congratulated me on my safe arrival in the West.'

Meanwhile, Brigadier Baines's policy of disregarding Soviet keep-out signs, unless they were part of a carefully notified area of restrictions agreed at high level, was adding to the tension. To complicate matters further, Baines recalled, 'the Soviets tried to force us to accept passes which included wording that brought in the GDR as an authority to control our movements. We refused and went on using out-of-date passes. There was a series of incidents including holding a convoy of Mission wives returning from Leipzig.' The Mission stood its ground and the Soviets backed off.

In the field, things were no better. On 9 February 1973 Squadron Leader (later Air Commodore) Brian Speed and his team – Sergeant E. Doherty and Corporal E. Roper – were shot at by a sentry in an East German suburb. Or, as the Soviet protest note later put it: 'Speed . . . again flagrantly violated the rules . . . when they entered the area of a military installation guarded by restriction signs, in the built-up area of Teterow. After this, Squadron Leader Speed approached the sentry guarding the target and provoked him into opening warning fire . . . It was only by lucky chance that Squadron Leader Speed's actions did not lead to more serious consequences.'

The same note referred to Corbishley's latest detention four days later and to the Saar episode the previous year. Baines met the Soviet liaison team on 15 February and, after a long discussion, said that he was 'glad to know that members of the Missions were not liable to be shot at whenever they were near Soviet or East German installations'. The minutes of the meeting record that, as it ended, Colonel Nyurin (representing SERB) presented Major K. B. D. Aitken (a Brixmis tour officer) with 'a Russian winter uniform hat, as a leaving present. The welcome and atmosphere throughout were most relaxed and friendly.'

The shootings continued. The liaison Missions' score-card logged a total of nine during 1973, five involving members of the US Mission, three aimed at Brixmis and one at the French Mission.

In West Germany, the blundering counter-espionage service, the Cologne-based *Bundesamt für Verfassungsschutz* (BfV) was at last focusing its sights on the spy in Brandt's office. In May 1973, a trawl through intercepts of East German radio signals recorded in 1956 and 1957 identified a coded message destined for 'G.G.' The message was anything but warlike; it was, 'Remembering you on your birthday.' The Germans take their birthdays seriously. Morale depends on it, even at the risk of compromising a top spy. BfV double-checked the record to see whose date of birth this was. They came up with Gunter Guillaume.

A surveillance operation began but, incredibly, was lifted again when both the Guillaumes accompanied Brandt on a trip to Norway in July. There they handled all Brandt's correspondence including twelve secret telegrams, some of them from Washington. Eleven months passed before Guillaume and his wife answered the BfV's knock early on 24 April 1974. Gunter Guillaume immediately revealed himself as 'a citizen of the GDR and its officer'. He did not exactly echo the phrase, to which the British Mission was now well accustomed, 'an authorized citizen of the GDR', but he did not need to. The only people who were surprised by this turn of events were those who had trusted the good faith of East Germany.

CHAPTER 8

Brezhnev's Xanadu

1976–80

In little more than a year, from 1976 to 1977, the Soviet leader Leonid Brezhnev binged on power. At the sixtieth anniversary of the Bolshevik 1917 Revolution, all the top military jobs were his. He was Marshal of the Soviet Union; Chairman of the Defence Council and Supreme Commander-in-Chief of the Soviet Armed Forces. All senior political offices were his also. He was chairman of the Presidium (that is, head of state) and boss of the Communist Party which – thanks to the new constitution he had just built to replace Stalin's – was formally recognized as 'the leading, guiding force . . . the nucleus of the political system'.

Yet still the new Kubla Khan's Xanadu was incomplete. 'Consolidating world socialism' and 'supporting national liberation struggles' were also inscribed on the Brezhnev constitution. No secret intelligence was required to discover that Soviet communism was entering upon another fit of expansionism, propagated – like some medieval religion – by the sword and proclaimed from the pulpit of *Pravda*.

Neither the man nor the society that fabricated these absurd illusions was remotely capable of making them come true. An already crippled Soviet economy was saved only through grain supplied by the United States. An already ailing leader was on a downward path towards Alzheimer's, or something very like it, in 1974. By 1982, as death approached, one insider noted the Supreme Commander's vacant stare, his disorientation: 'He would read notes to the Presidium specially prepared for him printed in large characters . . . the same sentences over and over again, looking around pathetically as if acknowledging his helplessness.'

His domestic arrangements were as surreal as his strategy. As the writer Jeanne Vronskaya noted in her obituary of Mrs Victoria Brezhnev in 1995: 'She put up with her husband's young mistress living in the house, a married woman with a child, as well as his nurse, who had a powerful grip over him during his last ten years. It was that "Mata Hari", the KGB's nickname for her, who made Brezhnev an addict to the tablets which eventually killed him.' When he was not in those hands, his bodyguard Medvedev had greatest control over the supreme leader.

Brezhnev had instigated the KGB coup that overturned his predecessor Khrushchev in 1964. Within four years he had nodded approval, like a caesar at the Games, to the rape of Czechoslovakia. He did not learn. As his brain shrank, his ambition grew. The result, in 1979, was the KGB assassination of the Afghan president and the invasion of that country: the first Russian adventure outside the communist bloc since 1945. The US, still licking the wounds of Vietnam, did not intervene. But these were not times to place much faith in détente or Kremlin promises. These were years in which the risk of world war by accident or misunderstanding was also greater than at any time since the beginning of the Cold War.

The West was not invulnerable. Since the oil crisis of 1973, it had discovered that former client states in the Arabian Gulf were clients no longer, but masters of the West's oil-guzzling economies. Any move by the Soviets towards Iran, whether through the new deep-sea Soviet fleet or overland, through Afghanistan, was viewed with alarm. The West's oil war would happen, eventually, in 1990–91 with the Soviet's erstwhile client Saddam Hussein as the adversary. During the 1970s, these things could be perceived only dimly, if at all. They were years, nevertheless, in which the original role of Brixmis – war prevention – merited an equal place on the agenda with intelligence-gathering.

On the ground in Germany, the three Western Missions were working together more effectively than at any previous time. In 1974, for example, three combined operations were orchestrated. Operation Pinocchio had as its target photographs and any other details to be gleaned about a new self-propelled gun. One of the Missions nabbed it as it emerged from the sanctuary of the

Letzlinger Heide training area. Under the code-name Spring Blossom, the Missions dogged the Soviet army's élite 9 Guards Tank Division to discern what level of recruits were being posted into it. Finally there was the familiar chore of watching Soviet troop rotations by train, known as Operation Troika. The numbers of men leaving ceremonially for Russia, garlanded by flaxen-haired German girls in a spurious display of solidarity, were sometimes fewer than the replacements that arrived unannounced, after dark, in cattle trucks.

The British team, meanwhile, was benefiting from its closer links with the American Mission when it received its first night-vision goggles (NVGs) from the US. By early 1975, they were standard equipment. The British had always treated the night as a friend. NVGs, enhancing ambient starlight in a pale green glow, removed much of the hazardous guesswork. The hazards included wild boar which were not invariably friendly. All teams now carried minia-ture tape recorders. Later in the year, Range Rovers supplemented Opels.

The RAF watch on Soviet aircraft was also sharpened up with 1,000mm lenses and motor-driven cameras, both useful in bagging pictures of the latest Flogger fast jet and Hind-D helicopter gunship. In May, the Backfire bomber was added to the growing 'butterfly collection'. Later, pictures of new missiles, including Apex and Aphid, were snatched.

The price to be paid was the usual one: entrapment by waiting Spetznaz heavies and a brutal beating with, among other weapons, a rifle butt. Since the missions never carried arms as part of the pretence that they were simple liaison officers, they were literally on to a hiding-to-nothing. On 27 September 1974 an air tour comprising Squadron Leader (later Air Commodore) Brian Speed, Flight Sergeant Cooper and Corporal Wimhurst was attacked by twelve Soviet thugs, their car broken into and ransacked, and their hands tied behind their backs as they were hurled into the back of a Zil-130 truck. It was twelve hours before the formalities were complete and the team was released. Speed was found to have a broken collar bone.

On 9 July 1975, under a hot sun, a team lead by Flight Lieutenant Davies was surprised at Zerbst airfield. Then, says a Brixmis report,

'They were placed in the rear of a GAZ-66 truck with the canvas body of the vehicle sealed in high temperatures for several hours.'

RAF teams who sweated blood to get their material were less than amused when some of their most prized photographs appeared in American aviation journals almost as promptly as at official top secret briefings. This happened at least four times in 1975. The leaks were never traced.

Army teams, more mobile than their RAF comrades, were sometimes exposed to even greater risk. Out of reach of the fist and boot, they got the bullet instead. Two of them were shot at during 1975. A Brixmis memoir told the story:

> On 18 February Captain [later Colonel] Robin Greenham's tour was operating in the neighbourhood of Reitz and observing a well-known tactical route when a Soviet soldier armed with an AKM [Kalashnikov assault rifle] appeared some 30 metres in front of the car. The tour drove up to the soldier who unslung his weapon. The tour made it clear that they intended to drive on and passed the soldier. He in turn told the tour officer to get out of the car and turn the engine off ... The tour officer replied that he had no reason to stop them ... When the tour had gone about 100 metres the soldier was seen to fire one round from the hip hitting the car and one from a standing position which missed.

The bullet penetrated the boot and hit a cross member where it fragmented harmlessly.

The second shooting occurred in the early hours of 24 April. A tour officer was carrying out what was described as 'a reconnaissance of a Soviet installation at Belzig', apparently on foot. He encountered a Soviet sentry 'who pursued the officer whilst firing wild shots, possibly to summon help. The sentry abandoned the chase after firing two final aimed shots and the tour were able to leave the area without further incident.'

These shots were not heard in London. On 19 March, Britain – the sick man of Europe's economy – announced defence cuts involving 38,000 soldiers over the following four years and withdrawal of the Royal Navy from the Mediterranean. Even well-upholstered officials at Nato's political headquarters at Brussels felt the shock-waves from that. The British, who had been in the Mediterranean since Nelson's victory on the Nile, were ceding the southern , maritime flank to Admiral Gorshkov's new expansionist Soviet Navy. They expressed what diplomatists like to call 'disquiet'. It made no difference. Brezhnev took note and prepared for further empire-building.

In Helsinki, the theoretical fruits of détente were codified in an elaborate agreement protecting human rights and guaranteeing early warning of troop movements. The Kremlin promptly breached both these arrangements. The following year, as Britain signed a consular agreement with East Germany (the first Nato nation to do so) the GDR secretly trained irregulars of the Baader–Meinhof and other terrorist groups to attack targets in the West. Soon the Stasi would open a training school at remote Schloss Wartin, where hijackers would learn to storm and seize civil airliners.

For Brixmis, 1976 was memorable for renewed rammings as well as some useful intelligence coups. On 6 April a tour car was deliberately hit by an East German Wartburg saloon, driven by a man in civilian clothes. Brixmis noted: 'The tour car, unlike the Wartburg, was able to continue on its way.' Next day, 'a Soviet UAZ-69A swerved across the road from the oncoming lane. In attempting to avoid it, the tour car hit a tree, severely damaging the vehicle.'

The Mission's senior staff officer (G-1) at the time, Lieutenant-Colonel Jerry Blake, recalled driving quietly in a tour car on a country road when 'this random East German army truck coming the opposite way suddenly drove straight at us. My driver took off the road, through trees and into a field. The truck followed us and came screaming along behind us. We scorched through the centre of Wittenberg and the truck still followed, determined to get us.'

Worse followed in September, the military exercise season. At six o'clock one evening near Finsterwalde, an Opel Admiral tour car with Major Simon Gordon-Duff and Sergeant (later Captain) R. E. M. (Bob) Thomas was forced off the road by two motor-cycles. As it tried to regain the road, the car was deliberately rammed by a 9-ton Ural-375 truck from a nearby East German installation. The Ural ran up the near side of the tour car, over the bonnet and the front right-hand side of the passenger compartment. A Mission report said: 'Its momentum carried it clear of the car where it turned over on its side.'

The tour NCO, Sergeant Thomas, was trapped in the wreck, his leg broken. Local civilians helped to get him out. East German soldiers who tried to help were called back by their officers. Thomas, semi-conscious, lay in the wreck for an hour, his right leg fractured in four places. He also had head and rib injuries. He wrote later:

> I have vague recollections of lying close to the car after I was dragged out, gazing at my right foot, which was facing my left ankle . . . Some time later I remember someone twisting my right leg and I passed out. I came-to, to find that I was being driven along a bumpy road, lying on the bench seat in the rear of a Barkas ambulance, with a maniac for a driver. On every corner he braked violently and I was shunted along the seat until my legs hit the back door. After the second or third burst of abuse from me, I passed out again. Later I recall lying on a concrete floor with water soaking through my shirt. The room was lit by an unshaded bulb and I could hear someone talking about me in German. A doctor then approached me and cut off my trousers.

He spent several grotesque days in an East German hospital where the surgeons bungled the process of pinning the fracture so badly that, a few weeks later, stepping off a pavement in England, Thomas felt his leg buckle beneath him. British surgeons found that the pin in his leg had rusted through. Meanwhile Major Gordon-Duff and his driver were left, 'severely shocked and bruised', to wait for help from their own mission. This arrived from Berlin about twelve hours later.

Through the rest of the year, the shooting continued and the victims were not only soldiers. On 6 August, for example, an Italian civilian lorry driver was shot dead by East German border guards in an episode opaquely described as 'a border incident'.

The reward for Brixmis bruises included a first sighting of the T-64 main battle tank and air support of ground forces by Flogger-B, Fitter-D and Hind helicopters. The T-64 and Hind were an 'item'. In battle, the tanks depended on close fire support from the helicopter gunships. The T-64 introduced automatic gun-loading, reducing the crew from four to three and ending a long-standing joke about Soviet tanks. This was that their catastrophic internal layout demanded 'a strong, left-handed dwarf' to load the main gun.

The mandarins of Military Intelligence in London, with a scant notion of what the Mission did, issued special equipment with which, they hoped, tour officers could touch the newest Soviet tank, the T-64, so as to analyse the depth of its armoured hull. It was regarded at the time as the best of Russian armour, the tank they would use against their Warsaw Pact Allies if those Allies turned against them. The anxiety of Whitehall to know about the composition of its armour was understandable, but as Lieutenant-Colonel Blake drily noted: 'Whitehall did not always appreciate that we were perhaps not in a position to rush on a T-64 to stick a gadget into it.'

In parallel with the nocturnal stealth, the ambushes, the violence there was, as ever, elegant protocol, the round of diplomatic ritual that marked the departure of one senior officer from the Mission and the arrival of his successor. These two incompatible elements came together unexpectedly when Brigadier L. A. D. Harrod OBE, the British head of Mission since 1974, moved on in October 1976.

Harrod was on his way in his official staff car, Brixmis No. 1, to the Soviet Army headquarters at Zossen Wünsdorf to thank the Russians with whom he had vigorously quarrelled about the beatings they had handed out to his men. The Soviet escort vehicle, leading his, broke down. Harrod invited the Russian captain to ride with him. As they approached the sentries and barriers across the road, the Soviet officer told them a secret. It was that one flick of the car headlights would convince the watchdogs that VIPs were coming. No identification would be demanded. The barrier would be raised without question. Harrod's driver tried it. The trick worked. Harrod was charmed. So were the rest of his team. The device, which could be described as Harrod's Revenge, was used for a long time after that.

According to a Brixmis memoir: 'This was incorporated into the touring tricks of the trade with great success. In particular, when approaching [Soviet] traffic regulators to gain an indication of which way the column was due to pass, a quick flick of the lights often produced better information than bribery with cigarettes and hot soup.'

In 1977 – the year they celebrated the diamond jubilee of the Bolshevik victory, the year of Brezhnev's power binge – the communists hit the West at several levels and got away with it through bluff, bluster and deception. First, there was the West's 'own-goal', the story of the enhanced radiation nuke, a tactical, battlefield warhead designed by Americans for use with the Lance missile in Europe. The energy of neutrons would penetrate tanks, killing the crews, but with less explosive power than other nuclear weapons required. The weapon threatened less potential damage to civilian areas around the battlefield. Its 'prompt' radiation dissipated rapidly. A *Washington Post* news story inaccurately described it as 'the neutron bomb'. The mythology grew, bankrolled by Soviet propaganda, that this was a weapon that destroyed life while leaving property intact. It was now a sinister paradigm for the capitalist system. Dutch church leaders leaned on their government. The Netherlands led the critics at Nato's Nuclear Planning Group. President Carter wobbled. The weapon was officially designated 'militarily useful but politically sensitive', and discarded. The whole episode was a triumph for Soviet 'psyops', advised by, among others, Kim Philby.

In Paris meanwhile, President Giscard d'Estaing assured Brezhnev that 'French forces are independent of Nato'. He seemed to have overlooked the co-operation between his Mission beyond the front line with those of Britain and the USA. A few weeks later, on 28 July, 100 Soviet submarines exercised a mass 'break-out' around Norway into the deep water of the Atlantic. The message was clear: a submarine blockade of Europe was still possible.

In the late summer, as Brixmis and others followed the Warsaw Pact manoeuvres in East Germany, a new, deniable form of warfare was unleashed against West Germany by terrorists trained in East Germany and Syria. The bluff was that this was the 'New Left', anarchist-syndicalist and anti-Soviet, rallying to Proudhon's battle-cry, 'Property is theft!'

It was truth that was hijacked, as usual. With the training and arms supplies in the GDR came, when necessary, new identities and sanctuary. Those benefiting from communist hospitality included Susanne Albrecht, a Baader–Meinhof and Red Army Faction terrorist who helped kill a banker friend of her middle-class family. She was one of many New Left terrorists, described by one author as 'Hitler's Children' on account of their anti-Semitism, arrested in East Germany after reunification.

In 1977, however, their kidnap and sadistic murder of Hans-Martin Schleyer, leader of West Germany's industrialists, followed by the Lufthansa hijack to Mogadishu, ended by GSG-9 with British SAS help, all seemed to represent a conflict with no links to the Cold War; a revolt by spoiled children of the middle classes against the idea of defending any advanced Western society, justified by the calamity of Vietnam. They succeeded, for the rest of the Cold War years, in absorbing the energy and attention of agencies which would otherwise have been paying attention to the KGB and East German HVA. Like the neutron affair it was a brilliantly managed campaign of destabilization through subversion.

Brezhnev's regime rounded off a stunning performance at the end of 1977 with a massive air- and sea-lift of arms and Cuban fighters to support Ethiopia, then at war in the Horn of Africa. America could only protest about 'illegal overflights'. Public opinion in the US would not have tolerated anything more emphatic. The difference between the superpowers, apart from America's economic superiority, was that the USSR had not yet been humbled by its own 'Vietnam experience'.

In this febrile atmosphere, the pressure was still on Brixmis. At the picturesque tourist town of Angermünde, in April, a Brixmis car was blocked by an East German army truck, then rammed by a police car. Soon afterwards, with the sun rising over a compromised observation post, Captain (later Lieutenant-Colonel) John Crosland MC, an SAS tour officer, legged it as the shots flew. The incident began, said a Brixmis account, 'a lively chase across country lasting until the afternoon when a dramatic detention was finally effected'.

Crosland was accompanied by another SAS soldier, Sergeant-Major (later Major) Nick Angus BEM, in an escapade aimed at stealing a Russian sign warning Allied Missions to keep their distance. (ATTENTION! Passage of Members of Foreign Military Liaison Missions PROHIBITED!) These were regarded as desirable souvenirs for the downstairs loo at home. The two noted some brand-new signs during a tour of the north-east. Angus said: 'We waited until it was dark and then crept towards the newest sign, on the edge of, or just inside, a training area and started work to remove it. We'd not done much when the night's peace was shattered by some extremely loud – and close – shooting ... Exit very quickly two of Her Majesty's highly trained, brave, etc., killers, sans sign!' Angus made good the loss later.

Two days after Crosland's detention, another tour officer, a specialist in map-making, was detained at Ludwigslust by the Soviet commandant in person. In a sophisticated display of *noblesse oblige*, 'the commandant produced a bucket of water and sponge with which to clean the car number plates. When satisfied with the result he released the tour car.'

As they ducked and weaved, the mission crews noted that a lot of new equipment was coming into the hands of the Soviet and East German troops around them. Potentially, the new equipment was as destabilizing as Baader–Meinhof subversion. Efforts to reduce European tension at the mutual Force Reduction talks were being undermined, as the International Institute for Strategic Studies (IISS), noted, 'by widespread Western concern that recent improvements in Warsaw Pact forces had given the East the capability to launch an attack with little warning'. The search was on for Confidence Building Measures (CBM) such as the right by Nato to fly reconnaissance missions over areas from which a surprise attack might come, in particular Soviet airfields nearest the Inner German Border.

Evidently unaware of the Western Missions, or their true purpose behind a camouflage of protocol and liaison, the IISS continued: 'Satellite reconnaissance will remain an uncertain way of monitoring movements of conventional forces. A more certain way would be to post observers (one's own, or neutral) on enemy territory. Assured observation together with measures to ensure that it takes longer to prepare for war – such as limitations of forward storage of ammunition or fuel – should reduce fear of short-warning attack. Restrictions on secure radio traffic, except on notified exercises, might also be reassuring since a sudden burst of coded radio traffic would indicate something alarming.'

In fact, one of the Mission's most valuable roles was to provide factual confirmation of what was learned from other, more secret sources including satellites and agents on the Foreign Office payroll. As Lieutenant-Colonel Blake explained: 'Very often we would produce something from our trips unaware that we were delivering collateral for someone else's work. You happened to photograph a kit train carrying, say, a new missile. This would be perhaps the first time people had proof that it was in East Germany. Alternatively, we enabled material gathered from some other source to enjoy a wider circulation. It was valuable.'

The Mission's forte was its use of a target of opportunity. Blake, who had occasionally suffered loss of face when detected, was released from detention late one night and set off home. Soon came the change of luck, the chance encounter: 'The whole of a Russian armoured division going through a little town and we photographed the whole of it by the light of a single light in the town square. When we ran out of film, at about 4 A.M. we "ran" the remainder of the column, recording what we saw on tape.'

Through 1978, as Brezhnev's condition visibly deteriorated, the Soviet arsenal increased. The IISS reported that, by the end of the year, 'Eastern Europe was waiting for the end of the Brezhnev era in Moscow' with 'a mix of uncertainty, hope and apprehensiveness'. After twenty passive years, the Kremlin modernized its medium-range (3,500 miles) nuclear missile option with a 35-foot mobile rocket named SS-20. The first of these, outside existing arms control agreements, were on Poland's border with East Germany by the end of January. By midsummer, 300 had been deployed. In May, as part of the continuing 'spy wars', American counter-espionage teams checked out their own newly-built Moscow embassy and found it to be infested with KGB listening devices. They then chose to stay in the old, unmodernized building.

Between 2 and 11 July, Soviet forces staged their biggest field exercise for three years in Central Europe. It gave Brixmis the chance to deliver to Nato the first warning of tracked self-propelled artillery guns, the 2S-1 and 2S-3 on German soil, in Soviet hands. The number of new, sophisticated surface-to-air missiles such as

SA-9 and SA-6 was growing and Brixmis was counting them in, in spite of the likelihood of detection, punishment and detention. The multiple rocket-launcher BM-22, armed with sixteen launch tubes and mounted on a lorry, came into service. A battalion of eighteen was reckoned to be able to fire 720 of these fearsome weapons in thirty seconds over a distance of eight miles: ideal for delivering a barrage of poison gas.

In the air, pilotless DR-3 drones and mine-laying HIP helicopters appeared in April and were duly logged by the British Mission. Brixmis recorded the addition of a new anti-tank missile ('Swatter') fitted to the Hind-D helicopter in September to be followed soon after by the Soviet equivalent of Awacs: an airborne command post operating from an AN-26 Curl air transport. As Brixmis itself put it, by mid-1979 the Soviet and East German forces posed on the border with the West had 'undergone a major re-equipment programme, enabling the Warsaw Pact to have a most potent forward air capability ranged against Nato ... Combined with modernization of the ground forces, this presented the West at the start of the new decade with a most formidable threat scenario.'

The winter of 1977–78 gave the airmen with Brixmis a chance to note something about Soviet air operations that contradicted the textbook guidance from air intelligence in London. At the time Air Commodore Mike Rayson was deputy Chief of the Mission. He explained: 'The official view was that Soviet helicopters such as the Hind could not operate in severe winter conditions with lots of ice, snow and slush because that affected the efficiency of the rotary blades on the machines. We went to take a look and saw the same helicopters flying in conditions which were supposedly unfit.'

The knowledge was to be of great importance when the Soviets invaded Afghanistan, in mid-winter. While the watch on airfields, live bombing and missile ranges and radar sites continued, so the RAF contingent of Brixmis remained at risk though, with their own airfield defences at home in mind, the British airmen sometimes wondered why the Russians never used guard dogs. Rayson, who liked to take his turn on 'air tours' (sneaking through the undergrowth to watch the opposition's tactics), was watching helicopter training. He was interested in the flight 'envelope' of these big machines. Suddenly they were spotted and the driver took off at speed, downhill, only to find that their car was surrounded. 'They tried to block us with their vehicles. We went for it. They had their guns levelled as we drove past. The driver took the car over a 5-feet drop, across a ditch, to get us out of it.' The 'air tour' was now airborne. The springs of the Opel Admiral groaned as the machine hit the ground.

The leader of the RAF group within Brixmis was no safer when flying the unit's two-seat Chipmunk trainer. He returned from one routine trip to discover a bullet hole in one of the propeller bosses. His colleague Squadron Leader (later Group Captain) David Williams OBE suffered a broken arm when his car was hit by a Russian vehicle. His tour of Brixmis was almost over but he could no longer drive his own car home to England. Rayson, due to deliver a talk to an intelligence training centre in England, did the job instead.

Nick Angus, the SAS representative on the Mission, remembered the stress and fatigue imprinted on the faces of a Dave Williams tour. 'The stress of touring was not only caused by the normal, run-of-the-mill accidents or enemy action, but from the sheer necessity of having to be awake, alert and observant all the time; all the hours of daylight, getting into your LUP [laying-up point] for a few hours' sleep, probably inside the installation or exercise area to which you were tasked, for first light.'

In spite of the stress, few people cracked. As Air Commodore Rayson put it: 'The guys took it as a challenge. We were doing a worthwhile job. It was really operational. It was magic. As a Group Captain I should have been sitting behind a desk, bored to hell. To go out on a ground tour or be one of the "flight of angels" around Berlin was fantastic . . . even though the Chipmunk was very cold to fly in winter. "Running" a [Soviet] convoy on the ground was one of the most adrenalin-pumping experiences I have had.'

One of those who joined the Mission as a tour NCO at about that time was Staff Sergeant Graham Geary BEM, a Royal Engineer. The tour NCO spent more time than most on the road, savouring the risk with the surprise, 'calling' (into a tape recorder) the identification of Soviet vehicles with the facility of a cattlemarket auctioneer. With Captain (later Lieutenant-Colonel) M. H. Auchinleck and Corporal Phil Roper – another Brixmis novice – driving, Geary was on his third trip. The destination was the industrial city of Karl-Marx-Stadt (Chemnitz), on the approaches to the Czech border. It was 'a prize target' and 'a hostile city to Missions'.

They arrived in the city at about 5 A.M. and began to establish an observation post. The Vopo arrived in a Lada, without safety-belts. It was still dark. The British car was showing no rear lights. A chase began.

Away we went at high speed, through K-M-S. Going past the station, things started to warm up. We came within inches of causing a fatality and almost knocked over an old lady ... The Vopo were hard behind us: sirens, lights flashing. The Boss called over to Phil, 'Are your brakes OK?' Phil said, 'Yes, my brakes are fine.' The Boss said, 'OK, wait till we get out on to the straight stretch of the road out of town and when I tell you, just touch your brakes.'

We hit the straight road. Vopo were right up behind us. Boss said, 'Do it now, Phil.' He put his foot on the brakes, probably a little too hard for comfort; the Vopo ran straight into the back of us. I could see through my mirror what happened next. As they were both unbelted the passenger put his head through the wind-screen; starred the windscreen badly. I could see smearings of blood all over the inside and on his face. By this time we had started to pick up again. We had got some distance down the road. The Boss looked over his shoulder. He said, 'I think we had better stop. We could be in serious trouble here, lads.' So we just pulled over to the side of the road. It couldn't have been more than five minutes later when four Vopo pulled up. Within ten minutes two cars pulled up full of MfS [Stasi secret police]. They started going about their normal business of photographing. The injured Vopo was reeling around, blood all over his face; troops trying to comfort him; the Vopo put a car behind us and a civilian car in front of us.

Both Phil and I were covering our faces, trying not to be photo-graphed, holding up maps inside the car, turning away from them, trying to make life as difficult as possible. Feelings were running high. We'd injured one of their guys. Their officer said to the policeman, 'If either of those two in the car move, shoot them.' I understood this in spite of my poor German. The policeman said he didn't have a problem with that. He unbuttoned his holster. They meant business. They were there for the kill. I wanted to get into the glove compartment for the duration and stay there.

After a tense hour, a Soviet officer arrived to arbitrate. Auchinleck, a Russian speaker, played the 'wartime comrades' card: 'The Vopos claimed we had stood on our brakes but they couldn't prove that. Our counter-argument was that they rammed us in an attempt to stop us from getting out of town. Eventually, the "Auk" was able to draw the commandant to one side and press his point. A bottle of Scotch was passed. This wasn't unusual. It was almost mandatory for the tours to carry a bottle of booze, 200 cigarettes and Mars Bars for the kids. There was no drinking on our part in the field. It was to smooth the way with commandants.'

The affair ended in a handshake between the British and Soviet officers.

A short time later, Geary was learning the finer points of close-up convoy observation from a roadside ditch near Wittenberge, near the Elbe frontier with West Germany.

Our car was backed into some trees; I was out in a ditch right alongside the road and just the other side of the bush was the tour officer, Captain [later Major] Ron Boryer. I was lying down so I was getting an up view of the vehicles as they rolled past my head. The Boss wasn't comfortable with our OP. I was too new to know any different. He was an experienced guy and he wanted to move across the road and into a wooded area where we could set up a more valuable, advantageous OP. He was going to get into the car, cross the road with the car, I was to run after him. It was a small country road, no big deal. He didn't get into the car. He waved it across into the woods, then got into the car. I then ran over the road.

As Geary trotted across the road he was spotted by the crew of a Soviet UAZ-469 military police truck. He got into the tour car, preparing for escape.

We started to drive around the wood. We drove on to a tree stump. It was sod's law. The driver's inexperience made no difference. It was a leafy, stump-bound wood. A Soviet colonel, tanks-on-black [insignia], I'll never forget, got out of the 469, walked round the car, checked it out, went to the back of the car, and removed our number plate. He then got back into his 469 and left. At that point, it was game set and match to the Soviets. We have no way of moving without that number plate. It was a pretty effective way of keeping us in one location ... There were no Soviet sentries but we didn't leave the car.

After about an hour, the Russian was back, with reinforcements. The Brixmis team occupied the waiting time photographing some new Soviet equipment as it rolled past.

It started to drizzle. They put a couple of guys around us. Les Eltherington [their driver] decided he wanted a cigarette. I told him not to open his quarterlight. He said, 'They're not going to do anything.' He 'cracked' his quarterlight to smoke his cigarette. One of the Soviet sentries saw this and put the barrel of his AK [Kalashnikov assault rifle] through the window. I realized that the weapon – now about 12 inches from Les's left leg – was the new AK-74. Heard a lot about them but it was also a first sighting.

I leant over and took the serial number off the weapon through the window; put that in the tape recorder; Les tried to push the barrel of the AK out while the Soviet soldier was trying to squeeze it in; I was also trying to make my point to him that he should have left the window closed. A young Soviet second lieutenant came along and told the guy to take the gun out of the window, which he did. We shut the window.

Until then, the only accurate image the West had had of the AK-74 was its brief appearance on a Moscow parade, in the hands of Soviet paras. Following the success of the American lightweight Armalite rifle, with its small calibre/high velocity bullet, the Russians had created a similar weapon. As one standard reference book put it in 1980: 'When it appeared on the parade, this totally new weapon had passed through design tests, troop trials and into production without a word leaking to the West. No official data has [sic] yet been published.' Corporal Eltherington's need to smoke, and Staff Sergeant Geary's professional habit of observing everything in detail, provided the mission with a uniquely close examination of the new gun.

Soon afterwards the Mission was asked by Military Intelligence in London to collect some live bullets for the AK-74. The task was passed to an adventurous pair of spirits: the youthful Captain Hugh McLeod and a hardened SAS veteran of the Dhofar war, Sergeant-Major Ken Connor. They drove north towards a Soviet training area near Neustrelitz in late summer. The main road ran conveniently near the rifle range. As Connor remembered it: 'We saw blokes walking up to the range with AK-74s in their hands . . . Perfect.'

Waiting for dusk before scouring the range for bullets dropped by careless conscripts, the British crew parked their vehicle in woods near a sensitive railway sidings, brewing tea from time to time. 'Then we drove back to the range where these people had been walking. We had heard them shooting and drove the Range Rover in that direction. Then we moved on foot to the firing point and started searching.' It was now dark. McLeod searched the ground around the trench. Connor jumped into it and gently swept his hands along the floor until his fingers touched something cold, metal and cylindrical, a bullet-shaped object even smaller, at 5.45mm, than the American Armalite. It was, unquestionably, what they were looking for. He tried again, passing his hand over the dark earth like a magician and found a second unspent bullet. Someone had been very careless. Possibly the Russians, unlike British soldiers, did not have to account for every spent cartridge and live round at the end of a live-fire exercise.

'We've got some here, Boss,' said Connor. McLeod, who would encounter greater adventures a few months later, asked how the older man had done it. 'Experience,' Connor said. In fact, as he admitted later, it was one of those lucky breaks.

This was, as things turned out, a lucky tour. At the sidings where they had spent the first part of the day a train of flatbeds had stopped, carrying the Soviets' new T-64 main battle tank. The composition of the tank's hull was vital knowledge before an anti-tank missile could be devised which would have a chance of stopping an armoured attack. Sensing an opportunity, three times during the day and early evening they drove up the main road which crossed the sidings by a bridge. This not only confirmed that the tank was still there and apparently unguarded, but it also enabled them to check the ground and make a plan.

The tank was located on a flatbed some 50 metres from a signal box across the sidings. This meant that their access to the tank would be limited but they reasoned they could still 'scratch' it. This was a technique which Brixmis often used. The object was to obtain a sample, on the spot, of the tank armour. The tool they used was a super-hard, tungsten-tipped 'pen' which, when scratched on the surface of metal, collected a sample on the cutting edge. Previous efforts had failed to penetrate the hardened paint, down to the metal. This time, the Mission crew planned to cut through the paint with a hacksaw. Such were their thoughts as they cruised quietly past their target. They were also able to confirm that they had found a reasonably safe route in, even though the signalbox would probably remain manned as darkness fell. Around midnight, they backed quietly down a track leading to the sidings. As they reached it, McLeod and Connor left their driver, Corporal Wayne Fury, with the 'One Eye' night viewing device as a check that they remained undisturbed.

McLeod and Connor then crawled down a ditch at the edge of the track, into the sidings, until they reached the tank. This shielded them from the gaze of a watchful signalman. McLeod cut the front of the tarpaulin and Connor, the expert in identifying Soviet fighting vehicles, reached inside to confirm that it was indeed a T-64. It was. It took only a few seconds for them to hacksaw and 'scratch' both frontal armour and turret. 'We were back in Berlin before first light,' Connor remembered, 'with two good "scoops" in a single eighteen-hour tour.'

A few months later they had the additional satisfaction of meeting an MoD scientist who briefed them in layman's terms on the results of the night's work. They had collected more than paint. The hacksaw had proved mightier than the sword.

*   *   *

Not every tour flowed so smoothly. On a track near Prenzlau, north-east of Berlin, on 11 December 1980, Connor was giving two Brixmis novices their first taste of the business of entering an area barred to the Mission, with the aid of a plausible alibi if they were caught. The trick was known as 'passing signs'. Essentially, it was a tortuous process of finding a way into the target area on unmarked roads. Prenzlau, he warned his pupils, was an East German army garrison. East Germans might tolerate nosy British interest in the Soviet Army but they were less sympathetic if their boys were targeted.

They had only just entered forbidden territory when their vehicle, Brixmis car No. 7, a usually reliable Opel Senator, caught fire. They were now sitting on a potential bomb, equipped with reserve fuel tanks. The fuel load, early in the patrol, was around 150 litres. Analysing the fault later, Connor believed that while travelling across country they had caught the underside of the vehicle on a rock and punctured a brake-fluid supply line. The system had then overheated. 'We grabbed what we could, got out and ran like blue-arsed flies. The cameras were the most important item. We ran some distance and hid those, then ran back to the car, by which time we had a full range of Stasi, Vopo and local civilians.'

Connor took off across country to find a civilian telephone, from which he called the Mission duty officer at Potsdam. A long interview with the local Soviet commandant at his headquarters followed, via an attractive female interpreter. Captain McLeod arrived with another vehicle. The Soviets and East Germans now had teams of soldiers scouring the countryside after dark in search of the hidden cameras. 'They knew there was something there,' said Connor, 'but they did not go far enough.'

During the long wait for diplomatic formalities to be completed, McLeod and Connor cruised off into the darkness, breaching protocol, and retrieved the cameras. They were only gone thirty minutes. There was a row when they returned to the kommandantura. They said they had been to buy food from a local shop. The story was implausible but the Soviet commandant knew there was nothing he could do about it. Like many before and after, he shrugged, said goodbye and don't come back too soon.

A Brixmis memoir filled out that picture somewhat. It asserted that the recovery operation involved a Soviet crane and that 'Soviet officers discovered hidden tour equipment and retained it in front of both tour crews under much protest. The bags [containing the equipment] were not returned until January 1981 after much correspondence . . . The incident gave the Soviets an incentive to go to any lengths to retrieve Brixmis equipment.'

As the SAS representative at Brixmis, Connor had his own, deeply secret agenda concealed even from other members of the Mission. This was the role of British special forces operating behind enemy lines in a European war. Since 1961 the volunteer reservists of two Territorial Army SAS regiments had been experimenting with light but strong prefabricated materials so as to dig secure underground hides in West Germany, near the border. When – if – the Russians invaded, the reservists would lie concealed while the war swept past them. They would then report by radio, in morse, on Soviet movements. At least thirty sites were earmarked for the hides. Though details of their location were top secret, the units' role was an open secret among many people in Rhine Army. By the late 1960s it was also known to the KGB and East German intelligence which tried, unsuccessfully, to penetrate one of the SAS teams involved.

Connor had other fish to fry. In an entirely separate operation the regular, battle-hardened special forces regiment known as 22 SAS, based at Hereford, had earmarked a squadron to penetrate through the front line into communist territory to watch the flow of Warsaw Pact columns at certain choke points and, if necessary, to attack them. This tactically offensive role was successfully kept top secret.

From time to time, as new information about Soviet war plans trickled through to Nato from agents, defectors and other sources, the SAS plans – locked in a safe at Brixmis' Berlin headquarters – had to be updated. That meant a visit to a covert observation post that might now be past its shelf-life. Little or nothing was said to the driver about the destination or the reason why. Such mysteries are a normal, need-to-know part of army life. Professional soldiers rapidly acquire the sense to know when not to ask questions. This was especially true of the sources of some information that Brixmis was asked to double-check. 'The Hill' was a source they all knew: a signals intelligence listening post working from a high point in West Berlin. Connor's successor, Sergeant-Major (later Major) Jeff Fairbairn BEM, recalled that when the operations officer told him to go to a particular place, 'You were never told why you were going there or what you expected to see. We would go to some railway sidings, such as the one at Stahnsdorf, at the appointed time and along would come a cargo train carrying a new tank. Or sometimes nothing happened. We were not supposed to know where the tip came from but often it was attributed to "The Hill".'

Connor's predecessor as SAS representative, Nick Angus, was asked to identify 'suitable spots that would be used as rendezvous points for downed aircrew or other escapers, or as agent-contact points'. Such places had to be 'easily found, immovable, natural, with good concealment and unlikely to be pre-targeted by any nasty [Nato] nuclear devices! An overgrown quarry would be typical. We had to choose the spot from a six-grid square location which were the same-sized areas allocated for SAS operations. The interesting thing about these locations was that I was "all right, Jack". I knew the areas to head for in case the crunch occurred, though I wasn't sure how nuke-proof the SAS OP areas were.'

Both SAS and Intelligence Corps soldiers serving with Brixmis were 'badged' as something else. The SAS tended to wear Parachute Regiment red berets. At a cocktail party, the Soviets dryly asked why the SAS didn't wear their own headgear. As Angus put it: 'Changing our berets and badges didn't deceive the Sovs. They knew who was who, just as we knew our opposite numbers in SERB. They were mainly GRU.'

In parallel with the special requests, if not from 'The Hill' or SAS headquarters or some arm of Military Intelligence, the Brixmis crews continued to use their initiative and take risks. Fairbairn's biggest trophy was a brand-new air filtration unit fitted to a bunker deep in Letzlinger Heide training area. This item, measuring 5 × 3 × 2 feet, was meant to exclude chemical agents. It was not proof against Brixmis. Fairbairn unbolted it from the floor and with help from others on the tour, including Major Nigel Wylde QGM, the Mission's technical intelligence officer, 'staggered back to the car with it, before taking it to our HQ in Berlin'.

From there the device was shipped to the biological and chemical warfare establishment at Porton Down to be tested. Part of the device was also analysed in the United States. Wylde said later: 'Our scientists concluded that the filter not only provided protection from chemical warfare agents but also against "particulate" munitions. They fall within a grey area between chemical [gas] and biological [germ] weapons. There was evidence at that time that particulate munitions had been used by the Soviets in Afghanistan but it was not conclusive.'

A second filter was then stolen for further tests. After the second raid, 'we had proof that the Soviets had protection from a "particulate" weapon. There could be only two reasons for this. Either they had a "particulate" weapon or they thought the US was producing one. We could not take any chances in the West so a programme to provide protection for UK forces, against these weapons, was devised.'

Not long afterwards, an M16 team operating in Afghanistan retrieved fragments of exploded chemical weapons that gave hard proof that the Soviets had indeed used particulates against the Mujahedeen guerrillas.

For the SAS representative Connor, after years of living on the edge in Dhofar jebel, fighting a savage war, the risks he encountered in Germany, even when shots were fired, engaged about 15 per cent of his nervous energy. Others who had been on undercover work in Ireland regarded the Brixmis posting as a working holiday, with wives and children close at hand. From a Brixmis standpoint, as one officer put it: 'Some of these men were no longer suitable for orthodox, regimental soldiering but they were ideal for our purposes.'

Man-for-man, they were also superior to the Russian conscripts who were expected to keep them at bay. Connor told a Soviet commandant who expressed surprise that Connor, a senior NCO, was given the dangerous responsibility of leading a Brixmis tour: 'In my army, you would be working for me!'

Dramatic improvements in the Warsaw Pact arsenal generated fear in the West of surprise attack from a standing start, without any of the early warnings that might come from observation of tanks, aircraft, fuel and men moving to the front line from Russia.

The front-line strength of the Soviet forces in Germany, Brixmis noted, was 400,000. Over the next two years, through 1980 and 1981, 'the Soviet training cycle was revamped to start two weeks earlier, with exercises more realistic and offensive in nature. Between 31 August and 4 September 1980, the annual Warsaw Pact exercise, Waffenbruderschaft 80, practised the pursuit of a fleeing 1 English Corps.' No. 10 Guards Tank Division played the role of the retreating British. With the new tactics came an impressive array of new equipment.

The surprise attack, when it happened, was not to the West, but to the South, into Afghanistan. Within a week more than 50,000 mechanized troops had stormed across the frontier. Many of them flew from bases in East Germany. In January 1979, Squadron Leader (later Wing Commander) Brook Blackford was an air tour officer who watched the trucks arrive with their frozen, already-tired young Russian soldiers to emplane and fly to a destination which he knew and they did not: 'It was a cold and boring job for us. We had to position the car so as to watch the road approaching the Soviet Falkenberg air-base, the airfield and the transport aircraft flying in. We had to be able to read the VRNs [vehicle registration numbers] on the trucks. As the aircraft only carried 200 troops each, the convoys were only up to ten lorries, not an uncommon sight. We were as cold as they were. Luckily we did catch the right lorries and were able to photograph the three or four aircraft taking off later.'

The painstaking business of identifying units by reference to VRNs was still an important part of the Mission's bread-and-butter routine. One of those involved was Bob Thomas, the NCO whose leg was shattered by an East German ramming attack. They needed a computer. The only one available was the one which usually handled US forces' pay in Germany. It was based at Frankfurt. Brixmis accessed its more peculiar numbers through the US Mission in Berlin. Not until 1984 did the Mission acquire its own computer.

After the invasion of Afghanistan the USSR was promptly treated by Washington and London as a pariah. The Western Missions including Brixmis were instructed accordingly. As Brixmis itself observed: 'The "Afghanistan Rules" were adopted by the Foreign and Commonwealth Office as guidelines for organizations dealing

with Soviet authorities on a routine basis. Essentially, they prohibited social and working contact at all levels. Yet this was the
very lifeblood of Brixmis liaison.'

Britain's newly elected Prime Minister, Margaret Thatcher, was
not unduly concerned about that. In Washington, President Carter
would soon be replaced by the Republican Ronald Reagan.
Thatcher and Reagan agreed from the beginning that the Soviet
Union was 'the Evil Empire'. The tread-softly-with-big-stick-
concealed fraternity within the British Mission did not all agree
that it helped to say so, out loud.

The Soviet–Afghan War gave the Mission new and macabre
tasks. One of these was to scour the rubbish bins of military hospitals used by the Soviets in East Germany to treat their wounded
out of sight of potential critics of the war at home in Mother Russia.
Brixmis also haunted Soviet military graveyards at the back of the
hospitals, carefully noting the names, numbers and dates of death
of Soviet soldiers who did not recover. Sifting through the detritus
of military exercises, including human excreta and worse, was a
valuable technique which sometimes produced gems of intelligence. It had long been sanitized within the Mission under the
code-name 'Operation Tamarisk'. 'To tamarisk' became a verb in
mission argot. Sergeant-Major Ken Connor BEM, the SAS representative on the team at the time, robustly described it as 'shit-
digging'. He and his successor in the role, Sergeant-Major Jeff
Fairbairn, also concede that even by their standards it was disgusting and awful. It required the theft of well-used hospital dressings
and other items fresh from the ward. These were packaged up and
sent to England for analysis or to the US Mission headquarters in
Berlin.

The samples revealed, for example, traces of metal from bullets
or missiles whose source would be revealed by another layer of
analysis such as gas chromatography. Fairbairn said: 'Outside the
hospital on Route One there were "Plague" signs. We would find
all sorts of disgusting things in them including someone's guts
removed during an operation and dumped on the rubbish tip. It
stank.'

A Chief of Mission during some of that time was Brigadier (later
Major-General) Brian Davis CB CBE, who confirmed: 'It was an

extreme strain on the boys to do that job. But it did produce what might be called surgical memorabilia which linked the stuff to battle wounds. These were not traffic accidents. You don't get shrapnel coming out of people if that is the case.'

For Connor, the 'shit-digging' detail led to a remarkable and enigmatic find at Neustrelitz, a quiet place in the north of the GDR famed for its parks, its castle, its peace and quiet. There was also a Soviet army barracks there which Connor liked to think of as 'my happy hunting ground'. Accompanied by Geary and Staff Sergeant Dave Picton as driver, he went to check on the rotation of Soviet soldiers. Theoretically, one-third of these went home at intervals to be replaced by the same number from the USSR. At such times, the departing troops dumped their rubbish on public land near the back gate. Connor ran his own 'tamarisk' operation on what they left.

Under the noses of the sleeping sentries, at first light they filled their Range Rover with oddments that might be interesting, then drove back and filed their report. A subdued tingle went through Mission staff when they looked at a private logbook, written in careful Russian and illustrated with technical drawings, which Connor had extracted from the pile. When he asked what was going on, he was told, 'Can't say. It's too secret.'

One of the most senior officers with the Mission, entrusting the find to no one else, acted as courier to take it back to London. Two weeks later a senior Military Intelligence officer arrived at the Mission to talk to Connor: 'He said: "Do you want to know about the stuff you brought back from Neustrelitz?" I said, "No. I don't know where I might end up in future." He said, "If I told you it was the most important thing we have had from any source for ten years, would you be impressed?" I said, "Yes." He said, "If the Mission's days were numbered, you've just multiplied them many times over. We would oppose any move to close the Mission after this." I still did not want to know what was in the stuff.'

The meticulously-kept manual caused a sensation in the back rooms of Nato's technical intelligence and set in train an emergency programme to acquire a new anti-tank missile know as the 'long rod penetrator' (official description: APDFS or 'armour piercing discarding-sabot fin-stabilized round') now in service with the

British Army. The Russians were known to be ahead of the West in fabricating such exotic metals as titanium for warlike purposes. The log that Connor found revealed top-secret data about the type of armour, the strengths and weaknesses of the latest Russian tank, the T-64, and even its proposed successor, the T-80. As a bonus, the Neustrelitz document described other secrets of Soviet armoured warfare including a plough attached to each side of a tank, to dig up and push to the side anti-tank mines.

Vastly outnumbered by the Warsaw Pact's tank divisions, Nato had to decide whether to fight tanks with tanks, or go for the more cost-effective option of investing hugely in anti-tank missiles. As one expert put it at the time: 'In this argument a given amount of money can be expected to buy more defence than offence.' Soon after Connor's operation, Nato decided to rush into service 1,400 heavy and medium anti-tank missiles by 1982, a 60 per cent increase, along with 2,500 hand-held anti-tank weapons and hundreds of other anti-tank devices.

Almost as impressive in its effects was the trawl undertaken by Lieutenant-Colonel Jim Orr OBE, a Parachute Regiment soldier doing a tour with Brixmis as a G-1 between 1980 and 1983. With Sergeant Tony Haw QGM, in 1981, he 'tamarisked' a training area near Cottbus being used by the Soviet paras, the Guards Air Assault Brigade. Here as elsewhere, the apparently omnipotent Red Army did not issue toilet paper and had to improvise. *Faute de mieux*, it used secret documents.

Some smelly papers were reassembled and analysed back in Berlin. They included documents revealing the brigade's training programme and, even more important, an Order of Battle booklet that revealed some units as 'shell' formations, to be manned from the reserves only when war seemed imminent.

To get this information, Orr and Haw lay concealed close to the Soviets. As they were scratching among the rubbish at first light, 'a Russian soldier came out to have a pee . . . He didn't see us. My heart was in my mouth.' Orr added: 'I seemed to get landed with a lot of tamarisk operations. Eventually I volunteered for them as a sort of masochistic pleasure.'

Nick Angus turned up reels of audio-tape in one of his digs. The area was 'the shit-pit used by Sov Sigint [signals intelligence] close to the Inner German Border. These were sent back to the UK for analysis. We heard later that the British units on exercise in West Germany at the time of the Soviet deployment got a rocket from on high about their insecure voice procedures. They never knew that the source of the criticism was interception by Soviet Sigint.'

Flight Sergeant Colin Birnie BEM was tasked to take some rubbish back to where it came from. 'We had two black bags full of the stuff and decided to chuck it into the River Elbe. It was dark and we threw it in. Too late, we realized that the river was frozen over. Our two bags sat on top of the ice. We had to try to get them back. I started crawling across the ice, but the ice cracked under me. We drove off to a laying-up point. During the night the temperature rose and it rained. We returned at first light. The bags had now sunk and we sighed with relief.'

Birnie was not lucky with tamarisk. He brought back what he thought was an unusual lump of metal only to discover that it was familiar to analysts at the Berlin headquarters: another tour had brought it in the previous week and had been asked to return it to the spot where it was dug up.

Through the edgy period that followed the Soviet invasion of Afghanistan, the airmen of Brixmis pursued their own stealthy campaign against selected Soviet targets. For one particularly sensitive operation, the three Allied Missions combined for three months until they got the photograph they wanted. This marathon reconnaissance – a continuous, covert watch on a specific Soviet airfield – became known as the Allstedt Saga. The Russians had just taken delivery of a swing-wing Sukhoi reconnaissance aircraft known in Nato circles as the Fitter G. There were, said one participant, 'incredible moments of adrenalin when you got results and incidents and chases as well as days and nights simply spent waiting and watching'. The agencies wanted to build a total picture of the Fitter's operation, including the logistical back-up needed to keep it serviced and flying. They wanted to know about the equipment carried by Fitter, including its missiles. They wanted to know about the trainer variant of the aircraft and what was in the special pods containing reconnaissance electronics. The prime pictures, when they were finally obtained, were the work of Brixmis.

One member of that team was Squadron Leader B. M. Blackford.

Because of his sense of timing, particularly his uncanny knack of pulling out of an observation post just before it was uncovered by the opposition, he was nicknamed 'Dodger'. For him the Allstedt Saga was just one adventure among many. During the bitterly cold winter of 1979–80, he took his crew to Retzow, an isolated spot where a railway skirted an air-force missile range. Driving through deep snow they came upon a pair of half-frozen 'reggies' and a military recovery vehicle, signs of a major military manoeuvre in spite of the conditions: 'The snow was very deep but we managed to find an OP. The Soviet columns moved past and we took "picc-ies". The opposition spotted us and gave chase with four BTR-60s [eight-wheeled armoured personnel carriers] and two BRDM-2s [armoured cars].' This was not the sort of rally that Range Rovers were intended for, but 'our escape route was planned and we beat the BTR-60s to the critical junction after which they could not catch us. Unfortunately as we got there so did three East German snowploughs which could not move out of the way because of the snow. We took to snow-covered fields, off the track. We got further than the BRDMs but unfortunately not as far as the BTR-60s, which had better ground clearance.'

They were now cornered. The Soviet commandant was summoned.

Meanwhile the Soviet captain who detained us showed me two mines which he placed under one front and one rear wheel, saying 'Do not go anywhere, Angliski!' We had a pleasant, warm evening curry in the car, watched by freezing soldiers. The whole event was treated as a game in which they had scored bonus points for catching us.

The Russians withdrew their armoured vehicles a few feet away. We deduced that if the mines were real, they would have stood further back but since we couldn't go anywhere anyway, we were not going to prove them wrong. Next morning, the captain removed the mines and smiled. He asked me to look at the mines. They were genuine containers, filled with stones and cement instead of high explosive.

Eventually the commandant arrived and the usual Akt [statement of guilt] was prepared. We were accused of being in a

'Wie heiss, Lilli Marlene ... by the barrack gates': the human face of the East German war machine, caught smiling, behind his army truck, by a Brixmis lens in the 1980s.

The Stasi narks who followed Mission tours sometimes joined the Brixmis target list. This agent, working a camera from within his inelegant Wartburg 'banger' was one of them.

Detention: scene one
The endgame, after many pursuits, was a stalemate. In this photograph – taken on a military 'tac route' used by tanks and other fighting vehicles – a Soviet kommandatura car has halted in front of the Brixmis vehicle to make an arrest. Beyond the cars, two tanks can be seen.

Detention: scene two:
Through the windscreen of his Mission vehicle, a familiar sight for the Brixmis crew as they begin a long and tedious process of detention: a Soviet officer has removed his cap and opened the file to write his report on the incident. He is guarded by armed soldiers some of whom take photographs of the 'Angliski espions'. Soon, the British team leader will be asked to sign an 'Akt', a statement admitting responsibility for breaking the rules. This the British will politely refuse to do. What then? If the crew are lucky, nothing worse than a long, boring detention at a Soviet base while negotiations take place far away to clear the air... But if they are unlucky, there might yet be violence. At this stage the crew just don't know.

Staff Sergeant Graham Geary BEM (right) completed two arduous tours with the Mission, the first from 1979 to 1981 and the second from 1987 to 1990. This photograph was taken as he was arrested yet again by the Russians. Geary retained a dry, self-mocking sense of humour during such episodes and in describing them afterwards.

ATTENTION! PASSAGE OF MEMBERS OF FOREIGN MILITARY LIAISON MISSIONS IS PROHIBITED!

ATTENTION! PASSAGE AUX MEMBERS DES MISSIONS MILITAIRES ETRANGERES DE LIAISON EST INTERDIT!

ПРОЕЗД ЧЛЕНАМ ИНОСТРАННЫХ ВОЕННЫХ МИССИЙ СВЯЗИ ЗАПРЕЩЁН!

DURCHFAHRT FÜR DAS PERSONAL DER AUSLANDISCHEN MILITARBINDUNGS — MISSIONEN IST VERBOTEN!

Both Soviets and Germans tried arbitrarily to limit the Mission's movements by declaring some areas off-limits without warning. As many as a thousand 'Mission Excluded' signs might be erected in one night. Notices were ignored by Brixmis patrols or stolen as souvenirs.

Photographer caught in action in wing mirror.

НАЧАЛЬНИК ШТАБА ГРУППЫ
СОВЕТСКИХ ВОЙСК В ГЕРМАНИИ

11 сентября 1972. № 155

Господин генерал,

6 сентября 1972 года члены Вашей миссии связи полковник авиации Джонс КОРБИШЛИ, майор Родни Карл СААР и капрал Дональд КЭЛВИН преднамеренно проникли в район советского военного объекта, ограждённого запретными знаками, где они были задержаны с поличным при фотографировании ими военной техники.

Такое поведение членов Британской военной миссии связи является грубым нарушением соответствующих положений соглашения МАЛИНИН-РОБЕРТСОН от 1946 года.

Главнокомандующий ГСВГ поручил мне заявить Вам, господин генерал, в этой связи решительный протест и объявить, что майор СААР, нарушавший и ранее положения указанного соглашения, не может более пребывать в составе Вашей миссии.

Главнокомандующий ГСВГ ожидает, что в отношении полковника авиации КОРБИШЛИ и капрала КЭЛВИНА Вами будут приняты самые строгие меры к недопущению ими в дальнейшем подобных действий.

В. ЯКУШИН
Генерал-лейтенант

Генерал-майору Д.Дж. ХАУСУ
Начальнику штаба Британской
Рейнской армии

Squadron Leader Rod Saar MBE in action with a 1000 mm lens purchased in Moscow, sent by diplomatic bag to London and then used to expose the secrets of the Soviet Zella Mehlis signals intelligence site. Saar was declared *'persona non grata'* in 1973.

Right: Russian letter confirming that Rod Saar was now *'persona non grata'*. It complained that Saar and his companions were 'caught red-handed whilst photographing military equipment, in gross violation of the Robertson-Malinin agreement.'

Below: Rod Saar's Soviet pass.

Permanently Restricted Area and behind keep-out signs. Our policy was to ignore them. After a long argument the commandant arranged for us to be towed out. Then we drove in convoy – the Soviet Army team, the East German Polizei and the narks in formation to the nearest sign that said [in several languages including English] that the area was off limits to Allied Missions. The commandant pointed at it and said, 'Look at this. Look at what it says.' I, of course, said, 'I am sorry I cannot see or read today because I have not got my spectacles.'

Blackford arrived back at the Mission headquarters, exhausted. Like many before him in similar circumstances, he was now called out to deal with an emergency.

Flight Lieutenant David Williams had crashed in the snow in the Rheinsberg Gap. I was asked, could I go and get him with a driver and trailer? I managed a quick change into dry clothes and set off again in the worst winter for years. We had snow for nearly a hundred days in 1978–79. When we got to the crash site we learned that David had been taken to hospital with a broken collar bone. Both the driver and tour NCO of the same crew were still there, battered, very cold and in shock. We tried to load their car on to the trailer with the help of a Soviet commandant and his GAZ-66 [a four-wheel drive truck]. The tour car was so badly bent by the tree it had crashed into that we couldn't move it in a straight line on to the trailer. Eventually the car was dragged into a field with the empty trailer. I was forced to send my car back with David's crew. They needed medical treatment. The commandant said, 'Goodbye. See you in the morning.' I was now left alone in the middle of nowhere, in freezing cold, in a useless car, with fourteen hours to wait until daylight.

Blackford's temper was not improved when he discovered the injured crew's exposed film under one of the seats. He had made sure, before coming out, that he was 'clean'. He had company of a sort, but the wrong sort. Stasi narks, in two cars, had parked nearby. He recalled: 'I could not cook because of the petrol leaking from the wrecked vehicle I was in. My supply of yoghurts had frozen. I was not a happy teddy bear. It was bitterly cold. I finally got to sleep but was woken by the village drunk, knocking on the broken window. Next morning the commandant arrived with a mobile crane and lifted the wreck on to the trailer. We then discovered that the trailer had a puncture. The mobile crane lifted the crashed car off the trailer and we managed to change the trailer wheel.'

An army colleague from Brixmis, Major Gavin Scott-Forrest, had arrived in an Opel Senator similar to the wrecked car in which Blackford had spent the night. The roadworthy Senator towed the trailer, on which rested the damaged Senator. They had covered five miles and reached the town of Rheinsberg where, ironically, they were impeded by a major Soviet military convoy on the move.

In the middle of the town the trailer began to wobble and we discovered that one of the wheels was coming off and was at a 30 degree angle to the road. The Soviet kit was still going past. We decided to leave Gavin sitting in the wrecked car, on the unroadworthy trailer, at the side of the road, while I returned to base. When I arrived there I discovered that I was the duty interpreter. Theoretically I had been back off tour the previous night. I ended up at the Soviet External Relations Bureau asking for a pass enabling us to bring a large British recovery vehicle from Berlin to go up to the Rheinsberg Gap to retrieve the wrecks. In the event permission was given and all ended well, after four cold, tiring days.

In 1981, ten years after Rod Saar's reckless penetration of Soviet radar sites, 'Dodger' Blackford and his crew, 'found a hole in the fence around a SAM-2 [anti-aircraft] site north of Parchim, drove to the centre of the site along a one-kilometre track unnoticed, popped into the open, quickly took the "piccies" and even more quickly departed. Looking back on it now it was a stupid thing to do as the danger of a shooting incident was high, but that's the Brixmis challenge for you!' The equipment they targeted that day was a radar known as 'Fan Song', its wings spinning round a vertical axis like a gigantic turnstile. The updated Fan Song, they noted, was also fitted with a television camera.

The crew watched and photographed 'good flying programmes

at Retzow range including fixed wing and helos; took some close
shots at Parchim of the Hind-E [helicopter gunship] with its Gatling
gun swivelled and depressed' and some useful night rail movements. The party was far from over. Both Nato and Warsaw Pact
planned to use motorways as tactical airstrips in wartime. The
RAF's vertical take-off Harrier was peculiarly suited to such operations. An unanswered question in Nato was how efficiently the
opposition could handle the same task using big fast jets. Blackford
and his crew were about to learn. It was now high summer.

We were in multi-relax and mega-pleased mode, looking forward
to a cool beer in the Mission house at Potsdam as we drove home
down the Rostock–Berlin autobahn. As we passed Wittstock, I
noticed a Soviet Curl transport flying low immediately over the
autobahn. It was a special version, rarely seen and only used for
checking ILS [instrument landing systems] and radar.

As we approached the Gadow Rossow range, where Soviet aircraft attacked ground targets, the East German police were erecting
barriers as if they were preparing to close the autobahn. It soon
became apparent that the Soviets were activating the Gadow
Rossow landing strip on the motorway, near the range. This was
an extremely rare event. No one on the Mission could remember
a precedent. As we drove down the autobahn the big parking and
picnic areas each side of it were being turned into aircraft refuelling
dumps. Mobile radar equipment for air traffic control was in position just yards from us.

Years later, Blackford could still identify the separate beasts he
glimpsed in this whirring, buzzing, nodding, humming electronic
menagerie, with its attendant generators, by their opaque Nato
code-names: HOME TALK, HAY series, and so on. 'An area radar site
with BARLOCK, SIDE NET, etc., was working. A SAM-4 site complete
with its radar systems was present and operating together with
extensive communications systems in the trees: CAT'S EYE and PAW,
R400/404, etc. Headquarters sites with BTR-60 armoured personnel carriers and other vehicles were out in the open being "cammed
up" under netting. We managed to photograph most of this but
because of the hostile reaction as we drove past we decided not to

try a second run, back up the autobahn in the other direction. We quickly returned to Berlin and reported.'

To Blackford's surprise, the intelligence cell at RAF headquarters in West Germany, knew – or professed to know – nothing of what the Brixmis crew had seen and 'could offer no advice'. This was part of an elaborate game of blind man's bluff, as played by the intelligence community. If – thanks to the signals intelligence team on 'The Hill' or elsewhere – a Mission crew was directed too precisely on to a target then what was happening, without a shadow of doubt, was orchestrated espionage by a diplomatic mission ostensibly cleared to conduct liaison duties. The spying had to be disguised, if only for diplomatic reasons. For that to happen, the Mission had to be nudged into an area where it would find what the intelligence chiefs intended it to find, but spontaneously and therefore in line with its rights as a liaison team.

As Blackford put it:

This was a perennial problem as many RAF tours were often sent on what seemed like normal watches unbriefed as to the true nature of what The Hill knew was about to happen. My predecessor with the Mission had been sent to Zerbst in 1976 for a routine watch on the airfield and its Mig-21 Fishbeds. The ops staff, however, knew that the new Flogger B [Mig-23] had just been delivered and would be operating. It was. He was, however, caught by Soviet special forces outside the car with all his equipment and roughly treated. If he had known the true state of events he might well have taken a different course, to avoid the precautions the Soviets and narks took whenever new aircraft were delivered.

The beer they had promised themselves in Berlin had to wait.

We returned next morning at 5 A.M. to an observation post near the strip, not knowing what was due. It soon became apparent as four Flogger G flew in from Koethen followed by four Fitter C from Templin and four Fishbeds from Wittstock. This was something big and we moved into close OPs to get good 'piccies'. These aircraft were turned round [refuelled, rearmed] and departed to be followed on to the strip by four Flogger D from Finsterwalde.

Eventually most Soviet airfields in the GDR sent in groups of four aircraft that day including a Foxbat [the newest Mig-25] and Brewer from Werneuchen.

We were mega-chuffed. We had the photos, flight paths and times of operations of the nearly thirty aircraft that went in. However, the continued appearance of a civilian UAZ-452 saloon and other nark cars forced us to move more in the open. It was summer and the fields were dry, with plenty of escape routes, but when they started to unload a number of fully 'cammed' individuals [combat troops wearing camouflage war paint] discretion became the byword and we left. We had to hide for some time before we lost them. We were lucky not to get caught. They didn't call me 'Dodger' Blackford in those days for nothing. I learned a very important lesson on that tour. You cannot cover everything all the time. Just go for the important event and don't get caught.

Their next port of call, on the same trip, was the Soviet Air Force missile range at Gadow Rossow, a mere six miles away. 'As we passed the main firing point of the range I looked behind me, in case we had missed anything. Then I spotted a group of HIP helicopter gunships approaching for an attack. This quickly became a formation of forty HIPs and HOOKs (big transport helos) which all attacked the range with rockets and guns in pairs at twenty-second intervals. We were forced to photograph from the side of the autobahn but they were so close we used only a 200mm lens. It was quite a sight!'

CHAPTER 9

Lifting the Lid on the T-64

1981

On May Day 1981 the Warsaw Pact threatened Nato Europe with 45,000 main battle tanks, a numerical advantage of two-to-one. Captain Hugh McLeod of the Argyll & Sutherland Highlanders and his tour NCO Sergeant (later RSM) Tony Haw QGM were interested in just one of those vehicles. It was a shiny sample of the new T-64 armed with a 125mm smoothbore gun and, as the Soviet Army caroused away a public holiday, the tank was safely under lock and key. Or so they thought.

McLeod, Haw and their driver Corporal Anderson drove deep into a tank gunnery range, broke into a locked hangar, found the tank, opened the turret lid with a forged key and pillaged the secrets within before making a successful getaway. An American Mission major, Arthur (Nick) Nicholson, who tried to follow their act four years later, when the T-80 had overtaken the T-64, was shot dead by a guard, prompting a crisis in US–Soviet relations.

McLeod, a Russian speaker, was briefed to cover three tank ranges and a Soviet Army rubbish dump. 'In my second year with the Mission, I was given the task of Rubbish Officer. A serious job! Promotion!' So, jokes apart, it was. This was Tamarisk territory.

'On May Day and other holidays we pushed our luck to the maximum; we knew their guard was down,' McLeod said. 'The Russians, although disciplined in many ways, could be very lax in their discipline if they had all been out on a holiday binge. They simply didn't have a presence at installations where they should have had a presence. I was unhappy about the dump I was given that day because it was one we didn't know much about and there was a railway there.'

The day before they left, McLeod and Haw put their heads together. 'We went to the wall map to plan the tour. We decided that the rubbish dump would have to be done just before first light and then we would do the tank ranges in a logical order. It then occurred to us that those three were in a straight line which continued towards a special tank installation at Parchim. So I thought I might as well have a go at that as well. So I went along to the ops officer and got his agreement.'

McLeod understood that T-64s were kept in a shed on a range at Parchim, a desolate patch of heathland. 'I thought, let's assume that we do actually get access to a T-64. Can we exploit this to the full? Answer, No. For a couple of reasons.'

The first of these was that the key to open the turret, held by the Mission at its Berlin headquarters, was not usually carried by the touring teams. The key, and its copies, had been forged back in England by a remarkable technical intelligence team. Brigadier Brian Davis, having recently taken command of Brixmis, knew that the key was very hot property indeed, and a political boomerang if discovered in a Spetznaz raid on a mission car in some isolated spot. So he withdrew them all.

McLeod and his boss had worked briefly together at the military intelligence centre at Ashford in Kent. They had a rapport. So when McLeod asked if he could take the Soviet tank key with him on this trip, Davis agreed. The key was carried in the tour car's toolkit, as a sort of camouflage.

The T-64 scam was now gathering momentum. McLeod envisaged the task facing him if he got inside the darkened tank; he would need photographs, since eye-witness data and 'I-was-there' stories were no use to the intelligence analysts back home. The standard Brixmis camera lens was not appropriate for anything closer than 15 feet. He was hoping to be inches from his material. He traced a couple of wide-angle lenses.

So we set out on our tour. They were just building a motorway up into that area and we tended not to be strict in our observance of East German traffic regulations. It was always one's intention to get to the targeted area without being spotted. An unfinished and unused motorway was a heaven-sent opportunity. We used this to get right up into the north-west area.

This was 30 April now, the first day of the tour. We thought we would have a look at the area of Parchim to see if there was activity there. We were driving along a road towards Parchim and we had just gone behind [keep-out] signs when we came across a convoy of about six Soviet trucks who were particularly alert. As soon as they saw us they deployed in a sort of herring-bone across the road, thus completely blocking us. There were ditches on both sides of the road, which had prevented us from going on to the fields. Corporal Anderson, a good driver, was still able to get us out of that. We decided not to go further on towards the tank range that day.

We then went off and 'sat on' a railway line as one tended to do, until well into the evening. When there was no activity one sat and had the evening meal somewhere where one might get a result. We spent our evening watching a railway line and then went off into the woods to sleep. At around 4 A.M. we carried out our task on the rubbish dump, which was as uncomfortable as we had expected. We spent five or ten minutes groping around in the gloom and none of us was happy with it because both I and Tony Haw had been obliged to cross a railway line away from the car to reach the dump right underneath the wall of a Soviet barracks. We both thought, 'No, this is silly.' We left.

We then went through the other three installations in order. In one of them the tank sheds were derelict. The next, the second, was in an area which was so exposed and visible to a main road that we felt that to go and slip around in what was then daylight, was simply not feasible.

The third one, we got a good cross-country route into it going through the danger area [the live firing range] because we were confident that on May Day they would not be firing and we got within about 600 metres of the sheds. These were open and didn't have any tanks in them. We had just breasted a rise and there was an exceptionally alert sentry there. The moment we put our heads over the rise he had his rifle in his shoulder and so we had to back off from that one as well. But that was interesting in that there were no tanks in the sheds and it was May Day and there was this sentry really on the button. And so to an extent that taught us a lesson, that you can't write rules about how you treat the Russian Army: they will react in totally different ways regardless of the circumstances.

So we moved on to Parchim. I had been there once before and had actually driven up to the back of the sheds but hadn't got out of the vehicle because the circumstances were not right. But at least I'd got close. I knew a good route, down a disused railway track. We parked on this railway track about 500 metres from the sheds. We were at this point right on the edge of Permanently Restricted Area. I'm sure a Russian would say the sheds themselves were in PRA. We would say that the demarcation line went right through the middle of the sheds.

We sat observing the sheds at about 11 A.M. for a full hour through a telescope and could see no sign of life whatever, but I knew from my earlier visit that if there was a sentry he would be on the other side of the shed. But I reasoned that to go up to the shed, see the sentry and drive away would be no problem so after an hour there was no excuse for not going further. So we bumped down the disused railway track over a heavily rutted tank track and round to the back of the sheds and there was no sign of life. We parked the car and Tony Haw and I checked the whole area on foot and assured ourselves there was no human life there at all.

There was a little sentry box built into the corner of the shed and that was an interesting lesson as well in that the guy who should have been on duty there was not allowed access to the tanks. The tanks were a highly classified item. The sentry was not allowed access. He just had a spy-hole into the sheds. Anyway there was nobody in that little box so Tony Haw tried the main entrance door and said, 'No, it's locked.'

[With their driver acting as look-out, they now considered how to break into the shed.] We tried levering away at the door without marking it. It was a heavy metal door for pedestrians at the back of the shed but we couldn't make any effect on it. We had a sledge hammer in the boot. We had nothing to lose. The driver and I started having a go at the wall but luckily we had only struck a

couple of blows when Tony Haw persisted in rattling the door and
it just opened. Obviously, the door had sunk on its hinges and the
officer who'd last been on duty the previous day had tried to lock
it, rattled the thing and said, 'No, sod it! I can't get it to lock and
I want to go off to the May Day party.'

So we backed the car right up to the door. We agreed a plan,
how to react if someone came up and joined us. None of us was
under any illusions about how we would be treated if we were
caught out of the vehicle. We agreed we would do everything we
possibly could to get into the car and get away. We also agreed
that if challenged we would probably stop because it was more
than likely that we would be shot at, that they would be shooting
right at the car.

The first surprise when they entered the hangar was that it contained five T-64s. McLeod started work by taking close-up exterior
pictures of the vehicle: 'There was one item on one of the tanks
which had puzzled us for about nine months. It was a T-bar on
the back of one of them ... We opened it up and it turned out to
be some strange winch arrangement. That took us five minutes.'

He now turned his attention to the interior. He had much to
think about as he pulled himself up the side of Russia's newest
tank. Would the turret key, a forgery cast in Berkshire, open the
lid?

The key is L-shaped. The turret itself has a commander's hatch
and a gunner's hatch. The latter has a hole where the key goes
in, a circle with two flats on it and so it was obviously the place
to insert the key. I shoved it in, twisted it and it sprang open. So
I immediately returned the key to the driver and again we had a
conference as to how we were going to play it. There we were,
with the tank opened and the ability to photograph it and because
of the limited size of the thing I had to do the whole lot. The driver
was to stay in the car. The tour NCO Tony Haw was to stand in
the entrance to the shed and to relay anything the driver had to
say to me [as look-out and getaway boss]. We agreed that I would
not have more than one film on me at a time and so every time
I completed a film I would call Tony Haw across, hand it to him

and we agreed places in the car where the driver could secrete the film just in case we were caught and turned over. Then we would still have a chance of some of the films being retained.

I thought about the consequences before I got into it. I was scared, frankly, getting into it because one was under no illusions what would have happened if we had been caught there. It would have been a severe beating up if we had been caught out of the car. If we had been in the car and had tried to escape, they would have shot at us, certainly.

I decided first to lean into the tank with a torch and talk into a tape recorder and describe everything that I saw. That didn't take very long. I'm a Russian speaker. I'm not a tank man. I don't know that much about British tanks. But nevertheless I made a methodical survey of the inside of the turret as I saw it. Again, I did all of that just in case none of the films came out.

I was reading out all the markings on the sight, the gun and all of the equipment in the turret. I then gave the tape recorder back [to Haw] and got my camera and still had my torch and got in and sat in the gunner's seat. It was pitch black in there and so I put my torch down on the commander's seat, to illuminate the interior. I took a whole series of photographs without considering what I was photographing. I then moved over to the commander's seat and repeated the process in reverse, covering the gunner's area.

The torch I was using was a standard British Army torch. I knocked it off the seat. It dropped down past the gun mounting right into the hull of the tank. I tried to get it out but I couldn't. At first I thought it didn't matter. Then it struck me that next day this tank might go back to Omsk or somewhere to be refitted, where a British Army torch would be found inside it. That was serious. I tried and tried to get it out. We had a long-handled spanner and with that, we eventually got hold of it. I have often thought since what would have happened if we had left it there and it was discovered during a refit.

Having got the torch back I photographed and recorded everything to do with the communications and weapon systems. I also wanted to try the driver's compartment, where I knew there would be valuable information. But his hatch was sealed and the only alternative access was to squeeze past the gun mounting inside the tank. This would have denied me any chance of escape and so I decided that the powers-that-be could find out about the engine of a T-64 from someone else.

McLeod emerged from the hull slowly and methodically, closed and locked the turret lid behind him, checked that he had not inadvertently forgotten anything and dropped softly to the floor of the hangar. He had forgotten something – footprints – but his NCO had taken note and dusted his boot marks off the tank.

McLeod was still not satisfied that he had scooped every last ounce of secret knowledge from this place: 'The Soviets also had a turret simulator in the shed, covered by a tarpaulin, for crew training. We took the tarpaulin off that. That probably gave us a lot more intelligence than the photographs from inside the tank because I was able to take detailed photographs of the whole of the simulator. We replaced the tarpaulin on that.'

Finally, the Brixmis team turned its attention to the Soviet training boards displayed in the hangar.

In Russian training areas they have big boards giving the outlines of a lesson. It's well organized; better than the British Army. If you have a platoon waiting to fire on the range then the platoon commander just goes to that training board and gives them a lesson using the board as a training aid. It's very efficient. There were a lot of training boards in the shed. They contain intelligence on tactics primarily but also there is some technical intelligence there. Having done that, we decided it was time for lunch. So we made a thorough check of the sheds to make sure there was no trace of our presence and we were entirely confident of that and left the area.

They drove as quietly as possible along the disused railway and then on to the unfinished motorway, without passing a single vehicle. There was no hot pursuit, no shots, no drama. 'We eventually pulled off the motorway and made coffee. This was the first chance to relax and relieve the tension that had built up over the last couple of hours. It was only then that the three of us realized what we had done and were able to talk about it and joke, particularly about the torch. We tried to invent an explanation for a worker in Omsk when asked how he came to be in possession of a British Army torch.'

A year later, he was awarded an MBE.

The team that fabricated the T-64 turret key was as remarkable as the team that used it. This was a minor branch of the Directorate of Scientific Technical Intelligence, known as DI51e. As one of its long-serving members blandly put it: 'It offered technical and instrumental support to our defence attachés and other accredited service representatives including Brixmis.' Staffed by three ex-service scientists, it operated under free terms of reference: 'DSTI management took the view, "Don't tell us what you are doing until you have done it and then only if you must. Whatever you do, don't land us, your customers, or yourselves, in trouble." In other words, we were deniable.'

These then were the loosely defined rules of what a director of DI51e affectionately described as 'The Game'. He enlarged on this:

Demands for our services could arise from any person in the intelligence loop, but most came from intelligence collectors or their taskers. Our purpose was to provide the collectors with kit which made their tasks easier or indeed possible. So as to avoid conflict with branches which officially issued equipment, we maintained all our kit in our own inventory: we lent it to our own people. Consequently our inventory kept growing.

Sometimes the equipment was purely 'domestic' in character: gloves, a hikers' tent, a bicycle here, a car there. For reasons which will become clear, most of the items we supplied were standard commercial products, unlike the funny kit James Bond took with him.

The director and his staff assumed that their customers were 'special guests' in potentially hostile countries where their rooms and baggage would be searched: 'Every item found in their possession had to have a normal use. Equipment which was purely for intelligence collection was therefore ruled out, unless the task was of exceptional importance. This was specially important for Brixmis, because a single incontrovertible spying incident could have consequences which would far outweigh the value of any information gained, not to mention the certainty of a swinging handbag' (as wielded by the British Prime Minister of the day).

The key carried by Hugh McLeod fell into the special category: 'One morning there appeared in my office a major, a video-tape, a photograph, a drawing and a request. The request was: Could we get eight of these made please?' 'These' were bits of steel bars, bent in the middle at a right angle, with specially shaped ends. The video-tape, recorded in Moscow, was from a popular Russian television programme entitled 'I Serve the Soviet Union'. It contained a fleeting glimpse of a tank commander opening the hatch. The photograph, taken from a Brixmis operator poised on a bridge over a railway, was of the top of a T-64 as it passed below on a cargo train.

All these data left the artist who did the drawing the interesting task of assessing the depth of the slot into which the key would fit: 'An inspired draughtsman, a Tech. Int. Army man, had put it all together on his drawing. All we had to do was to find a manufacturer and ensure that they got paid. A light engineering company made the devices for about ten pounds each.'

From time to time, the feedback of information from the 'customer' to DI51e was at least as valuable as anything constructed in the department's workshop. One of the more dramatic innovations of the 1980s – the Star Wars years – was the use of laser, a narrow beam of light so intense as to be a weapon in its own right. It was ideally suited as a ranging device, fitted to anything from a holidaymaker's camera to a tank gun. The director recalled:

The first real information we obtained on the opposition's laser came when a Brixmis tour was zapped by a Soviet rangefinder. At the time, the tour officer had the rangefinder in the field of view of his camera. The NCO was a short distance away looking through binoculars at the rangefinder. The officer saw a bright red flash and later was found to have a mark on his retina. The NCO saw the rangefinder flash a bright red. The driver was looking at the tour car at the time and was not aware of a flash. The camera's mirror was found to be damaged where the light from the laser had hit it.

This disturbing incident told us, first, that Warsaw Pact forces were not above using military lasers on personnel from other countries. Second, the laser light was reportedly red in colour and gave us a probable identity for the medium being used as ruby. Third, when we tried to replicate the damage to the camera mirror we found that the energy pulse had been only just sufficient to lift the aluminium coating off the mirror. By making some reasonable calculations, based on the diameter of the camera lens, its focal length, the laser's distance and the probable divergence of its beam we concluded that the laser's output pulse probably lay between three and thirty joules.

The technicians collaborated urgently to create a filter to be fitted to the eyecup of a camera viewfinder, with a cautionary word that there were no guarantees that it would work. The risk of blindness was now added to the inventory of potential horrors facing Brixmis teams.

The Chief of Mission presiding over many of these adventures was Brigadier Brian Davis, a breezy Gunner who infected others with his sense of operations-as-fun. With the SAS representative on the team, Jeff Fairbairn, he broke into a desolate ammunition depot which was thought to contain nuclear warheads. They found a spot where a stream passed beneath the wire fence at the perimeter and enlarged it. It was bitterly cold. The stream was wide and frozen. They decided to take the tour car in, driving on the ice so as to leave no tracks. Fairbairn and the driver were in the front, the Chief in the back. Fairbairn was concerned that the driver was taking things too fast and said so. As he explained later: 'As tour NCO you never wanted to get caught in a compromising position with the Chief in the back. At the same time they didn't like you to be overly protective.'

The Chief recollected:

We were going along quietly, extremely alert, and suddenly the ice broke and the whole shebang went to the bottom of the stream, about two feet deep. The engine cut at once and the water came up to the level of the seats. I immediately opened the sun roof. Jeff leapt out through that and jumped ashore. I was moving cameras up to the roof of the car to get them out of the water. My seat was pretty wet by this time. We were sitting there like lemons with water all round us, about two yards either side of the car. I said to Fairbairn, 'You're bloody SAS. You're trained to sort this sort of thing out. Do something intelligent.'

He said, 'Hang on, Chief, I'll just fix this.' I was now sitting on top of the car with my feet over the windscreen with water all round. His reaction was to take a picture of the Chief in the shit! We were all a bit nervous at this stage and pretty exposed.

They prepared to extract their car with a hand-winch and a cable running round a tree. This would not be easy. Their car, an over-loaded Opel Senator fitted with under-body armour, was very heavy. Then they got lucky. A civilian forestry worker employed by the Soviets came along with a tractor. He helped to tow them out, but they knew that as soon as he was out of sight he would fetch somebody. They tried the Senator's engine. It backfired 'like fourteen mortar bombs', but they got it going after a fashion and got away.

Such misadventures gave the Brigadier a special degree of empathy with the tour crews. He learned to enjoy the surge of adrenalin when, unexpectedly, a Soviet convoy appeared:

You think, 'Kit! Wa-hey!' They had these tactical routes running right across Germany, not roads but tank tracks in great swathes across the country, usually in training areas. In the summer you could see the dust trails miles away. Other times you had an eye for the heather.

On the roads we might see their traffic regulators wearing black boiler suits and Soviet hats with a red stripe round them, holding these little direction-waving sticks. They might be there for a week with a little wood fire burning. When you saw traffic regulators, opportunity knocked.

The other clue was broken-down military vehicles. The Soviet failure to maintain their vehicles was appalling. If an armoured division had moved across country, through villages, across roads and on to 'tac' routes you could trace their route by looking for the Frog [mobile missile] or a couple of tanks, a communications vehicle or whatever, broken down beside the road. If you could see nothing, you could often smell them. They used cheap fuel, the odour of which hung in the air for ever.

Brigadier Davis's approach sometimes created its own hazards. On one occasion his tour had pulled off Route 2, near Luther's historic centre of Wittenberg, to brew a coffee. By tradition, this was the tour officer's task. For a change, the Chief did it. Suddenly a big Soviet column appeared, led by escorts with winking blue lights and a heavy low-loader with flashing orange lights: 'Kit! I chucked my scalding coffee out of the window but the window was shut. It hit it and splashed back over me. Worse, it had covered the window. We usually kept it closed in case someone chucked something in at us. This time I operated the camera – a Nikon with motor-drive – with the window down as we ran the column from the front, straight down. It was a convoy of surface-to-surface missiles.'

There were more targets than ever during the late summer exercise season, when the first harvest was in and before the winter wheat was sown.

We came upon a para drop. We had seen the aircraft circling. Out came the paras, to a drop zone half a mile from us. We were separated from that by a cornfield. The corn was four feet high. Beyond that we could see the air controller's radio aerials.

We wanted to get close enough to the vehicles to identify the unit involved. Were the paras Air Assault troops or Spetznaz? In a typical Brixmis manoeuvre we turned off the road, down the bank and straight into the cornfield. We went flat out through the corn. We couldn't see anything. We paused and heard the paras shouting. They'd twigged what was happening. We shot out into a clearing on the other side within ten paces of the troops and took some nervy pictures. We immediately turned about and followed our own trail back. After a mile the car started smoking.

Every conceivable part around the Senator's engine was stuffed with corn and it was overheating.

Davis's adventurous approach won applause from Washington and ruffled feathers at the Foreign Office.

Hugh McLeod's operation gave real pleasure to the intelligence community but that was relayed to us from Washington, not London. Our approach was to get away with what we could. That was not always seen that way by intelligence or military circles within HQ BAOR, or the civil side of the JIC (Joint Intelligence Committee) in Bonn which was usually chaired by the Minister or his number two in the British embassy there. The Foreign Office was very good at reporting information but no bloody good at taking decisions. We often entered on rather dodgy tasks on the authority of the Chief. Had I indicated to them what Hugh McLeod proposed to do there would have been a bloody great panic and the answer would have been No!

The 'authority of the Chief' was something the Soviets also had to come to terms with. In spite of the limited contacts in Europe that resulted from the Afghan War, it was customary for the Brigadier to be present when the Russians took their turn at guarding Spandau Prison, in the British sector of Berlin, where Rudolf Hess was the only prisoner. Brixmis provided interpreters for the contacts, such as they were, between Hess and his gaolers. What was more, the Mission was accredited to the Soviets and its Chief was invited by the Russians as part of their protocol. As Davis put it: 'The ceremonial Soviet guard-mounting at Spandau was by SERB, the people we knew, the people who arrested us.' The 'lunch' – really a drinking marathon – that followed the ceremony was a useful chance to do some information horse-trading.

We'd had a very bad week. We'd had two tours detained. Some were still out there somewhere. So I was at the lunch with my interpreter. We were the only non-Russians there. Over a drink, old Alex Rubanoff, our liaison officer, a full colonel, said, 'The Mission has been awful this week. I had a call this morning that we arrested Nigel Shakespear and his crew on the Elbe, the third this week. What the hell's going on, Brian?'

I said, 'Don't tell me. I'll tell you what happened. Nigel was down on the Elbe with a camera. Some of your bloody heavy-footed soldiers came along. He tried to run for it and he was captured.' Rubanoff was dumbstruck because we don't talk frankly and don't admit to carrying cameras.

I went on, 'Another typical Russian cock-up. Listen Alex, the white stork is due to return to the mudflats around the Elbe. I sent Nigel out this morning and gave him my express, personal permission to go down here and get some pictures of those lovely birds. I told him to keep clear of any Soviet military activity because that wasn't his business. I told him he was there for the white stork and nothing else. Nothing to do with military stuff.'

Rubanoff slowly sipped his vodka. He had not known that the English brigadier was a keen bird-watcher. He had not yet discovered the truth, that – as Davis admitted when it was safe to tell the tale – 'a white stork wouldn't be seen dead within ten miles of the place because of the Soviet bridge-building activity there. We had heard they had a new snorkel fitted to their tanks, enabling them to traverse the river submerged. We wanted to know how much time it took to prepare the tank for this operation.' The detained crews were promptly freed on Rubanoff's instructions, by telephone.

Lunch followed but there were signs of disfavour, in particular the absence of the usual Armenian brandy bearing a Mount Ararat label. That afternoon they had to make do with vodka, beer and mineral water.

'About 4.45 P.M. there was a great grin from Alex. In came a platoon of Russian waiters with trays with brandy bottles on them; and glasses. They poured me a glass but made sure I couldn't see the label. Then Alex stood up and proposed a toast. "To the white stork!" At the same time, he showed me the label on the bottle, which was White Stork Brandy.' Why the delay in serving the brandy? 'Rubanoff had sent a messenger all the way back from Berlin to his own headquarters at Zossen. He wasn't going to let me get away with that . . .'

A more potent source of misunderstanding than the location of the white stork was the direction of Soviet policy towards Poland. The emergence of Solidarity, a trade union independent of the communist regime, was perceived by Moscow to be a threat to its control of all its satellites and, ultimately, the subject peoples in the USSR. The crisis in Poland – which the Russians described as 'the Polish disease' – flared up and down like a political abscess. In the autumn of 1980 the politbureau (average age seventy-something) had started to build up the forces in the western military districts of the USSR to begin a process of apparent blackmail. In December 1980 Nato's foreign ministers, recalling their failure to respond coherently to the Soviet invasion of Afghanistan, decided to convene immediately if the Soviets invaded Poland. One question in the minds of Nato planners was whether the Russians would also use their army based in East Germany to attack Poland from the West. What would then ensue? A wholesale mutiny by the Polish Army and an internal war within the Warsaw Pact that would be impossible to contain?

The portents were not good. With the end of the usual autumn field exercises, Soviet forces in East Germany as well as those in western Soviet Russia remained at a high state of alert, as did two Russian tank divisions in western Poland. Special exercises were staged in East Germany, Czechoslovakia and western USSR. As the IISS noted: 'By mid-November, a force of 25 to 30 divisions had been prepared to a high state of readiness in case the order should be given to invade Poland. Moreover, General Ivanovski, the former C-in-C of Soviet forces in East Germany, and one of the Soviet Army's most experienced senior commanders, was put in charge of the Belorussian military district, from where an invasion into Poland might be directed.'

Brixmis spotted a division of East German tanks assembling on the Baltic coast at Rügen Island, apparently preparing for a repeat of Germany's invasion of Poland. This was a sick as well as an ironic spectacle. Lech Walesa, the Solidarity boss and the only strike leader to win the support of Mrs Thatcher, growled: 'Soviet tanks can occupy the country but they will not get it to work again.'

Brixmis was tasked, in Operation Spahi, to assess what was being planned. Davis said: 'We were looking for communications exercises, troop movements, covert activity on the Polish border. All movement on the River Oder to East Berlin was to the Polish border. In many places we couldn't get within three miles of the border since it was declared a restricted area. The routes to the bridges were blocked by snow six feet deep.'

The Mission ran its patrols anyway. Signals traffic and everything else pointed towards normal, low-level activity by the Soviets. What was missing, however, was the human contact with the Soviets which would offer some better clue to their real intentions. Davis had stretched his political brief already by getting close enough to Rubanoff to share the white stork joke.

The Afghan invasion [in December 1979] had upset the West so much we were told we couldn't attend any official Soviet functions; no present-giving. We couldn't invite them, as had been the custom, to the Queen's Birthday party reception. The Foreign Office said that the SERB could only have six bottles of whisky that year instead of the usual twelve. That seemed so petty that I sent the usual dozen bottles anyway. Now, the Foreign Office instructions about whisky for Russians was a highly secret piece of information! Nevertheless I had a message back from the SERB commander. He was pleased to receive my gift of whisky and he hoped I would be allowed to keep my job because I had sent him more than the permitted quantity.

Since we couldn't entertain the Russians in our homes after Afghanistan we used the Mission House in Potsdam. I remember that during one good evening Alex Rubanoff said, 'Brian, let's take a stroll in the garden.' There was two feet of snow out there. When I gave him a funny look he said, 'I need some fresh air and so do you. We will hear the birds, look at the lake.' Out we went, out of bugging range.

Standing in the snow, in the dark, Rubanoff came straight to the point: 'Brian, I have to tell you we have no interest whatever in supporting anything that is going on in Poland with our GSFG [Group of Soviet Forces in Germany].'

The brigadier got the message, which was, 'You are wasting your time.' A few months later, the Polish crisis was contained through the imposition of martial law by the Polish government, using Polish forces. Rubanoff was to be vindicated, but the West was not prepared to take his word. For fourteen months, until 13 December 1981, the three Allied Missions shared the burden of watching for 'target indicators' (signs of trouble) defined in advance. Brixmis patrolled the E74 autobahn up to the Polish border. The French worked the E15, E22 and Cottbus–Finsterwalder railway line. The Gallic Mission's railway 'sleeper' was still feeding them information which they shared freely with the British. The US Mission shared some local chores, patrolling round Potsdam, to free the French for more enterprising work on the rail network.

Brigadier Davis handed over command of the Mission in 1982 to Brigadier (later General Sir John) Learmont after two years in which the team had suffered eight or nine serious injuries. These resulted from beatings, rammings and even harassment by Hind helicopters. A Brixmis memoir laconically summarized some of these:

On 25 August 1980 at the Merseburg airfield a tour tried to make good its escape from an OP overlooking the approach path after being spotted by a Soviet UAZ (patrol car). The UAZ approached . . . a Soviet officer got out and threw a rock at the car breaking the rear right window. The UAZ then rammed the tour vehicle twice before the tour vehicle eventually made good its escape.

On 12 March 1981 a shot was fired at a tour car, possibly at the tyre, but missed and the tour evaded subsequent pursuit.

On 15–16 April a tour was moving into an OP at Wittenberg when three shots were fired over the top of the vehicle. The tour left . . . drove along the E22 autobahn near Cottbus when two UAZ attempted to detain the car by blocking the road. The tour car glanced off one of the UAZ and made good its escape.

On 3 July in Wildau a tour stopped to buy ice cream (a favourite pastime). A Vopo officer tried to detain the tour car . . . following a pursuit the tour was blocked by another Vopo vehicle and rammed from behind.

On 10–11 August a tour encountered exercise traffic . . . After an accident the tour was threatened by an armed officer. The tour NCO and driver were manhandled, the key to the car taken and

all tour equipment stolen. The tour, comprising Major (later Brigadier) P. A. Flanagan, Sergeant (later Staff Sergeant) I. M. McColl
BEM and Corporal Jones, were held for fourteen hours.

On 1 September a tour was leaving the Eupen training area
having observed a Scud deployment when a sentry ran towards
the vehicle and fired seven rounds at the car. The tour left the
area along a different route.

This tour was led by Captain (later Major) Nigel Shakespear,
who got so close to the highly sensitive business of practising Scud
launch precedures that serial numbers on some of the weapon's
containers could be read without difficulty. The photographs make
a dramatic sequence, from arrival on the carrier to the vertical
erection of the missile ready for firing.

The final incident of 1981 occurred on 14 October. An air tour
was returning to Potsdam when it met a column moving east at
Freyenstein. The tour car was rammed twice by an MAZ-537 tank
transporter before escaping.

A tank transporter is a very large vehicle. In a collision, it would
have the same relationship to a Brixmis tour car as a size 16 boot
might have to a black beetle. It should be no surprise that not
every member of the Mission was ready to be sacrificed so as to
vindicate the Robertson–Malinin Agreement of 1946. As Major-
General Davis, now in retirement, confirmed: 'We had a flight
lieutenant who was beaten up by people using pickaxe handles.
He was very badly shaken and he really lost his nerve for the
business after that, understandably. In another case an RAF warrant officer – a master air loadmaster – was the tour NCO in a
forced traffic accident. He became a casualty.'

In the soured atmosphere following the Afghanistan invasion of
1979 and the Polish crisis soon after, and under a hawkish new
commander, General Zaitsev, the Group of Soviet Forces in Germany from 4 December 1980 demonstrated that it was not just
senior NCOs and junior officers who were on the hit list. When
Davis left in 1982, the Chief's official shiny black car with its one
star and Union flag on the bonnet and 'Brixmis 1' on the back –
the embodiment of protocol – was one of the few Mission vehicles
still untouched.

CHAPTER 10

'Hand-to-Hand Liaison'

1981–85

In the early 1980s, it seemed as if the Cold War was spiralling into one of its periodic East–West crises, trials of strength, that had characterized the Berlin blockade and the Cuban missile affair. As Brigadier (later General Sir John) Learmont, Chief of Mission, wrote in his 1983 report: 'During the last twenty months I have witnessed the biggest re-equipment programme undertaken by GSFG (Soviet Forces, Germany) since World War II. The improvement is both qualitative and quantitative. The threat presented now is totally different from that presented in late 1982. Western nations would be unwise not to comprehend fully what has been achieved in the weapons field in recent months.'

The difference between this and earlier crises was that it was less than clear who was in charge of the international poker game. Martial law was imposed on the Poles on 13 December 1981, de-stabilizing much Warsaw Pact planning and calling into question some of the Pact's most cherished assumptions. Leonid Brezhnev finally expired on 10 November and was succeeded by another ailing geriatric, Yuri Andropov. Andropov, a former KGB boss, lasted a mere fifteen months. Most key government posts in Moscow were now filled with KGB professionals, while control of the Group of Soviet Forces in Germany was assumed by General Zaitsev, who seems to have adopted as his credo a Soviet 'folk-saying', ironically quoted by a leading dissident: 'We will fight for peace until there isn't one stone left standing on another.'

The GDR's Stasi secret police – a private army of 85,000 – also tightened its grip on the citizens of East Germany, tapping 1,000 telephones at a time, storing five million names on its computers, filling 18 kilometres of shelving with yet more personal records.

Brixmis forged its own ironic *bon mot* to match the spirit of the age. It was now practising 'hand-to-hand liaison'. As the IISS report for 1981–82 put it: 'The stalemate in East–West relations continued and procedures for effective crisis management remained woefully underdeveloped . . . According to Western opinion polls, the fear of nuclear war had seldom been shared by so many since the Cuban missile crisis of twenty years before.'

The sharply increased pressure on all the Western Missions can be traced to the appointment of the bear-like General Zaitsev – a charismatic officer known among Western Missions as 'Big Z' – on 4 December 1980. Zaitsev had joined his army, of which he was passionately proud, in 1939. He had been a tank commander through the Second World War, was at the forefront of the Battle of Berlin and bore the scars of a head wound. If he had one fixed belief it was that Germany would never be given another chance to invade his country.

This simplistic view conveniently overlooked the cynicism of the Nazi–Soviet pact which held until Hitler betrayed it in June 1941. Churchill, whose country had stood alone against the Nazis since 1940, had warned Stalin of what was to come. Stalin, cherishing the pact with Germany, disregarded the warning. For British as well as Russian communists, what Russians still describe as 'the Great Patriotic War' started not in 1939 – when the Soviets were invading Finland with Berlin's approval – but in 1941, when Wehrmacht Panzers struck at Russia.

A 1982 Brixmis memoir noted:

The impact of Zaitsev's character and ideas were absolutely key. He expounded his thoughts quite openly to the Chief at a meeting in Zossen Wünsdorf when he talked of 'future conflict procedures'. He didn't want to fight a war but he remembered personally the loss of twenty million of his countrymen in the last one and damn well wasn't about to let it happen again.

This robustly simple view was efficiently and ruthlessly put into practice throughout the tenure of his command. He corrected the infantry and artillery weaknesses. He lengthened and directed the training cycle. He appreciated the significance of firepower delivered by air, expanded the attack helicopter inventory and reckoned that 50 per cent of his total firepower would be delivered by aircraft. By 1983, GSFG had become a new and more dangerous animal.

Brigadier Learmont, Chief of Mission 1982–84, respected Zaitsev, whom he got to know through many meetings: 'He was a great patriot and a formidable leader of men, very impressive.'

Zaitsev, like many Soviet commanders, was secretly convinced that Nato, using the Germans, would repeat the shock of 1941. Not only history but Marxist theory also taught that the capitalists were doomed by their political system to resolve their cyclical economic problems through the catharsis of war. The Western Missions were licensed spies, the precursors of the invasion. He intended to curb them. He gave his divisional commanders strict instructions that they were to tighten up on mission tours. The commanders were ordered to file regular reports on the number of detentions they had achieved. More serious, from a Brixmis standpoint, was the increase in the number of Permanently Restricted Areas imposed on the Missions in May 1984 and notified in advance as being out of bounds to the tours. Such areas, marked in yellow on mission maps, spread remarkably.

The new policy of containing the missions began violently in August 1981 with the theft of a Brixmis tour car and its equipment and the detention of Major Flanagan and his crew for fourteen hours (see pages 233–4).

The tension was not relieved in mid-March 1982 when an American mission car, manned by two officers unwilling to experience 'hand-to-hand liaison', was ordered to stop by a Soviet officer on a bridge overlooking railway sidings at Dallgow-Döberitz. The bridge was a good vantage point for Allied train-spotters. It was also a favourite spot for catching them. On this occasion a US Marine Corps officer who had just joined the American Mission was learning routes and techniques from a colleague. When they were told to stop, they were surrounded by a Soviet Army platoon. The Marine Corps was not trained to take orders from real, live, three-dimensional communists. The US tour vehicle, a Mercedes

Geländewagen, was driven at the Soviet officer and then over him. Fortunately the ground clearance beneath the G-wagen was enough to avoid crushing him, but he was severely concussed and hospitalized for a time before returning to duty. The episode would have ended fairly peacefully, as just another routine detention, if the Marine Corps spirit had not come into play. As it was, both Americans were PNG'd and relations with the US Mission soured. Much worse was to follow, with loss of life as the logical outcome of a growing process of tit-for-tat.

On 28 June a Brixmis air tour – comprising RAF personnel spying on Flogger operations at the Soviet airfield at Merseburg and led by Flight Lieutenant Dick Hart – was ambushed by about a dozen Soviet guards, probably Spetznaz. The driver, Corporal Steve Jones, took his vehicle through them. They scattered. There were no casualties. There was just one problem: the tour NCO, Flight Sergeant Colin Birnie BEM, was still outside the car. Birnie was a good athlete with a reputation for using his fists. He had been ambushed in this area before and was lucky to escape injury when a Russian threw a rock through his car window.

To elude the latest ambush, he 'ran to the centre of the field, followed by a Soviet soldier and leapt into the Range Rover as it passed'. The soldier grabbed his foot. Birnie kicked him in the face with his other foot. They drove off, pursued by ten Soviet soldiers.

Birnie and Hart knew the ground well enough to be aware that the number of escape routes was limited. Behind them was a Permanently Restricted Area which it would be fatal to penetrate. Ahead lay the River Elbe. They found one rat-run which seemed clear but after little more than a mile they discovered a Soviet truck blocking their way. They made a U-turn. Birnie remembered: 'I had one escape route left, over the Elbe. We thought we had made it when over the hill came a UAZ-469 [jeep]. I said to Steve, 'Let's go for it!' He jinked our car left and right but the UAZ hit us sideways-on. We careered down a twenty-two-foot bank into a ditch leading to the Elbe. This was a well-orchestrated ambush and we were trapped.'

After some time, the flight lieutenant got out of the car, now surrounded by armed Russians, one of them smoking near the leaking fuel tank. They claimed that his team had driven over one man and that the jeep driver had severe head injuries. Birnie took his turn outside their car. A Soviet warrant officer stood close to him.

'He stank of booze. We had a bit of eye-to-eye contact.' Birnie, the veteran of several recent fights in the army sergeants' mess where he was accommodated, was not flustered by the prospect of another fight, but then he had a bright idea.

It was World Cup time. Scotland was due to play the USSR that week. I explained, using a lot of sign language, that I was a Scot. I told him that he might have smashed our vehicle but Scotland were going to smash the USSR at football. His mood changed immediately. He was saying 'Oleg Blochin,' 'Kenny Dalgleish,' 'Joe Jordan' and so on. In no time at all we were like brothers. He was now on our side to such a degree that he punched one of his men for smoking near our vehicle.

The Soviets eventually pulled us out and allowed us to proceed. I was invited back by their warrant officer for a night on the vodka. We limped home to Berlin.

The following month a tour car on the E-8 autobahn, following the progress of a big Warsaw Pact exercise (Hauptstoss 82), found itself under simultaneous attack from the air and on the ground. A mere ten feet above the car a HIP-C helicopter angrily buffeted the roof with its powerful downdraft while a Soviet jeep repeatedly crossed both sides of the autobahn, regardless of oncoming traffic, in its efforts to ram the Brixmis vehicle. The Mission memoir claimed: 'Local East Germans were so impressed by the tour's tenacity that they informed them where other major exercise movement was going on!'

Flight Sergeant Birnie had an even closer encounter with a helicopter gunship: 'We were outside our car, an Opel Senator, at Retzow, an aircraft weapons range in the north of East Germany. We were aware of a Hind flying very low towards us. Setting ourselves up for the intelligence photo of the year, we waited for the Hind to make its approach. Through the binoculars I could see that it was getting mighty close and low. I shouted to the tour officer that it was going to land. We got into the vehicle to escape. As we did so the wheels of the Hind bumped the roof.'

He also acted as guide to a new Chief of Mission. To get the Boss into detention was to lose much face, so Birnie chose as a target a radar site which was tucked away in a tranquil and usually unguarded spot near a place called Dahme. The Boss insisted on shooting an extra few frames of film. It wasn't their day. Birnie recalled:

> I noticed the guards pointing rifles at us. A UAZ-469 exited the site. A ZIL-131 truck approached from the rear and a URAL-375 truck blocked the road in front . . . The Range Rover shot forward with the Chief entangled in assorted films, cameras and motor drives. I remembered a small road I'd passed many times, marked on my map as 'No-Go'. It seemed worth a try. We hurtled along the road with half the East German Army chasing us. The escape route led to a cemetery. I asked the Chief, 'Are you religious?' 'Not particularly, Flight,' he said. That was good. We went full speed ahead, through the front gates. How we avoided the headstones and graves in a Range Rover I'll never know. There was a gap just large enough to let us out. We escaped and cruised quietly back to the Mission House.

The Russians knew that they could not depend upon their satellites. At their backs, in Warsaw, 30,000 Poles had taken to the streets in defiance of martial law to demand the release of the trade-union leader, Lech Walesa. Poland was on the brink of three days of street fighting in four major cities. To secure communications between their East German garrison and Mother Russia, skirting round Poland, the Soviets were obliged to develop a huge port on the Baltic coast of the GDR at Neu Mukran, near the former Nazi holiday camp at Prora (see Appendix IX). This did nothing to relieve their cultural isolation. Around the Soviet Army, East Germans expressed their contempt with sullen silence. Junkets set up by 'Soviet–German Friendship Clubs' were attended by a few Communist Party clones. Like Romans outnumbered by the barbarians on the edge of empire, the Russians lived in an atmosphere of

242

increasing fear and isolation. The only targets on which they could vent those emotions were the Western Missions. The East German Volksarmee (the NVA) followed its example.

No one was immune. On 12 August Brigadier Learmont, Davis's successor as Mission Chief, was one victim. As his shiny black staff car, with its Union flag proudly displayed on the bonnet, passed an East German radar site near Quedlinburg, an NVA vehicle roared through the gates in a carefully planned 'accident' to hit the British car squarely behind the front offside door, forcing the car against a tree. Two weeks later Sergeant Tony Haw QGM and his driver Corporal Anderson (accomplices in Hugh McLeod's break-in of a T-64) with Flight Lieutenant (later Squadron Leader) Alan Bouchard MBE, were watching a train of anti-aircraft missiles known as SA-9 and the latest tracked infantry carrier, the BMP-2, being unloaded. The place they had chosen for this was a favourite corner of the railway sidings at Neubuckow. They were spotted by a Spetznaz ambush team who broke into the car and hauled out Bouchard. Next they grabbed Anderson and beat him up. With his officer and driver hauled away he knew not where, Haw stayed put. There was another fight which continued until Haw, too, was finally extracted from a vehicle which, according to the rules, enjoyed diplomatic immunity.

The crew was held effectively in detention, under arrest, for five hours. Meanwhile Soviet soldiers helped themselves to the car's contents. The British protested at the highest level, to Zaitsev's staff, but it cut no ice.

Not surprisingly, drivers who could shake off pursuers were becoming highly valued within the Mission. Among them, Corporal Paul Hartley, Royal Corps of Transport, became a legend between 1981 and 1983. Driving an Opel Senator saloon car he was being hotly pursued by a Soviet BMP armoured personnel carrier across farmland. The Russian-hating farmer, taking in what was happening, opened a barn door and waved the Brixmis car through, then shut the door as Hartley made good his escape on the other side. An angry Russian followed, through the now-closed doors, wrecking much of the building. That episode was one in a ten-hour attempt, which did not succeed, to arrest the crew driven by Hartley. On another occasion he was cornered in a field by eight Soviet Army vehicles: 'After twenty minutes I lured them to one end of the field, then slipped through and escaped.'

In 1982, responding to an 'agency' request combined with a tip-off, his team chased a Soviet military train for 120 miles until it stopped in a siding at 8 A.M., where they photographed it. 'We never learned what it was carrying,' Hartley recalled years later. 'I took it to be a nuclear "command" train of a type I had not seen before. I think it would be used as a command centre in a nuclear war. To stay with it we had to drive fast . . . It was vital to catch it up before the train reached the Czech border, where we could not follow. The map-reading had to be spot on.'

Hartley calculated his risks. Training drivers new to the Mission, he told them to control their adrenalin. 'Otherwise,' he said, 'on a straight track you will start at 50 m.p.h. and soon hit a bend at 120 m.p.h. and kill everyone. In traffic, leave enough room to escape towards the front, since most attacks come from the rear . . . Be vigilant; spot potential escape routes.'

Those who could not flee so effectively used camouflage. Major Jeremy York, an accomplished Operations Officer with the Mission from 1982 to 1985, remembered 'carrying a Royal British Legion wreath on one or two occasions so that if caught in a tight spot I intended to step out of the car, lay the wreath against a barrack wall, or whatever, salute smartly, get back in the car and drive off.' His other evasion techniques included 'canoeing out as a highly effective way of getting a head start on the narks; visits to cemeteries, ice-cream stops and "miniculturals".'

One British tour officer was now attracting special attention from the opposition. Captain Bob Longhorn, a Royal Corps of Transport officer who later transferred to the Intelligence Corps, had a knack of getting under the skin of the Stasi. It is thought they became so irritated that they asked the Russians to make an example of him, *pour encourager les autres*. Longhorn was to enjoy the distinction of being the last Brixmis officer to be declared *persona non grata*, but his first encounter with the opposition, by the standards of the day, was not unusual.

On 13 August 1982, the day after Learmont's staff car was rammed, Longhorn and his team were 'train-spotting' at Satzkorn sidings and were chased by two six-wheel trucks, Soviet ZIL 131s.

The Mission crew thought they had the situation licked when a third ZIL intercepted them. As they weaved through the trap, one of the chase vehicles caught up and dented the front passenger door. It was a minor event. Longhorn carried on touring without trouble, until 28 December when he was chased by a four-wheel Soviet lorry, a ZIL-130. He shook this off, unscathed. Later in the day, as he paused to take a coffee break in a car park at Bad Berka, the same Soviet vehicle charged past a 'No-entry' sign on the wrong side of the car park and rammed Longhorn's vehicle. A chase followed and, surprisingly, an apology from the Soviet commandant at Weimar.

On 10 August 1983, Longhorn glanced in his car mirror and saw a Stasi Lada following him. He and the crew stopped to brew up. The Lada's occupants photographed them. Longhorn, says a Brixmis report, 'went to remonstrate with the driver (a common ploy) and emphasized his point by tapping the vehicle windscreen with a small stick, causing no damage'.

More months passed and 'on 17 January 1984 a Soviet URAL-375 drove head-on at his tour car deliberately ramming it in the rear door, damaging the vehicle beyond repair'. Eight days later, East German soldiers detained Longhorn at Havelberg and two days after that he was involved in a genuine traffic accident with a local civilian vehicle. The tour car was a total write-off. As if that was not enough, the Brixmis car sent to pick up the Longhorn crew was also involved in a crash with an East German vehicle. Longhorn's history now began to acquire a unique, almost slapstick flavour. He avoided any sort of arrest or ramming throughout February, but on 1 March he was rammed by the irate crew of a Soviet SA-8 mobile SAM missile system. This vehicle, while not in the same league as a tank transporter, is a six-wheel truck capable of crippling a car without recourse to the missiles it carries. The Russians now began preparing a case for Longhorn's expulsion.

The *persona non grata* notice was signed by Colonel-General Sviridov, Chief-of-Staff at the Group of Soviet Forces German headquarters on 16 March and was addressed to the British Chief-of-Staff, Major-General Mike Grey. It said:

The number of serious violations by members of your Mission has steadily increased. In two months of 1984 there have been six detentions of Brixmis crews. The actions of Captain Longhorn are particularly shocking. He engages in active reconnaissance of units and installations of GSFG, so creating situations that endanger the health and life of GSFG soldiers and GDR [East German] citizens.

On 17 January, whilst observing military equipment, he created an accident situation as a result of which there occurred a collision between Brixmis Car No. 6 and a Soviet military vehicle. On 25 January 1984, Brixmis Car No. 11, commanded by Captain Longhorn, was detained by NVA [East German] troops for carrying out reconnaissance of a local installation; the installation was bordered by signs forbidding entry to members of foreign military liaison missions.

On 27 January this same vehicle violated traffic regulations and collided with a Kombinat tractor. The collision caused considerable damage to both vehicles; the tractor driver sustained bodily injuries. On 1 March Captain Longhorn's crew, in Car No. 7, three times approached a column of vehicles in order to obtain intelligence; he ignored demands by GSFG soldiers to stop. Attempting to escape detention in the village of Reuden, the mission car drove on to a pavement where building work was being carried out and collided with a pile of bricks. Such an incident is outrageous. Crew members of Car No. 8 stopped a passing car driven by a GDR civilian. Captain Longhorn went up to the car and banged on the bonnet; he then hit the windscreen several times with a piece of wood. Subsequently the crew of No. 8 attempted to ram the car and push it into the ditch.

In all, Captain Longhorn penetrated permanent and temporary restricted areas seven times. He was detained by GSFG personnel four times for illegal activity, for which the relevant 'Akts' were made out by representatives of Soviet Kommandanturas.

The letter demanded action to halt 'illegal actions' by mission teams including reconnaissance, traffic violations and disrespect of 'the rules regarding foreign citizens in the GDR'. It concluded: 'For systematic and malicious violations of traffic laws and for actions incompatible with the status of a Mission member, I suggest you remove Captain Longhorn from the staff of the British Military Mission. Otherwise the High Command of GSFG reserves the right to remove Captain Longhorn's accreditation to HQ GSFG.'

For Longhorn, the doubtful honour of being PNG'd might have been a life-saver. Six days after Sviridov wrote his expulsion letter, on 22 March, a tour officer was murdered in one of these jaunts. The victim was a French regimental sergeant-major, Adjutant-Chef Mariotti. He was travelling in a French tour car at Halle when an East German Army URAL-375 truck approaching from the opposite direction swept across the central reservation of a dual carriageway to smash into the driver's side of the vehicle. A Mission report put it: 'The force of the collision was so great that the URAL mounted the French tour vehicle, coming to rest on its roof. Adjutant-Chef Mariotti was killed instantly.' Brixmis veterans still regard Mariotti's death as a premeditated homicide.

Only a few days earlier, the BAOR chief-of-staff had warned the Soviet Army headquarters in Germany that this game of 'car wars' was becoming lethal. The Soviet soldier hit by the American tour car would have said amen to that. The role of the East German Army in Mariotti's death was specially disturbing. They now seemed to be working to their own agenda with no control by the Soviets. Brixmis itself observed:

> On the face of it, the Mariotti incident appeared wholly unprovoked by the French and unplanned by the rammer. That it was deliberate is unquestioned. However, there was much speculation that the East German soldiers were not what they appeared to be and that they were in fact either members of the MfS (Stasi secret police) or the Soviet anti-mission units (Spetznaz) based near the GSFG headquarters at Zossen Wünsdorf. If that were the case then the killing would appear to be both deliberate and pre-planned. Given the current intelligence success of the Allied Missions at the time, particularly the French, and given the general professional and hostile increase in anti-mission activity . . . this action was a deliberate statement of intent to crack down.

If the danger signals were clear to one side, they should have been clear to both. The US Mission did not read it that way. Almost a year to the day after Mariotti's death, Major Arthur (Nick) Nicholson, a popular member of the Mission, with his driver Sergeant Schatz, was probing the secrets of the training area known as Ludwigslust 475. Nicholson had been a star on the pre-Mission training course run by the British at a secret centre in the UK. He had impressed his British peers, as well as others, with a twenty-four-hour stay inside a T-64b tank hangar. Now he was trying to crack Ludwigslust 475, an area too large to enclose with secure fences. The Russians did not bother. As a British report noted: 'The area is easily accessible by forest roads and tracks, often used by East German civilians.'

The civilians, in warm weather, occasionally removed all clothing to indulge in the favourite East German pastime of sunbathing. In a repressive communist state this practice was subversive because a naked human being would not be carrying identity papers. It was defended by citizens of the GDR as one of their last freedoms, so much so that officials sent to enforce the law forbidding nudity were overwhelmed by large numbers of naked, angry people. A tradition of tolerating nudity on the beach or in the forest gradually grew up until, after the reunification of Germany, tourists from West Germany objected.

While the Cold War was at its height, to soften the outlines of close-up photographs of Soviet weapons systems, Mission crews would occasionally also take pictures of the sunbathers. In due time naked German nymphs decorated parts of the army's intelligence centre back in Britain. The paradox of Ludwigslust training area 475 was that it was also a highly sensitive military zone, the home of a T-80 tank regiment and over-cultivated by the French as well as the Americans. The tank gunnery range, where the T-80's main gun was not fired but supplementary machine-guns were used, with live ammunition, proclaimed itself a dangerous place to be. The message was reinforced by the presence of armed Soviet guards who routinely shot at uninvited visitors. In October 1984, the French Lieutenant-Colonel Manificat had come under fire there. According to a British report:

The US tour approached the sub-calibre tank range at approximately 1520 hrs on 24 March. After an initial probe to the edge of the wood line 200 metres east of the sheds [where Soviet tanks including the new T-80 were thought to be parked] they made a second approach and exited the wood line directly north of the sheds. After stopping and listening the tour drove up to the sheds to recce for security personnel. No guards were evident. The car was positioned by a storage shed 200 metres south of the tank shed. Major Nicholson left the vehicle and photographed the poster [training] boards with a Canon auto-focus camera whilst the NCO undertook a look-out.

Major Nicholson re-entered the vehicle and the tour moved around to a position ten metres north of the tank sheds. Major Nicholson left the vehicle and the NCO stood in the vehicle hatch as look-out. A Soviet soldier standing in the northern wood line was observed by the NCO aiming a weapon at him. He turned and shouted, 'Sir, get in the car!' Before he was able to finish the warning he heard a round go past him. He dropped inside, started the vehicle, unlocked the passenger door and started off in reverse. He heard two more shots and a scream. When he looked back Major Nicholson was lying on the ground.

Those who knew Nicholson agree that he was not a 'cowboy', a trophy-hunter, but a cool, professional soldier. Sergeant Schatz, it is believed, left the car to give first-aid to his wounded officer but was ordered at gunpoint back into the vehicle and forced to remain there, under pain of death himself, as Nicholson bled to death. This scene, like some of the killings alongside the Berlin Wall, provoked horror as well as indignation among the Western Missions.

One of the first senior Soviets on the scene was none other than Zaitsev's chief-of-staff General Krivosheyev. He was far above the rank structure represented by the Soviet External Relations Bureau with which the Allied Missions routinely dealt, usually in a spirit of co-operation. Zaitsev was a hawk among hawks. First Mariotti, now Nicholson, had been murdered. The timing, as a Brixmis analysis noted, was sinister: both deaths had occurred just before the end of the Soviet accounting year, as had the PNG notice served on the British Captain Longhorn.

The day after Nicholson's killing, representatives of the missions, part of a 'tripartite rapid response committee', convened in Heidelberg, the US Army headquarters in southern Germany. The committee advised that the three Western commanders-in-chief in Germany should protest to the Soviets. All social and liaison work was cancelled forthwith. The Soviet Mission, Soxmis, would not be permitted to tour when a memorial service was held in Berlin on 28 March; nor on 30 or 31 March, while Nicholson's funeral was taking place in Arlington, Virginia, in the presence of Vice-President Bush. New limits were imposed on Soxmis movements throughout West Germany. On 26 April Washington expelled the Soviet military attaché, Lieutenant-Colonel Stanislav Gromov, in a further gesture of displeasure.

The Nicholson tragedy resonated long after that. In Washington, as a Brixmis memoir observed, it rankled until 1988, when the Cold War was accelerating towards the buffers. As a contemporaneous Brixmis report put it: 'Relations were curt and acrimonious. The continued existence of the US Mission was even questioned, given that the Americans argued themselves into a corner over Permanently Restricted Areas and the obeyance [sic] of all Mission Restricted Signs.' For the first time since the missions came into being in 1946, the British adopted an independent national policy. 'Brixmis broke with Anglo-US solidarity in order to preserve the Mission role, continued to press for reductions in PRA and preserve the traditional non-observance of Mission Restricted Signs.'

Should the British and French Missions have gone out of business as a protest? The doomsayers' credibility was strengthened on 4 June 1985, less than ten weeks after Nicholson's death, by more Soviet brutality on a country road near Schorbus, south-east of Berlin. This time a British patrol was the target. At 7 A.M. a tour officer named Captain Guy Potter, with his NCO Sergeant (later Warrant Officer 1, or Sergeant-Major) Nick Rowles and driver Corporal Paul Roberts were studying military convoys from a stationary observation post 100 metres from the road and at an angle to it. Almost certainly the NCO was calling the numbers and types of vehicle into a tape recorder while the officer used a motor-driven camera or camcorder.

Suddenly a medium-sized GAZ-66 truck turned away from the column and drove at speed towards the parked British car, apparently to ram it head-on. Corporal Roberts started his engine and swung away. The Soviet vehicle caught them a glancing blow. The Brixmis team went into evasive-driving mode, chased by the GAZ-66. Having opened some space between themselves and the Russians, they tried to make a three-point turn. This was insufficient. A Brixmis report said: 'The GAZ-66 caught up and rammed the tour vehicle in the side at approximately 40 k.p.h. (about 25 m.p.h.). The force of impact lifted the tour vehicle off its wheels, moving it sideways and in so doing removed two of the vehicle tyres from the wheel rims. Soviet soldiers then assaulted the tour vehicle with shovels and bricks.' The British team remained inside their car, still doggedly determined to get away. 'Despite the vehicle damage the tour departed rapidly, given the persistent and life-threatening actions of the limpet-like 66.'

They reached the tiny town of Schorbus, a mile or so away, and found a garage whose owner agreed to do a quick repair job on their battered car. This was hoisted on jacks and without one wheel when 'the Soviets found them again and deployed troops around the vehicle, having first ostentatiously issued live ammunition which they loaded into weapons, cocked and removed safety catches'.

Although the GAZ-66 had come from the local Soviet HQ, the kommandantura, Captain Potter and his people were initially relieved when the regional Soviet commandant arrived from the town of Cottbus. Cottbus, if not the centre of the universe, was at least on the map, unlike the obscure place in which they were now trapped. Furthermore, the commandant was the official conduit through which such situations were usually brought under control while tempers cooled. In this case that did not happen. 'The Cottbus commandant arrived eventually and the situation resumed an air of normality until a Soviet major, under the eyes of the commandant and behind the [British] crew's backs, stole the NCO's tour bag and ran off with it. The tour officer protested in vain at this action. The tour finally left minus tour bag.'

A diplomatic row rapidly escalated in Berlin. An invitation to Soviet officers to attend the Queen's Birthday Parade on 7 June was withdrawn. The Foreign Office sat on its hands and left the Chief of Mission to bring things under control. The Mission had its own problems at the time. The Chief had just left prematurely. His deputy's health had failed. This left a senior staff officer, Lieutenant-Colonel (later Colonel) Roy Giles CBE to take on a full-blown diplomatic rumpus with an opposition several ranks above his own. Headquarters of British Army of the Rhine in West Germany was also happy to delegate this hot potato to the acting Chief of Mission. Matters were further complicated when someone, probably in the US Mission, leaked to the Berlin bureau of Reuters news agency word of the last-minute British withdrawal of the invitation to the Queen's Birthday celebration.

The only truly helpful gesture came from the Commander-in-Chief of French forces in Germany, who offered to write from his Baden Baden headquarters some word of reproof to the Soviets. Brixmis, though grateful, felt that this was a case of 'least said, soonest mended'.

Since 1979, the British Mission crews had been rammed and detained twenty-five times, and there had been four shooting incidents. It was a matter of luck that none of these was fatal. In four more instances, Brixmis crews had been beaten up or otherwise assaulted. In almost every case, the only British response that was authorized was a protest by the Chief of Mission or the deputy or the deputy's deputy.

A luminous exception was the successful campaign by Brigadier Learmont to persuade BAOR to PNG the most effective Russian officer serving in West Germany with Soxmis at that time, as a reprisal for the unnecessary action against Captain Bob Longhorn. As Learmont sharply reminded the Soviets, Longhorn was virtually at the end of his service with Brixmis and would not serve in East Germany again. This diplomatic overkill cost the Soviets their most knowledgeable officer on the Western side.

An acute observer of what was happening from 1982 to 1984, was Major (later Lieutenant-Colonel) Nigel Wylde, an explosives expert. Fresh from staff college, he was posted to the Mission as its weapons intelligence officer. He also went on the road as a tour officer on 270 days.

Wylde, as meticulous as his trade implied, tried to recover a plough attached to a Soviet tank, from a wood. The plough's purpose was to clear anti-tank mines. Wylde spent twenty-four hours trying to retrieve it. There was one problem: the plough weighed 1.5 tons. Wylde had to settle for detailed photographs and technical measurements instead.

He delved into the multiple layers of signals equipment used by the Soviet Army during exercises to test the command and control of their forces including those armed with gas and nuclear weapons. He scoured the area used by one signals regiment and found a list of code-words used in an exercise that had just ended. British Signals Intelligence had recorded what the Soviets were saying during the exercise; they could now understand what was said.

In February 1983, Wylde photographed a new artillery gun, the M1976, at a railway station where it was under armed guard.

Back at Brixmis headquarters, Wylde co-ordinated the vast flow of intelligence scooped up by others in the Mission. The RAF Chipmunk team now had its own dedicated staff: two aircrew, a photographic interpreter and back-up clericals. 'Under the tripartite agreement Brixmis was allowed three operational flights per week at 500 feet and took photographs over barracks and training areas,' Wylde recalled. 'That way we got perfect photographs of Soviet tanks exposed for maintenance, with turrets off and the ordnance – missiles and shells of various kinds – laid out on tarpaulins. The type of ordnance carried revealed the role of those particular tanks.'

The aircrew also briefed the 'Local Tour', before it left for a twenty-four-hour reconnaissance around West Berlin. This run was part of the constant surveillance maintained during the Cold War by the missions in their check on 'Indicators of Hostilities', a necessary precaution, given the elaborate plans made by the East German Army to seize West Berlin with 32,000 soldiers if that became necessary. Among the chilling assumptions built into the East German war plan was the belief that the Allies would defend West Berlin with thirty-two nuclear weapons.

Technical intelligence reports on the latest Soviet equipment with pictures to illuminate them were circulated around the Western intelligence agencies. Brixmis produced more than two hundred of these reports each year, many as a result of Chipmunk flights. These were now run in a more stringent, professional fashion with a switch from part-time air duties by some of the Mission's airmen, to full-time flying by a team who did nothing else.

As one of them explained: 'We became the eyes and ears of Rheindahlen [the headquarters of RAF Germany]. The fiction that RAF officers with the Mission needed to keep their flying skills current, to qualify for aircrew pay, was dropped.'

Not only were the aircrew dedicated exclusively to Brixmis reconnaissance missions, they also attended the Mission's recognition classes and scored well in the tests that followed. The observer/photographer now flew in the front seat, the pilot in the rear, so as to give the camera a clearer view of the target. Aerobatics over the Berlin Control Zone were out. The two aging Chipmunks – airframe numbers WX 862 and WD 289 – remained unchanged. Their maintenance benefited, perhaps, from the absence of stress imposed by loops and spins.

On the ground meanwhile, the RAF's patrols (air tours) worked to get even better photographs of the underside of Soviet aircraft as they lifted off, heavy with weapons and radar pods. The British airmen had the satisfaction of knowing that the highly secret pictures taken by US satellites, in orbit 200 miles high, could not match what they were seeing from below. They also visited RAF squadrons whose wartime mission would be to hit targets in East Germany to offer photographs of the places already earmarked for attack. 'We told them,' said one veteran, '"If you have targeted a particular bridge, we can photograph it for you."'

The man co-ordinating most of this was the Squadron Leader, Operations ('Slops'). From February 1987 to October 1988 that was Squadron Leader (later Wing Commander) Andrew Pennington. In a private memoir he described how the job was done.

The actual decision as to which target a tour would be sent to and in which order, came down to gut-feeling and experience on the part of the Squadron Leader Ops. He liaised regularly with the intelligence staff at headquarters, RAF Germany at Rheindahlen and with the Defence Intelligence Staff in the Ministry of Defence. Each week he met the US and French Mission Air Ops officers to exchange information, plans and requirements.

In choosing airfields he was helped by the fact that both Russian and East German airfields flew to a generally fixed pattern. For instance in area B (the south-west corner of East Germany) the airfield at Zerbst only flew on Monday, Wednesday and Friday whilst its sister airfield at Koethen flew Tuesday, Thursday and Saturday. By playing these flying days with the [bombing and air missile] ranges, which were open most days, Squadron Leader Ops tried to work out a route which kept the Air Tour [patrol] busy and generally got them pointed back towards Berlin on the last day of the tour. If the tour came up with something more interesting or of a higher priority for int. collection en route, then the tour officer was at liberty to use his common sense and ignore the plan, so long as he could justify his decision on his return.

There were attempts to use this system the wrong way. If a tour had been allocated a set of potentially very boring static targets along the Czech border there was always a temptation to find something more pressing that would save them from going all that way.

Detailed map planning followed. 'OPs at airfields were almost self-selecting, since the needs of photography meant having the sun behind you, ideally on the approach to an airfield where the aircraft would follow predictable paths and be relatively slow.' For static targets such as radar sites, the full history of previous visits by Allied Missions was reviewed. This included 'notes concerning access, nark activity and general alertness and reactions of the sentries'.

The individual members of the tour crew then assembled their kit (see Appendix II).

Once everything was packed, the driver drove to each of the homes of the tour NCO and the tour officer, loaded their personal kit and then drove to the Brixmis offices in the Olympic Stadium, Berlin. Here the crew collected camera kits and tour bags containing maps, etc. and then checked with the Duty Watchkeeper for latest messages.

The last duty was to sign out in the Tour Log and then the tour was officially under way. After crossing the Glienicke Bridge, the tour always called at the [Potsdam] Mission House in case of any last-minute messages, and then set off. Normal time for air tours to leave the Olympic stadium was about 2030 hours, so exit from the Mission House ended at about 2130. The route towards the first target was normally navigated by the tour NCO, leaving the navigation to the Z-platz [sleeping area] to the tour officer. The tour was always alert for ground forces movement or activity en route, but the tour officer, for some unaccountable reason, tended to sleep.

This was considered to be OK (at least among the tour officers) as long as he could wake up instantly and operate a camera. Since the first indication of activity was normally a sharp application of the brakes by the driver, followed by the hunting cry of the Mission – 'Kit!' – some drivers would test the alertness of the tour officers by tapping the brakes very lightly for the fun of hearing the tour officer burst into wakefulness, ask what was going on, and say that he wasn't really asleep but only sitting with his eyes closed.

About ten miles from the pre-selected Z-platz the tour began evasive driving, using cross-country routes, pausing, doubling back to discover whether a nark tail had joined them.

It was rarely we saw any late at night and the use of cross-country routes combined with night vision goggles normally deterred casual followers. Actual penetration into the Z-platz was carried out with lights off, using night vision goggles, or very dim 'Trabby' lights.

This surreptitious approach did not always work. On one occasion I was tour officer on a ground tour where we were tasked to observe the barracks at Schotheim in anticipation of a major move out. I was not particularly familiar with the area ... I deferred to the tour NCO ... It was about 1 A.M. and the Z-platz was in a thinly wooded area on a steep hill virtually on top of the barracks. It was raining heavily and had been for some days. The driver drove through the trees, lights out ... down a slippery track to where the Z was to be, right on the tree line where we were assured of a good view of the barracks should anything happen overnight. The ground was too bad to guarantee a quick exit should it be necessary.

The ground was too slippery to turn the G-wagen safely on the slope, so the tour NCO secured the electric winch to a tree to help pull the vehicle round. At the whispered command to take up the slack on the winch, the driver pushed what he thought was the winch control toggle, which immediately turned on the 4-way flashers . . . A minor panic set in to get the flashers switched off. In the confusion the driver managed also to sound the horn. Feeling very exposed, we managed to turn the vehicle and flee before we woke up the sleeping troops in the barracks below us.

That was not how it was usually done. In the darkness, the tour would make a quiet reconnaissance to ensure that they were not trying to camp next to a Soviet deployment (which once happened to Pennington).

The first move was for the driver to get out for a pee, after which the Tour Officer and NCO got out with their bed-rolls, leaving the vehicle free for the driver to sort out his bed inside it. Normally the other two would erect their tents within about 10 metres of the vehicle but this could be further depending on whether there was a snorer in the crew. Having found an appropriate site, largely by feeling with the feet, an experienced tourer could get his tent up and be in his sleeping bag within about a minute. I always slept extremely well but there were a lot of animal noises at night in the forests and these affected the more nervous bodies.

Flight Sergeant Birnie had his own way of dealing with that problem. He persuaded one nervous tour officer 'that he should urinate around his basha because it keeps the wild pigs at bay and to watch out for rabid squirrels'.

As Pennington saw it:

There was no point in getting up early just to sit around waiting for the flying to start, particularly since the narks had a habit of driving round likely OPs and Z-platzs early in the morning. It was much better to stay hidden until the aircraft appeared. This was complete anathema to the army, who subscribed to the centuries-old tradition of getting up for the Dawn 'Stand-to' . . . In 1985–86 the Soviet Air Force regularly started flying at 0430 hours in the summer but as time went on they started later and later. This might have been in response to East German complaints about flying noise. In 1987–88 there was a major reduction in night flying, reported in the East German press as a response to public complaints.

Once the flying had started, or earlier if the tour really couldn't manage to stay in bed any longer, the vehicle was moved carefully into the OP, parked in a direction which gave the driver the best view of potential routes into the OP by unwanted visitors . . . Once in position it was normal practice for one or other of the crew to take a walk around the immediate area, checking either for narks, Sovs [Soviet snatch squads] or [the opposition's] prepared OPs. During one tour, our driver took a walk, spotted the narks in a hide, grabbed their bag and found a camera with a 200mm lens and binoculars. The narks then grabbed the bag [back] and fled through the woods.

Recording the Soviets' flying programme, like every other aspect of the air tour, now followed a well-rehearsed drill.

The driver stayed in the vehicle, providing security, and also acting as log keeper. The officer and NCO stood outside but near the vehicle with the window partly open and the camera and binoculars on the seat inside. As soon as an aircraft was spotted the NCO used his binoculars (normally 15 × 60s) to identify the type, see the bort [side] number and alert the officer to weapons or anything that deserved special attention photographically.

The officer, using his 1000mm lens, plus doubler, if necessary, then took between five and thirty-five shots of the aircraft, depending on the type and its weapons. Because we used a mirror lens with a fixed aperture the only controls available were ASA [film speed] and shutter speed. Using 400 ASA film it was rare that you could set the camera at less than 1600 ASA even in summer. During the winter months, it was invariably stuck on 6400 ASA.

In spite of all the rule-book advice on using long lenses, we were unable to use tripods mainly because of the need to exit the scene rapidly when disturbed. The conventional wisdom that your shutter speed should be always equivalent to the focal length of your lens (i.e. 1,000mm lens × 1,000th/second shutter speed) had to be almost completely ignored.

The general exposure for aircraft in the sky was set and then if additional exposure was required because the NCO called interesting weapons or pods underneath, the officer could only adjust the shutter speed in mid-shot. All officers had to work out their own minimum shutter speed through practice. Mine was 1/250th with a 1,000mm lens.

As soon as the aircraft had passed out of view the officer called the [film] frame numbers to the driver, who entered them in the log whilst the officer and NCO took over the security look-out. The NCO then gave the aircraft type, bort number, weapons and any other details to the driver. The officer changed his film if he had used more than fifteen to twenty exposures, ready to take a full film of any 'scoop' should it turn up as the next item. At the same time as taking an air programme the tour was also alert for ground activity. It was not unknown for an RAF tour to photograph a road column and a kit train at the same time as reporting the air programme.

As flying ended, the RAF tour would move out, if they had not been rumbled already, and set a course for the next target, stopping overnight beside a railway line. 'Watching railway lines was a regular evening occupation. In winter a crew could end up sitting on lines from about 1600 hrs until midnight without seeing any [military] kit trains. This gave opportunities for outrageous bets, along the lines of, "I bet you one Eastmark that the next train will be a passenger train with eleven carriages, coming from the left." During an eight-hour rail watch, using double or quits, this could end up as an expensive pastime even in Eastmarks, with a conversion rate of between seven and ten Eastmarks to the Westmark.'

When the tour had completed its programme it returned to Berlin by way of the Potsdam Mission House.

At the House, the chance was taken for a cold drink and to pick up any messages to be taken back [by hand, for security] to Brixmis headquarters. The driver also cleaned the windscreen, lights and number plates and, if necessary, patched any minor scratches or dents with sticky tape ... to save a long wait on the Glienecke Bridge, since the Soviet guards would spend ages phoning around to establish whether the damage to our car had been caused by collision with Soviet or East German military or civilian traffic.

Having crossed the bridge the tour's next stop was the US Mission near Clayallee, where a quick highlight report was written and distributed. Then we went back to the stadium area, where personal kit was first dropped at home. Then the crew reported back to headquarters to book in and leave films, cameras and other items. Although that marked the end of the day for the officer and NCO the driver still had a major task in cleaning the vehicle inside and out, to prepare it for servicing the next day. The vehicle could get absolutely filthy on tour. That was encouraged since it added to the camouflage effect and often obscured our distinctive number plate.

The ideal weather for a driver was warm and dry for the tour with pouring rain on the way home, to clean the car. All tour officers made a point of marking river fords on their maps since a number of fast runs through a ford cleaned the underside of the vehicle extremely well.

Next morning, the debrief began with photographs that had been processed overnight into prints. The pictures were carefully checked to identify weapons, pods and anything else unusual. 'The report was then written to describe the tour activity ... providing a log and tying the film and frame numbers to each [aircraft] airframe. Any new weapons seen were selected and made into slides and large prints for rapid distribution around the intelligence community. Once the report was finished, planning started for the next tour and the cycle continued.'

In spite of the growth in violence against mission crews, some of the Brixmis team continued to take hair-raising risks, only slightly reduced by increased use of the dark and infra-red flash photography. Warrant Officer Ken Wike, a Gunner, was the tour NCO with a crew led by Captain (later Colonel) Peter Williams OBE, Coldstream Guards, when they saw a military goods train halt near their chosen tea-break/observation post. The train carried the new BMP-2 tracked infantry carrier. The team knew that the calibre of the gun on this vehicle – a new weapon, not previously seen in Europe – was on MoD's 'wish-list'. It had been spotted in Afghanistan, a long, snake-like barrel that had an arc of fire through 90 degrees. Now, an entire trainload of the beasts was standing waiting for a roving Brixmis team to admire it.

While Captain Williams took photographs, Wike clambered on to the train. Once there, he realized he had nothing with which to measure the cross-section of the barrel. Then he remembered his unfinished snack, and an apple he had been keeping for a quiet moment.

> I went back to the tour car and picked up the apple. Then I got back on the BMP, prized off the cover and got an indentation of the barrel by pressing the apple against it. To measure it I put my miniature tape recorder on top of the flash eliminator at the end of the barrel while Captain Williams took a photograph. We knew the size of my recorder. We could then calculate, by making a cross-reference from the picture, the dimensions of the gun. But I looked pretty silly on the picture, with an apple in one hand and the cord of my tape recorder held out with the other, on top of a BMP.

Wike then removed the cover from a new rangefinder fitted to the top of the vehicle. He dismantled part of it and stuck it inside his jacket. 'We were disturbed by an East German car coming down the other side of the train. Soviet soldiers were in an accommodation wagon. The East German blew his horn and waved. This alerted the Soviet soldiers, who ran down the track towards me. I dropped off the train and ran like hell through the brambles back to the car and away.'

He brought with him the first officially secret apple since the Serpent's operation in the Garden of Eden. Unlike Adam, Wike was awarded a British Empire Medal for his ingenuity, having demonstrated that the gun had a 30mm bore.

The Mission Chief, Brigadier Learmont, now had the job of patching up the diplomatic damage this episode had done. Tech-Int

This Soviet soldier was not amused when a Mission crew crept up on his signals unit vehicle as he tried to get some sleep. He heard English voices, grabbed his assault rifle and came out snarling. Brixmis stayed just long enough to take his photograph and then left, smartly.

Below: Brixmis officers had other reasons for 'legging it', running away or 'making a tactical withdrawal'. As one of them put it, 'It might not seem very dignified but it makes sense to me.' This was the scene after one Mission OP was compromised. Leading the field, Captain (later Major) J.A. Wallis with WO-1 Michael Corcoran, Weapons Intelligence.

Another escape-and-evasion manoeuvre, this time by a Brixmis Opel Käpitan tour car, racing away at full speed.

Above: The Brixmis building at Potsdam in East Germany, an elegant mansion that was the forward base for the team's spying operations.

Left: Out of public view, Anglo-Soviet parties were occasionally exuberant. The signal for everyone to start to relax was the moment when the Russians unbuttoned their uniform jackets and loosened ties. Here Brigadier (later Major-General I.L. Freer CBE, Chief of Mission 1989–90, goes one step further and entertains Soviet guests with guitar and song. No balalaikas were in evidence, though the Cold War was effectively at an end.

Below: The fatal shooting of an American tour officer, Major Arthur 'Nick' Nicholson, aged thirty-seven, on 24 March 1985 at Ludwigslust provoked a crisis in US–Soviet relations. President Reagan said: 'We are resentful and it is an unwarranted tragedy.' This was the scene as his coffin arrived for a military burial at Arlington, Virginia, a few days later, carried by US Mission officers.

Supper, a feast to which every member of the tour crew was expected to contribute some ingredient, was an important ritual at the end of an arduous day. Sometimes it was cooked inside the tour car and eaten there. When it was safe to do so, crews would cook in the open, using Army mess tins over a hexamine-driven field cooker.

Right: Tour crews took their hospitality into the field. They carried cigarettes, beer and whisky as a means of lubricating relations not only with the Russians with whom they did business but occasionally to win hearts and minds of East German civilians. Towards the end of the Cold War, Mission crews were increasingly popular among the Germans, except for members of the now-threatened Stasi. This crew – RAF warrant officer (and Master Air Load Master) Mal Girling (front) and Corporal Glyn Bromham, RAF tour driver, 1985–9 – used their Range Rover as a platform for an impromptu party with two local girls.

Farewell barbecues in the forest – the Mission's main operational habitat for forty-four years – became a standard feature of Brixmis life and a normal courtesy to departing Mission chiefs. This one marked the departure in 1987 of Brigadier WT Dodd OBE, a radical, innovative but low-profile commander (right of picture).

This ramming might have been fatal but was not, thanks only to the good luck of the driver, whose door took the full impact. The lucky survivor on 12 August 1982 was the British Chief of Mission, Brigadier John Learmont; the attacker, an East German Army Tatra–148 truck.

Above: Such attacks could be lethal, as this ramming, on 22 March 1984, demonstrated. The East German Army driver, at the controls of a heavy Ural-375 truck deliberately crossed the central reservation to crush a French Mission car travelling in the opposite direction. The victim, Adjutant Chef (regimental sergeant-major) Mariotti was killed outright.

Right: One tour veteran has compared the charge of a Kraz heavy Soviet truck, rolling towards him on two-metre diameter tyres, to that of an angry water buffalo. This example has abandoned its load – a pontoon bridge – and trails the securing cables for that load alongside, in its haste to ram the Mission team who took the photograph.

in London were pleased with the apple operation but the mission car number was taken by the guards as Williams's crew escaped. They were lucky to reach the sanctuary of the Mission House at Potsdam, to hide their loot, without being intercepted.

Learmont, whose staff car had been rammed only three weeks into his period of command, had been formally denounced by the Russian Chief-of-Staff as a 'Hooligan'. This, in the diplomatic arena of the Cold War, was the opposite of a decoration or merit award; the word carried an adverse status. He had not yet formally presented his credentials to the Soviet supremo, Zaitsev, and pushed for a personal audience with him in order to do so. This was granted. Learmont tried a joke: 'The Hooligan wishes to present his credentials, General.' Zaitsev was not amused, but he was interested in this new figure on the landscape. The formalities were complete within a minute or so.

Having been tipped off by his translator, Captain Dimitri Trenin (later an occasional BBC commentator from Moscow), that if he commanded less than thirty-five minutes' worth of Zaitsev's time, he would be deemed by the Soviet top brass to be a lightweight, Learmont then prodded Zaitsev to defend the failure of Soviet equipment in the Middle East, where the US-armed Israelis usually won. The encounter continued for almost three hours. Learmont's stock rose.

A week later, Williams and Wike raided the BMP train and Learmont found himself being carpeted by an unusually angry head of SERB, Colonel Alexei Rubanoff. Learmont waited for the storm to pass, then coaxed Rubanoff – usually a sociable, urbane man – to come down to the Mission House officers' mess for a gin and tonic. When Rubanoff had cooled down, he suggested a walk in the garden: that is, out of reach of Stasi listening devices. Then he told Learmont: 'In an odd way, we Soviets take professional pride in the fact that you British pull off something like this. It was a very good operation.' Learmont thanked him and, with a flash of inspiration, promised that Williams and Wike would not appear in East Germany again for a month. This mollified Rubanoff, who asked mischievously, 'Was it Captain Williams or James Bond who pulled this operation?'

Learmont's spell as Chief had an eccentric postscript. With the complicity of the senior staff officer, Lieutenant-Colonel (later Acting Chief of Mission and Colonel) Roy Giles, the Russians arranged to 'detain' the Brigadier as he drove away from Potsdam for the last time, towards the Glienicke Bridge, in 1984. There had been a farewell party at the Mission House. He recalled:

> I had had a lot of champagne and was not driving my car. I was just closing my eyes when a Soviet soldier waved our column off the autobahn. We got out. They said I was going to be detained. A team of Sovs arrived with an 'Akt' which they started to read. By now I was steaming with anger. Roy translated the 'Akt' sentence by sentence at my request. I was charged with 'Conducting the affairs of the British Mission with professionalism and elegance.' My sentence was a farewell drink with my Soviet friends. Round the corner came a whole group of their senior officers. They gave me a party at the roadside and sent me on my way. That was my last detention.

In 1986, Captain (later Major) Tim Spacey MBE and his team drove into a railway siding near Magdeburg. It was a hectic time, with much movement by the Soviet 11 Guards Tank Division from exercise back to barracks. The biggest of the tanks was the T-80, weighing in at 42 tons and the pride of the Red Army. This beast was moved from training areas to barracks by rail. Just before midnight a military train drew in and stopped almost alongside the tour car. Spacey, taking the first watch that night, peered up at the load.

> It was full of T-80s and other new kit. I couldn't believe my eyes. I woke up the others. Two of us got out. We knew that Russian guards were at the front of the train. My companion, an RAF flight lieutenant, kept watch while I cut through the camouflage net covering the nearest tank. Then I climbed up to the turret. I tried to open the hatch and it moved. It wasn't locked. I got inside with a camera and using flash I shot an entire film.
> It was a senior captain's tank. He had left his briefcase inside. It contained a lot of useful stuff about the exercise his regiment had just completed. I took that back to Berlin. Our people were

particularly interested in details of a wire-guided missile fired through the 125mm tank gun.

I then came out of the turret to take pictures of the optics on the sighting head. Outside the hull, the flash might just have been noticed. An East German signalbox was about 150 yards away. I made sure I pressed the button to coincide with the flash generated by passing electric trains. Their flash masked mine.

Spacey then noticed that the same train was loaded with BMP-2s as well as T-80s. He leaped from one flatbed to the next and checked the hatch on the armoured carrier. It was locked. He paused. 'I realized I had never done anything like this before. If the train had moved off I would have had to jump for it. I checked my watch. I thought I'd been on the train for about ten minutes. In fact it was thirty-five minutes and I was sweating and tired.' Spacey, an enthusiastic marathon runner accustomed to monitoring his own physical and mental condition, realized that it was time to leave. He had known the American Major Nicholson as a comrade-in-arms and he knew also that Nicholson had been shot dead for less than this.

Before leaving the train, Spacey rapidly photographed the optical sight of the BMP's missile/gun system, slipped out from under the camouflage net and back to his car. They left as soon as they could.

They still had to cross the Glienicke Bridge, out of East Germany into the British sector of Berlin. Spacey was carrying compromising film and a stolen briefcase. What if someone had reported them to the Stasi? All it would take was one telephone call. The moment of truth came as they drove up to the barrier, showed their passes and were nodded through. He woke the duty officer at the Mission headquarters and briefed him about the operation, then caught three hours' sleep in the mess. He took the films to bed with him.

Tech-Int were not entirely satisfied. 'I was asked what was the colour of the inside of the turret. Was it metal or lined with some other material on the spall [fracture] line?' Spacey was awarded an MBE all the same but, like Hugh McLeod and others decorated for their work with the Mission, he never saw the citation attached to it. (This is conventional in top-secret operations, since details of the citation itself must be held in an official safe.)

At the diplomatic level, the Mission's theoretically self-contained world, covered by a unique agreement between two military commanders, was in practice disrupted regularly by some Cold War crisis over a far horizon. On 1 September 1983, a South Korean Boeing 747 civil airliner which strayed into the Far Eastern airspace of the USSR was shot down with the loss of 269 lives. Group Captain R. D. Bates AFC, deputy Chief from 1981 to 1983, said: 'The Mission was told not to have an annual cocktail party for the Soviet External Relations Bureau. Nor was the Chief, Brigadier Learmont, to entertain any Soviet officer at his house in Berlin. We did not think that was a sound policy. We felt that the worse the situation was, diplomatically, the greater the need for dialogue.'

The job of liaison was sometimes humanized by history, and British goodwill mattered at a personal level. Bates acted as host to a senior Soviet officer who wished to see for himself the Plötzensee prison in West Berlin where his father had been executed by the Nazis during the 'Great Patriotic War': 'There was no other mechanism for the visit, except through Brixmis. I remember the numbing chill at seeing, in the prison museum, the Führer's cordial invitation to his VIP guests to witness the execution, with refreshments to follow.'

Lieutenant Colonel David O'Connor, senior interpreter with Brixmis 1967–71, was approached by the Soviet External Relations Bureau deputy chief, Colonel Grishel, 'in some trepidation, with a request. His son had been diagnosed in Moscow with a serious blood disease. Would the Chief get the written diagnosis checked at the British Military Hospital in Berlin? This was a desperate move for a Soviet citizen to make, acknowledging as it did a Western medical superiority and leaving Grishel open to pressure. He realized that his position had been compromised. He reported himself to his superior. An elegant English compromise was arranged. This was a tea-party in the Mission House, with three from each side, at which the matter would be lightly but publicly raised and dismissed. I suppose if it had been the other way round they would have applied the pressure. The diagnosis was, sadly, correct.'

As the Mission watched the flow of new military hardware into East Germany and rehearsals for river crossings ominously pointed towards the West, it was not yet obvious that the Soviet empire was ailing. In a favourite Marxist phrase, it carried the seeds of its own destruction. (Marxists applied this analysis exclusively to the capitalist system; some still do.) First, there was the simple fact that a gerontocracy suffers a high degree of natural wastage. Brezhnev had gone in November 1981. His successor Andropov died in February 1984. Andropov's successor Konstantin Chernenko went on terminal leave five months later and died in March 1985 after thirteen months in office. Defence Minister Dmitri Ustinov died on 20 December 1984 and was replaced by Marshal Sergei Sokolov, aged seventy-three.

One white hope was emerging from Moscow: a former tractor driver, party manipulator, law graduate and self-made hero, Mikhail Gorbachev. At fifty-four he was the youngest member of the ruling politbureau. Three months before Chernenko died, Gorbachev was already setting a new style of détente politics. As head of a Soviet 'fact-finding' delegation on his first overseas trip, he met Prime Minister Thatcher at Chequers. When he was appointed leader of the USSR he praised détente and called for arms reductions.

The plain fact was that the arms race was ruining what was left of the Soviet economy while, politically, the satellites were slowly but surely breaking ranks. Solidarity was alive and kicking (usually communist policemen) in Poland and even East Germany's leader, Erich Honecker, set up a visit to West Germany which was cancelled only under Soviet pressure. Attrition, financial and political, was bleeding the Soviet system white. It was time for a change.

CHAPTER 11

The War We Would Have Funked

1985–90

The years 1985 to 1990 were ones in which the Cold War ended with bewildering speed, to be replaced briefly by America's paper tiger, the 'New World Order'. Antique tribal hatreds, long suppressed in Eastern Europe, emerged like a forgotten medieval virus from Asiatic Russia to the Balkans. The only common factor of the New World Order was that the victims were invariably unarmed and were usually women, children and the aged. Lethal force was exercised with total commitment upon unarmed non-combatants by young men drunk with the power of the gun.

The liberal West discovered an Achilles' heel that made it unfit to intervene anywhere. This was the political penalty incurred by heavy casualties, in open democracies exposed to the horrors of the battlefield in 'real time', as they happened, courtesy of satellite television. Body-bags meant low popularity ratings for politicians back home. As a consequence, the remaining superpower and its European allies found themselves pinioned by the political imperative of the bloodless victory. It was a choice between that or the bloodless defeat. This was a sobering discovery, the fruit of the brief war with Saddam Hussein in 1991 and with a ragged band of Somalis soon afterwards. During the seven months of Saddam's occupation of Kuwait from August 1990, and the ponderous build-up of a US expeditionary force of 500,000 men and women, all that was required to tilt public opinion sharply away from support for combat in the Gulf was a realistic re-creation on American television of the American Civil War of 1860 to 1864, reinforcing the more recent Vietnam experience. The agonies of Gettysburg reminded a volatile American public of General Robert E. Lee's dictum: 'It is well that war is so terrible [lest] we should grow too fond of it.'

What if the Warsaw Pact had attacked the West as a means of relieving its economic sickness? Could any Western leader have pressed the nuclear button? Would the West have had the will to fight back without recourse to nuclear weapons? With the wisdom of hindsight, the common-sense answer to both questions is 'Probably not'. The Germans would have seen no point in destroying their own reconstructed homeland. As a military reservist exercising in Germany at that time, I worked alongside Bundeswehr officers who made no secret of the fact that they and their families had their own evacuation plans ready. They had already bought the hideaway cottage in Brittany or Galway and they had to hand the emergency supply of gold coins to help them get there. One air force officer even had his own telephone alert code with which to warn the family to get the Mercedes out of the garage, ready to roll West.

During the mid-1980s the introduction of short-range nuclear weapons by both superpowers had been bitterly opposed by people who did not regard themselves as 'peaceniks'. As late as 1989, a Nato 'command post exercise' – essentially one of crisis-management within the bunker, in which military and civil leaders are pressured by sleeplessness and tough decisions in a simulated war – led to virtual mutiny by a senior West German participant.

According to the exercise scenario, Warsaw Pact tank divisions were breaking through Western defences. The proposed American response was a strike with twenty-one nuclear warheads each of 100 kilotons on East European targets, the equivalent of 160 Hiroshimas. The German official playing the role of Chancellor Kohl protested to the real Chancellor Kohl who said: 'Stop this idiocy.' West Germany, according to a detailed newspaper account, pulled out of the exercise three days early.

The French, it may be assumed, would have proved as pragmatic about a fight to the death as they had been in 1940. The British would have supported a defensive European war initially, as they supported the Gulf and South Atlantic conflicts, out of habit and because this war was close to home, though opposition would not be limited to those who had made a career out of anti-war protest. The Americans – witness the Gulf experience and its sequels – would not have accepted the slaughter of their forces in Germany.

Fortunately, the issue was never tested in Europe. There is an alternative argument. This is that a European war would have happened with great speed and little warning and would have ended quickly, unlike the slow-burn that preceded the Gulf campaign when doubts built up at home in direct ratio to the prolonged movement of reinforcements into the war zone. Until the end of the Cold War, the Soviets believed, perhaps too readily, in Western resolve. So, at the time, did most professional Nato soldiers. Saddam Hussein and the Somali warlord Aideed did not. But until the Berlin Wall was shattered on 9 November 1989, Nato seemed as solid as the Wall itself. The lessons of the Gulf, Somalia and the Balkans were part of an unknown future for which no contingency plan existed.

In May 1987 when Brigadier (later Lieutenant-General Sir John) Foley KCB, OBE, MC became Chief of the Brixmis Mission, the Gorbachev reforms were like the bright light of virtue in a dark, naughty world. Initially suspicious of the new Soviet leader and his version of Camelot, the West had just started to believe that Gorbachev was serious about reform, but 'perestroika' (reconstruction) and its tool 'glasnost' (openness) were a mixed blessing. For a start, they made the Soviet Army in Germany, cut off from home by a potentially hostile Poland, nervous. There was a joke current in Brixmis at the time about a Polish soldier facing invasion from Russia and Germany simultaneously. Would he kill a Russian first or a German? 'I would kill the German first.' Asked why, he replies: 'Business first, then pleasure.'

The Soviet high command was unamused by such dynamism. A Russian general told Foley: 'I want to know what "glasnost" means. If I open the door to let in some air and a gale blows through I might not be able to control it. I don't think our political leaders understand that. How would you handle it?' The British brigadier made a sympathetic but non-committal reply to this odd invitation. It did not inhibit another senior Russian, Colonel Pereverzev, head of SERB, from telling him: 'This glasnost is nonsense. It is rubbish.'

The threat assessment Brigadier Foley received as he took over

the Mission in May 1987 was that Gorbachev might yet be destabil-
ized. That happened, eventually. Gorbachev was replaced as president by Boris Yeltsin. When Foley assumed command, Yeltsin was
a fierce critic of the Gorbachev reform programme and was sacked
as chief of the Moscow City Communist Party as a result.

Foley was in no doubt that if it became necessary for the Russians
to attack, they would do so. The senior Russian officers he dealt
with at SERB told him so. They would attack pre-emptively if the
Nato threat – as they saw it – was likely to overwhelm them.

> I used to talk to the Soviets about it. I would say, 'You're not really
> going to do this?' They replied, 'Of course we'll do it if the political
> situation requires. If we see Nato about to attack us, we will pre-
> empt it.' The whole mindset of their military was backed by confi-
> dence that they had a good machine and they could do it. Many
> of them genuinely believed that the West was preparing to attack.
> It was possible that there could have been a whole series of miscal-
> culations leading to the conclusion, 'Let's strike before they strike
> us.'

This meant that the original purpose of the Mission, to act as a
fail-safe mechanism that prevented war by mistake, was back at
the top of the Brixmis agenda. But in Soviet eyes, signs of potential
Nato aggression could include a too-adventurous approach by the
Western Missions themselves in their pursuit of the other objective,
the collection of intelligence. The biggest mission of all was still
Brixmis.

It was clear to Foley that the days of aggressive touring were
over. A serious provocation by a mission team would now be a
hostage to fortune in a bigger political game, to give credibility to
the enemies of Soviet reform. Yet the job of intelligence-gathering
still had to be done, since Brixmis could not fulfil its basic job of
preventing war by accident if it did not know what was going on.
Foley admits that they trod a narrow, ill-defined path through
a diplomatic minefield. 'Gung-ho' touring, no longer acceptable,
included 'driving at excessive speeds, or over people's gardens, or
inserting oneself unnecessarily into the middle of Soviet convoys and so on'. The risk–gain equation meant that some risks

were still worth taking, if they had been carefully calculated in advance.

We told the Mission teams that when they had a split-second decision to make about getting a scoop, a coup, whether photograph or video, to keep in mind the famous risk-versus-gain equation of the intelligence world. If the risk is out of proportion to the gain – and the actual decision might have to be made in the time it takes to say that – then the advice was: 'Don't do it because there will be another opportunity.' A minor incident involving the Mission would have gone very quickly up to ambassador and commander-in-chief level. In Moscow Gorbachev's enemies would say: 'Here are these people behaving in this aggressive fashion.' I would get a rocket on my side. Up would go the alert states on the Russian side.

My instructions from the Foreign Office and Ministry of Defence were, 'There is a slightly different situation. You might have to adapt to it.' It was too early to say that the danger had passed. The 50,000 Soviet soldiers moved out of Eastern Europe after 1988 was a drop in the ocean. They still had tremendously powerful conventional forces on the Warsaw Pact borders. They had and still have their nuclear arsenal. There was no slackening of their security. They were all still extremely good.

We developed slightly different touring techniques. I remember saying to people: 'You've got to stand further back because it's going to cause an upheaval which would be unwelcome politically if you are too forceful about going in to get information.' The techniques we developed were longer lenses and camcorder videos mounted on stabilizing gyros inside the tour cars. In so far as there were problems, they were with second or third tourers, with previous experience of Brixmis, who were accustomed to going in pretty hard. I explained they had to tour in a slightly more subtle way. We didn't want anyone deliberately inducing traffic accidents, for example.

The challenge of more Permanently Restricted Areas imposed by Zaitsev was met by accepting that the tour car must be replaced by an all-terrain vehicle. In general this was the Mercedes G-wagen, a cross-country invader that made the task of controlling mission movements so great as to require an army dedicated to that alone. Meanwhile, touring techniques as taught at the military intelligence centre in England remained unchanged by the 'new' doctrine.

In Brigadier Foley's eyes, the essential difference was not one of content but style, a move towards the light-fingered and away from the heavy-footed. The Mission continued to respond to the 'wish-list' from various parts of the intelligence apparatus known collectively as 'the agencies'. Some of those activities were so sensitive that they are still classified Top Secret.

The brigadier, an SAS veteran, accompanied by an SAS NCO rebadged as a para in Brixmis, avoided excessive caution:

> I enjoyed touring. As an SAS officer I was unhappy if I wasn't out for two nights a week. It was such fun as a brigadier – after a desk job as Director, Special Forces and a year at the Royal College of Defence Studies – to sleep under the stars, in the snow, two nights a week. We brewed up these amazing curries. It was like being back in the SAS with top-class British NCOs, the best in the world.
>
> I toured a lot. I got detained a lot. It became a joke in the Mission, but a joke in the right way. I was caught in the middle of a Soviet column and interviewed by a Russian colonel. I showed him my Brixmis pass. He said, 'Why on earth is a brigadier doing this, out here, in the middle of the night?'

With one of his SAS companions, Foley penetrated an underground Soviet Army command bunker. This was a big complex, on several levels.

> We rooted around and took a number of photographs. We came out to see two Soviet sentries standing either side of the tour car, with a very worried driver sitting in it, chatting them up as if we had every right to be where we were not supposed to be. This was a shock. The car was 25 yards from the entrance. The only thing to do was to go towards the car and take charge.
>
> My Russian wasn't very good, but I remember going back to the car and saying to the Soviets: 'Good! Everything is in order. Thank you. We will now leave.'

The bluff was assisted by Foley's height, 6 feet 5 inches, as well as an extremely sharp, eagle-like gaze. He loomed regularly over certain SERB officers, one of whom complained that he was being pressured by Foley's habit of standing too close. This time, the sentries stood aside and saluted as the British trespassers drove away.

Foley's departure from a forbidden zone was not always so elegant. One of the intelligence agencies wanted to know the identification codes, batch numbers and industrial origins of small arms and machine-gun ammunition stored in a Soviet depot. Foley and his NCO 'went through the wire, over a couple of obstacles to get to where the containers were stored'. After they had been there for about ten minutes they rounded a corner and saw two Soviet soldiers, with their weapons to hand. 'It was shock-horror-dismay time again but on this occasion we ran like hell out of it. I remember ripping my trousers so badly that they flapped, exposing one's arse.'

The pursuit of intelligence scoops, if conducted with greater caution, was still a main part of the Mission's work and no less successful. Staff Sergeant (later Captain) Dave Butler BEM spirited away a section of the latest Soviet reactive tank armour. This was a major coup. The answer to modern tank-busting missiles was the modern equivalent of an outpost in front of an ancient fort: a type of armour that would take the first force of an incoming missile, exploding the warhead. That job done, the outer, reactive shell would fall away to leave the main hull of the tank unscathed. Nato was shocked to learn that the Soviets had developed such armour for the new T-80. Bringing home a sample of this was the first step towards Nato's solution.

Some people were still sorting through Soviet garbage and finding malodorous intelligence truffles. A series of reports detailing Soviet sickness statistics, gently removed from a military hospital, provided a vivid insight into the reality of the Russian war machine. The Red Army, it seemed, was hampered by everything from hepatitis to shrapnel wounds sustained in grenade 'fragging' attacks by angry soldiers who used fragmentation grenades against their officers as the officers slept or dined. That information was neatly supplemented by further reports on Soviet Army disciplinary offences.

Another useful scoop was camcorder video footage of the 2S6, a twin-barrelled anti-aircraft system, combining a gun with a missile, carried on a tracked vehicle. As Foley recollected: 'The agencies asked us to get it. We spent a lot of time and eventually cracked it with video, good close-ups of the communication and gun systems. I remember getting a very nice note back from London on both the reactive armour and 2S6 operations to say, "Brilliant ... well done."'

In June 1986, after protracted negotiations, the Soviets re-opened to Allied Missions many of the permanent training areas closed off in 1984. This was a reciprocal move for a Western concession to their Soxmis teams. The Soviets went even further in some areas. A Brixmis report on air operations that year said:

The reduction exposed many areas around airfields that had historically been well protected by PRA. A number of important radar and SAM sites became visible again and although access to the two most important air/ground ranges was made more difficult and details of weapons harder to get, it is still possible to observe the attack profiles. The more favourable situation near airfields, combined with the introduction of new aircraft types and marks, led to airfields' receiving a very high priority. Furthermore the style of touring has altered slightly. It is now possible to move more quickly between airfields and use a greater number of OPs, thereby increasing the 'opposition's' surveillance problems. The Air Element's efforts to exploit the new map have been rewarded by the acquisition of better technical-quality photography and a better feel for Soviet and East German air operations.

This bonanza resulted from delicate negotiations among the four headquarters – Soviet, American, British and French – on ways to reduce the risk of unnecessary violence, following the killing of Major Nicholson.

There was another, undeclared Soviet interest in this unexpected charm offensive. A year earlier, to the surprise of the Soviets, Western Europe had accepted the controversial cruise missile (based at Greenham Common, England) after six years' debate. There was still a feeling among liberals in the West, however, that

274

Nato over-rated the communist threat. As the IISS survey for 1986–87 put it:

> Most socialist parties in Nato member states pledge support for Nato ... Nonetheless, most of them have come to question the wisdom of Nato doctrine, which many view as inconsistent with the idea of a 'defensive' alliance. [Alternative defence strategies were wanted.] Nato's assessment of a Soviet bloc numerical superiority in heavy weapons in the central region should be discounted, on grounds of the technological inferiority of Soviet-bloc weapons, undermanning of Soviet units, low levels of education and training (especially in electronics), a dearth of initiative in the Soviet forces at junior levels of command, and the unreliability of East European troops. Explicit also was the view that Moscow would not initiate hostilities unless provoked by the West.

West Germany, it was noted, now had twice the number of tanks that were available to Hitler when he attacked the Soviet Union. In those circumstances, it would make good sense for an intelligent Russian leader, such as Gorbachev, to use the Western Missions to reinforce that message in the West. The Brixmis report on air operations for 1986 suggests that the gambit, if that is what it was, worked:

> The Soviets and East Germans [in the air] have been observed 'recovering' in poor weather, by day and night, and they exhibit some confidence in their equipment but they certainly lack style and flair. Their pattern of range operations is routine and on the whole repetitious. On the other hand they are capable of organizing large numbers of aircraft and executing intensive programmes, and are seen to have few missile failures. However, their low-level flying is far from impressive. The low-level transits by fixed-wing Nato aircraft and helicopters that are commonplace in West Germany are never seen in the East and it can only be concluded that they do not practise aggressive, low-level flying. It is therefore very doubtful that they would be capable of flying competently at low level in war.

How did they fly in peacetime? Fencer, the swing-wing, low-level strike aircraft feared by the West for years, appeared in Germany. Brixmis dismissed the Soviets' fencing skills as 'lacklustre'. Like tank formations on the ground, air sorties depended on numbers to overwhelm the opposition: 'They still attack the air/ground ranges at vulnerable heights, although they do attack in streams of twenty or more aircraft.' Floggers and Fitters, the backbone of Soviet ground attack aircraft, were using television and laser-guided bombs, unconvincingly. The new Frogfoot was also marked C-minus. 'Perhaps the most disappointing (or should it be pleasing?) feature of the Soviet fixed-wing force is the employment of Frogfoot . . . Infrequent activity at ranges dull and boring,' said a secret Brixmis report.

The exception to this image of mediocrity was the new Fulcrum team. No fewer than forty of these powerful machines were moved into the East German bases at Wittstock and Merseburg during the first few months of 1986. Fulcrum was Russia's answer to the Tornado. Fulcrum pilots threw their aircraft around the sky like happy cavalrymen playing polo. As Brixmis put it: 'During the initial observations it was assessed that some aircraft were giving special aerobatic demonstrations for spectators at the airfield but it was subsequently found that many normal sorties ended with a short [spontaneous] display. Such general flair and style had never been seen with other aircraft. Fulcrum pilots were pleased with and confident in their new and advanced machine.'

By 1988, however, even this fizz had gone flat. The Mission reported: 'The Fulcrum team have shown little of the flair and aggression that was expected . . . The initial exuberance shown by pilots flying aerobatics over the airfield has, like vodka, steadily evaporated and the aircraft is handled, like all the others, without flair.'

Defence analysts, gurus and commentators of whatever political persuasion in the West, on the basis of such reports, might have justified opposition perceptions of the Soviet threat and concluded that it was over-rated by Nato's hawks. By opening up more ground to the licensed, partly-controlled spies of the Western Missions, the Kremlin assuredly redressed the balance in favour of Nato's peaceniks.

As it happened, the most useful secret of Soviet air defence was extracted not from a flying programme but on the ground. The target was the latest Russian radar system known as TIN SHIELD, the multi-winged spindle that turned and twisted like a slow dervish. Brixmis reported:

> In April 1986 a tour took still photography and video of the TIN SHIELD at Marksuhl. For the first time the Mission obtained imagery of the rear side of the radar sail but, more significantly, the video showed that during rotation the sail was able to tilt by at least a few degrees . . . In June a tour obtained extensive and extremely close cover of the TIN SHIELD at Salzwedel, previously in PRA. Notwithstanding the considerable amount of information obtained about aircraft and helicopters, the superlative photography of TIN SHIELD will possibly be regarded in future years as the most significant product of 1986.

The reason for that was self-evident. In any Nato air attack on the Warsaw Pact, the first targets – as in Iraq in 1991 and Bosnia in 1995 – would be radar systems. Had the doves of Western Europe known that, they might have screeched like seagulls instead of merely cooing nervously.

Squadron Leaders Brook Blackford and his colleague Andrew Pennington were at the forefront of the latest operations. They were now getting better early warning about impending Soviet operations from signals intelligence on 'The Hill' and from Rheindahlen, headquarters of RAF Germany. Blackford recalls that to get the first clear pictures of Fulcrum at Wittstock, 'Pennington and I, with separate teams, staked out both ends of the airfield over a period of fourteen days.' The surveillance started, auspiciously, on Blackford's birthday.

> We now had direct contact each morning with the radar squadron at RAF Gatow [Berlin] so the Mission's squadron leader ops could ring up to see who was flying and where. If it turned out that a Soviet exercise at Gadow Rossow range was a TASM [tactical air-to-surface missile] we rushed up there assured of a flying programme. It was only ninety minutes away if you were on standby!

This period also marked a great change in the 'tip-off' procedure [by the agencies]. In 1986, some of us were authorized to carry scanner radios on tour. These transformed our operations as we could sit in a quiet area with the local air frequencies and ranges on scan. As soon as we got a signal on the radio we knew that they were flying and where. Off we went to guaranteed action, instead of waiting around on spec. It did not matter that you could not understand what was being said. The radios gave you the steer you needed.

If there was no flying activity you could safely go and do technical [ground] targets and the scanner would tell you when to go back. This and the RAF radar squadron tips transformed RAF touring. A TASM attack was an extremely rare sight during my first tour, from 1978 to 1981. It became a regular feature in my second (1985 to 1986), including the ability to video these missiles before they were fired.

Encouraged by the new climate, airmen from the three missions ran some tri-national operations to improve their coverage of Soviet air-to-ground attacks at the air-ranges of Gadow Rossow and Retzow. Normally, each Western mission would work its agreed patch for an agreed period, after which everyone would take a new area in rotation. Now they operated in the same area as one co-ordinated team. From the ranges they moved on to a clutch of Soviet fleet air arm bases at Werneuchen, Falkenberg and Welzow, each mission taking one base as its target. 'A useful byproduct of this [new] activity,' Brixmis reported, 'is that by disregarding the usual allocation of areas to Allied Missions, we may have caused our friendly MfS some confusion and a few late nights working out what we were up to.'

In 1987 an American team pushed its luck in a sensitive area overlooking the west end of a runway at Neuruppin. Technically open to the missions, the area was still sensitive enough to provoke shooting at the Americans by Soviet guards. In August 1988, nervous perhaps that they had conceded too much to Western eyes, the Soviets restored some of their PRA zones, off-limits to the missions. It was all too late. By now the German front line that had mesmerized the high commands in Moscow, Washington and

London for forty years was becoming irrelevant. Armenia and Azerbaijan, on the southern fringes of the USSR, were in a state of uproar. The Red Army was shedding blood and treasure in Afghanistan until early in 1989. The Soviet system was breaking down.

The Soviet military establishment, through their newspaper *Red Star*, decided to circulate a sort of health warning about the virus the Allied Missions now represented. On 11 January 1989 the journal described how soldiers travelling through East Germany might meet 'camouflaged, solid-looking Mercedes, Opels, agile cross-country Land Rovers and Fords. Not on all roads, it is true, but on those that pass close to military installations of GSFG [Soviet Forces, Germany]. They are also found on military ranges, near railways on which military equipment is transported and "escorting" military columns. In many cases they represent a danger to road traffic. Who owns these vehicles, whose index numbers are not registered with East German police? Why do they complete more than 3,000 (scarcely tourist) trips to military establishments of the Socialist states each year?'

The Western Missions, created in 1944 for liaison between the wartime commanders-in-chief, it said, 'have been turned into subsidiaries of the military intelligence services of the USA, Britain and France. They include specialists trained at intelligence centres such as the US Army Russian Institute in the West German town of Garmisch-Partenkirchen; the Institute of Eastern Languages in Paris and the Beaconsfield Intelligence School in Britain . . . Training in military attachés' offices in capitals of the Socialist states . . . military intelligence units and special purpose forces (Rangers and Green Berets).'

The teams carried 'a rich store' of spy equipment in vehicles 'with excellent cross-country capabilities'. They often ignored the boundaries of restricted military areas.

During the years 1987–88 alone, Soviet personnel stopped prohibited activity by Western military crews on ten occasions. A persistent offender . . . was US intelligence officer Captain Bennet McCutcheon . . . who violated the boundaries of restricted areas sixteen times in the course of which he performed impertinent and hooligan escapades. The spying career of this captain ended after a subsequent, specially insolent act. Following a protest by the Soviet Commander he was posted ahead of schedule.

A British officer, Flight Lieutenant David Browne [an air tour officer with the Mission 1987–90], was caught unawares at his work by Soviet servicemen. A large quantity of spying equipment was confiscated from the Englishmen including night observation devices, a video camera and recorder and cameras with special attachments. All this spying material was described by the British Chief of Mission, Brigadier John Foley, as 'authorized equipment'. To the Soviet Commander this represented proof of the intelligence-gathering nature of Browne's activities and the Commander-in-Chief of Soviet Forces, Germany accordingly made a written protest to the British side.

Captain Stephen Harrison, another British officer, 'repeatedly sought to establish contact with Soviet military personnel, trying in conversation to gain information'.

Among the French, Lieutenant Saby, Warrant Officer Bock and Sergeant Brune were trapped while spying on military aircraft.

When caught, the Western observers 'distort the truth to lay blame for incidents on to the Soviet side. An example of this was ... when American Major Nicholson entered a Soviet military installation and did not heed a guard's commands, with tragic consequences. In March 1988, French military intelligence-collectors under the command of deputy Chief of Mission, Lieutenant-Colonel Demay, followed a military column and ignored the demands of a Soviet traffic regulator to stop. The regulator ended up on the Mercedes bonnet. The Frenchman then increased speed and only stopped after driving three kilometres into a forest.'

While factually accurate, the *Red Star* article, like the symbol on its masthead, was irrelevant to the real world. It reflected an almost private competition between the isolated Group of Soviet Forces, Germany and the Western Missions watching them. The year 1988 was the turning point, one in which Gorbachev, in a speech to the UN in December, promised that the Warsaw Pact would, once and for all, restructure itself to become purely defensive. He was as good as his word. Soviet forward-deployed air and ground forces were reduced so as to make any surprise attack on the West less likely. Britain's Prime Minister, Margaret Thatcher, with monumental conviction, pronounced the Cold War to be over. When that became apparent, some months later, it caught everyone in Brixmis and Soviet Forces, Germany, by surprise.

Gorbachev sensed what was happening. He also knew that he could not trust the old guard commanding the Soviet forces in Germany. A staff officer with Brixmis in 1989, specializing in close liaison with the Russians, was Major John Walker, an Intelligence Corps officer. He recalled: 'The Soviet Commander-in-Chief, General Snetkov, disappeared towards the end. He was an old soldier, a tank man since 1943. He was very opposed to the Soviet withdrawal. He had an old soldier's ethics. He was concerned about his troops and their families. He knew they had nowhere to go back home in the USSR.'

As the end came, morale sagged within Brixmis also. The British Mission noted that, in West Germany, the Soviet team known as Soxmis was unmolested while Brixmis, ordered to 'pussyfoot', still suffered prolonged detentions in which their vehicles were covered by tarpaulins – a process known as being 'tarped' – for hours while they were still inside.

The night the Berlin Wall was breached – 9 November 1989 – was one of those operatic moments in human experience when symbolism, theatre and real change all occur simultaneously. History usually cheats and delivers symbolism without change, as at Versailles in 1918; or change without much evidence that anything significant has happened, as at a nearly empty Kitty Hawk beach, North Carolina, in 1903 when the Wright brothers' Flyer took off. Occasionally however – as at the Bastille in 1789 or Hiroshima in 1945 – symbolism, theatre and real change line up together unmistakably. Major John Walker was a staff officer with Brixmis when the people of East Berlin at last started to break out of their prison publicly and openly, daring their countrymen to shoot them down.

For months, the turbulence and defections had grown, the rattling of chains inspiring headlines around the world. For some days, Mission cars on tour were being glad-handed by East Germans who had formerly telephoned the Stasi to report their presence.

On 8 November, Major Walker had returned to Berlin from his last trip. Tour crews were instructed to log any demonstrations they saw but to keep their distance. Walker concluded that the demos were not very widespread. At home next day, packing his kit to prepare for the journey by road and ferry back to England, he listened to British Forces Radio. Just after lunch, the newscast said crowds were gathering on both sides of the Wall. Wearing civilian clothes, he went out to see what was happening and spent six hours watching history unfold.

'The atmosphere was electric, like the sky just before a storm. There were hundreds of people there. Suddenly they started climbing on the Wall.' Then came the tidal wave of East Germans. 'I was kissed by half a dozen people of both sexes. They all asked the same question: "Where can I buy a map of West Berlin?"' In the prison they had just left, such maps were unobtainable and, if acquired, probably illegal.

Next day he tried to drive home. The whole of East Germany, it seemed, was also driving west. 'There were traffic jams for 40 kilometres [25 miles] filling both lanes of the autobahn, moving at a speed of 100 metres every thirty minutes. I left Berlin at noon, believing I would be in Düsseldorf by 6 P.M. I finally got there after an eighteen-hour journey.'

By a nice irony, the second day of Germany's freedom was also the anniversary of the armistice marking the end of the First World War. Next day the British Chief of Mission, Brigadier (later Major-General) Ian Freer CBE, was summoned from a Remembrance Day service at the Anglican St George's Church in Berlin to deal with an urgent message from the Soviet External Relations Bureau. The Soviets, it turned out, were concerned about demolition of the Wall, particularly at Potsdamer Platz. Security of the Soviet War Memorial in the Tiergarten was also causing concern.

An emollient reply was sent back referring to an exchange of messages between President Gorbachev and Prime Minister Thatcher, adding, 'I understand also that a direct link has been established with the people in the Soviet Sector of Berlin and the Western Sectors.' The implication was clear enough: that the process of German reunification had started, regardless of diplomatic niceties. Furthermore, to the very end, Brixmis – with its continued use of the phrase 'the Soviet Sector' – made it clear that it still did not recognize the legitimacy of the East German government. But to soothe General Snetkov's feelings further, Brigadier Freer added: 'The British Commandant fully understands General Snetkov's concerns about the situation, particularly over the Soviet War Memorial. The British authorities have been in touch with the West Berlin police who have considerably increased their presence. The [British] Royal Military Police are also closely monitoring the situation.'

The end was now in sight. On 2 October 1990, eleven months after the Wall was breached, ten Brixmis tour crews met in a forest near Klein Behnitz, twenty miles west of Berlin for a barbecue to mark the suspension of the Robertson–Malinin Agreement. Feelings were mixed. As one veteran put it: 'Time to rejoin the regular British Army!' The wives knew the emotional problems of readjustment to 'ordinary' soldiering. Lady Foley, wife of Sir John, still describes it as 'the post-Brixmis Blues'. Ex-Flight Sergeant Colin Birnie BEM, a tough Scot notoriously ready to use his fists, said: 'Brixmis is like a disease. It gets into your skin and you can never really rid yourself of it. I left the Mission almost twelve years ago ... It took me a long time to settle back into "normal" RAF life. I was very restless and unhappy and longed to get back.'

The barbecue over, the last crews returned to the Potsdam Mission House to entertain senior Soviet officers from SERB. An official signal pronounced the last rites:

At 1815, after a short speech by Chief Brixmis acknowledging end of RM Agreement but not end of essential functions of liaison and communication, all moved outside front of Mission House to witness lowering of Union Jack to Last Post played by a bugler of 1 Royal Welch. Inside House, Chief Brixmis presented Soviet officers with Brixmis plaques and mementos ... At 1915 all ten vehicles crossed Glienicke Bridge in line astern to sound of car horns and good wishes from those Potsdamers out on streets. All measures to lower Mission profile have now been implemented and Union Jack will not be flown until further instructions received.

If there was a sense of anti-climax in Brixmis after the forty-four-year campaign, the emotional hangover among the Soviets was greater. As the final signal put it: 'Soviets are tired and dispirited and rather shellshocked by events.'

The break-up of the old order created a new instability within the Iron Curtain territories. Tensions did not evaporate. A special West German team took over the functions formerly exercised by the Allied Missions, operating with a self-confidence not seen since the days of the Third Reich. One crew pushed its luck in trying to examine a bunker containing Soviet nuclear warheads, still under Russian guard. The guard, obeying his orders, fired at the intruders, one of whom was wounded in the arm.

Dismantling the communist arsenal under the terms of CBM (confidence-building measures) in the turbulence that followed the collapse of the USSR sharpened the need for trained, Russian-speaking military observers from the West. Former Brixmis soldiers and airmen found their skills as observers-for-peace much in demand. As Lieutenant-Colonel Wylde argued: 'The unique observation skills developed by Brixmis and the other Allied Missions have been put to good use in the various CSCE [Conference for Security and Co-operation in Europe] and SALT [Strategic Arms Limitation Treaty] monitoring units in the UK and at least a dozen other European countries including Russia and the Ukraine, whose officers have been trained by former Allied Mission staff. Similar confidence-building organizations are now springing up in Africa, the Middle and Far East. Most owe their existence to the success of the former Allied Missions in East Germany.'

He and others also asserted that, in the light of the Mission's experience, it is time to rethink the current approach to intelligence, or rather, the way the apparent product is analysed and evaluated. The Brixmis experience was that the Mission's reports and those of Sigint (signals intelligence, including the data culled from the airwaves by GCHQ at Cheltenham) were often at variance. 'Brixmis tours had observed events the Sigint staff had monitored aurally. Yet the Sigint events would be invariably believed because they were of a higher security classification.' Frequently, a Brixmis report would be graded merely 'UK Confidential' while a less significant item from GCHQ in the same area would automatically be graded 'Secret' or 'Top Secret'.

The snobbery of the access lists to high-level intelligence overlooked some plain facts. The SIGINT staff were professional Intelligence and SIGINT monitors. They probably understood about 70 per cent of all communications they monitored. Then they attempted to interpret what they had heard.

The analysis of what is being said on radio nets is not an easy task even for somebody who understands the tactics being employed, so an accuracy rating of 50 per cent would be fair. This gives an overall probability of the SIGINT's assessment being right of about 35 per cent.

Whole divisions of [Soviet] troops would roll out of barracks to their emergency deployment areas under radio silence, observed only by the Allied Missions. The Russians made full use of the civil telephone network to control their moves. Our professional intelligence-collectors were frequently surprised by this fact, but they should have realized that it would happen as a matter of routine in a real emergency, just as in the West when units of 1 (British) Corps crashed out on emergency deployments, again under complete radio silence. It took until the late 1980s, just before the Berlin Wall came down, [for the intelligence community back home] to realize that this state of affairs was absurd. Tasking of intelligence assets in a given theatre is now usually controlled by one organization.

The Brixmis experience also changed the quality of staff employed in military intelligence posts: 'High-quality staff officers now control and run the intelligence branches and task the professional intelligence staff.' That change is a momentous shift of control over such operations from the man or woman whose experience has been exclusively devoted to the hermetic world of intelligence, to the person who has long experience of soldiering in the field, the air and at sea.

There is one other, somewhat touching, legacy. The special experience of the British Mission was better understood by some of their Russian adversaries than by their own colleagues, uneducated in the ambiguities of life on or beyond this particular front line. An impressive number of Brixmis veterans now commute from Britain to Moscow. Some even have apartments and businesses there. In a world of bewildering, fast change, there is much reassurance in the company of the devil you know ... but in a few cases the 'new' relationship with post-communist Russia is remarkably like the old one. In March 1996, for example, a former Brixmis soldier, settled with his family in Moscow, was abruptly put on an aircraft to London by local security officials, without explanation. According to Alexander Golitsin, a senior Russian Foreign Ministry official, he was not expelled. 'His visa was terminated,' said Mr Golitsin.

Why? It seemed that the Russian security services had found 'negative elements in his activities' which were 'not compatible' with his status as a businessman. The British Foreign Office said it was mystified and would seek a fuller explanation. Back in London, the veteran rejected any suggestion that he had been a spy. 'I categorically deny it,' he told a newspaper. 'The charge is totally unjustified and totally unfair.'

In the spring of 1996, he arrived back in London just in time for publication of a report from the House of Commons intelligence committee. This found that Russian spies had started to target Britain again for the first time since the Cold War ended. The committee also identified another disaster for Western intelligence.

Committee chairman Tom King, a former Defence Secretary, said that the 'massive treachery' of the CIA traitor Aldrich Ames might have enormous repercussions for British security. The lives of agents and some of Britain's most closely-kept secrets might have been compromised by Ames. British ministers, the committee suspected, had relied on 'tainted' intelligence provided by agents whom Ames had betrayed over a ten-year career of treachery beginning in 1985. Ames had handed Moscow the identities of thirteen CIA agents, nine of whom were executed and three imprisoned. In 1996, it seemed, the great, ugly game was beginning afresh.

EPILOGUE

Throughout most of its history, Brixmis charted the Orbat (Order of Battle) – the regiments, air squadrons, their equipment, locations, war roles, leadership cadres and battle-readiness – of 95 per cent of the Western Group of Soviet Forces in Germany. The Western Group was the front-line pride of the USSR, the first resort in any war with the West. At the end of the Cold War it comprised 380,000 men formed up in eleven tank divisions, eight motor-rifle divisions, an artillery division and specialist forces. Soviet airfields in Germany held 400 fighter/bombers, 305 fighters, 65 reconnaissance and 15 electronic counter-measures machines.

Keeping track of this vast garrison – its deployments in and out of exercise areas and its regular rotation of regiments – was itself an extraordinary undertaking. The area involved was almost equal to the whole of England. By comparison, the entire regular British Army had less than half the Russian strength in Germany; the RAF had about 260 strike aircraft in its entire inventory, just over half the equivalent Soviet assets in this single arena.

The Allies had other sources of knowledge about what was happening just beyond the front line, but none was foolproof. Satellite cameras could not penetrate dense cloud or smoke. Intercepted radio signals, courtesy of GCHQ at Cheltenham or the US National Security Agency, could be spoofed by bogus transmissions or by a stealthy deployment by a division from its barracks to its combat assembly areas in radio silence. Even agent reports (Humint) could not always be trusted, while most defectors, including some from the KGB and at least one from Spetznaz, often had an axe to grind that diminished their credibility.

In 1994 (in his book *Looking for Trouble*), General Sir Peter de la Billiere described the 'stay-behind' role of 21 SAS, a territorial regiment committed to reconnaissance in Germany, as follows: 'Again and again, we demonstrated the crucial importance, in intelligence work, of having human beings on the ground. No matter how sophisticated spy aircraft and satellites may be, they are no substitute for pairs of alert eyes which function, whether the sky is clear or cloudy, at night as well as by day, in rain, snow and even fog – and we proved this so many times that after a while the [1 British] Corps Commander came to regard us as indispensable. Time after time on the major exercises ninety per cent of the best intelligence emanated from our hides. We became so popular that we could not furnish enough teams.'

Sir Peter's words were at least as apt a description of the Brixmis role, with the difference that the Mission performed not just for a fortnight or so during the annual Corps exercise in the reassuring atmosphere of friendly West Germany, but 365 days a year in the treacherous environment of the GDR.

Checking the Orbat was the basic bread-and-butter of the Mission's programme. It was refined by reference to Indicators of Hostilities (IoH), events or signs which revealed how awake was the Russian bear and how aggressive. Typical of these IoH events was the deployment of 25,000 Soviet troops from their barracks to an assembly area, usually concealed in dense woodland near the border with the West.

This was one intimate way in which Brixmis took the temperature of the Cold War at the point of confrontation. Another was the prolonged, close study of the senior Soviet officers themselves. How serious were they about a way with Nato? 'We know their capabilities; we do not know their intentions,' was the refrain at Nato's operational headquarters at Mons. The mood of the Soviet high command, detected at armpit's range, changed dramatically and was, perhaps, the most important Indicator of them all. Brigadier Miles Fitzalan-Howard, during his period in charge (1957–59), never believed that the Soviets would attack the West. This was not a popular view at the time: in 1958, CND was founded in response to the perceived peril of imminent nuclear war. From 1987 to 1989 another Head of Mission, Brigadier (later Lieutenant-General Sir John) Foley was in no doubt that the Soviets would strike pre-emptively, if necessary, to eliminate what they perceived to be a Nato threat to their security. They told him so quite plainly and he believed them.

These tasks were the big ones, long-term and strategic in their effects, together with the intangible benefits of the constant contact between Brixmis officers and the Russians. Usually, the communication was less than human. It was compressed into the cultural straitjacket of a KGB-orchestrated reception or some other form of communist mindset. Suddenly, in implausible circumstances, real humanity broke through, often aided by the catalyst of Scotch whisky. On such occasions, the intolerable burden of weighing every word and gesture was too much for those Russians – and there were many – who preferred a party to The Party. Then they poured out their frustration (and sometimes their secrets) to the British whom, it turned out, they much admired. Nothing better illustrates such moments than the Soviet team which had just arrested, with some force, a Brixmis air tour and which was then persuaded, while everyone waited for a senior Russian officer, to perform some Russian songs and dances.

The impact of Brixmis intelligence scoops can never be properly assessed. To do so would require a godlike overview of which agency acquired what information and when. The Mission's work was assuredly unique and uniquely important. It was not only a matter of obtaining close-up photographs of the latest Soviet radar system, though that was the sort of thing that prompted congratulations from Washington as well as London. The best contribution was probably the clinical and professional reports the soldiers and airmen of Brixmis wrote on the way the Russians handled their equipment. When they went on to the offensive, how did they drive their tanks? Brixmis showed that they drove them in Indian files across the country, regardless of attrition. Was it true that their attack helicopters could not operate in below-freezing temperatures? So it was believed in the West, until a Brixmis air tour watched the Russians prove Nato pundits wrong.

Some of the scoops were unquestionably momentous. Ken Connor's acquisition of a secret Soviet manual, apparently describing the latest tank armour (c. 1980) was one example. Hugh McLeod's breathtaking burglary of the T-64 tank, locked in its hangar in a Soviet battle training area, was another.

The level of technical knowledge from which such scoops were achieved was itself awesome. The Mission produced its own

Recognition Book, 'to assist touring personnel to identify the most common items of military equipment seen whilst on tour in the GDR'. The volume is the size of a small telephone directory. One section itemizes 350 separate pieces of equipment, ranging from 'Grid Iron', a VHF aerial system, to 'Prayer Wheel', a portable direction-finder to intercept Nato radio signals. Another section, dedicated to intelligence requirements, set the watcher's agenda when he encountered one of these items. In the case of the BM-21 – a rocket-launcher mounted on the back of a truck – the advice was: 'Look for evidence of improved ammunition and warheads. Colour imagery of rounds and packaging where possible. Look for evidence of extended range capabilities in addition to missile changes. Watch for improved targeting systems: target designators, new Met radars.' The feat of memory required would test a good academic mind. The synthesis of hardware-spotting and tactical literacy was what gave a Brixmis report its very special flavour.

Soviet officers came in for the same orchestrated scrutiny. One Brixmis department specialized in 'Personality Research', recording 'all personalities encountered by the Mission'. A personality questionnaire devised by the Mission covered nine separate areas with the assistance of fifty questions. Areas of interest included appearance; health; character traits; social behaviour; habits ('Has he any bad or perhaps odd – but perhaps unobjectionable – habits?') work ('What ambitions has he?'); personal and family background ('What is his wife like and is their relationship happy?') and politics ('How strong are his ties to the Soviet Union, to "Mother Russia", or to the particular Republic from which he comes?') Perceptive veterans of the Mission believe that this attempt at personality profiling was a reconnaissance too far, beyond the remit, usually not done well and altogether 'naff'.

Every working day, Mission teams knew that if the Soviets launched an attack on the West which they did not foresee, they would be the first victims. Plans were laid on both sides for that eventuality. The key element would be the seizure of West Berlin, inside East German territory. This was to be carried out, after what one authority described as 'a covert preparatory phase to get all the attacking forces into their assembly areas', by the East German army, the NVA. The assault plan was code-named 'Operation

Centre'. It was to start with an attack in the dark by a heliborne battalion of the 40th Air Assault Regiment to seize two Western airfields, at Tegel and Tempelhof. Up to 100,000 troops would be needed to swamp the area. In 1989, as the Cold War ended, the NVA high command was still polishing its invasion plan. Had it ever happened, the Mission would probably have gone to ground to become the first Nato stay-behind team of the Third World War. It can take much credit for the fact that this final role remained hypothetical.

The Brixmis 'Trophy Cupboard' of Intelligence Scoops

Throughout its forty-four-year history, the Mission collected a vast amount of intelligence about Soviet and East German military secrets. Much confirmed or added detail to what was gleaned from other sources. Some of it enabled the more general circulation within the Nato intelligence community of data which had been tightly restricted initially to protect the original source. Data restricted almost as much by the West as by the Warsaw Pact itself were clearly of limited value. The collateral sourcing of Brixmis released such secrets for circulation and enhanced their value to the West.

These considerations have led other agencies to conclude that the Mission achieved few, if any, genuine intelligence 'scoops' of its own. The argument goes that if the Secret Intelligence Service or GCHQ Cheltenham or some other august team of lifetime professionals in intelligence did not know about a given secret, then it could not be particularly important. This is as inaccurate as it is arrogant. Though the methods adopted by Brixmis were crude as well as direct, they were unquestionably effective.

Almost as important as the discovery of a new piece of Soviet equipment was the first sighting of it on the front line in Germany rather than at a site 1,500 miles away in Russia, under development. In other words, the *first deployment* of a new tank, radar, anti-aircraft or radar system could be of as much importance to the West as the initial knowledge that it existed somewhere over the horizon.

The movement of personnel was another major intelligence job. Every six months, the Red Army moved around 80,000 conscripts into and out of East Germany. The Mission – with a strength averaging 100 men, only thirty-one of whom carried passes enabling them to rove around the country – had to record the process to identify changes in Soviet strength. A former Chief of Mission has admitted: 'This was not an exact science by any means.' The total strength of Warsaw Pact forces in East Germany was about 500,000 men.

Mapping the Soviet Army's Emergency Deployment Areas – which allowed units to get out of their garrisons to an operational stance – was another process hard to evaluate at any given time, since it was part of a continual monitoring process by Brixmis. The Pact could have mounted an attack on the West at forty-eight hours' notice. Knowing the alert state of the Soviet EDAs day by day was vital and one of the Mission's Indicators of Hostilities.

Another contribution, difficult to quantify but obviously valuable, was the part played by the Mission in enabling defectors such as the KGB officer Aleksei Myagkov to abscond to the West.

The full catalogue of Brixmis' scoops is still held under lock and key. Many revealed the evolution of Soviet nuclear and chemical warfare preparations. The latest gas-masks were stolen and smuggled out of East Germany, along with much else. What follows is a selection taken from the personal accounts of people whose experiences contributed to this history.

During the last decade at least of its existence, as Lieutenant-Colonel Wylde QGM pointed out: 'We "raised" 200 Army technical reports and about 50 air force technical reports every year. Every one of them was an intelligence coup.' In the early 1980s, the surge of new Soviet equipment increased the Mission's workload dramatically. An internal Brixmis report confirmed:

The term 'scoop' was first coined in the 1984 Annual Report ... Operations and supporting research were radically altered in the early eighties to cope with the apparent expansion of the Soviet and East German armouries, their increased training cycles and new and improved operational techniques ... By 1982 both ground and air touring had become all-weather, day and night, 365 days a year intelligence-gathering operations. New targets were continuously being added to the list: Emergency Deployment Areas, formation level command posts, bunkers and fixed communications sites to name a few. Tri-mission operations [with the French and US Missions] by now had become commonplace and efficient . . . Operations Sorbet, Tetragon, Renaissance and Sacristan were the tri-mission code-names for coverage of major exercise movements [by Warsaw Pact forces] between training areas and restricted areas. So great was the required intelligence effort that the then Chief, Brigadier Learmont, established the Chief's Directive on 1 January 1983. Essentially it prioritized the collection requirement for a much stretched organization . . . The Soviet training cycle stampeded on unabated. Whilst touring personnel were being stretched and tested on the ground the support staff back in Berlin were being thoroughly swamped with information.

Statistics from the photographic 'special section' staffed by the RAF plot the increase. In 1963, a total of 1,100 films was developed. By 1984 the total was 7,324. The number of photographic prints grew from 63,000 in 1963 to 343,386 in 1984.

This, then, is a very incomplete catalogue (employing Nato code-names for Soviet equipment) of the trophies in the Brixmis cupboard.

Date	Scoop
1948–49	Detailed reports on state of East German rail system revealed that the West's counter to Berlin Blockade was working and that East German steel production had plummeted.
1949	JS [Josef Stalin] 2 heavy tank, aka IS-2 seen and detailed measurements of armour taken.
1949 onward	Spiral code of registration numbers on Soviet vehicles decoded. On the road, Mission tours 'ran' Soviet columns from the rear, checking the vehicle numbers and often being rammed while doing so.
1955	Major Chris Hallett photographed first T-54 tanks in East Germany; first AK-47 rifle and first missile.
	Hallett recorded first firing of main gun on PT-76 amphibious tank as it 'swam'.
1957	AI radar inside nosecone of Soviet Flashlight fighter photographed.

| 1959 | Photographs taken of 85 per cent of Soviet front line 24 Air Army aircraft based in Germany, later increased to 100 per cent. |

1959   Photographs taken of 85 per cent of Soviet front line 24 Air Army aircraft based in Germany, later increased to 100 per cent.

     Maps and other items taken from crashed Soviet Ilyushin-28 bomber.

     Soil and other samples taken from Soviet Air Force runways to enable Nato to design ordnance capable of disabling airfields.

1962   Photographs taken of first SAM Guideline missile deployed by Russians in East Germany.

     First photographs obtained of T-62 main battle tank.

     Pictures taken of new 'Big Mesh' radar.

1963   Details noted of T-55 tank snorkel for river crossings.

     Details noted of PMP (prefabricated pontoon) bridge in action in Germany.

1965   First deployment observed in Germany of Scud-B missile.

     Appearance/first photographs snatched of 122mm artillery piece known as the Halle gun.

1966   Electronics, engines, airframe composition of Yak-25 Firebar stolen and analysed after crash in Lake Havel.

July 1968   First warning given that East German Army would take part in an invasion of Czechoslovakia.

August 1968   New radar systems photographed during Warsaw Pact invasion of Czechoslovakia including Long Track (surveillance radar) and Thin Skin B (height-finding radar).

     New electronic equipment noted on T-62 tank.

1970   First sighting of SPG-9 recoilless gun in action.

     New warhead spotted on Frog-7 mobile missile.

     Photographs taken of SAM-4 and 'Fan Song' attached radar.

     Samples of new 21mm ammunition fired by

Fishbed-J aircraft and 30mm aircraft ammunition collected from Soviet Air Force practice range.

First photographs taken of tactical air-to-ground missile carried by Fitter bomber.

Details of SAM-2 radar equipment noted.

Soil samples taken from runways of new tactical airfield.

New electronic pod carried by Fishbed reconnaissance plane photographed.

First joint East German Air Force deployment with Soviet Air Force witnessed at Erfurt.

East German troops watched while crossing river at night using tanks fitted with snorkels and mine-ploughs.

Joint Soviet/East German nuclear warfare training observed at Hainichen.

1971   Fitter aircraft seen making nuclear low-air burst simulation.

First Soviet tactical air-to-ground missile (AS-7 Kerry) fired from Fishbed F interceptor aircraft and observed by Brixmis. (Fishbed was normally armed with air-to-air Atoll missiles.)

First sighting, Fishbed firing 23mm cannon.

1973   Photographs of SA-6 missile radar system taken.

1974   Details of new Soviet self-propelled gun (2S-1) obtained during Operation Pinocchio.

Photographs obtained of latest bombers Flogger and Backfire, and Hind-D helicopter; plus pictures of new missiles including Snatter, Apex and Aphid.

1976   First sightings in Germany of T-64 tank and supporting aircraft, exercising with the tank, including Hind helicopter, Fitter D and Flogger B aircraft.

1977   First sighting in Germany, at Priort Sidings, of SA-8 SAM missile. This mobile system made its public debut on parade in Moscow in 1975.

| 1978 | T-64 tank spotted as Soviets start massive re-equipment programme in Germany. |

Other new deployments included: BM-22, a 16-tube multiple rocket-launcher; new satellite communications system, Nato code-name Park Drive; BRDM-2 tracked reconnaissance vehicles.

| 1977–78 (Winter) | Soviet helicopter gunships seen flying tactically in 'unflyable' weather. |

| 1978 | Confirmation of presence on German soil of new self-propelled artillery gun, 2S-3. |

Rapid build-up of new SAM missiles including SA-9 and SA-6 reported.

Pilotless drone DR-3 and mine-laying Hip helicopters spotted along with airborne control system, AN-26 Curl (similar to Nato Awacs).

Swatter anti-tank missiles seen fitted to Hind-D helicopters.

| 1979 | First pictures obtained of Fitter G reconnaissance aircraft in combined tri-mission operation known as 'The Allstedt Saga'. |

T-72 tank noted in hands of East German Army.

Soviet Air modernization in Germany included arrival of Flogger G interceptor and Hind-E assault helicopter.

AK-74 assault rifle comes into service, spotted by Brixmis, but more information was required. This was obtained in 1981.

| 1980 | Close observation made of Soviet aircraft using autobahn as a tactical airfield. |

Documents revealing that some Soviet front-line units were 'shell' formations to be reinforced by reservists obtained through Tamarisk operation.

First photographs taken of Mig-23/27 Flogger aircraft fitted with reconnaissance pods. Flogger G ground attack aircraft and Fitter H recce aircraft new in theatre, identified.

Entry of BTR-70 armoured personnel carrier into Germany noted.

New 35 Guards Air Assault Brigade kept under surveillance at Cottbus, discovered to have variant of BM-21 rocket-launcher; much airborne forces' equipment identified as part of Soviet modernization.

New communications kit delivered, including the truck-mounted Twin Ear radio relay and tropo-scatter system and the reconnaissance battalion's mobile radio monitoring device known as Turn Series.

Three new air bases – for helicopters at Laage and Hohenmoisen and for fixed-wing aircraft at Holzdorf – were found to be under construction. Between 1979 and 1982, hardened shelters were photographed as they were built; samples of concrete in these and runways taken for analysis along with measurements of earth levels.

1981   Close-up details of new assault rifle, AK-74 described and sample bullets for this weapon retrieved.

Samples of T-64 tank armour obtained for analysis.

The Neustrelitz Document, a Soviet notebook revealing details of Russia's latest tank armour, recovered from barracks garbage.

Photographs taken of interior of T-64 tank including fire control system.

Latest variant of T-64, the T-64B, with new laser range-finder and enlarged sight, spotted and photographed at Neustrelitz.

T-72 tank and other new equipment identified in hands of East German Army.

Satellite communications system known as Wood Bine seen arriving to replace Park Drive.

New IFF radar system to distinguish friendly from

enemy aircraft (Nato code-name Dog Tail) identified at Pritzwalk.

Electronic warfare (jamming) gear brought into use includes a system (Brick Shell) only spotted hitherto at sea aboard Soviet spy trawlers.

Paint Box, a proximity fuze jammer was also identified.

Various aircraft, notably close-support Fitter and Fishbed interceptors, were upgraded.

New Soviet self-propelled 152mm howitzer, the 2S-5, identified in railway sidings.

Air defence missile and gun system SA-13 identified as it appeared in theatre.

Tracked nuclear warfare and chemical contamination monitoring vehicle, RKHM, spotted during divisional exercise.

1982   Filtration unit stolen from nuclear bunker reveals existence of 'particulate' weapons.

Soviet use of laser as weapon against Brixmis enables UK scientists to analyse composition and likely source of beam.

Photographs taken of Soviet nuclear warfare train/command centre.

SS-21, an 80-mile-range battlefield missile, followed as it deployed into East Germany.

Anti-tank AT-7 missile, similar to Nato's Milan, recovered and brought back for analysis.

Aircraft newly transferred to Germany, identified by Brixmis, included Fencer C, Foxbat E and Fitter K.

Radar innovations included End Curve, an aid to the static air defence missile SA-3.

1983   Photographs of new M1976 152mm towed howitzer taken at Gross Ammensleben sidings.

Impression of new BMP-2 gun obtained and gun-barrel dimensions recorded by use of apple as a mould.

New main battle tank, T-80, spotted by US Mission on low loader under canvas; later by Brixmis on rail transport at Halle.

PMM-2, a portable pontoon bridge, identified at Glau. The escort vehicle, an amphibious PTS-2, chased the Brixmis team and in so doing revealed its own secrets.

Hind F helicopter gunship watched, to reveal its role as 'deep assault against armour' rather than close air support of Soviet ground forces.

An adapted fast, tracked vehicle (MT-LB M-1983/ 2) spotted fitted with the latest AT-5 anti-tank missile as it boosted the power of 3 Shock Army.

1984   First evidence of Soviet tank fleet in Germany – notably T-64B – fitted with Explosive Reactive Armour. ERA reduced the effects of incoming missiles. The Mission's signal enabled timely warning to be given to Nato. Deployment of tanks so fitted outside barracks was thought to indicate 'hostile intent'.

BMP-2 – a tracked, light-armoured personnel carrier – seen to be fitted with appliqué armour on turret sides and under gun mantle, effectively doubling its protection. Even at the end of the Cold War, tour crews were advised: 'Large samples of this armour are required: small scrapings of the surface are insufficient.'

First photograph of T-80 tank 'untarped' (without a tarpaulin cover) taken at night in July as the tank was carried on a military train.

Nuclear warfare (NBC) detection vehicle known as K-611 photographed at Magdeburg. The basic tracked vehicle was familiar; the sensors on top of it were not. They identified effects of a nuclear burst from a distance.

Air defence improvements spotted included new radar systems.

Tin Shield, a new radar towed by a Kraz truck, spotted on its deployment among Soviet and East German armies.

Fitter K close-support aircraft on the air war range at Neuruppin seen to use a lobbing technique known as a 'toss bomb' run, simulating a tactical nuclear bomb 'that produced the necessary simulated mushroom cloud over the town of Neuruppin!'

Laage airfield checked as it opened for business: four new helicopter squadrons seen. At Brandis, a ground attack aircraft known as Frogfoot identified in Germany for the first time.

New airborne jammer carried by Hip helicopter, seen at Cochstedt.

Oddest sighting of the year: a Hind-G1 helicopter with a 'nuclear testing scoop' – a device needed after a Chernobyl-style disaster – flying towards Mahlwinkel. An official report asked: 'What was this variant doing in East Germany?'

1985   Telescopic lens photographs taken of T-80 tank with explosive reactive armour at Gross Ammensleben sidings.

T-80 tank with ERA 'boxes' noted on tanks outside barracks.

A 'chemical protection canister', EO-18, known to the Soviets as 'the secret respirator', along with another type of gas-mask (EO-62 K), were picked up. As the Mission's guidance reminded tour teams: 'Acquisition of respirators, canisters and NBC suits remain a very high priority. All recoveries should be brought directly to the weapons office for a decision on their disposal.'

First ground photography of construction work at SA-5 missile sites at Kraatz and Grubkow.

Arrival of Fitter G aircraft at newly opened Laage airfield recorded.

First photographs of Curl transport aircraft carrying external bombs.

First photographs of aircraft-tracking TV camera fitted on Fan Song Air Defence Radar.

First close-up coverage of Tin Shield radar showing detail of antennae feeds, cables and connections.

1986   Recovery of documents giving details of T-80 main battle tank, as follows:

Gun:	125mm smooth bore
Rounds:	38 (6HE; 15 HEAT; 10 APDFS; 7 AT-8 missiles)
Weight:	41 tonnes
Width:	3.65m
Height:	2.19m
Engine:	Gas turbine
Fuel consumption:	700l per 100km
Range:	350km
Wade:	1m
Snorkel:	5m

Surface-to-air (anti-aircraft) system 2S-6 – mobile, self-propelled weapons array – was spotted soon after being brought to the front line. It combined guns with missiles. Brixmis was the first to note that it was armed with four 30mm cannons as well as missiles and was 'an important upgrade of capability at regimental level'.

First sightings, photographs of SA-11 anti-aircraft gun; 2S-9 and 2S-11 guns and MT-LBu radar variant.

First sighting of PRP-3 recce vehicles variants, confirming that the Soviets used a number of reconnaissance vehicles and co-ordinated their output.

First photographs and analysis of role of ten Command & Control variants of MT-LBu vehicle.

First photographs of Fulcrum and Foxbat F aircraft.

Close-up photographs of T-80 tank taken on military train.

1987   Section of reactive armour stolen from T-80 tank, parked in a railway siding. This was one of the great coups.

First photographs of SS-23 mobile nuclear missile deployed in East Germany in response to the US deployment of Pershing missiles into Europe. A former Mission Chief said: 'Sighting one of these missiles was a strategically important factor for Nato, part of an intelligence build-up leading to implementation of the Intermediate Nuclear Forces treaty in 1987 which resulted in withdrawal and supervised destruction of all these categories of missile both in Warsaw Pact and Nato.'

Confirmation of grouping of SS-21 short-range nuclear missiles with army brigades: previously these weapons had been controlled at divisional level.

Recovery of four TM-62 anti-tank mines.

An ARS-14 chemical decontamination vehicle observed siphoning colourless liquid from a railway wagon: sample obtained by Brixmis, analysed in UK and identified as trichloroethylene. It was not previously known that this organic solvent was in the Warsaw Pact inventory.

First photographs of more than twenty different types of Electronic Support Measures (ESM) and Electronic Counter Measures (ECM) vehicles. ESM includes radar detection/analysis and Sigint. ECM jams the opposition's signals.

1988   Confirmation that Soviets were withdrawing SS-23 missiles from Jena and Weissenfels, without saying so in public.

First photographs of new 152mm gun howitzer M1987 as replacement for D-20.

First use of thermal-imaging devices to collect

thermal 'signatures' of Soviet equipment for recognition and battlefield file purposes.

First photographs of Mainstay, the Soviet Airborne Early Warning & Command System (AWACS) in East Germany.

First sighting of T-80 tank snorkelling.

First photographs of new reconnaissance pod fitted to Flogger J aircraft.

Identification and photography of twenty-three variants of the 'Silver Box' mobile headquarters vehicle.

First photographs of Soviet Copper Log computer vehicle.

APPENDIX II

Tour Kit

The equipment carried by Brixmis tours had to cover every contingency from the need for a quick getaway to survival under canvas in winter temperatures of minus 30 degrees. Since arrest and detention for hours, or even days, in an unheated office at a Soviet kommandantura was a likely end to the reconnaissance, a large book was also vital, as was a pee-bottle for those trapped inside their vehicle and 'tarped' (under tarpaulin) in the yard of a barracks or police station. An elaborate first-aid kit including morphine was carried alongside whisky as a bribe for Soviet officers as well as a winch to crank the car out of a bog, snowdrift or even a river.

This was the gear used by SAS Sergeant-major (later Major) Nick Angus BEM in the late 1970s and by Squadron Leader (later Wing Commander) Andrew Pennington in the mid-1980s:

VEHICLES. At the beginning of its existence the Mission used Humber 'Boxes', jeeps and Humber Snipe staff cars. By the early 1950s the favoured vehicle was the Opel Kapitän, painted in black until 1957, then in khaki matt. The Kapitäns were replaced by the larger Opel Admiral, which frequently bogged down and had to be winched out of the mud, sometimes with the help of German farmers. Only in 1980, with the arrival of the Range Rover, did the Mission have a truly reliable off-road vehicle. Later in the decade the Mercedes Geländewagen (G-wagen) supplanted the Rover, but if a low-profile vehicle was required then a specially strengthened four-wheel drive Opel Senator was used. In 1989 a trial of 4×4 Audi Quattro cars found that the Audi was not robust enough for the treatment it got during mission tours.

The cars were driven for 37,500 miles and Range Rovers for 56,000 miles before being disposed of to the military Staff Car Company in Berlin. The disposal mileage was usually reached after six to nine months. Some vehicles were a total write-off before then as a result of high-speed accidents or rammings. The cars were rewired to a special console enabling brake lights and front light combinations to be switched so as to resemble, in the dark, a local Lada or Trabant. Extra fuel tanks were fitted, enabling the cars to run for an additional 625 miles.

NIGHT EQUIPMENT. Drivers were equipped with night-vision goggles (NVG), enabling them to drive along autobahns at 125 m.p.h. or faster without lights to escape Stasi tails. One veteran said: 'Although the GDR roads were fairly free of traffic I did wonder about the effect of passengers in a Trabant when they were passed by a vehicle without lights moving at that speed.' From 1985 the tour NCO also had NVG. The team carried, if necessary, a thermal imager. Before 1985, infra-red photography was used to provide some nocturnal coverage. It was rarely a success. Neither was the image intensifier tried for a period. All this specialist equipment was provided by the department known as DI51e.

CAMERAS. The tour officer carried:

Nikon F2AS camera plus 180mm f2.8 Nikon lens (main camera lens)
Nikon F2AS camera plus 500mm f11 Nikon reflex lens (both cameras fitted with motor drives)
Nikon F2AS camera plus 85mm f7 Nikon lens
Nikon f87 1,000mm lens
Additional Nikon 2,000mm lens
30–40 rolls of 400 ASA Ilford HP5 film
10 rolls of colour transparency film

From the early 1980s onward, the F3 camera was used. For some years, this equipment was carried in a photographic case purchased in East Germany, where it was cheaper. In the early 1980s a custom-built carrying case replaced the old East German one.

After 1985, a camcorder (video) was also used. For some years before that, cine-cameras and clumsy, heavy early video cameras had been employed from time to time.

MAPS. A full set of 1:50,000 scale maps of East Germany plus a copy of East German road maps overlaid with PRA, shaded in yellow; Soviet original PRA map; 1:25,000 scale target maps.

OTHER NAVIGATIONAL EQUIPMENT. EZB compass; tripmaster.

TAPE RECORDERS. Two Sony mini cassette recorders.

BINOCULARS. Zeiss 8 × 30b (Angus's personal equipment); Pennington carried one pair of 15 × 60 binoculars and one pair of 10 × 40 binoculars.

REFERENCE MATERIALS. Copy of Robertson–Malinin Agreement.

WRITING MATERIALS. Pens, pencils, coloured mapping pens, notebooks in an RAF navigator's briefcase.

SURVIVAL EQUIPMENT. Sleeping bag with waterproof outer cover; ground sheet; two stainless steel vacuum flasks; East German mini petrol stove; food (sandwiches and digestive biscuits); 'brew kit' (for tea, coffee); electric razor: all carried in a parachute bag. Pennington also carried chemical heating pads, charcoal hand-warmer, sunglasses, morphine syrette, large aerosol can of mosquito repellent, small torch with red filter, spare cassette tapes, batteries, adjustable spanner, screwdriver, GDR version of Swiss Army Knife, micrometer and thick winching gloves in his rummage bag.

TENTS, ETC. Pennington noted: 'Until about 1984, tours had used "bashas" made from Australian ponchos but we converted to one-man Goretex tents with built-in ground sheets, used by the SAS. Everyone made his up differently. Mine was equipped for comfort in all weathers. The tent was attached to an external extra ground sheet which gave extra insulation and protected the tent from ripping when opened in pitch dark on top of a sharp branch. Inside, the bottom layer included a mat made from foil-backed foam blanket, designed to be stuck on walls behind radiators to reflect heat. This was wrapped in a commercial "space blanket", again to provide insulation. On top of those was an East German inflatable airbed and on top of that the sleeping bag. We each had two sleeping bags, one of summer weight and the other, Arctic capable. In mid-winter, when the temperature in the GDR regularly fell to minus 25 C, most of us used the winter bag inside the summer one. All this was kept inside the tent, which was rolled up with the tent hoops already in place, but not secured. The roll was secured with bungees and, with practice, could be erected in pouring rain at 2 A.M. and occupied in less than a minute.'

FOOD. The Pennington approach was to carry 'enough tinned food for the number of planned nights out on tour, plus spare tins to allow for unplanned extensions. On tour, individuals provided their own breakfast and lunch but the evening meal was communal and "all-in". My breakfast consisted of Jordan's Crunchie cereal washed down with black coffee. Some made fried-egg sandwiches. Group Captain Keith Harding, when he was deputy Chief, took marmalade sandwiches, which tended to get soggy after a couple of days and attracted wasps in summer. For lunch I took crackers and cheese. Occasionally we would stop at a baker's and buy fresh bread rolls. A favourite diversion was to buy cakes to eat with coffee. Air tours were devoted to ice cream during the summer months and suffered a traumatic period after the Chernobyl reactor explosion since an edict was issued by the Chief that all dairy products were to be avoided because of possible radioactive pollution.'

The evening meal was cooked and eaten after the tour had settled for the night beside a railway, to conduct a watch on the traffic using it. Each member of the party solemnly offered up his tin of meat and vegetables to the collective pot.

Every two hours, in principle, the tour would stop to brew tea or coffee. This was a ritualized process. 'The Brew Kit had to include teabags, coffee, sugar and Coffee Mate ... This consisted of four empty screw-top coffee jars, taped together and refilled after each tour, with a teaspoon secured in the middle. The coffee had to be real Nescafé granules. Cheap powder substitutes were spurned as "Naafi Dust" ... The first brew was always made by the tour officer, then in sequence by the tour NCO and the driver. Each tourer had two vacuum flasks which he filled with a total of six litres of boiling water during pre-tour preparations. One flask was enough for six brews per twenty-four hours.'

CLOTHING. Tour crews were not supposed to wear camouflaged clothing since their ostensible job was liaison, not covert intelligence-gathering. Both soldiers and airmen in British crews usually wore: beret; olive-green shirt; olive-green lightweight trousers; green jersey; RAF flying boots; Canadian green parka plus – in winter – long underwear, green quilted parka inner liner, green quilted trouser inners, thin leather flying gloves, padded gloves, thick winching gloves, green woollen balaclava, green quilted socks.

Pennington recalled that because air tours spent a lot of time operating outside the vehicle in air OPs, they suffered from winter conditions more than others. 'We used Canadian Air Force mukluks in snow, which kept the feet wonderfully warm. I bought and used, strictly illegally, a Swedish government surplus sheep-skin-lined grey canvas coat which I used with the mukluks in winter OPs. Whilst you could barely move in this combination, it was warm.'

HYGIENE. Toilet paper was used to wipe eating utensils as well as bodies. 'Wet wipes' were employed instead of soap and water for washing. 'The ultimate treat in summer was to wait until it got dark and then find a lake or river in which to have a nude swim, generally whilst fighting off the mosquitoes. In winter it was . . . unwise to disturb the layers of clothing by washing. On a five-day tour a tacit agreement existed that we would all smell the same.'

CREW RELATIONS. Relations between officers and NCOs on a Brixmis tour were informal yet disciplined, as in the Special Forces. First names were not usually used by the officers to the NCO and driver but 'when you are in a car for twenty-four hours continu-ously the conversations covered everything imaginable. The atmos-phere was relaxed but professional. This was a very close-knit team of about sixty who, regardless of rank, were able to talk freely.' Senior officers rediscovered the pleasures of being back in the field. Angus recalled 'Brigadier Elderkin saying that he was the only brigadier in the British Army at that moment lying in a damp ditch, trying to get some sleep and thoroughly enjoying it.'

The Map-makers

For its first twenty-three years, Brixmis was obliged to use maps which could not be trusted either as a guide to what was on the ground they had to cover (an area equal to 83 per cent of England) or politically. The first shortcoming was a nuisance; the second, potentially lethal if a tour strayed into a Permanently Restricted Area (PRA). As Major Alan Gordon, a surveyor who joined the Mission in 1974, put it: 'We were using essentially prewar, unrevised maps to carry out tasks in a hostile environment.'

Official East German maps gave little away on 'small-scale maps which showed . . . that Dresden is south of Berlin (together with a multi-lingual condemnation of the Allied bombing of that city).' Even Nato, supplying one designated map, could not help. 'The effects of opencast mining in the Cottbus area created a "lunar" landscape for miles . . . The building of new towns and roads such as the Grimma and Rostock autobahns made navigation, particularly at speed in the dark, difficult and sometimes extremely hazardous.'

Early in 1974, an added twist to the problem was that the Soviet liaison office (SERB) changed many of the PRAs from which Allied tours were excluded. The SERB maps were hand-drawn, one for each mission, and they were not consistent. A road might be within a PRA on the version handed to the French (and therefore off-limits) but outside PRA (legally accessible) on the British or American versions. When that happened, the three Missions got together to produce their own master copy, taking advantage of every anomaly in the originals.

The problem of outdated maps was still unsolved in 1974. Over the next three years, crews sent on special mapping tours surveyed virtually every road and track in East Germany not enclosed by PRAs. The data that were collected included, as well as obvious features such as bridges and railway crossings, favourite cake shops, parking places and kilometre marker stones. Marker stones were particularly important because a tour NCO, spotting a convoy of Soviet kit ahead, would start his recorded report, for example, as follows: 'Halle Autobahn, going south, K-stone 34, 1040 hours: three BTR-60 . . .'

Collecting the data was one thing. Assembling them as a coherent map was another. This was the job of a Royal Engineer survey specialist, Staff Sergeant (later Major) Alan Gordon and a small staff. They collected the information and drew it up in a form ready for the printers in BAOR to over-print on to the only available – but out of date – 1:50,000 maps of East Germany. The result was used for the tourers' 'strip maps', carried on the road and for a vast master map which ran along a circular inner wall of the Olympic Stadium building where the Mission had its Berlin head-quarters. By the end of 1977, some 208 out of 214 sheets had been surveyed and over-printed.

Gordon also did a deal with the Map Library run by BAOR at its West German headquarters, Rheindahlen. That library held a copy of almost everything ever produced. Gordon offered to supply the library's map research officer with everything Brixmis trawled up, in exchange for a constant supply of dyeline copies of the library's originals of maps unobtainable elsewhere. They included for example a larger scale 1:25,000 map used to record details of Soviet bloc installations in East Germany.

Looking back on the operation years, Gordon said it was difficult to convey the scale of the problem: 'Over the first three years, a handful of tourers travelled virtually every single road and motor-able track in an area roughly equating to England south of Yorkshire.'

One experienced tourer, Sergeant Major (later Major) Nick Angus BEM added: 'All tracks and roads were graded as passable by two-wheel drive, four-wheel drive, tracked vehicle, etc. I spent quite a few hours mapping the NE of the GDR border region record-ing all the forest track conditions and what could be used on them. I also noted the direction of travel of any wheeled or tracked vehicle that had used the area and any trackside tactical signs' (which would be in temporary use during a military exercise).

A civilian team achieving results akin to those of the Mission's tiny cartographic unit would probably be nominated for an award by the Royal Geographical Society. By contrast, the armed services expect their technicians to perform miracles without complaint or reward.

How They Lived

Members of the Mission had two bases: a main headquarters in the offices of the circular Olympic Stadium complex in Berlin and at Potsdam, East Germany, an elegant centre of aristocratic life surrounded by lakes and forest. 'Home' for Brixmis personnel was the comparative freedom of a married 'quarter' – a flat or house – in West Berlin. The Mission House, a mansion beside a lake in Potsdam, sometimes known as the Villa, provided temporary accommodation for the duty officer, for tour crews on standby and for emergency cases. It also housed an officers' mess. It was provided by the Soviets in December 1958 after a rowdy political protest caused severe damage to the compound used during the first twelve years (see Chapter 3).

The Mission House routine was controlled by a warrant officer (sergeant-major) and his wife, living permanently in their flat. At weekends a duty officer took over so that they could take time off in West Berlin, a mere thirty minutes' drive away across the Glienicke Bridge but culturally and politically on another planet.

The domestic staff were all East German, employed by the Soviets, usually picked and controlled by the KGB or Stasi secret police, who expected them to report anything they heard or saw that might be of use to GDR Intelligence. The British knew this. (See Appendix VI.) The *modus vivendi* that met this otherwise impossible arrangement was that some of the Mission team would ensure that innocuous titbits were fed to the staff, most of whom they liked. The Germans, given treats and small gifts not available in the GDR, were usually more loyal to their British employers, dangling the carrot, than to their stick-wielding political masters. Nevertheless, it was an uneasy lifestyle, one in which the Mission servicemen and their wives had to assume that their every conversation, however intimate, would be recorded. As one Brixmis wife said: 'It wasn't uncommon to find a wife such as myself talking loudly to the electric light fittings.' When it was necessary to discuss anything sensitive, then the conversation would have to take place 'in the garden' – a long way from the house – in pouring rain, if necessary.

Facing the front of the house was the 'goon-box', a shed with opaque windows, concealing a member of the Volkspolizei who reported the movements of the British and their visitors to the Stasi. A short distance away, plain-clothes Stasi narks, usually clad in black leather and – such was their fear of being on camera themselves – sunglasses, waited in cars to follow the Mission tours as they drove out of the compound. The Stasi also filmed, or made video recordings of diplomatic parties at the Mission House to identify links between, say, intelligence officers attached to the French Mission and their British or American opposite numbers. At French Mission parties, such recordings also tracked the progress of Stasi 'plants', some of them attractive women, among the staff serving canapés and cocktails.

Loyalists among such domestic spies were expected to believe, as the official GDR guidebook to Potsdam put it: 'It is a well-known fact that during the period of the Cold War against socialism, reactionary forces in the USA, Great Britain and France violated the Potsdam Agreement of 1945. They supported the West German big bourgeoisie which had recovered its strength and helped to split first the economic and then the political integrity of Germany.'

Entertaining Russians was always a challenge. Access to Brixmis parties by the Soviets was strictly controlled by Russian intelligence officials. As one veteran put it: 'We did not know in advance who was coming or how many were coming. Those who did come appeared often not to know what it was they were coming to. One group brought along to a dinner night at Potsdam had already taken dinner before they arrived.' A film night bristled with protocol traps. There had to be no political implications. Musicals and recordings of royal occasions such as a wedding were popular.

Lieutenant-Colonel David O'Connor, senior interpreter with Brixmis from 1969 to 1971, was one of many people on the team who had a compassionate understanding of the human dilemma the domestics represented. He recalled the team and the atmosphere of his period, when – as a good Russian and German speaker – he dealt with them as president of the mess committee, the ultimate boss of the British officers' mess at Potsdam.

'They were very nice people who were employed by the Russians. We knew that, as part of the privilege of having the job, they had to make some contribution to the security effort. Thus, if you left a letter lying around it would be taken advantage of. However, it did not go much further than that and was part of the rules of the game. Four of the women were jolly ordinary working people who enjoyed the fun and the spirit in the Mission House and I think they genuinely liked us. The woman in charge of them always had a problem. She was a good housekeeper, a pleasant and decent person, but I believe she was a genuine and dedicated communist. She liked us too, but didn't think she should and her attitude was always ambivalent and restrained. The rest of them couldn't give a monkey for communism.

'The event where all this came out most clearly was the Christmas dinner which, in the traditions of the Army, was cooked by Mrs Gooch [wife of the warrant officer in charge of the Mission House] and served by the brigadier, myself and Mr Gooch. As the presents were given (wrapped Lux toilet soap was an incredible luxury to them) the drink took effect and carols were sung. They all became maudlin-sentimental. There was a great shortage of men in the GDR and they were all once married but now without their husbands, who were in a buyers' market. Out came the personal stories and the tears.'

Things were rarely what they seemed. O'Connor recalled 'a US Marine Corps officer who was in the US Mission just after I left. There had been a boilerman called Herr Lutzelburger, who "did" all the mission houses, but who was rarely well. He died and the American, who spoke fluent German, decided to go uninvited to his funeral. He turned up to find the Mission House staffs all dressed up as sergeants in the Volkspolizei and Lutzelburger's police cap resting on his coffin . . . Great embarrassment all round.'

There was no inclination on either side to engage in 'hanky-panky'. The domestic staff had good jobs. 'They wanted nothing to rock the boat. We made up their wages. However, in early 1971 a young and attractive girl joined the staff unexpectedly and

appeared to be making a beeline for the Royal Signals radio operator whose boring task it was to man the high-frequency link back
to the British base at Krefeld in West Germany. These boys came
from the Signal Squadron in Berlin and spent two weeks living in
at the Mission House. They had little to do except make scheduled,
routine radio checks.

'It was clear that the older women were not happy with the
situation that developed. The young girl did not fit in. She was
accused of stealing from one of their pockets and disappeared as
rapidly as she had come. I know of no attempt to suborn any
member of the Mission apart from this episode.'

Driving through East German towns, the presence of the Mission
was a symbol of hope for a better tomorrow. As Colonel O'Connor
said: 'To be cheered and waved at by the workers, who had nothing
to lose, was as good for them as it was for us. They knew they had
not been entirely abandoned to "the Friends"' (from the East).

How They Trained

Everyone who joined Brixmis, from its raw start in 1946 to its end in 1990, was already trained within his own service as a soldier, a sailor, an airman or a Royal Marine. Many were also qualified in some special area such as the Russian or German language, or in technical intelligence or electronic warfare. But it was 1971 before some sort of formal training specifically tailored to the demands of the Mission was introduced. Initially, tour officers and NCOs alike learned on the job. The only test of their suitability, having been summoned to Whitehall to be informed of their new role as spies, was to be sent on to the street with a camera and instructions to photograph some inconspicuous target such as Nelson's Column. By the mid-1950s, however, some Brixmis officers did attend a training course for military attachés where they learned how to inspect and photograph factories.

In 1971 and 1972 selected officers posted to Brixmis were sent on the Service Attaché Course at the military intelligence centre at Ashford, Kent. That experience identified the need for a dedicated Brixmis course. The first of those ran from 22 October to 10 November 1972. In the next two years, four courses were run. Thereafter three courses were staged each year. In 1982, the length of the course was increased from three to four weeks, to meet the increasing demands of touring. The last course, No. 49, ran from 18 June to 13 July 1990. From 1976 onwards, four members of the US Mission were trained at Ashford each year and, after 1983, a few French team members also.

This pre-Brixmis training was described as the 'Intelligence (Special Duties) Course', a description which, it was hoped, would distance the ostensible role of the Mission as a diplomatic liaison team from the darker world of military espionage.

Virtually everybody joining the Mission was expected to take the course, regardless of whether or not he was to be an official touring officer. The course covered three main areas of work: equipment-recognition, photography and touring techniques. The first two weeks consisted almost exclusively of classroom training in these subjects while the last two weeks were dedicated to practical touring exercises against military targets in Britain. During the first exercise, students were led and taught by members of the course directing staff (DS) travelling with them in the same vehicle. On the final exercise, the students operated solo. The DS team then worked against them, simulating narks. Almost invariably the novices were arrested and given a hard time by an angry 'Soviet' commandant.

Group Captain K. O. Harding OBE, deputy Chief of Mission in 1986–88, recalling his training, said: 'We did recces of American air-bases and Porton Down [chemical warfare establishment]. I had a very good exercise on Salisbury Plain which became rather more realistic than we anticipated because we got mixed up in a cruise missile convoy. There were police all over the place. The directing staff, running our course, knew that a tank exercise was taking place on Salisbury Plain. They did not know about the cruise missile deployment there. When I got mixed up in that it added a touch of realism.'

Most of those who went on to experience the reality of touring against a real opponent in East Germany found that experience much harsher than anything they encountered on the Intelligence (Special Duties) Course. The best preparation was a real conflict such as Northern Ireland or Oman. Yet the Ashford training had its strengths. Every student, regardless of rank or service, was obliged to pass a rigorous recognition course covering 950 items of Warsaw Pact equipment. Each equipment had an intelligence 'requirement', which had to be learned also so that priority could be given to one item, in preference to others, when the cameras were brought into action in the field. Even more important, the tour crews had to learn what was significant and what was not. As one veteran pointed out, 'There was no point in chasing a T-55 tank in 1982, since we already had several of them in the UK.'

Tour officers learned another valuable lesson at Ashford. This was that certain equipment proclaimed the role of a unit or formation. Brixmis agents would be expected to know, from the equipment deployed, what was going on. In an African game park, an experienced warden would know which watering hole was the best bet for anyone wishing to watch and photograph wildebeest. So, in a similar way, the Mission crews tracked and watched their quarry and sometimes got there first, to await its arrival.

Drivers, usually drawn from the Royal Corps of Transport, were given a special two-week course in off-road, evasive driving in the Grunewald forested training area in West Berlin.

How the KGB Watched Them

In 1990, a former lieutenant in the East German secret police, the Stasi (also known as MfS), told Brixmis what he knew about efforts to spy on and otherwise control the Allied Missions. The defector was known as Frank. His British handler concluded that, 'in essence, all Mission House staff members were being run by either the MfS or KGB, to varying degrees of success, as a precondition of continued employment. Handling rights were worked out between the KGB and the MfS Commanding Officer at Beyer-strasse, Potsdam, on a fifty–fifty basis. The situation was not without discord. Staff members being run by the MfS who proved to be too adept at producing quality information were resented by the Soviets and in some instances, sacked from their jobs!'

The breakdown of British Mission House staff by the employing service suggested that the Stasi and KGB each had four agents there.

The nine-page debrief report which emerged from Frank's revelations provided a unique insight into the way the Stasi operated until the very end of the Cold War and, arguably, still do function under the surface of a reunified, democratized Germany. It also illuminated the thoroughness of Europe's most efficient secret political police service. This is what it said:

INTRODUCTION

1. Subject is a thirty-year-old former lieutenant in the MfS. Despite having joined the Stasi in 1978 he was not fully employed until just prior to its demise, after a protracted period of probation and training. At the time of the dissolution of the MfS [in 1990], subject was employed in the small eavesdropping unit based in Potsdam, targeting Allied Mission phone calls into and out of their Potsdam Mission Houses.

2. [. . .] He readily agreed to be debriefed about his knowledge and experiences within the Stasi. His motivation is largely ideologically based in

that he now sees clearly the faults and excesses of the old regime and the part played in it by the MfS. He now feels no loyalty to his former organization or its masters and wishes to 'purge his soul' in an almost confessional way . . .

RECRUITMENT AND EARLY LIFE IN THE MfS

4. Subject's ambition from the age of fourteen was to join the NVA [East German Army] as an officer specializing in air defence. Students pledging themselves to the NVA were guaranteed secondary education up to degree level. Subject had made contact with the schools liaison organization in Potsdam.

5. At age seventeen, however, he was approached by a Stasi officer who worked out of the Wehrbezirkskommando [army recruitment office] in Potsdam . . . He agreed to join the Stasi in preference to the NVA . . . Subject met the officer several other times whilst still at school. In this way he learned more about the Stasi while still not understanding in which department he would work. The Army was not happy on learning that one of their candidates had been poached by the MfS . . .

8. On 1 October 1978 he formally joined the Stasi. He attended a two-month basic training course in Glienicke, north of Berlin. This consisted entirely of basic military skills. Students received no special-to-arm intelligence training. On the last day of the course, a car picked up subject and took him to Potsdam, to Beyerstrasse. (This was where subject was employed in the eavesdropping unit on the dissolution of the MfS . . .)

10. In 1981 [after a probationary period as a guard] he was asked if he was prepared to learn a foreign language . . . from April 1981 to November 1983 he studied at the School for Foreign Languages in Schönewalde, based in buildings next to the castle . . . All students were members of the MfS (some were candidates for the Foreign Intelligence Service) as were the teachers. The majority of teachers had served abroad . . .

[The debrief, curiously, does not specify the foreign language but this was almost certainly English since 'during the 1981 summer break his class was employed looking after American children at the Pioneer Republic summer camp in Altenhof, north of Berlin. They posed as students and found the exercise valuable language training.']

11. In November 1983, subject returned to Potsdam, to Beyerstrasse where he was introduced to the eavesdropping section.

12. In 1986, subject began a course at the Hochschule in Eiche in Potsdam . . . for management positions . . . During this period students were attached to other departments to receive on-the-job experience. For

example, subject spent six months attached to a surveillance team. The course covered political indoctrination, international law, penal law and more operationally related skills including clandestine photography, recruiting and running agents. [Stasi insiders referred to agents as 'Unofficial Members'.] The subject completed this course early in 1990 just prior to the Stasi's disestablishment.

13. Subject's work in the eavesdropping section was a prelude to his ultimate transfer to the Analysis Cell, also based in Beyerstrasse. Its function was to sift through the raw data pertaining to Allied Mission activities and identify factors that could be exploited.

PERCEPTION OF ROLE OF ALLIED MILITARY LIAISON MISSIONS (AMLMs)

14. The MfS perception of AMLMs was that they were intelligence-gathering units closely linked to their national intelligence organizations. Not all Mission members were believed, however, to be professional intelligence officers.

15. The major tasks carried out by the Missions were perceived to be:

   a. Collection of military data, primarily Soviet-related but including NVA targets. This included ground installations and deployments, radar and communications sites, airfields and aircraft. When targeting aircraft it was believed the AMLM vehicles could intercept air-to-ground communications. It was also believed that seismic sensors were used to detect the movement of ground equipment.

   b. Collection against certain economic targets of strategic interest, e.g., the uranium mining operation in the Weimar area.

   c. Recruitment and running of agents in the field. The running of agents was believed to include direct contact, e.g., receipt of tactical tip-offs from Deutsche Reichsbahn [East German State Railway] employees concerning rail movements, or reports from factory workers and indirect contact including the servicing of DLBs [dead letter boxes].

   [The British debriefing officer added his own comment: 'This belief was held at a senior level and was not shared by subject.']

ANTI-MISSION OPERATIONS

16. The effort expended by the MfS against the AMLMs involved several different departments or 'Referat' using different means. Monitoring the Missions involved mobile surveillance teams on the ground, telephone eavesdropping of Mission House calls and the use of Unofficial Members' (agents) sightings, e.g., shopkeepers, petrol station attendants, residents near military installations. The whole anti-Mission operation was directed from Beyerstrasse in Potsdam. The fundamental

322

problem was that so much raw information was collected that the effective processing of it was not possible.

17. The MLM unit worked to Abteilung 5 of Hauptabteilung VIII in HQ MfS in East Berlin. It consisted of seven Referat employing approximately eighty-five people:

   a. Referat 1. Ran all Unofficial Members working against the AMLM including the Mission House workers.

   b. Referat 2. Worked to develop awareness of AMLM activity amongst the East German population. They also liaised with HQ MfS on matters of army counter-intelligence.

   c. Referat 3 & 5. Deployed the surveillance teams.

   d. Referat 4. Included the analysis cell and eavesdropping section.

   e. Referat 6. Oversaw all admin matters.

   f. Referat 7. Controlled the surveillance teams on the ground using radio.

18. The aims of the MfS anti-Mission operation were:

   a. Prevention of espionage against military targets. It was perceived that the Missions mainly but not exclusively targeted Soviet military activity and installations. By harrying Mission vehicles with surveillance teams it was the Stasi's intention that they would be forced to abort efforts to gather intelligence on military targets. Sometimes the Soviets would provide the MfS with prior warning of new equipment entering the GDR in order to protect it. MfS would then mount an operation deploying surveillance personnel to the deployment area to prevent Mission attack. Such operations could last several weeks. Surveillance operators would live in tents or caravans in the area of the target and deploy from there. The team would be briefed on the basis of an appreciation by the Analysis Cell in Beyerstrasse. They would consider who from the Missions would be likely to attack the target based on perceived specializations and how the target would be approached by the Mission crew based on routes, Op locations, etc.

   b. Prove Mission espionage activities. Another role of the mobile surveillance teams was to photograph or video Mission teams photographing targets. The aim of this was to provide the Soviets with proof upon which to base official protests, through SERB.

   c. Deliberate planned detentions. One of the main aims of mounting deliberate planned detention operations was to prove a direct link between the Missions and national intelligence services in the form of captured equipment or documents. The decision to mount a deliberately planned detention operation – as opposed to opportunity detentions executed by troops on the ground – was based on one of two factors. If a Soviet Mission crew was detained in West Germany the order would be passed to the MfS in Beyerstrasse by the KGB department in Potsdam to attempt a reciprocal detention . . . Alternatively, on the basis of analysis, if a member of the Missions was deemed to set patterns whilst touring that could be exploited, he would be targeted. An officer in the FMLM [French Military Liaison Mission] was successfully ambushed and detained because he persistently approached an identified OP from the same direction. A special squad was set up based in Zossen Wünsdorf [Soviet garrison headquarters] composed of either GRU [Soviet army intelligence] or Spetznaz [special forces, similar to British SAS] personnel.

[The debriefing officer added the comment: 'This squad may still be in existence.']

Because the Soviets did not have the necessary analytical section to plan detention operations they relied on the MfS. Additionally, the special detention squad would be supported on the ground by MfS personnel dressed in Soviet uniform. The Soviets did attempt to continue planned detentions after the demise of the MfS in February 1990 . . . Latterly, even prior to February 1990, little was done to detain Mission crews because of the complexity of mounting the attempts, the scant gain in reward and the reluctance to risk embarrassing the Soviet leadership in its dealings with the West.

d. Gathering information on Mission personnel. One aim of observation of AMLM personnel on the ground was to determine if they had any specialist skills or interest in any particular type of target. Uniform or insignia worn by members were disregarded. Personality files were produced by the Analysis Cell in Beyerstrasse on all Mission members and passed (unofficially) to the Foreign Intelligence Service by the Colonel and to ZAIG.

e. ZAIG 5 (Central Analysis and Information Group) was based in East Berlin and controlled by the Deputy Minister for State Security [i.e., MfS]. Its role was to liaise with friendly intelligence services and in the case of Allied Missions to aid identification of ex-members who reappeared serving abroad in their national embassies or other agencies. Two ex-AMLM members traced in this way were Colonel Huet (an ex-French Mission Chief) who was posted to the French Embassy in Moscow and Colonel Le Joy (ex-US Mission Chief) who was posted to the On Site Inspection Group for Medium Range Missiles.

SURVEILLANCE

19. Surveillance operations tasked against the AMLMs were directed by the Central Department in Potsdam. There were two Referat surveillance teams, 3 and 5, one deployed in the north of East Germany, the other in the south. They were controlled by radio direct from Potsdam. When working against a Mission target the surveillance controller in Potsdam would relay information via the KGB in Potsdam to SERB and thence to the commandant in the area.

20. The aim of surveillance teams was to follow the Mission vehicles clandestinely, monitor and attempt to record their activities on film or video. Their surveillance reports would then be used by the Analysis Cell to enhance future tasking.

21. A surveillance vehicle would normally have a three-man crew, a driver, a navigator and radio operator. They had the capability to perform number plate changes in the field.

22. Formerly, teams would attempt to maintain surveillance on a Mission vehicle throughout the length of its tour in East Germany. This was, however, perceived as being too difficult. Consequently tactics were changed and through analysis, choke points and likely targets were identified which surveillance teams could stake out and hope to get behind an Allied Mission tour . . .

23. To augment the efforts of covert mobile surveillance, the MfS operated an extensive system of static surveillance posts manned by Unofficial Members run by Referat 1. A number of people in the Seestrasse area of Potsdam were recruited to observe the French and British Mission houses particularly when receptions were being held. No long-term OPs were maintained for fear of compromise. The Volkspolizei posts opposite each Mission House and the Soviet checkpoint on the Glienicke Bridge were tied into the surveillance effort. Each had a phone/radio link to Beyerstrasse. In this way a comprehensive all-informed net existed to monitor AMLM movements.

TELEPHONE TAPPING

24. The telephone eavesdropping operation mounted against the AMLM houses in Potsdam was conducted by two MfS departments. The technical installation and maintenance of the intercept capability was the responsibility of Department 26, based in Hegel Allee, Potsdam. The monitoring and recording of intercepted information was done in Beyerstrasse, Potsdam, part of Hauptabteilung VIII in HQ MfS East Berlin. Although each region had an eavesdropping section, Potsdam was tasked exclusively against the AMLMs.

25. The installation of the 'bugging' equipment was done by agents employed in Deutsche Post. They used an 'inductive' method whereby the actual telephone lines were not touched. This meant the Mission phone-users heard no tell-tale sign as they spoke. In all, six lines were 'bugged': three GDR Deutsche Post lines going out of the Mission Houses and three West Berlin lines coming into the houses. All six lines passed through Hegel Allee. They were then diverted and extended to the monitoring room in Beyerstrasse. Subject was not aware of any technical eavesdropping devices planted actually inside Mission Houses.

26. The operation in Beyerstrasse was technically unsophisticated. Latterly cassette recorders were used to replace reel-to-reel machines, one per line. Each was voice activated when a telephone line became busy. The line in use was highlighted by an electric light board.

27. During working hours calls would be transcribed directly from the telephone line by the two officers employed there, subject plus one. Once a day the important calls would be typed up into a daily report. During silent hours the calls were taped and transcribed the following morning. If important traffic was passed during the night the duty officer would call out a transcriber.

28. The daily report listing traffic was passed directly to the supervisor, a lieutenant-colonel. He made three copies. One went to the KGB office in Potsdam, one to the Analysis Cell in Beyerstrasse and one to the Colonel. He annotated to what end information should be used, e.g., a separate report, an AMLM members P [personal] File, etc.

29. All numbers dialled from the Mission Houses to West Berlin could be worked out. If they were not known they would be rung by Unofficial Members in order to identify them and attempt to gather more information. In this way a number of Mission members' home phone numbers, mainly from USMLM [the US Mission] were known. Unless stated by the caller, the originating numbers of callers from West Berlin could not be worked out. (The subject was not aware of any monitoring of telephones in West Berlin but he presumed another department was active in this field.)

30. The tapes of recorded phone calls were kept for two weeks then wiped clean. Monthly and yearly reports were written by the Analysis Cell and kept for ten years. With the dissolution of the MfS all the old reports were passed across to the KGB in Potsdam.

31. This operation was deemed, especially by the Soviets, to give some valuable intelligence, particularly of a humint [human intelligence] nature. Most was given away by USMLM. FMLM consistently maintained the tightest telephone security.

32. The subject was not aware of any penetration of the Allied military including the Allied Military Liaison Missions. (The Soviets would have run any such case.) However, former East German civilians employed in the Mission Houses as domestic staff were being run by the MfS (Referat 1 in Beyerstrasse) and Soviet Potsdam KGB detachment as agents.

33. In the case of the British Mission House staff they were certainly regular providers of copies of the Berlin Bulletin. (Copies were also obtained by the Colonel through his contacts in the Foreign Intelligence Service.)

34. The only case of a recruitment attempt mounted by the Soviets against an AMLM member concerned a USMLM Warrant Officer. The MfS in Beyerstrasse was able to build up a large and comprehensive file on this man, based on the extensive 'business' dealings he conducted from the American Mission House in Potsdam over the telephone. The Soviets were confident that they could exploit the Warrant Officer's business connections. The Americans became aware of the Soviets' intentions and decided to let the play run in order to gain an insight into their methodology. The affair ended with two Soviet officers being apprehended. (Subject's knowledge of this incident is limited to hearsay and is consequently sketchy and quite possibly inaccurate.)

FOREIGN INTELLIGENCE SERVICE

35. Subject had no personal contact with the Foreign Intelligence Service. He did know, however, that the Colonel maintained unofficial links with them.

36. Subject is not aware of the identities of any Foreign Service personnel and was not approached by them at any time. He knew one officer who worked in a counter-intelligence department who was approached after ten years' service with a view to recruitment. He was eventually rejected because although married, he had a girlfriend.

KGB IN POTSDAM

37. The KGB detachment in Potsdam worked out of offices within the Soviet Army barracks on Friedrich Ebert Strasse. (This installation is thought to be Potsdam 283.) Access to the KGB building was carefully restricted. Subject never entered it ... The detachment consisted of a military counter-intelligence section and a section of ten to fifteen officers monitoring the Allied Missions.

38. Although all contact between Beyerstrasse and the KGB was conducted

by the Colonel, subject knew the first names of two officers, Yuri and Nicolai. They never used their surnames.

39. The KGB also had an officer working in SERB. Subject does not know his identity.

DEMISE OF THE STASI

40. There was some optimism prior to December 1989 that the Stasi would survive the tide of change sweeping through the GDR. This was short-lived. An attempt was made by reformers to occupy the Beyerstrasse station. This was successfully deflected by the Colonel, who persuaded the demonstrators that the offices were used solely for military counter-espionage work.

41. By the end of December 1989 all surveillance and eavesdropping work against the AMLMs had ceased. In January 1990 it became obvious that the pressure on the Stasi was too great and the organization would collapse. Whilst waiting to be told that their jobs were to go, the Stasi operators in Beyerstrasse caught up with paperwork, shredded material and generally found jobs to do to keep busy.

   The end was announced by the Colonel in February 1990. At lunch time the offices were locked up and everyone went home. By then, the Station's entire paper holdings [archives] had been moved by lorry to the KGB office in Potsdam.

42. Since February 1990 the Soviets have attempted to approach a number of ex-Stasi officers in Potsdam including the Colonel but excluding the subject, with a view to persuading them to continue working for them, or at least to divulge information they require. There is a fear amongst this group that the Soviets, or indeed the BND [West German equivalent of the CIA] may resort to blackmail in order to persuade them. The Colonel point-blank refused to co-operate with the KGB and has advised those others who have been approached to do the same. He has also spoken to a number of Mission House domestic staff advising them what to do if they are blackmailed by the Soviets into aiding them.

43. In November 1990, subject again met the Colonel as he does period-ically. The Colonel reported that he had been again talking to members of the KGB department in Potsdam. They claimed to be relatively inactive with little to do. It was expressed that hopefully a military coup in Moscow will not be long in removing Gorbachev from power.

How They Communicated

Although the Stasi and KGB expended much effort in bugging the telephones used by the Allied Missions in Potsdam, it is not clear how successful they were in intercepting the other communications available to Brixmis, USMLM and FMLM. Since the missions were ostensibly diplomatic and liaison groups, their communications were unclassified.

Under the Robertson–Malinin Agreement of 1946, each mission had a 'wireless' station for communication with its own commander-in-chief. In practice, the communications available to Brixmis comprised an ancient High Frequency radio link to the British headquarters at Rheindahlen in West Germany; a Very High Frequency link to the Mission headquarters in West Berlin; a West German telephone supplied specially to Potsdam to the missions and to the SERB, and an East German telephone. No radios were carried in tour vehicles.

The KGB would have felt that it was falling down on the job if, by some means, it did not have access to all these systems.

The Robertson–Malinin Agreement, 1946

AGREEMENT REGARDING THE EXCHANGE OF MILITARY LIAISON MISSIONS BETWEEN THE SOVIET AND BRITISH COMMANDERS-IN-CHIEF OF ZONES OF OCCUPATION IN GERMANY

In accordance with Article 2 of the Agreement of 'The Control Machinery in Germany' of 14th November 1944, the Soviet and British Commanders-in-Chief of the Zones of Occupation in Germany have decided to exchange Military Liaison Missions to be accredited to their respective Staffs in the Zone and to confirm the following points regarding these Missions:

1. The Missions will consist of 11 officers assisted by not more than 20 technicians, clerks and other personnel including personnel required for W/T [wireless telegraphy].
2. The Mission will be placed under the authority of one member of the Mission who will be nominated and termed the 'Chief of the Soviet/British Military Mission'. All other Liaison Officers, Missions or Russian/British personnel operating in the Zone will accept the authority and carry out the instruction of the Chief of the Mission.
3. The Chief of the Mission will be accredited to the Commander-in-Chief of the Forces of Occupation. In the case of the British Zone this means Air Marshal Sir Sholto Douglas. In the case of the Russian Zone this means Marshal of the Soviet Union Sokolovsky.
4. In the case of the British Zone the Soviet Mission is invited to take up residence at or near Zone Headquarters (Bad Salzuflen area).
5. In the case of the Soviet Zone the British Mission is invited to take up residence at or near Karlshorst or Potsdam.

6. In the case of the British Zone the Chief of the Soviet Mission will communicate with the Deputy Chief of Staff (Execution) Major-General Bishop or his staff.

7. In the case of the Soviet Zone the Chief of the British Mission will communicate with the Deputy Chief of Staff Major-General Lavrentiov.

8. Each Mission will have similar travellers' facilities. Passes of an identical nature in Russian and English will be prepared. Generally speaking there will be freedom of travel and circulation for the members of Missions in each Zone with the exception of restricted areas in which respect each Commander-in-Chief will notify the Mission and act on a reciprocal basis.

9. Each Mission will have their own [sic] wireless station for communication with its Commander-in-Chief. In each case facilities will be provided for Couriers and Despatch Riders to pass freely from the Mission HQ to the HQ of their own Commander-in-Chief. These Couriers will enjoy the same immunity as diplomatic Couriers.

10. Each Mission will be provided with telephone facilities in the local exchange at their HQ and given facilities for such communications (post, telephone, telegraph) as exist when [words missing] are touring in the Zone. In the event of a breakdown of the wireless stations the Zone Commander will give every assistance in meeting the emergency by providing temporary facilities on his own signal system.

11. Each Mission will be administered by the Zone in which it resides in respect of accommodation, rations, petrol and stationery against repayment in Reichsmarks. The building will be given full immunity.

12. The object of the Mission is to maintain Liaison between the Staff of the two Commanders-in-Chief and their Military Governments in the Zones.

The Missions can also in each Zone concern themselves and make representations regarding their Nationals and interests in the Zones in which they are operating. They can afford assistance to authorized visitors of their own country visiting the Zone to which the Mission is accredited.

13. This agreement is written in Russian and English. Both texts are authentic.
14. The Agreement comes into force the moment letters have been exchanged by the Deputies to the British and Soviet Commanders-in-Chief of the Zone of Occupation in Germany.

(Signed)

B. H. ROBERTSON Lt. General,
Deputy Military Governor, CCG (BE)

M. S. MALININ Col. General,
Deputy Commander-in-Chief,
Chief of Staff of the Soviet Group
of Forces of Occupation in Germany

Berlin, 16th September 1946

Rügen: Hitler's Sinister Paradise

Rügen, the isolated Baltic island zone in which Brixmis teams had many adventures, was described by East German propagandists as just another seaside holiday resort, where sons and daughters of socialist labour could rest awhile, thanks to Papa Ulbricht. An official GDR travel guide, published in 1983 (when the regime was sharpening up plans to seize West Berlin), mentions the deeply indented coastline, the neo-classical nineteenth-century hunting lodge of Granitz and the nearby resort of Binz. A few miles north 'the more than 100-metre-high cliffs descend steeply to the sea. The white rocks shining brightly through the verdant trees and shrubs and the bluish green sea provide one of the most beautiful views along the whole Baltic coast.'

The guide does not mention the most remarkable structure on this, or most other, isolated parts of the coastline of northern Europe. At Prora, north of Binz, the Nazis built the longest building in the world for use as a holiday centre and a concrete monument to the Strength Through Joy (*Kraft durch Freude*) programme. The plan was personally approved by Hitler, after he had studied a scale model, in 1936.

The following description is by Lieutenant-Colonel N. N. Wylde QGM.

Rügen, the most beautiful island in Germany, typifies the tragedy of the Nazi era and the subsequent occupation of East Germany by the victorious Red Army. The island was chosen by the Nazis as the site for the first of five massive holiday developments to 'Strengthen the Nerves of the German People for the approaching Storm of their Lives'.

The site chosen was Prora, at that time a mere hamlet beside the finest beach on the island. Under the direction of Reichsleiter Dr Robert Ley, who was to commit suicide during the Nuremberg Trials, building started in 1936.

The buildings were built in typical Nazi style on a massive scale and in such a substantial manner that they would have lasted for 1,000 years of Hitler's Reich. The grandiose monstrosity stretched north from Binz, 90 metres from and parallel to the sea, for some 5 kilometres. Every kilometre or so there is a gap above ground to allow people passage from the beach. Two separate accommodation blocks, each 2,000 metres long, would house a total of 20,000 privileged workers. Between the blocks it was intended to construct a massive square and hall where organized entertainment would be provided. A new railway was built to deliver the happy holidaymakers for a week-long break. Unfortunately the Storm of Life began before the building was completed when, in September 1939, Hitler ordered the invasion of Poland. Building work was stopped at once. It resumed in 1944 under the direction of the Mayor of Hamburg as an emergency measure to house some of the thousands of homeless from his city. In 1945 when the war ended, the main accommodation blocks were intact even though only partly completed. The occupants from Hamburg had fled West to escape from the wrath of the Red Army.

The Soviets arrived in May 1945 and spent three months looting anything that was removable. They then set about the task of destroying Hitler's Holiday Monument. The buildings defied all the attempts of the Soviet engineers to destroy them, so solid was their construction. So they put the buildings to another gruesome use.

In late 1945 the Russians started to round up all landowners. They were particularly active in Sachsen and Thuringia as the landed gentry and farmers in those two States had not fled West like the majority of Junkers in the North. Camps were set up in Mühlberg, Sachsenhausen (the former concentration camp), Bautzen (where the prison continued to hold political prisoners until 1990), Coswig and Prora. The two largest were Coswig and Prora. Between 1945 and 1950 about 120,000 people were arrested and sent to the camps.

Some 40,000 of them died in captivity, mostly of illnesses contracted in the camps. It is thought that the original Russian plan . was to deport the majority to Russia but that this was, at least in part, prevented in late 1945 by the 'British Mission in Berlin'. A British officer from one of the search teams boarded a train and insisted that it stayed in Germany. It was eventually diverted to Prora where it was followed and inspected by the same or possibly another British officer as it crossed the Rügendamm on to the island. Prora served as a prison camp for just a few months before the Soviets decided it was time to abandon the place.

Prora, the Nazi holiday paradise that makes Benidorm look like Utopia, then became a problem for the East Germans. Until 1949 it was used to provide building material for the local area. The Germans took on the task of destroying the structure but even though they used much more explosive than the Soviets they were just as unsuccessful in destroying this legacy of Nazism. At the end of 1949 the East Germans admitted defeat and ended all attempts to destroy the buildings. In early 1950 a police training institute was established by the East Germans in Prora. A Soviet division occupied the northern buildings in 1956 while a fledgling East German division moved into the southern part of the complex. After training their new-found allies to fight like Soviets, the Red Army withdrew in 1962 and left the buildings in the hands of the East Germans. The East German Army occupied parts of the complex at various times during the early 1960s and '70s before an East German tank division took up permanent residence at the end of the '70s.

Prora was used in 1981 as the holding point for the many thousands of East German 'Solidarity Troops' who were being assembled to go to help their socialist friends in Poland by putting down Lech Walesa and the Polish Solidarity movement. A number of brave East Germans refused to go and fight the workers of their fellow Warsaw Pact member. They were arrested and imprisoned at Bug, on the western side of Rügen, before being executed for treason.

However, so many people objected to the proposed action against Poland that the East German regime was forced to form a Conscientious Objectors' Brigade.

This brigade was soon put to work in the construction of the new ferry terminal that the Soviets had told the East Germans to build so that rail communications to Russia could be maintained while avoiding sending military equipment through Poland. Thus began the construction of Neu Muckran rail and ferry terminal. The regime was determined to punish conscientious objectors, so no mechanical equipment was provided. The massive complex of sidings and buildings measures about 2 × 5 km and was constructed entirely by hand.

In 1996, the future of Prora is as unsettled as at any time in its past. Part of it is likely to be converted into flats for the many families in the area made homeless by the policy of Helmut Kohl in allowing people who fled West, or their descendants, to reclaim their old family homes in the East. Neu Muckran is likely to be converted to *the* port of the Baltic. Massive sums of money will be needed to convert the facility into a modern and efficient port and it will be many years before the conversion is finished.

GLOSSARY

Agencies, the: Friendly intelligence agencies, usually British.

BAOR: British Army of the Rhine (with RAF Germany, the main British force stationed on the potential front line to oppose Warsaw Pact forces).

BCZ: Berlin Control Zone, the airspace 20 miles around the Berlin air safety building, an area of 1,200 square miles, within which the RAF was allowed to fly routine 'training' missions by Chipmunk trainer aircraft. These became spy flights.

BfV: Bundesamt für Verfassungsschutz, Federal Office for the Protection of the Constitution. West Germany's counter-espionage agency, run by the Interior Ministry.

BIOS: British Intelligence Objectives Sub-Committee, an intelligence policy team directing the work of field investigators in Germany immediately after the defeat of the Third Reich.

BND: Bundesnachrichtendienst, Federal Intelligence Service, West Germany's foreign intelligence agency.

Brixmis 'Sandwich': A formation in which a mission crew and its vehicle were trapped fore and aft by Soviet vehicles, often armoured or heavy trucks. To escape, mission drivers often drove off the road and across country.

Chipmunk: Two-seat light trainer aircraft used by RAF members of Brixmis, ostensibly to keep their flying efficiency current, ensuring that they still qualified for flight pay. In practice, the Chipmunks (there were two airframes) were equipped with spying devices to supplement the work of the observer, who took photographs with a 1,000mm lens camera while leaning through the open canopy of the machine at low level: too low, probably, for a parachute to be of use if he fell out. The crews were ordered to 'torch' the aircraft if they made a forced landing in East Germany.

Comms: Communications.

CPX: Command Post Exercise. An exercise played out in a bunker, or series of bunkers, in which commanders were fed signals requiring them to take decisions and give orders to non-existent forces. A CPX tested signals, liaison and intelligence procedures and much else, as well as the ability of senior officers and civil servants to make sound decisions while stressed and sleep-deprived.

DI51e: A branch of DSTI, giving specialist technical support including the provision of keys and gadgets to field operators (regarded by some as the source of James Bond's fictional scientific adviser).

DST: Directorate for the Surveillance of the Territory, French counter-intelligence agency run by Ministry of the Interior.

DSTI: Directorate of Scientific Technical Intelligence, part of the British intelligence network.

EDA: Emergency Deployment Area.

FIAT: Field Information Agency, Technical, Western Allies' liaison teams, to identify German war-making assets immediately after the Second World War. (The teams recruited German military scientists and investigated the fate of important Western agents and service people still missing in Europe.)

FMLM: French Military Liaison Mission, the French equivalent to Brixmis.

FTX: Field Training Exercise, usually by a large military formation on the ground and in the air, often 'fought' against a friendly formation playing the role of enemy.

G-1 or GSO1: General Staff Officer Grade 1 (senior staff officer).

GCHQ: Government Communications Headquarters, Cheltenham. British signals intelligence unit, intercepting and decoding radio signals of all kinds including telephone calls transmitted by microwave link.

Grepo: Grenzschutzpolizei, border guards.

GRU: Soviet Military Intelligence, similar to US Defense Intelligence Agency or British MI. GRU worked closely with Spetznaz.

GSFG: Group of Soviet Forces, Germany: twenty-six divisions, hundreds of aircraft, comprising the Soviet front line facing Nato across the border of a divided Germany.

Highlights: The most important discoveries made by a Mission crew, reported to the US Mission headquarters as a priority for dissemination around other missions.

'Hill, The': Teufelsberg, or 'Devil's Hill', a mound in West Berlin, built from rubble after the devastation of the Second World War. On this high point, more than 300 feet above the surrounding flat lands, the British set up a Sigint unit whose information was sometimes used to send mission crews into dangerous, if potentially valuable, situations.

Humint: Human Intelligence, usually a code for a secret agent or informer. Stasi-speak for such people was 'Unofficial Members'.

HVA: Hauptverwaltung Aufklärung. East German foreign intelligence service.

KGB: Soviet foreign intelligence service, similar to the American CIA and British MI6.

Kommandantura: Local Soviet military headquarters in East Germany; the point of contact for Brixmis crews detained by Soviet and East German security teams. The headquarters was run by a commandant, usually an army lieutenant-colonel.

MAD: Mutual and Assured Destruction, a primitive doctrine of nuclear deterrence, replaced by Flexible Response once the Soviets had achieved nuclear parity with the US.

MI: Military Intelligence.

MRS: Mission Restricted Sign. These signs, in four languages (English, German, French and Russian), were not sanctioned by international agreements and were used by the Soviets as a means of deterring Allied tours from sensitive areas. The signs were invented by the Soviets in 1951 to guide Allied Mission crews away from PRAs in East Germany. British crews collected individual Soviet signs as souvenirs.

Narks: Members of Stasi engaged in shadowing and pursuit of Mission tours. These contacts often ended violently.

NKVD: Narodny Kommissariat Vnutrennikh Del, or People's Commissariat for Internal Affairs, a political police force that routinely used state terror.

NVA: East German Army, not recognized by Allied Missions but their activities, like those of the East German Air Force, were targeted by Allied tour crews.

Orbat: Order of Battle. The weapons, vehicles and command structure which comprise the sinews of war of an individual military unit, usually a division of around 15,000 to 20,000 men.

PRA: Permanently Restricted Area. Areas declared out-of-bounds to mission tours, notified by Soviet main headquarters to Brixmis and marked in yellow on hand-drawn maps. Missions looked for anomalies on the maps they could exploit but required special, high-level permission from their own high command to breach one deliberately. When they did so they were hunting an unusually important target and risked being shot. At one point during the Cold War, 40 per cent of East Germany was under PRA.

RIAS: An American-run German-language radio propaganda station broadcasting from West Berlin.

RMP: Royal Military Police.

SERB: Soviet External Relations Bureau, the liaison group which was the official link between Allied Missions and the Soviet high command.

SHAPE: Supreme Headquarters Allied Powers Europe, the operational headquarters of Nato.

Sigint: Signals Intelligence. The product of intercepted Soviet and East German military communications whether by radio or landline. The Soviets countered the threat by broadcasting tape recordings of old exercises. The only counter to that was a mission tour, to catch them at it.

Soxmis: Soviet Exchange Mission, the Soviet equivalent of Brixmis, operating in West Germany.

Spetznaz: Special Forces group, similar to British Special Air Service Regiment or US Delta Force. Used to ambush mission crews caught spying, notably near Soviet Air Force bases.

Standing orders: A code of military instructions drawn up on a contingency basis in advance of events.

Stasi (or MfS): East German Secret Police, a private army and intelligence service numbering at least 18,000, whose authority was never recognized by the Mission. Worked against mission crews in collaboration with KGB and Spetznaz.

Tac-signs: Tactical route-markers to guide military formations on routes, many off-road, used for warlike training.

Tamarisk: The name given to clandestine recycling, for intelligence purposes, by Brixmis of Soviet military rubbish dumps. The work carried with it serious health risks. Gloves and masks were often worn. It generated such jokes as: 'We are the people who wash our hands before we go to the toilet as well as afterwards.' It produced some brilliant intelligence coups.

TRA: Temporary Restricted Area. Imposed for the duration of big field exercises or strategic crises such as the Czechoslovak invasion. Signs indicating these were easily circumvented by nimble minds.

USMLM: The United States Military Liaison Mission, the American equivalent to Brixmis.

Vopo: Volkspolizei, or East German Police, not recognized by missions.

VRN: Vehicle Registration Numbers, one means by which Brixmis logged patterns of Soviet military activity, particularly at times of international tension.

Wash-up, Hot: The debriefing and analysis, usually verbal, that took place immediately after an important military exercise.

BIBLIOGRAPHY

Author's note: This bibliography is somewhat sparse, for a book of its size. That is because most of its sources are original, first-hand accounts.

GENERAL

Billiere, General Sir Peter de la, *Looking for Trouble: SAS to Gulf Command* (HarperCollins, London, 1994).

Boldin, Valery, *Ten Years That Shook The World* (Basic Books, New York, 1994).

Frankland, Mark, *The Patriots' Revolution (How East Europe Won its Freedom)* (Sinclair Stevenson, London, 1990).

International Institute for Strategic Studies, *The Military Balance*, 1961 onward; and *Strategic Survey*, 1966 onward (IISS, London).

Lichtnau, Bernfried, *Prora: Das erste KdF/Bad Deutschlands* (Verlag Axel Dietrich, Peenemünde, 1993).

Mercer, Derrik (ed.), *Chronicle of the 20th Century* (Jacques Legrand/ Longman Chronicle, 1988).

Remnick, David, *Lenin's Tomb (The Last Days of the Soviet Empire)* (Viking, London, 1993).

Ruhmland, Dr Ullrich, *The Warsaw Pact Dictionary* (Bonner Druck und Verlagsanstalt/European Military Press Association, Bonn, 1988).

Travel Guide, German Democratic Republic (Zeit Im Bild Publishing House, Dresden, 1983).

Wylde, Lieutenant-Colonel N. N. QGM, Gibson, Captain S. D. MBE et al. *The Story of Brixmis 1946–1990* (privately published by The Brixmis Association).

INTRODUCTION

Kemp, Anthony, *The Secret Hunters* (Michael O'Mara Books, London, 1986).

Low, Vera, 'Day an evil war was over for me', *Daily Mail*, London, 3 February 1995.

Sommer, Theo, 'Germany's Long Shadow of Guilt & Shame', *Observer*, London, 3 September 1989.

344

CHAPTER 1: BLOCKADE

Jackson, Robert, *The Berlin Airlift* (Patrick Stephens, Wellingborough, 1988).

Lashmar, Paul, 'The Night the RAF "bombed" Russia', *Daily Telegraph*, 7 February 1994.

Onderwater, Hans, *Second to None: The History of No. II (AC) Squadron, Royal Air Force 1912–1992* (Airlife Publishing, Shrewsbury, 1994).

Royal Air Force Historical Society, *Proceedings 6* (September 1989).

van der Aart, Dick, *Aerial Espionage* (Romen Lochtwaart, Holland, 1984).

CHAPTER 2: MARCH ON BERLIN

Dewhurst, Brigadier S. H. OBE, *Close Contact* (George Allen and Unwin, London, 1954).

Fontaine, André, *A History of the Cold War* (Secker and Warburg, London, 1970).

Johnson, Paul, *A History of the Modern World from 1917 to the 1980s* (Weidenfeld and Nicolson, London, 1984).

Neubroch, Squadron Leader H., 'Germany Between East & West: The Reliability of an Ally', *RUSI Journal* (London, 1958).

Roberts, Sir Frank K., Foreword to *The Cold War Past and Present* by Richard Crockatt and Steve Smith (Allen and Unwin, London, 1987).

CHAPTER 4: THE BLAKE EFFECT

Ind, Colonel Allison, *US Army: A History of Modern Espionage* (Hodder and Stoughton, London, 1965).

Nunwick, Wing Commander Harry, MBE, *The Nightriders of Berlin* (unpublished memoir).

Wright, Peter, and Greengrass, Paul, *Spycatcher* (William Heinemann, Australia, 1987).

CHAPTER 5: THE NIGHT THEY SHOT CORPORAL DAY

Alsop, Joseph, 'Far Worse Than Quemoy', *New York Herald Tribune*, New York, 7 September 1962.

Andrew, Christopher, 'Covert action man at the CIA' (Review), *The Independent*, London, 5 February 1995.

'Harold Macmillan: Interview', *Daily Telegraph*, London, 28 August 1961.

Taylor, Edmond, 'The Forbidden City', *The Reporter*, Washington, 13 September 1962.

Whitney, Craig R., *Spy Trader* (Times Books/Random House, New York, 1993).

CHAPTER 7: THE DOUBLE-CROSS YEARS

Childs, David, 'Gunter Guillaume', obituary, *The Independent*, London, 14 April 1995.

Myagkov, Aleksei, *Inside the KGB* (Foreign Affairs Publishing Co., Richmond, Surrey, 1976).

CHAPTER 8: BREZHNEV'S XANADU

Menaul, Air Vice-Marshal Stewart, CB CBE DFC AFC, et. al., *The Soviet War Machine* (Salamander Books, London, 1980).

Vronskaya, Jeanne, 'Victoria Brezhnev', obituary, *The Independent*, London, 11 July 1995.

CHAPTER 9: LIFTING THE LID ON THE T-64

Reid, C. D. OBE, *From the Back Room: A Personal View* (unpublished memoir).

CHAPTER 10: HAND-TO-HAND LIAISON

Pennington, Wing Commander Andrew, *Brixmis Air Touring, August 1985–October 1988* (unpublished memoir).

CHAPTER 11: THE WAR WE WOULD HAVE FUNKED

Catterall, Tony, 'Nuclear exercise rocks Western alliance as Thatcher flies to Germany/ War game "idiocy" fires Kohl resolve', *Observer*, London, 30 April 1989.

Leonidov, Major Yuri, and Zheglov, Captain M., *Western Military Missions* (trans. Flight Lieutenant A. G. Cohen MBE), *Red Star* Newspaper, 11 January 1989.

INDEX

Printed by RR Donnelley at Glasgow, UK